CATS BRIGADE

The First Miss Licky Tale

Jeremy Cope

woodlord

For Michael

CHAPTER 1

I am a Maltese cat who for the past few years has led a very charmed life. Little did I know that overnight my life would be turned upside down.

Most of the time I had lived on board a yacht, the *Sun in Splendour*, moored at Vittoriosa Marina on the small island of Malta, deep in the Mediterranean. My owners, Eric and Daisy from Yorkshire, England were in their mid-sixties and seemed to have been married forever and a day. They were a free spirited couple with a sense for adventure and a challenge in life. Happily retired, financially secure and with no ties to England and its miserable climate, Malta was now their home. The *Sun in Splendour* was their pride and joy and had proved a great source of pleasure for all three of us.

Eric and Daisy had retired to their cabin unusually early. It could have been no later than 9.00 pm and all was quiet on the *Sun in Splendour*. I was sitting up on the main deck glancing carelessly at couples, husbands and wives and their children, strolling along the quay side. They appeared mainly Maltese folk, though there were a few obvious tourists toting cameras, taking pictures of each other, back dropped by fine yachts like our own. I suspect I have probably featured in many of these photos whilst perched on the top of the slightly raised gang plank. However, the *Sun in Splendour* was by no means the most coveted yacht to have in the back ground for these eager tourists. Though 47 seven feet in length, she was dwarfed by some super yachts a little further down the quayside whose pedigree suggested Premier League Football Clubs and Russian Aluminium smelting Oligarchs.

After an hour or so of people watching, I took a little stroll myself. I needed to stretch my legs, as I had been on board all day long. I had always favoured evening walks in preference to venturing out in the day. The heat during the day in June could be quite unbearable. Also the quayside traffic was far too dangerous in sunlight hours as pedestrians skirted with oil tankers and fruit vendors plying their trade, next to the busy quayside restaurants.

The restaurants, intertwined with the old Maritime buildings to my left were still full as diners entertained family, friends and some very noisy children. I fairly raced by this threatening kindergarten until I came to a stop outside the Maritime Museum. It was then that I noticed something most odd. One of the two enormous oaken doors was slightly open. At this time of night something had to be amiss. A sign to the left of the door clearly stated that the Museum closed at 5.00pm.
I slowed to a halt under the massive limestone eves abutting the museum. My curiosity was aroused. I moved forward and popped my head round the door and peered in. I could see an area bathed in low light. Curiosity I know has been known to *kill the cat* and I should have sensed danger ahead if I actually entered. I stupidly sneaked indoors.

I came across a cool flag stoned area, with a reception desk ahead of me. I moved further forward for a closer inspection. The desk had a till neatly positioned to the left and countless brochures in a stand to the right. I walked on by and turned to go behind the unmanned reception desk. I jumped onto the chair to peek at the historical pamphlets lying on the desk which would be given or sold to the daytime visitors who of course would queue to buy entrance tickets. I browsed and learned something of the history of this place.

I was suddenly stopped in my studies by the sound of uneven heavy footsteps. The place echoed and even my keen senses could not tell where these ominous sounds were coming from. I froze for a moment, realising that I was an intruder. I had no right to be here in the Maritime Museum out of hours. In fact, I would probably have no right being here at any time of day. The footsteps were now all around me as I crouched behind the desk. Then they passed and grew softer and less threatening.

I heard a loud creaking noise followed by the slamming of a door and the turning of a lock. One, two and finally the third great and final groan as the key engaged with the final spring. All was silent as I peered onto the passageway and realised the lights had been switched off. My eyesight was still keen however as some light could enter the museum through windows and gaps around the stone and wood. I was now alone in the building, trapped and locked in probably for the rest of the night. That sign outside had stated the museum opened at 9.00am.

At this moment I did not consider my circumstances to be too dire. In awkward moments I had learned to keep a level head, so I sat back for a moment and pondered all my escape options.

Step one would be to search the entrance area for a possible exit point. I initially walked over to the entrance doors and looked up. They were fiercely impenetrable and would not yield to any other force than that of the returning key. So I could stay here and position myself close to these doors. Dart out the very moment the first member of staff arrived and race across the road and back to the yacht.

An awkward thought suddenly struck me. What if tomorrow was a Bank Holiday? My mentors Eric and Daisy taught me that Maltese Bank Holidays were highly unpredictable and fall on the most peculiar of days. The calendar date remains the same year in year out and if a Bank Holiday date falls for instance on a Sunday of that year, there it shall remain. The museum might well be closed the next day. The very thought sent a shiver down my spine. The museum staff would all have the day off, visiting sandy beaches with their families, whilst I was locked away in a museum. What a hideous thought. I decided to put this to the back of my mind and seek an alternative way out but with renewed vigour.

Step two must be to walk around the entire building, looking for any open windows or portholes within

7

jumping distance of the ground. I could leap great distances when push came to shove.

My unplanned and unofficial exploration of the Maritime Museum commenced at about midnight.

CHAPTER 2

My feline skills were inherited from my mother who taught me survival strategies which certainly helped move my status as a stowaway on the yacht up to house guest. I am a female and approximately five years old – that is of course in human age terms. In cat terms I seem to be about 35 years old. As I now scour the museum secrets I can ponder my own secret history and share my thoughts with you as we move forward.

My early years were heaped with difficulties and uncertainty – infinite sadness when I was born and was forcibly parted later from my brother and sister. We were born triplets. We were not parted at birth, but something much worse. It was one year later that we were parted and I have missed them terribly each day since. On that same day I lost my mother too.

Now I must take care not to think too much about those events. I had already been too cursory as I paced the corridors of the museum, to find an escape. When I am safe and out of here and back on the *Sun in Splendour*, I shall share more of these earlier and unhappier times with you all. I suspect that the more human beings understand my story, the better the chance shall be that one day someone may help reunite us.

My house guest name is Miss Licky and has been, since I joined the crew of the *Sun in Splendour* several years ago. Proof of my name is on the brass name tag around my neck, with my owner's mobile telephone number. These adornments could prove helpful if I am ever found here. In my present meandering situation, it all became a little meaningless, since there was no one here to find me and no one to return me.

Many house guests have asked Eric and Daisy about my name. They have explained the reasoning countless times. I have found it a little embarrassing having the origins of my christening explained as it has been. Of course I am aware this is simply an aspect of the survival gifts I inherited from my dear mother. God bless her. You see, I have developed a liking for licking my best human friends. My two owners, Eric and Daisy, are inevitably the immediate object if my affection. For reasons I do not understand, the upper back part of their necks are most attractive to me. The favoured moments are usually in the evenings, when Eric and Daisy are seated together on the upright couch, watching television. I can perch myself on the ledge behind them, near the porthole, and lick to my heart's content. I think they have learned to understand why I do this, as they have spoken about it more than once. However, they have grown to accept this as my way of saying thank you for everything they have done to keep me alive. So 'Miss Licky' it must be.

They first sensed that my lickings stemmed from a salt deficiency in my diet. Now I do know humans in hot climates can and do exude minerals of a salty nature. However the salt was never the issue. They then moved towards another theory, which put them almost on track. They came to the conclusion that I thought they were my babies or my siblings. Maybe I had siblings and as a female my mothering instincts had transformed them into my surrogate babies. Maybe I was simply washing them. Well they were partly correct.

The truth I think lay with the loss of my brother and sister. I always licked them each day to keep them clean, tidy and presentable. The licking and tidying procedure for my owners is also my way of telling them I love them. I cannot communicate verbally although I have a sufficient vocal repertoire to aid their understanding. Scratching doors and plaintiff soft meow sounds normally prompt an early rising. The cabin door would open, and a swift roll on my back would encourage the first tickle and cuddle of the day; the precursor to breakfast.

I have learnt to understand English and can hear as clear as a bell and I can also read English. But I can only meow, which just seems so unfair. I imagine we were born this way, to ensure that we could not over step the mark and forget our place in life. Well I suppose this makes some small sense, as we would be running off to the police to report animal cruelty and seeking legislation in Parliament.

Still I would love the luxury of speech instead of this pitiful meow business, but now I needed to concentrate and get back to the business in hand, that of escaping my sore predicament, that of my incarceration in this dark and musty museum. A voluntary bondage if ever there were one and all of my own making.

CHAPTER 3

I moved back towards the reception area as all other escape routes had been explored but dismissed. I entered into a large room - the 'Anadrian Hall' – so described on the inscription above the entrance. Something occurred to me as I made my way across the floor into this vast room containing exhibits of the engine room machinery of the Anadrian, a steam-driven grab dredger English built in 1951 for Malta by Fergusson Brothers of Port Glasgow. What if the museum was alarmed?

This could have been excellent news for me. Set off the alarms and people would come scurrying to investigate. I would then seize the opportunity and slip out amongst the melee. The moment those massive doors opened, I could dart out around or between their legs, unnoticed. Freedom would be mine!

I could run amuck amongst the exhibits, swishing my tail with loud meows and even scratching. I began swishing my tail from side to side and then paused to listen. I heard no alarm bells ringing from either inside or out. A better idea occurred to me. I leapt up onto the largest machinery part I could see and started to gyrate as noisily as I might. I walked atop the length of the exhibit whilst furiously waggling my tail. All remained quiet. This strategy clearly was not working. Maybe the alarm system was not working. Had it been switched off while those builders worked against the scaffold windows? Maybe the museum had no alarm system at all.

Or perhaps there was an alarm system and it had been set to be 'cat friendly' and therefore could not be set off by me. A frightening thought entered my head. Supposing the museum had a resident cat that lived in the building. The idea put me into a completely rigid state, with my backbone arched and tail erect. I had no fighting skills whatsoever and instinctively flew out of the range of any pugnacious feral brethren. There was little room to evade such adversaries here. I felt a degree of paranoia setting in. I had to focus on finding an exit from this unlit and lonely building.

Common sense told me to patrol the first floor again. Maybe my consternation had led me to overlook an obvious exit route. I castigated myself for dwelling on past memories and possibly missing a clue.

As I ascended the large limestone steps, I reflected on their age. This building hailed from the 1840's and became the British Naval Bakery at Vittoriosa. The bakery was the hub of the Victualing Yard and supplied the Royal Navy with its daily requirements of bread and biscuit. All of this information I had gleaned from the pamphlets held at reception.

I reached the first floor, and found myself presented with a display of the Merchant Navy and exhibits of detailed ship replicas and paintings illustrating 19th and 20th century vessels, most of which served on the Malta run.

It was also my first close encounter with the windows in the building. There were three individual windows, all symmetrically tall and with matching window ledges. I leapt onto the first ledge of these three windows and peered out. These large windows were firmly locked. I inspected all three and knew my luck was not in at this point. It was time to move on into the next room, named the St Angelo Hall.

This was quite different to where I had just come from. I was in the museum's events and lecture room, decorated with an array of colourful ship badges. And it had a fine window facing the marina, with a full length pair of curtains, with tie backs. They hung from the ceiling to floor. Once again I leapt onto the window sill to see what I could see and what I saw made my heart flutter. I had a semi side view of the *Sun in Splendour*. There she lay at berth, in total darkness, as were almost all the other yachts at this time of night. The view was encouraging, but I was immediately disheartened as I pressed the tightly locked windows to reveal the slightest of openings - none appeared. I started to take stock of the situation and let reality prevail.

13

The likelihood of my getting out of this place before staff arrived was by now pretty well non-existent. There were a few more rooms to investigate, but optimism was not my friend this night. I leapt down from the window sill and strolled across to the Main Hall.

The Main Hall housed illustrations of developments from ancient times to the end of the rule of the Order of St John of Malta. There were portraits which set the scene for the Navy of the Order of St John. The display included paintings, weapons, uniforms, anchors, maps, models and other artefacts dating from 1530 to 1798. I did take a cursory glance at some navigational charts, as I had seen similar on the *Sun in Splendour*, but in much better condition. I had been told a number of times by Eric not to sleep on them in the cockpit. The only thing that was missing in the Main Hall was windows, and alas pretty much the same in the next room, the Customs Hall. No windows but a farrago of standard weights, measures and other objects.

I left this room more disheartened than ever. My only hope lay with the coming morning and making my great escape just as soon as the staff let themselves in. By this time I had banished all worries about Maltese Bank Holidays. I felt the best place to retire to would be back in the St Angelo Hall, where I could sleep on the window ledge behind the tied back curtains, and keep watch on the outline of the *Sun in Splendour*.

Thirst suddenly overcame me as I felt the need to drink something. There would be no option but water, and I knew I should find a toilet. In previous adversity, I had learned how to drink water from a toilet bowl without falling in. Please don't be alarmed by this choice of refreshment, but I do not have the strength to move taps. So my intuition led me back down onto the ground floor, where most conveniences are placed. Elderly people cannot climb rambling staircases in extremis, so ground and basement levels dictated the plumbing arrangements in fine old mansions and museums and often the rest.

The ladies' and gents' toilet doors were marked with signs I recognised. The gents' toilet door was propped open with a mop and bucket. A clear sign of a recent clean which made me feel better. The ladies' door was closed so I was forced into the gents'. I have never understood why both types of toilet have nearly identical insides. Why do humans not have one toilet for all? I have noticed on the Cottonera waterfront queues of ladies' forming to enter their toilet — some with pained expressions. There would be no queues at the gents' and in contrast I had witnessed men striding in and out with a cheery look about them. So bearing all this in mind, I had no qualms about using the gents' toilet — and anyway who was here to know? Ignoring the etiquette, I jumped over the bucket and strolled straight in. I looked up at the highly polished basins where I heard a faint dripping noise. By this time I was very thirsty but the jump seemed awkward indeed. Maybe the toilet bowl would be the better bet. I peered into the bowl but even severe thirst would make this bowl a desperate last resort. Thus I took the gymnastic route and skated into the first wash hand basin before jumping on to the next where the drips could now be seen. I gingerly crouched beneath the tap then lowered my lips under, my whiskers gently brushing the tap. I immediately caught the water and stayed still for several minutes until my thirst was nearly quenched – then I experienced a complete and utter shock.

The tap erupted, drenching the whole of my face and saturating my sensitive whiskers. Instinctively I leapt backwards. Obviously I was not alone. I scoured the room for signs of the villain who understood the plumbing arrangements. Surely someone had deliberately set the tap to full flow to force me to flee.

Of course there was no one else present. Just me and a rebellious squirting tap. I approached this turbulent tap with stealth just hoping it would maintain its gentle flow. I stretched my right paw cautiously towards and beneath the tap, hoping to at least catch a drop or two on my paw and then lick it off. And then once more it exploded into full flow. I used my paw to grab what water I could but it barely whetted my tongue. The water mystery was quite beyond my feline understanding. However my curiosity had been aroused and caused me to ponder what magic might cause taps to squirt and stop whenever cat paws approached them.

I tried again and wiggled my claws close to the nozzle. Nothing happened. However as I waved my paw underneath the nozzle a sudden a jet of water flew out. I pulled back and pushed forward several times and noticed exactly the same thing was happening. Paw in — water out. Paw out- water in. I jumped into the other four basins in turn and tested their taps. They all behaved the same. Clearly these taps knew I was close by and wanted to help me. I knew human beings always left water outside their doors for stray cats. Maybe a cat loving engineer had created these automatic cat nozzles to make sure we could never go thirsty. Especially when trapped in unoccupied buildings as I was today.

I remained very thirsty and wondered whether I could sit on the round chrome stopper and trap enough water to have a good drink. Perhaps this was not such a good idea. I hate the rain and normally I would run away from it. However thirst is a great teacher, so I tried pushing the stopper with my right paw. It moved down. I then wiggled my left paw under the nozzle and hey presto. Out flowed the water until sufficient was collected to let me drink to my heart's content. I moved my paw away and the water flow stopped. I was happy I had learned how to get water in this place.

I now really needed to search for another way out or at least find a window with a good view of the harbour and the *Sun in Splendour*. I might be seen at least by someone who could help.

On leaving the gents' toilet and approaching the limestone steps leading to the first floor, I suddenly noticed something I had previously missed during my museum travels.

The hairs on my back, my tail, the nape of my neck, were standing on end. I could not believe what I was seeing. Under the first large step was a half empty bowl of milk. A premonition of danger overwhelmed me. There must be another cat present in this building. Why else would this bowl be here? I now knew I had to be very vigilant indeed as I was clearly not alone. Maybe the museum had no need of an alarm. Maybe the cat was an aggressive security guard cat with biting teeth and razor edged claws. Or was there a dog present? Do dogs drink milk? I shuddered and raised my guard and listened acutely for the slightest sound.

It must be a cat. Cats and dogs do not mix and that bowl was surely a cat bowl. The museum obviously employed a resident cat, and that cat would have had to earn its keep. It would not be just any old cat for sure. It would be a trusted and very well trained cat in the art of catching mice - a Mouser and old bruiser of a cat to be sure. If true, this would prove very bad news for me, if I encountered him. I say him, because I could not imagine a female cat chasing mice. Or rats. I always avoided the things.

So a Mouser it probably was who would realise I had no right to be in the museum. I certainly had no fighting skills to defend myself from a sudden attack. I first noticed my more docile side after I had been taken to the premises of what I deemed at the time to be a cruel man who was called The Vet. He had kept my brother, sister and myself in his surgery for a number of hours, and did things that perplexed us all. We all slept through whatever happened to us but that needle did hurt. Why he wanted to hurt us remains a mystery. Still this was no time or place to hark back about an almighty injustice all that time ago. I had to concentrate and think on my own four feet very quickly. I just hoped that the old Mouser was fast asleep somewhere in this large and foreboding edifice and would stay that way until I had made my escape.

I ran swiftly and without a sound up the stone staircase and made my way as quickly as possible to my perch behind the tie back curtains.

I sat on the window ledge and looked out to the marina. Nothing stirred and the only occasional sound that could be heard was the gentle creaking of those tall masts of yachts, swaying in a light evening breeze. The dawn was rising very slowly over the Grand Harbour, and that meant it was about 4.30 am, so nothing would be stirring for some hours to come. Eric was always the first up and routinely fed me before 7am. Much later than this and I would scratch at the bedroom door and cry for attention. That always worked as he came out and stroked me on my tummy. I had learned to roll over at such times which ensured no rebuke from him about my persistence. This suited me just fine. If he arose before me he would come out of their cabin in his dressing gown, flick the on switch of the kettle, and then come over and give me a lovely tummy tickle.

It was a routine that had been played out countless times, and I adored it. As soon as I heard their cabin door open, I would wake up and instantly roll over on my back from my sleeping position, which was usually but not always on the cushioned bench seating adjacent to the dining table. There I would wait for my tickle. The most significant part of this tickle was the promise to come immediately afterwards - my breakfast. Eric would proceed to fill my bowl with cat biscuits, then open the fridge door and add a spoonful of Whiskas from the tin. After breakfast, and before there was any serious movement along the quayside, I would race down the gangplank and trot along to the Casino Di Venetia for my morning constitutional and ablutions.

Now I should make one thing clear. I am not a gambling cat and I have never ventured into a casino. Anyway at this time of the morning the place was always closed unless an early delivery of food or drink had been organised. No, the reason for my early morning visits to the Casino di Venetia area was to visit the area and attend to my own business. I am a very clean and tidy cat and never needed to make use of the litter tray on the yacht which had become redundant, unless we were all at sea of course.

Some years ago and probably just before my 'adoption' the casino refurbished the wide frontage and placed some large terracotta pots there. These had been filled with earth and a variety of flowers. For toiletry purposes I found these most convenient and I was always most careful to heap the soil back into place and hide my activities. Obviously timing was the art to nature's call, and at such an early hour there was never anyone around, except the sleepy security guard in his little front office to the right of the casino entrance. So the litter tray was always the very last resort. Most cats are very well mannered and hygienic as me I am sure. Making a visit to the toilet is a very personal thing and should be done as discreetly and sparingly as possible.

Dogs are in a category of their own. No lamp post is safe from their behaviour. I have never seen a dog tidy up either. Just walk away as though nothing has happened and leaving others to clean up behind them. What is that all about? There should be a law about it. Actually things are a little better in recent times, as I have seen some dog owners walking their dogs, armed with a plastic glove and a plastic bag. My carers never have this trouble of course and with plastic bags at Lidl costing 20 cents a time I think I am very good value. Some crafty dog owners I have seen pretend to scoop up the mess when they know other people are around. However they do nothing of the sort. They bend down and *pretend* to scoop something up and pop it in the scoop bag, and then walk away.

I did not have a cat's chance of getting back to the boat before Eric rose and found me on the missing list. An early breakfast was clearly out the window, and the visit to the Casino toilet was a non-starter. Well there was no urgency here at least. When Eric found me absent, he would assume I had taken a rare nocturnal walk. However he might worry as I cannot remember when I had been that impolite as to not turn up for my breakfast. So it started to concern me more. By 9.00am he would certainly be very concerned. Or so I hoped. Then the search would begin. But no, surely I would be out of here and scampering across the narrow road and onto the quayside by then. One hop and leap and I would be back on board, with breakfast at the ready. In case you are in any doubt, I do enjoy my breakfasts. I should also let you know should you suspect I just live for my food that my main pleasure in life has been companionship - with Eric and Daisy - the absolute opposite of the here and now, stranded in this frightening museum.

I looked out one last time through the window pane, and felt that the best thing would be for me to try to sleep. After all, I had been awake all night. So I curled myself up behind the tie back curtain, whilst watching for a while and worrying if I could sleep with one eye open, less a museum cat made an unannounced leap into my position. I drifted off into an uneasy sleep, which would be short lived. My real nightmare was not to come in sleep nor from a museum cat.

CHAPTER 4

I must have dozed off for no more than thirty minutes, before being woken by a strange noise. Was I imagining that faint *squeak, squeak* sound? Was it a mouse?

I sat up quickly and warily peered around the curtain. Everything seemed normal. I moved back behind the curtain and surveyed the harbour. What I saw filled me with alarm. The *Sun in Splendour* was fully lit and it was just 5am. And what else was I viewing just a meter or two from the yacht, along the quayside? I put my nose to the window to see more clearly. My eyes were not deceiving me one little bit. Besides the yacht being lit up, there was Daisy running back and forth along the quayside. I could just make out that she was calling my name. What on earth was going on?

'Licky, Licky, Licky. Miss Licky where are you?' She was pacing back and forth looking very anxious. She turned around and walked the few meters back to the yacht and stopped in her tracks and called out to Eric. 'She's nowhere around. Oh my god, of all times for her to go missing. I can't believe this.' Eric appeared on the back of the boat, calling out my name several times.

'Where did you leave her last night? Surely you had the sense to lock her in the salon before coming to bed?' Daisy's voice was full of frustration.

Eric stood there with his legs apart with both hands on his hips.

'Just calm down as I am sure she shall turn up any minute. We can delay sailing until 6am, so we still have an hour for her to get back on board.' Eric's posture and the tone of his voice did not sound very optimistic. 'I was sure she was in the salon when I closed the outer door before coming to bed.'

Hmm... I thought to myself. Now Eric you know in your heart that you had not checked properly before locking up for the night. When the outer door leading from the back deck was closed, I was sitting perched up on the half lifted gang plank, which was nothing unusual,

21

as I often stayed out on deck all night, and would sometime pop ashore for a half hour stroll. But now things were becoming abundantly clear.

How stupid I was for not having picked up on things in the past few days. Both Eric and Daisy had been far busier than usual on the yacht. They kept returning from shopping trips with many more provisions than usual, which included tins of Whiskas, boxes of cat biscuits and all enough to feed the entire cat population of the Three Cities for a week. One day, Eric returned in his little Kia car with about fifty litre water bottles. Another time with raw vegetables, frozen meats and box loads of Ghirgentina blended wines he loaded on board with a further case of Whiskas. In pussy cat terms this meant 60 cans of cat food with two dozen boxes of dried cat food, and 2 large sacks of cat litter. A staggering effort if they only intended to continue mooring here.

The gravity of the situation was now becoming all too clear. They were going on a voyage and it looked like they had a schedule to adhere to. Eric's remark rang in my head. *We can delay sailing until 6am, so we still have an hour for her to get back on board.* No chance of that happening. I was the Prisoner of Zenda in some ancient museum, with little or no chance of escape. It might be 7am or 8am at the earliest if I was very lucky. If no cleaners came first, then it was more likely to be closer to 9am, when the museum officially opened.

'Daisy, you keep calling her name, and I will finish off below deck.'

And so as Eric vanished out of view, I pressed my face up against the window, and the doleful tones of Daisy's voice drifted through the air. 'Licky, Licky, where are you? Come on Licky.' I began to meow, a painful and low keyed meow, which I emit when I am in a state of distress. A meow, however, that was not audible enough for anyone to hear at this distance and with a pane of glass between me and the outside world.

If only Daisy would glance up at the Maritime Museum and look to the first floor, surely she would see me. Logically I knew this was a non-starter, since the museum was in darkness and I could only make out

Daisy's presence because of the background of the illuminated *Sun in Splendour*. I continued to softly whimper as I looked forlornly at Daisy pacing up and down the quayside, repeatedly calling my name. So close and yet so far from home and happiness, I pined to myself.

I started to try and conjure up comforting thoughts. Perhaps they were just off to the other Maltese island, Gozo, for the day. We often made this trip and usually returned early evening. We always made the trip on sunny days and with the wind blowing. Eric was fanatical about hoisting the sails and cutting the engine the moment we got out of the Grand Harbour. The *Sun in Splendour* was truly his toy and he was the captain and in full command. He would bark orders back and forth, left right and centre to Daisy, and she would scurry around the yacht, trying to get things right - ever one to please.

'No you silly moo, you are raising the jib far too quickly.'

Occasionally we would moor up overnight, in the cove on the south side to the island of Commino and come back the next day.

Well I would be okay for a day or two on the quayside, whilst I waited for the *Sun in Splendour* to return. Oh please dear God let this be the case, I thought to myself. And then those dark thoughts returned. What had been going on in the past few days with all the activity? I remembered what happened last year, last June, when we all three set sail, with me at the time none the wiser. I would not see my home shores for another three months. What a trip that had been. I felt I had seen half the world on that voyage of discovery.

My thoughts returned to my situation and the prospect that it was I, who had cast myself adrift. On the land! How would I survive such an ordeal? For the past four years I had been one third of a very happy family, smothered with affection and loved to death.

The survival skills I had been obliged to learn when I first came into this world, were now long forgotten and far behind me. It looked from where I was sitting, that I was in deep trouble. I observed Daisy relentlessly marching up and down the quayside, calling my name

23

repeatedly. It caused me to let out another painful meow, actually much louder and even more pitiful than my last cry. However loud, no one could hear me. If I had been on board the yacht and I had let out such a sound, then both Eric and Daisy would have searched for me and attended to the cause of my distress. It had only happened a few times, when I spied another cat getting too close to the yacht or the odd dog perambulating along the quayside.

My ears suddenly pricked up. There was that noise again. It was one quick squeak after another. What on earth was going on? I turned from the window and cautiously peered around the curtain, to receive the shock of my life. If I hadn't already endured enough horrors these past few hours, this one turned my imaginings into the new and very real nightmare.

Before me, merely perhaps ten feet away and built like a true alley bruiser, sat the most enormous black cat I would ever wish not to encounter. And in its mouth, was a lovely grey mouse, squeaking in abject terror to mirror my own. Its backside and tail were flailing from either side of a Mouser's mouth. The Mouser caught sight of me in a flash, and his jaw fell open in astonishment. This gave mousey the chance to run for its life. He fell to the floor and then managed to run up the curtain and hide. I felt happy to have assisted the rescue but now feared retribution. The Mouser gave me a venomous look, a look of abject hatred. Then he let out an almighty hiss.

My instinctive reaction was to put as much space between myself and this inhospitable black brute as was humanely possible.

With every sinew in my body wired to their limits, my two front paws grasped the curtain and raced me to the very top where a moment earlier the mouse had started its escape. My back legs fed the momentum upwards. The thick curtain material took on a mind of its own, as it swayed from side to side. Just before I reached the very top of the left hand curtain, supported by a heavy thick brass railing, I was overtaken by mousey. He had moved to the railing and proceeded to scamper along the brass rail to the top of the other curtain. Obviously fearful this second cat, me, was about to strike.

Amidst all of this chaos, I caught a fleeting glance of Daisy down on the quayside, still calling my name. The museum cat continued hissing spitefully and added to my impending sense of doom. I was swaying like a trapeze artist on the curtain, having also banged myself twice against the window pane, and all I could think about was that surely Daisy below would hear the bedlam over her head and take positive action to help me.

The sway of the curtain slowly came to a halt, leaving me looking down, cat to cat, eye to eye.

'Well then? What do you think you are doing up there? More to the point, what are you doing in my museum? How did you get in? How long have you been here?' He continued to hold my gaze. Then momentarily he licked his lips and looked away. My stare appeared to have had been disconcerting to him. I was quietly relieved. He was now muttering something about the encounter being way out of order and wholly unexpected and what if anybody found out a mouse had escaped his grasp?

'Oh goodness gracious me, I do apologise. It's been an awful mistake on my part, and I'm terribly sorry. No offence was ever intended,' I replied in the most conciliatory tone I could muster. Cats have clever accents which can both conceal and reveal the truth, learnt from thousands of years of close contact with humans. That is why we are such survivors and manage to avoid harmful contact between ourselves.

'It's all very well being sorry, but it doesn't answer any of my questions. How come you are in here of all places?'

Apart from having to hold on tightly to retain my precarious balancing act high up on the curtain, I nevertheless felt a shade calmer. Dialogue was being established. I needed to keep this going at all costs. My mind was still racing. Just stick to the truth and tell the facts.

'Ah well you see, I just happened to see the main entrance door half ajar just as I was strolling past last night.'

'The main door half ajar you say? What time would that have been then?

He looked back up at me and then turned his head sideways for a moment and then back towards me.

'Oh I know what's happened. Its old peg leg Sam, popping in for a few minutes to put out my bowl of milk and a top up of cat biscuits. It's all a ruse you know. All that could be done when the museum closes at 5pm and the staff are preparing to leave.'

Mouser appeared to pontificate over his logical explanation, perhaps musing at the same time that I was not a threat; merely a nuisance. He began licking his lips and turned and smiled in my direction. What was he thinking? Problem solved? No real threat here and anyway a pretty and well turned out cat whose pedigree seemed beyond doubt?

'Oh I see,' I replied lamely, not knowing what else to add.

'Aha but you don't see!' Black bruiser retorted somewhat triumphantly. 'It's me that sees it all and Sam's being doing it for years - ever since the thing was installed. A perk of the job I suppose he would call it, but all a bit petty and unexciting if you ask me. He does it every night. Set your clock by it I can guarantee. Well not exactly but almost and almost is good enough.'

'Well pardon my ignorance but what does he do each night ever since the thing was installed.' I determined to expand the conversation and patronise Mouser as much as I should before either I or the curtain railing collapsed under the stress of it all.

'He fills up two empty plastic litre bottles with water of course! Sometimes even three, if he is feeling greedy.'

His declaratory tone made it sound as if this was the most obvious thing in the world that I should have known already.

'He takes it out of the Premier water dispenser installed near the reception desk. San Michel pure drinking water, wouldn't you know. It's there for staff use during the day. For years I have heard the odd comment from staff as to how the big thirty litre plastic bottle on the top of the machine seems to empty so quickly in a week. Hmm, hardly surprising when old Peg Leg Sam's helping himself to about half of it each week.'

'Well, he must have some thirst on him then.' I recalled my time in the gents' toilet and I was starting to take a shine to Peg Leg Sam. Thirst is a horrible thing to tackle. I took a quick glance out the window and down to the yacht. Things looked ominous. There was now no sign of Daisy, nor any sound of her calling my name. I looked back down at Black Bruiser, realising that I needed to cut to the chase. Curtail this small talk and get back onto firm ground.

'I am feeling thirsty and…. 'I started to say but got cut short.

'It's not his thirst that he is just quenching; it's his whole family that live up the back end of Birgu that he's watering. You work it out for yourself - if he was going into one of those fancy supermarkets and buying 15 or 20 of those litre bottles of water each week. Think of the cost of it nowadays. He's got a nice little scam going, I'm telling you. Work it out for yourself matey.'

He then shut up for a moment and looked up at me inquisitively and with his head cocked to one side. I needed to seize my moment and get a word in edge ways and hadn't he just called me matey? I sensed some common ground had been established. I needed to reinforce this bonhomie now, if I had any chance of getting out of here and back to the yacht before it left.

'Can I be so forward and ask whether you have a name?' Black Bruiser looked up at me with a quizzical expression and replied instantly.

'Mouser of course and pretty obvious I suppose. I got christened with that name by the museum staff before I actually moved in. Hardly surprising with the amount of mice I use to deposit outside the museum door. Oh yes, Mouser by name and mousing is my game. That's me!' Mouser appeared extremely pleased with his answer.

'And you? You must have a name. Your appearance gives it away. You are far too well groomed and pardon my French a little bit too well fed if I might say so. There's no alley cat in you. You have a nice home somewhere I bet. Well taken care of and no doubt utterly spoiled. You look lucky to me.' Mouser gave a sigh as if he had gone into some dream world of his own.

'Yes a nice warm comfy home. And your fur coat, so well groomed. I bet your owners take you to one of those pet parlours for a makeover. You have lovely markings on your coat too. All that heavy white fur with those vivid dashes of ginger patches. I presume it is all natural. What did you say your name was again?'

Oh if only Mouser would give me a break and let me get a word in edge ways. Time was decidedly against me and I needed to avoid all of this chit chat like the plague. I took one quick gulp and seized the opportunity.

'My name is Miss Licky, and I live on the yacht down there by the quayside, which you can see if you pop up here on the window ledge below where I am hanging at this moment in time. And Mouser, dear Mouser.' I was determined to lay it on with a trowel at any cost. 'I urgently need your help. Yes I stupidly popped in through that open door last night and before I knew it I found myself locked in. We now know what happened. Peg Leg Sam must have been doing his nightly water bottle collection and the rest is history. I was a victim of my curiosity and his greed.'

I was determined not to pause for breath, lest Mouser started gibbering on again and side tracked me from the real business of the day - getting out of here and back on board.

'Now I urgently need to leave here and get back to the yacht. You see, Eric and Daisy who own the yacht that I live on, are about to leave the island. I know this because they have been frantically calling my name this past hour looking for me. And I heard Eric say to Daisy that they could delay setting sail until about 6am. We must be nearly there by now. So please, please dear Mr Mouser, can you help me? I'll do anything to pay you back.' I thought for a moment and then quickly added, 'Within reason.' After all I knew nothing of Mouser but I had, by now realised that he and I were from different sides of the track. He was from the wrong side. Poles apart I feared.

Mouser was looking up at me most attentively. And for the first time I noticed a quite prominent black quiff of fur above his right eye. It stood quite erect and proud. It had not arrived there naturally but was there by design. What a strange thing for an old bruiser like Mouser to lend himself to and then I thought about it no more.

'Ah well this is a problem. This is a real problem, Miss Licky. What a funny name that is. Why Miss Licky?'

Oh my goodness, here we go again I thought. Mouser is away with the fairies again on yet another tangent.

'Oh Mouser may I explain all about that another time? Time is really pressing. I've got to get out of here, now! And another thing, if you wouldn't mind, I would be grateful if I could come down from this ridiculous hanging position and at least sit on the window sill. What do you say?' I gave my most appealing and sincere expressions as I said these words.

'Hmm, well yes, but providing you bring down mousey with you.' Mouser was squinting up just above my head, running his stare along the length of the brass curtain rod. 'I can't see mousey anywhere.' He liked his lips gently, twice over. 'Can you see him?'

Actually I could, out of the corner of my eye. He was on top of the end part of the brass railing but on the inside of the curtain, so therefore not easily visible to Mouser.

'No I think he's scarpered.' I was lying.

Mouser looked up and then away and then turned round a full half circle, looking to his left and right. I seized the opportunity and turned to mousey and whispered 'stay right where you are until I get Mouser to show me the way out. You then make yourself scarce and back to your mouse hole. Not a squeak.'

Mousey was much calmer now and did not appear to have any serious injuries from her time within Mouser' jaws. She was no longer shaking. She peeked at me and then let out two little squeaks of thank you. 'Sssssh.'

Mouser turned around instantly and looked up at me with a very serious expression on his face.

'What was that? I thought I heard mousey. Are you sure he's not up there? Is it my imagination or were you just whispering something to someone?'

My heart sank for a moment. I had to bluff this one out. Goodness gracious me, what was this morbid preoccupation Mouser had with catching a poor little mouse?

'Yes you are imagining it. Come up here and see for yourself if you don't believe me.' Now this had become a real game of poker and here was surely my last bluff — see me or fold. Mouser looked at me most offended.

'Oh leave it out. You know that's a fair impossibility. Look at me. Do you think I would make it up to the top of those curtains where you are in my state? Not a cat's chance. I'm far too out of salts for mountaineering and swinging from ledge to ledge nowadays. Look at the weight I've put on over the past few years. And I am considerably older than you'.

Mouser gave one big sigh that seemed to spell dejection. 'Well it looks as though fish heads are out the window for supper today. And if you don't mind me saying, Miss Licky, that's all down to you, thank you!'

'Well I am sorry if I startled you when you had mousey between your jaws. I can assure you it was not intentional. But anyway what is the connection to mousey and a fish head supper? What's that all about?'

Mouser looked at me for a moment as if I had taken leave of my senses. 'Oh God help me. You don't think I work here for free do you? I am one of the staff here at the museum. 0k I am not working officially on the books, but then that's Malta for you. It's a strictly quid pro situation, whereby I catch a mouse or even more than one mouse per night shift, and I get an extra fish head and other fishy bits thrown in for my supper. Old Peg Leg Sam collects the leftovers from the restaurant nearby. It's the old carrot and stick scenario for me in life, but I'm not complaining.' He gave a weary little sigh. 'Yes, dried cat food I guess for me tonight.'

I really felt very sorry for Mouser and for just a fleeting moment, wondered whether I should give up mousey to ensure Mouser had a full fish supper. I realised instantly that I could not be party to murder, fish heads or no fish heads!

'So Mouser can I please, please beg you to help me with my predicament, and get me out of here now?'

Mouser looked up at me and appeared to have a genuine empathetic feel to my situation.

'Yes of course I want to be as helpful as possible to the situation. Not that it will earn me any extra brownie points, or any extra fish heads.'

Oooh, don't go on about those bloody fish heads again Mouser, I thought to myself. Just get on and suggest a helpful way forward. *Get me out of here* I screamed in my head.

'Yes well the best thing is for you to first come down from the curtains. You must be exhausted, hanging up there all this time. Come and make yourself comfortable down here with me.'

Some progress was being made and this was the first sensible piece of advice I think I had managed to garner from him.

'Well that's very kind of you Mouser, and I don't mind if I do. Here I come.'

I gingerly clawed my way backward down the curtain, avoiding the violent rocking motion I felt earlier on with my lightening ascent. I dropped to the window ledge.

'Phew, that's better.' I stretched all four legs simultaneously, to shake off the cramps that had started to set in with all that curtain hanging. 'Let me just check this out Mouser. I need to see what's happening out there on the yacht front.'

I peered hard through the prison like glass. Oh yes, there was Daisy again, just stepping off the *Sun in Splendour*, and scooting along the quayside calling out my name.

'What do you see Miss Licky?' I turned in Mouser' direction, determined to put my cards firmly on the table and put him wholly in the picture. In an instance he might realise that he held all the important cards and it was up to him to play them with all the skill he could muster.

'Mouser, the yacht is almost certainly about to leave. It's got to be around 6am now. I have to get out of here immediately. What's the answer? There must be a small exit that I can squeeze through somewhere in this building?' My voice sounded shaky as I expressed all the urgency I could. My plight was by now desperate. 'Just tell me where it is and I will be gone. But I promise I shall never forget you and your kindness and I promise to see you again, if for nothing but to thank you for your help.' Mouser's attention was firmly held, as he gazed intently into my eyes.

'Oh Miss Licky, I've got to be straight with you. I know this museum inside out and I can tell you that there is no way of leaving until the place opens up for business. And that's not for at least a couple of hours. All the windows are firmly latched shut and each ground floor window is locked, together with the front entrance and a couple of doors rarely used at the back. The doors and windows are also alarmed but not the building. They chose this system as it was cheaper and it allowed me to patrol without hindrance. Don't worry, you will be as free as a bird, once the first member of staff arrives, but until that time, I am afraid you will just have to stick it out.'

I looked down at Mouser and found myself speechless. I was truly a prisoner of my own misfortune. I turned away and looked out the window for any further change. What I saw made me shudder and I gave out a most pitiful cry. The *Sun in Splendour* was on the move. It was inching out from its moorings, its engines gently throbbing. Eric was at the wheel, calling out instructions and Daisy was running along the jetty, letting out ropes and the like, and moments later, with Daisy now on board, the *Sun in Splendour* was passing by all the other sleepy yachts. She carried onward out of Vittoriosa Marina and into the Grand Harbour and set fair for the open sea. I craned my neck to see the last image of my home disappear past Fort St Angelo.

I turned towards Mouser and once again I let out a low meow and then my eyes starting welling up with tears. What was to become of me now? Where would I live? How would I survive? When would I ever see those two best human beings in the world? Were they just on a day trip and returning this very evening? In my mind I knew the answer only too well. Too many preparations had been undertaken the past few days for it only to be a short trip away. I flicked my right paw over the top of my head and down across both eyes, clearing the fog caused by my crying.

'Miss Licky. What's the matter? Come down here beside me. Now come on, things can't be that bad.' Mouser looked genuinely concerned for my plight, but it held little condolence for me at this moment in time. 'Have your people left? Has the yacht set sail?' Oh my goodness, come on down here and don't fret. We'll sort things out.'

And with no other immediate offers of comforts in sight, I hopped down from the window sill and walked slightly nervously over to Mouser. We almost touched each other's noses for a second, and then I sat down about two feet away.

'Now then Licky. Can I call you that? It seems less formal without the Miss.' He did not pause for a reply. 'Things are going to be alright. Trust me. We'll get through this together.'

I sat there in amazement and said nothing, merely thinking on what he had just said. *We'll get through this together.*

And I guess from that moment on, so my unconventional adventures began.

CHAPTER 5

Mouser was sounding more positive as he led me down to the ground floor and into the reception area. Not that he had any idea about how I could reach the yacht. Even if he did have a concealed escape route at the back of his mind, it was now too late. My home was gone.

He led me down the limestone steps and at the bottom we stopped. Mouser suggested I take a little refreshment from his half- finished bowl of milk. I was grateful and encouraged by his thoughtfulness.

Once in reception, he outlined what was to be done. Peg Leg Sam with the wooden leg would most certainly arrive around 8.00am. Mouser explained that he had suffered an unfortunate accident at the Malta Dry Docks many years since. He had been working around a crane — lifting material onto the ship when the crane twisted due to an unbalanced load. That caused Peg Leg Sam to leap backwards. An unfortunate reflex action as the load crashed onto his two legs — totally smashing the one and doing serious injury to the other. Amputation was his reward for the one totally lost leg. However the other limb was saved.

So Sam would be the first to arrive. He would open up and switch on the lighting around the building. Then at 8.30am the cleaner would be the next in. Peg Leg Sam would grant admission in and relock the main wooden entrance door. Just before 9am the two reception staff would arrive and then the main door would be fastened back. Shortly after that, the museum would be open for business and the first tourists would make their appearances, some in scant dress which caused some slight upset but money was needed and the employees saw the entrance fee as atonement.

'Now normally I scamper out when the cleaner arrives, or maybe a little later when the receptionists set up shop. Peg Leg Sam always gives me a light breakfast when he starts his day here. Dried cat food biscuits out of a packet kept in that cupboard over there.' He pointed with his paw towards a small pinewood cupboard built into the side of the reception desk. 'Once he has done that, he legs it up around the museum switching on the lights. So you can then join me and share my breakfast. How does that sound?'

'Well that sounds most generous of you Mouser. But I must say at present I have no appetite at all because of everything that has occurred here in the past few hours.' My sole intent lay in getting out of here and back to the quayside.

'Now, now Licky. You must eat something to conserve your strength. In my world you don't look a gift horse in the mouth. If, and I only say *if*, your adopted family does not come back in the immediate future, you are going to have to live off your wits. And believe me that takes some getting used to. I've had to do it all my life. Oh yes, life did became simpler once they took me on at the museum. But it is miles away from where you have been. You can't take anything for granted when you are an "old tom" like me.'

I mused on what Mouser had just said. At least he did not mince his words and he did not stand on ceremony when he called himself an old tom. Still, I was more interested in learning how he would get me out of this mausoleum. I brought Mouser back on side.

'So how do I get out of here?' I interrupted.

'Now be patient. I was coming to that Licky. There is no big deal at all. Once the museum is officially open at 9am, you put yourself quietly behind the glass doors. Then you wait for the first tourist to push open one of those doors and you slip out just as they move to step in. Bob's your uncle as they say and as easy as pie.'

He gave one enormous lick of his lips, totally content his escape plan was water proof. For me, I was more than happy to be receiving such simple advice. After all I was at his mercy now and was grateful for Mouser's help. I stopped thinking about these past few hours of strife and instead planned my escape. Mouser had up to now, shown me every courtesy, apart of course from our first encounter, when he had sent me scurrying up the curtain in fear of my life. I had grown to trust him. So I came to terms with the prospect that his kindness would be my crutch in the days ahead or maybe forever, if my owners chose not to return. A shudder tingled down my spine, as I pondered on my exit.

'And what I shall do, is wait and let you go first through the glass doors, and then I will give Peg Leg Sam a meow a few minutes later and he will automatically let me out. It's no good you and me waiting together at the entrance as we could get spotted. If Peg Leg Sam for a moment thought that I had been entertaining overnight, there would be hell to pay. He deals with trespassers with a metal spade.'

'Entertaining overnight?! Wherever did you get that idea from!?' For a moment I shocked myself by the tone of my surprise. 'I only came in here by mistake. The classic case of curiosity killed the cat, maybe, but I certainly did not come in here to meet someone for pleasure. Heaven forbid, nothing was further from my thoughts.'

Oh dear me, perhaps I was sounding a little bit harsh here. Mouser's expression revealed hurt, offence and confusion. He now looked very sad. I needed to recover the situation.

'Mind you Mouser, I am eternally grateful for everything you have done and I won't forget that easily. Rest assured you have been the model of a perfect host.'

His eyes lit up and he gave an instant purr for pleasure. 'Ah well Licky. You really do not mind if I call you that do you, Licky?' Of course I did not mind. I was growing happier with the sound. 'What I meant was that Peg Leg Sam would almost certainly view me as distracted, lazy and derelict in my duties, if he thought I had a lady friend. My failure to catch any mice and place them behind the milk bowl would and will make things worse for me. I am in trouble for sure.'

'Oh Mouser yes of course I know where you are coming from and I apologise if I slightly over reacted and I caused your distraction during the night with mousey and his escape. Thank you for your help so I can leave the building in a few hours. What's the time now?'

I need not have asked as there was a clock opposite me on the wall in reception. It was getting on for 7.30am. 'Yes, not long to go now,' I added as an afterthought from seeing the clock. 'And what are your plans for today Mouser?'

'Well I can join you shortly after you are out of the museum. Let's say on the quayside where your yacht is normally moored.'

I had not really expected such an answer. It made me feel a little uneasy. I hoped he was not thinking of the pair of us spending the day together. I had things to do, like sitting patiently on the quayside waiting for the *Sun in Splendour* to sail back home. I had to be there the moment the yacht came in to give Eric and Daisy total assurance that I had not run away from home and abandoned my owners.

My worries started to well up. It could be an awful long wait. Maybe days, maybe weeks, maybe months or years! I just managed to avoid crying out aloud at this thought. I did not want to let myself down again in front of Mouser.

And so it came to pass, just as Mouser had predicted. My opportunity to exit the museum came shortly after 9am when the first tourist pushed open the inner glass doors and entered, I slipped out unnoticed.

I darted from this sun starved museum across the service road and onto the quayside where only hours earlier my home had been moored. I sat there looking across the marina and towards the Grand Harbour exit. A large cruise liner was being escorted in by one of the harbour tugs, which brought no comfort to my situation. My wait could be a long one. But wait I would.

CHAPTER 6

I had been on the quayside no longer than fifteen minutes before Mouser came bounding out of the museum. He skirted around the delivery vans and raced across the service road to where I was sitting. He came and sat next to me, leaving a respectable space between us.

'Phew! Well that was simple enough wasn't it? All went like clockwork, just as I had predicted; not a hitch and no one any the wiser about your overnight stay.'

Mouser was content that his labours had resulted in such a happy outcome. He had learnt how to be a chaperone in times of crisis. A new lesson embedded in a new friendship.

'Now we must decide what to do today. What would you like to do Licky?' Mouser was full of the joys of spring.

I was confused by this out of the blue, maybe contrived question. My real intent was to sit here all day, all night. As long as it might take until my owners returned. That seemed the only right thing to do. Sit tight and wait.

I turned to Mouser and spoke my thoughts, explaining my intentions. He remained unimpressed and was far from slow in expressing his opinion.

'Now Licky, let's look at this sensibly and please pardon my bluntness but your people have gone somewhere and are not likely to suddenly reappear in the next few hours.' He paused for a second and then continued. 'Maybe not even days or even weeks, it could be even longer. Who knows? Perhaps, *maybe just perhaps*, they are only out for a day trip to Comino or Gozo, but how can we be sure? When I see boats leaving for these local trips, they normally start later in the morning. Not at six. An early start like that signals a much bigger adventure at sea. Am I making sense?'

Mouser was sadly making every bit of sense. Sense I could have done without. No matter. I had to pull things

38

together quickly. Take stock and start to plan ahead. Dwelling on the errors of the past hours and crying over spilt milk was no answer. Feeling sorry for myself gave no answer. Mouser gave me a quizzical look. I collected my thoughts.

'Yes you are making sense, and I guess I must now be practical. Look at the options. I haven't had time to think what I should do today. Do you have any suggestions Mouser?' To be quite truthful, I was in no mood to share his company. Depression leads to a need to be solitary. It would be churlish of me to share my selfish side with Mouser so instead I said nothing. I wanted to avoid causing any offence. After all, he had proved very obliging, up to now. Mouser's eyes appeared to light up to my question. Perhaps he saw this as a sign that *together* we could move the heavens in my quest to recreate the happiness I had so recently lost.

'Now that's more like it Licky. A good question indeed, if you don't mind my saying so, and the first thing to say is that I always take account of the weather early in the morning. Not to say that there is much accounting to do now, since we are in June. Every day shall be the same for the next three months or so - an unrelenting heat wave that shall give no quarter. It will be scorching hot right the way through to September and I doubt the island shall see a drop of rain until September at the earliest. Still I can always find us a shady spot at a shake of my cat's whiskers.'

I queried this last statement. I can always find *us* a shady spot. He did seem to be jumping the gun a little. Was this audacity or just simple concern? I avoided an answer in the hope Mouser would revert back to my original question. What to do today to move things forward.

'I normally take a stroll along the quayside and wait for that end restaurant to open up.' He turned his head in the direction of the row of five or six restaurants behind us and just down the road. 'It's the only one of the lot that opens quite early. About ten o'clock. It captures the early birds, mainly tourists visiting the area for an hour or so in one of the tourist coaches. Not that the restaurant is a great place for leftovers. It is vegetarian can you believe! Not a scrap of meat to be found. I think it must be the only vegetarian restaurant on the whole of this island.'

I had suspected something was different about this restaurant, through my occasional forays off of the *Sun in Splendour*. I had strolled pass many times and my sensitive nose had never prompted me away from the quayside. Mind you, my life aboard the yacht was complete. Pangs of hunger were things of a long distant past. So why should I stray into restaurants? Be tempted there by a sense of smell that belonged elsewhere? Oddly, there was also something in my mind that had singled out this place as different to the other restaurants. It's clientele. They were slim, often of slight build, pale and with an absence of rosy cheeks. That seemed to sum up the vegetable eating clientele.

'But they serve up fish there, don't they Mouser?' I was certain I had caught an occasional whiff of fish on my travels.

'Oh lord yes, later in the day from lunch time onwards. They are not completely mad. They haven't gone the whole hog yet.' He chuckled to himself. 'Can you imagine if that was the case? Vegan I ask you. No good at all for us.'

I hadn't a clue what he was talking about. What was this Vegan business? Mouser was evidently a human mind reader. My facial expression showed confusion with a question attached.

'Vegans don't even eat eggs or cheese, or even fish. Anything connected to living creatures is taboo. No milk. No yoghurt. No cheese. Nothing but vegetables, what a hoot. Well thank my furry feet that this restaurant has not gone so far. Whilst it not a gastronomic paradise for me there are tit bits to be had early on as this is always the first restaurant to open. Timing is vital. Jump on the table as the diners leave and before the waiting people have a chance to shoo you away. Much better though to return later when other bistros are sizzling steaks on volcanic rock. Huge portions meeting Maltese diners' great expectations. Too much happily for the tourists, who willingly share the excess with pliant cats. Secreting cut- offs underneath the table. Anyway we can take a stroll to our next port of call in about half an hour. The early morning breakfasts will be cooking and some free scraps of bacon and sausage shall be ours for the begging.'

Mouser's suggestions though helpful, simply piled further doubt onto my own parlous state. What was I to do if the yacht did not return? Live a life on the streets, foraging with those other feral creatures? My hairs were on end. Had things really come to this - my foolish error of yesterday leading me to having to beg and even pilfer wherever I could?

My early past started to flash before me. The life I was born into before my adoption; hanging around in alleys, searching for safe havens from the winter winds and other cats. Evading people who were then not to be trusted. I was facing a living nightmare. Despite the brightness of the sun I felt so chilly.

'Mouser, please don't think I am ungrateful for your advice but I really don't think I am up to it.' Mouser looked at me in disbelief.

'Not up to what?' he exclaimed in astonishment.

'You know, hanging around restaurants for tit bits and all that. I just don't think I've got it in me anymore. You see I have been living a new life for so many years now that I've lost all the skills I need to survive back in my original world.'

There I had said it, and plainly spoken. The idea of reverting to a hobo pussy cat again and at my time of life was impossible to handle. Begging for food and shelter was something so daunting and plain disheartening, that my soul could hardly take it. There had to be a better solution. The yacht would be back soon and that would be that. Problem solved. I squinted under the questioning gaze of Mouser. My argument was not convincing him.

'Licky, let's get wise here and call an ace an ace and a spade a spade. I'm going to talk plain and simple to you. Ask me what you want but you must be realistic. Plan for the future in the hope the yacht will return sooner rather than later. Either way you must survive and plan for that.'

41

Mouser looked more serious than I had seen him since we first met, when he caused my first panic attack and accidentally taught me vertical curtain climbing. His steely stare gave me no alternative but to sit up sharply and take note of what he had to say.

'Now I should not have to spell out the situation again Licky. At present I fear the odds are stacked against you regarding your patrons returning with the yacht in the near future. I may be wrong, and if so that would make me very happy. However at present we need to weigh up those odds and make contingency plans. It's no good relying on your ship coming in. That's like playing the lottery - hoping for that winning combination.' Mouser paused for a moment as if to take stock with what he had said. 'What ties your owners to Malta? Yachts come and go every day I know. Living on a yacht means that they can go and live anywhere. They could find a new berth in a pleasant land and even remain there forever.'

Mouser's understanding of language was surely born of a long history of curiosity. Listening to words like vegan and lottery. Learning their meanings, and educating me about new things in life. At least I had an answer to his latest question.

'Oh yes they have a small red Kia car here in Malta, so they wouldn't abandon that. They also own a lovely apartment down past the casino, just before you get to Fort St Angelo.' Mouser looked quite astonished by this latest revelation. Probably not so taken aback about the car aspect, but by the fact that they had an apartment nearby.

'I often stay there, especially when the weather is not so good - sometimes for quite long periods. I consider it my winter home. It has a nice large balcony that I have use of during the day, taking in lovely views of the Grand Harbour entrance. I see all the cruise ships coming and going. They visit for just the day and then leave late afternoon or early evening. And then there are the continuous Captain Morgan tourist boats that also roam the waters talking loudly through a tannoy about history.

"Over to your left you can see the quaint village of Kalkara, and straight ahead is the original hospital built by Nelson and

42

long ago abandoned." Yes I hear all this time and again when I am sitting on the balcony in the sun.'

'Ah well Licky, this put's a different perspective on things altogether. You are not only a boat cat. You have two different homes which is a luxury indeed! This is why you lack familiarity with your surroundings here in Vittoriosa. You are sometimes on the yacht and then at other times based in the apartment. How long would you stay in the apartment?' Mouser was not shy in posing questions and always straight to the point.

'Well it depends. Sometimes I would stay four to five months, as the yacht does not get used much between November and March when the weather can be treacherous. They will take it out for short sailing trips depending on weather reports and wind conditions. Mostly I stay in the flat at these times when they know they will return later that day. I do not worry then as I have learned to expect them home in the early evening. It is during the fine weather months that they pop me in the cat box and walk me up to the yacht, or go in the car, and I will often stay on board for months at a time. Unless they are making one of their flying trips back to the UK to visit their family and friends. Then I am back in the apartment whilst they are away, and the next door neighbour pops in each day to feed me. It all works out very well and I certainly have never had any complaints.'

I felt I had given Mouser enough information for him to better advise me what to do next. If I made things sound too rosy then I feared he too would plan his own adoption strategy when the yacht returned. And I could be cast aside.

Mouser looked at me with raised eyebrows. They lowered gently. I could not help staring at that extravagant quiff on his forehead above the left eye.

'Back to basics Licky, as we are still nowhere near to a plan, as you are suggesting the yacht could be away for a long time, especially if it does not return this evening. Your luxury life style might be out of the question for some time to come. Then day to day survival becomes critical. That brings me back to today. It is no good sitting here all day in the vague hope that your people might

43

return with their boat. You will need to eat and drink. So again do you fancy taking a leisurely stroll along the marina, keeping close to the restaurants for any pickings? Come on, you might as well. There is nothing to gain by sitting here and feeling sorry for yourself.' Mouser stood up and stretched his legs, and I found myself doing exactly the same.

'OK Mouser you lead and I will follow.'

It was Mouser who first spotted it. We had not yet moved from where we had been sitting. He let out a squeal of amazement.

'Licky just look at that. I cannot believe it. It's you, yes it's you.' He was looking directly up at the lamp post above our heads.

'You are on a wanted poster. That's a picture of you. You are famous! It's a nice picture too.' I peered in disbelief. Sure enough there was this poster with a picture of me in full colour. How extraordinary! Mouser's actual description of me being on a wanted poster was not however strictly true by any means.

'Can you read what it says Licky? Come on, read it out to me.' I peered up at the poster and tried to make out what it was all about.

'Well for a start Mouser it is not a wanted poster. The word in big letters at the top says *MISSING*. That is my photograph as I have seen it framed on a wall in the apartment. Something about a reward for any information leading to my safe return. There is a phone number underneath.'

'Well what a piece of luck Licky. I don't know about it not being a wanted poster. It seems all much of the same to me, a *MISSING* or *WANTED* poster. You are *missing* and they *want* you back. And there is a reward being offered too. Well I saw it first and I know your whereabouts, so I should claim the reward.' Mouser, with no shame that I could detect, licked his lips at the very thought of what might be on offer. Fresh salmon crossed my mind.

'And just how do you think you shall pass on this information to claim the reward? If you knew how to use a telephone, which you don't, you certainly could never make yourself understood to the people on the other end of the line. And that's a fact. Human understanding of cat language is basic to say the very least. A meow from me, followed by a few more in quick succession, usually dictates that I am hungry. A gentle meow as I press against my owners legs when they are seated down reading a book or something, usually means I want a stroke. Apart from that, our cat language has to be the least understood language in the world, except of course amongst our fellow cats. So I think it fair to say we can scotch any idea of you gaining very much at all. However many euros are on offer, neither of us can eat euros. Let alone change the things into anything remotely useful.'

Mouser looked most dejected by my response, but not for long. He looked up briefly again at the poster, before coming up with another of his bright ideas.

'It's simple. We hang around under this poster until someone comes along and reads it, and at the same time realises that the picture on the poster is you. Then hey presto, they will use one of those pieces of plastic that everyone nowadays talks into, and make a call to your owners. Then whilst they are talking to your owners, you start meowing like hell, and your owners will hear you. The caller might even lower the talking device down to our level and you can give a few more meows just to reinforce the evidence, that it really is *you*.'

Mouser' confidence in his new plan really defined belief, as far as I was concerned. At the end of the day, one meow sounded like any other million meows, from a human's point of view— of that I was certain. They simply have very poor hearing.

'Mouser I really don't think this will work. I can tell you that these bits of plastic you refer to for talking purposes, are called mobile phones. Now my owners have a mobile phone, but they only work when the boat is close to land. So if they are out at sea, there will be no signal. It will not work, and I am still puzzled as to how you expect to claim the reward. The person who made the call would be the rightful claimant, don't you agree?'

Clearly this gave Mouser food for thought, as he pondered my question.

'I suppose I could try to get the message across on one of these mobile talking things. That it was me that spotted the poster first and persuaded a human being to make the call. But I agree — probably a hopeless effort. But if I succeeded I would hope the money could be lodged at that Italian restaurant across the way. I could then enjoy free fish lunches until the money ran out.'

I was right about the fresh salmon. He paused for a brief second.

'And of course Licky you would be included as my guest.'

I was amused but perplexed by his add on comment, to include me in his fanciful spending spree. Free fish lunches until the money ran out. Hmmm!

'Well thank you very much Mouser for your kind thoughts, but thinking things through logically, why would I rely on promises of free fish lunches, when presumably I would be back safe and sound on my owner's yacht? Free lunches and dinners are guaranteed seven days a week - whether I am on the yacht or in the apartment.'

Mouser looked clearly miffed by my response, and I softened.

'Let me say Mouser and don't get me wrong. I would love to join you for the occasional lunch, but circumstances do change in life and who knows what tomorrow may bring.'

Mouser instantly perked up. He gave the poster one last look and then turned back to me.

'Alright, well sitting under this poster all day is not I guess the answer. It will get far too hot shortly. I think the best thing to do is to go and get some breakfast. Up to Birgu Square where hospitality bustles between the band clubs and the bistros. Skip the vegetarian restaurant, which is far too slim on the pickings right now. In the alleys leading to the square are plenty of bowls of food left for strays, and bowls of water too.'

'Strays in Birgu Square? I am not a stray. I wouldn't call you a stray either. After all you have a job and you live in the museum. The night watch cat as I recall.'

'Well Licky you must be a stray, because you strayed from the yacht last night and now you are stranded. You are going to have to accept these facts for what they are. At present you will need to adopt the mentality of a stray and live off your wits. Now we know you were a stray from birth, until you strayed onto that yacht.'

An admonishment from Mouser or was I just being selfish and boorish - probably both.

'Oh Mouser yes that may be true, but I hate dwelling on my own short but painful past. I thought those early chapters had been closed many years since. The page there had finally been turned, once and for all. I do remember Birgu Square and the pleasant streets running parallel with the square. But I only visited them through necessity in those days. I can truthfully say I have not walked back up to that square since the day I moved aboard the yacht. Birgu holds too many past and sad memories for me.'

I felt my eyes starting to water and could barely conceal my distressed thoughts.

'Now Licky, don't get so emotional. Let's treat this all as an adventure and take it day by day. You won't get into any trouble whilst I am around. Nobody messes with Mouser or anyone who is with me.' Mouser paused for a moment and then said something odd.

'There is something I have wanted to ask you Licky."

I wondered what this might be. The tone was suddenly quite serious and strange.

"Shall we take a stroll?'

I nodded coyly; Mouser said no more about that something he wanted to ask me, as we padded off the quayside and up the steep hill, to Victory Square.

CHAPTER 7

I followed as discreetly as I could behind Mouser, wondering what it was that he wanted to ask me and also wondering to my shame, if other onlookers were asking similar questions. What was I doing here?

Whatever it was, it was fast paling into insignificance. My current predicament was upper most in my mind. Here I was, heading up towards Birgu Square - familiar territory in years long past. This was a place I really did not want to revisit after all that had passed.

The memories of this area were those that I thought I had lost many years before; memories of painful days and great loss. Something I had never wished to share with anyone. Remembrances I had bottled these past 4 years. Time had supplied the veneer concealing my earlier anguishes - a forgetfulness I had been grateful for. That had made it easier to move forward with my own current life. Now I was being led forward into Birgu. Would the veneer splinter, exposing my own frailty? I feared bad memories would implode with each step of my paws.

Perhaps I should explain this to Mouser. I really could not stomach re-visiting this area. I could I suppose, make up some other stories to convince him of the danger. Or could I? The idea of spinning a yarn to Mouser became less and less attractive. He was an inquisitive cat at best. He would no doubt smell a rat and drill down into my reasoning, putting me in an invidious position of untangling lies and re thread them as truth. Perhaps I should just stick with the truth. Tell him the real reason why I needed to abandon this painful trek. But then I did need to eat and Mouser knew how best to find food. He was the one in control and in fairness he was making a great effort to look after me. I could not spurn his camaraderie by simply saying I did not want to go with him into Birgu.

We passed under the limestone arch, where a number of old men sat idly on stone steps opposite the Freedom Monument. A coach load of nationalities, almost certainly a party from one of the cruise liners, started to disembark onto the quayside and gather together following the guide's umbrella held aloft, into Birgu and on to other sites of interest.

A very elderly, weather beaten faced Maltese man tried to tempt some of the tourists for a quick trip in his colourful Lutzu boat around the harbour. There were no takers as the tour guide leader made her presence felt. She quickly marshalled her group into a straggling queue and urged the party to "see it, snap it, and move on." Time was everything as the Cruise Liner would wait for no waif or stray. Wind, tide and harbour fees controlled the Captain's timetable.

Mouser led the way past the Freedom Monument, and across the square towards the steps of the St. Lawrence Parish church. He turned to check I had kept up with him. Satisfied, he then sat down in the shade and turned to face me. I mounted the last few steps and joined him in this shelter from the glaring sun.

The tour guide and her followers were by now gathered below, standing in the road and looking up. Not at us I imagined. She was speaking in English and providing a running commentary about the church. I learned it was one of the oldest on the island - founded in 1090 AD. That St Lawrence was the parent church of those in Cospicua, Senglea and Kalkara, known as The Three Cities. In 1530, the Order of St. John took possession of the church and established it as their Conventual Church. Then it would witness important events surrounding the monastic life of the Order, such as investitures of Knights, Grand Masters and even Grand Inquisitors.

She rehearsed the victory over the Turks after the Great Siege of 1565, and then told her *students* that the Bishops of Malta held this church in great esteem. So it was that they conferred on it the title of "Post Cathedralem Ecclesiam dignorem sibi vindicate locum". Nobody understood this expression. She decided to explain the meaning. 'This Church', she exclaimed — in slight exasperation, 'was held as the principal church after the Cathedral in Valletta.' She finished off her unfathomable speech by telling everyone that on the 900th anniversary of the foundation of St. Lawrence church in 1990, Vittoriosa was visited by Pope John Paul 11. She did not explain why.

She opened her small umbrella, raised it above her head and commanded everyone to follow. Amidst the continuous clicking of camera shutters and flash bulbs, I wondered why on earth Mouser had chosen this place of all places to take a seat. We were surely not on a freeloading culture tour. I watched as the last of the tourists scampered after the flag toting guide as she disappeared up the narrow steps and into Birgu Square.

'Well, Licky, sorry about all of that ballyhoo. I was looking for a bit of quality time for us both - a place far from the maddening crowd. Still that's the Three Cities for you. It is a never ending endurance test during the summer months for humans who live here. Coach loads of tourists looking for culture and photos to share. Phew! You should see what it's like when the Japanese come. They live for photography and I know I must be in thousands of photo albums. If I could have charged a tip every time I was captured on film - some white bait for every photo! Think of all those tiny fish on a plate garnered together into a great pile.'

This story revived my faltering interest in the breakfast adventure.

Mouser licked his lips and gave me a ridiculous look of surprise. Had he really decided to become a photo-shoot backdrop for passing tourists who would sponsor his appetite for fish? I needed to get him back on track. Breakfast! Now! That was the priority and I had no need for any quality time. Maybe later we might ponder how best to move that thought forward. Such ideas I truly believed are best left to strolls in gardens and public parks, after hunger and thirst have been truly sated.

'Mouser, if you don't mind me asking, what are we doing here? I thought you wanted to take me up into Birgu Square. We need to talk about that as maybe we could take a different route, indeed to a different area. One that maybe I know nothing of and that I have never seen before."

I was hedging for time, as I found it difficult to say why I did not want to return to Birgu Square. I had no wish to push other noses into my own worries, and be a trouble.

'Oh yes Licky, that's right. I almost forgot why I stopped here. Yes I wanted to ask you something. That's it! All those ridiculous tourists with their flashing cameras quite put it out of my head.' He pondered.

Mouser gave one of those bedevilling long glances, which I would soon learn was his occasional practice - always and just before he said something of importance. Perhaps however, he had simply lost his train of thought. I hoped it was nothing worse.

'Ever since I came across you in the museum and we came here into these open spaces, I have felt something strange. A question continues to haunt me and it will not go away.'

'Oh Mouser please put me out of my agony. What is it you want to ask me?'

I truly hated to be pushed into asking this. Did it involve matters of romance, attachment and a future for us both? I was still a fiercely independent soul and wanted to remain so. Keep calm. Say nothing. Let me hear his proposal and hope it would not compromise my own aspirations. I remembered my time at the vet. Afterwards things changed and I saw the world differently, which included other cats. I had no interest or desire to join their tribes. I sensed Mouser had never met the vet. He seemed to be something of a loner.

Normally, I would have avoided the company of a Mouser, but now nothing was normal. I had become a surrogate and would probably remain so until my boat finally came back to Port. He was becoming my Tramp to his Lady and maybe that was not so terrible. However, I still felt this temporary affair was simply that and something to an end - whenever that might be - the sooner the better.

'Let me tell it to you as it is Licky. I have wanted to ask you this.' Here was yet another of Mouser's pauses, which gave me more time to feel embarrassed. What might he say - maybe something simple and nothing to do with me, or us or anybody special?

'I admire your stylish and elaborately patterned white and ginger coat. It is almost unique, the flow of those radiant patterns amongst that thick white fur. Your face continues this flow and I see an intense whiteness, blending with a light and ginger softness. When we first met in the gloom of the museum, I saw this radiance. But I may have seen it before.'

Where Mouser was going was anyone's guess. My sense of discomfort was suddenly heightened as I rarely spent time looking into mirrors and I had certainly never seen what he was now seeing. I felt uncomfortable.

'Mouser, thank you for your compliment, but I am still confused, as I thought you wanted to ask me something.' I was embarrassed. Please, please ask me something. Then I could answer and make the situation plain. Move forward — even if that should make us part company.

'Compliment you say? You misunderstand me.' Mouser hesitated for a moment. 'Oh I understand. Yes that sounded rude of me. I do apologise. What I meant to say was I had noticed something about your appearance which made me think. Ponder. Ask this question...'

Mouser paused for a moment as he scrutinised the canvas he had drawn. Me. Then he finally posed the question I had been waiting to hear.

'Have you got a brother and a sister? Are you one of triplets?'

The question chilled me to the bone. I was completely stunned by his question. I sat there with my mouth wide open. I could not believe what I had heard. Why was he asking me this? What did he know?

'You look shocked Licky. Are you shivering? Oh I hope I have not offended you in any way.'

I sought to compose myself, but I felt my eyes welling up with tears. Cats can and do cry.

'You see, you resemble two cats who I know live here in Birgu. In fact you are so similar I sense you could be related. The more I look at you, the more you remind me of them.' Mouser gave me a quizzical look, his head slightly cocked to the right. 'Are those tears I see Licky? I did not intend to upset you. But the likenesses...' Mouser hesitated for a moment and then continued.

'I could of course be wrong. If I have touched on a nerve then I regret it. Silly me, I do have these intuitions now and again but I would be wrong to say nothing. If there is any chance these other cats are a part of your family — maybe you should meet. Maybe become reunited. Your parents could be lying close by too. Who can say?'

I turned and looked at Mouser, gently using both front paws to clear away my tears.

'Oh Mouser, today you may have made me the happiest cat in the world. I remember my brother and sister but they disappeared from my life so long ago. We were born together. Triplets as you so rightly guessed. You really believe you may have seen them here in Birgu?'

Mouser looked at me and replied with utter conviction. 'Oh yes.' Mouser paused as though to assemble his thoughts. 'Oh yes. I am now certain it is true. It has to be them. And you will be reunited...'

CHAPTER 8

We sat on the top steps of St Lawrence Parish church, as I recalled things about my past, and shared these thoughts with Mouser.

I was born about five human years ago; one of three triplets, in an underground dungeon called the 'Oubliette'. I learned this was where misbehaving Knights were placed at Fort Saint Angelo. Why my mother chose this place as our sanctuary was a mystery to me and my siblings - foreboding but perhaps safe. Dank walls were covered with faded carvings of imprisoned hopelessness those many centuries ago. A constant dripping of water, an echoing place, this would be our home for the first six months of our lives. Yes it must have been the seclusion which led my mother here. Instinct told her that her time was near to give birth and she must get away from those humans in Birgu Square and its alleys. We adapted quickly as we knew no other way. We would dart from the darkness of our dungeon into the sunlight at every opportunity, but never too far. We learned those danger signs, such as footsteps and engine noises. We would then scurry back, never daring to turn.

We never strayed far from home, but just far enough to gaze across the noble harbour views from Fort St. Angelo, perched on this hill, tipping into the Vittoriosa promontory. We could see the boats, the ships and the people coming and going. Loading and offloading crates, people and pets as the waves licked the anchored boats, down beneath us in the Grand Harbour.

Our mother had made friends with the Order of St. John, our close neighbours in the castle. Scraps of food would be left out each morning and evening just outside our dungeon. Whilst we were all fearful of most human approaches, we learnt not to fear these actors of charity. So we would not scurry away but would accept the occasional stroke and their smile as they stooped to refill that bowl. These were happy days, skipping in the sun light along the bastions, under the watchful eye of our mother. Playful taps of the paw, jumping back and racing forward, mutual licks; and then one day everything changed.

We were fond of the man with the slight beard who often called to pay his respects. He was always in the vestments of the Order of Saint John. This morning he appeared and cleared the tray of old scraps as was his custom and this reassured us that all was well.

We slowly padded our way to the dungeon entrance, and gathered ourselves together as the food was spooned into the tray.

Our mother watched attentively a little distance away. We were sharing the scraps when we were suddenly caught off guard. There was no warning of danger. We heard a slight rush of air and then a large net enveloped us all in one swoop. Mother was spared as she was seated about two yards away just inside the dungeon entrance. She leapt to her feet and let out the most menacing of hisses, advancing to and fro, as all three of us vainly struggled with the mesh, seeking freedom from the net. Our claws became enmeshed in the net, betraying our fight for freedom.

The hours, days and then the weeks that followed proved tortuous and terrifying for all of us. It started as all three of us were bundled up together in the net, hoisted into the air and carted off down to the lower parts of Fort Saint Angelo. Our mother instinctively followed, hissing like a cat possessed. How carefully she had kept us from harm, until now. We were placed in the boot of a car in complete darkness as the lid closed down upon us, heading for oblivion.

The journey seemed to last an eternity. In reality it was probably no more than twenty minutes or so. I believed then and now that my brother and sister were more scared than I. I remember having to constantly assure them that things would be alright. I was not so sure, but someone needed to calm the situation. What fate was in store? Were we to be murdered? No. Keep these thoughts aside. I must not share them. Maybe we were going to a better home, a safer place. Their plaintiff cries resonated in the boot and dulled the drone of the engine. I was to be their protector in this time of crisis. Not for the first time had I acted this role. Many times I had herded my brother and sister back home, away from danger. Our mother expected me to help with their welfare, ensuring they did not get too playful or stray too far from our home, the dungeon. I would coax them back whenever they did.

The car came to an abrupt halt. The lid of the boot was raised and sunlight streamed over us. A kindly figure, I hoped, lifted up the net gently and carried these three crying cats up a short flight of steps, into a building.

The secured net was gently lowered to the floor. I could see three people, their legs next to boxes. I saw three other cats, each peering out of a box through plastic grating. We exchanged greetings and I sensed they were as perplexed and as fearful as we were. However each cat looked very well cared for, and their owners kept on talking to them. The only unwelcome guest in that room was a terrier dog, sitting bolt upright. Fortunately he paid no attention to us cats but rather to his owner who continued to stroke him. A chewy biscuit appeared from a pocket and the dog wagged his tail as it devoured the treat. No treats from our catcher. He spoke briefly to the lady at reception, and then abruptly left.

What happened next is very unclear. We were taken in turn to a bed and our fur was checked. Not stroked. The fur to the back lower part of my head was plucked together and I felt a sudden jab of pain and then nothing. All three of us woke some time later feeling sleepy, sore and confused. Terribly drowsy, we could not remember for a moment who we were or where we were.

We looked at each other and then at the bald patches where we felt some soreness. Each of us had similar scars just below our tails at the end of our tummies. Obviously something strange had happened to all of us but as we were asleep when it happened, we had no explanation to offer each other.

It was only an hour or so later that we were collected by the same person who had brought us here in the first place. By this time our sleepiness was diminishing a little. We were all placed together in a proper cat box, with a thoughtfully placed towel on which we could lie. This time, we did not travel in the boot of the car, but on the back seat, making the journey much more comfortable.

Once again it was about the same length in journey time back to what turned out to be the centre of Birgu. The car stopped, just off the main square. We were outside a large double fronted house, close to what I learned later to be the Inquisitor's Palace. Our captor jumped from the car and walked up to the front door of the house, and gave a loud knock on the polished brass ornamental knockers. I vividly remember noticing these resembled two leaping cats. We were now at a total loss as to what was happening and still drowsy and in a sad and sore state.

A minute or two later, a very elderly lady appeared with our captor, and peered into the back of the car. The man smiled as he lifted the cat box with us in it and placed it squarely on the bonnet of the car. The elderly lady looked through the cat box grill, and then suggested we all go inside her house. Once there, we found ourselves parked inside the cat box on top of a large and darkly coloured table. The three of us took in our new surroundings. The walls were decorated with large oil paintings framed in gilt. There was a tall grandfather clock ticking gently in the corner. I had never seen anything like it before in my life - the grandeur of it all. Little did I know that I would never see it again.

The old lady shuffled around the cat box, supporting herself with a walking stick. She seemed to be almost purring at us. 'How sweet, how lovely, how sweet.' What was so sweet and lovely was a mystery to me. During these past few hours, we had been taken from our mother, netted, assaulted and now brought here.

The old lady suddenly stopped. She held on to the table with one hand and raised her walking stick with the other. She pointed her stick at my brother and sister, saying we all three looked much alike, but she could only handle two of us. We had been paralysed with fear from the day's events thus far, but the final and enduring shock was yet to come.

In an instant my brother and sister were removed from the cat box, and then the grill was firmly closed, leaving me alone inside. They were placed on the dining table, and were now pressing their noses up against the wire mesh separating me from them. The old lady lent over, looked at me and then at my brother and sister and then started all over again. This time though her tone of voice sounded sorrowful. 'Oh how sweet. Now say goodbye to each other. Oh you poor thing. I would love to take you in, but I can really only cope with two cats. Never mind, I'm sure you'll soon find a nice home.'

By this time my brother and sister were crying uncontrollably and I was almost out of my mind. Was this truly our last goodbye to each other? Could life deal us such a cruel blow? What had we done to deserve this?

There was no time for me to answer and certainly no more time to bid each other even a wretched farewell. The cat box was suddenly lifted into the air and I was forced to hang on to the grill with my claws. Before I knew it, I was rushed to the rear seat of the car where the cat box was placed. The car door slammed shut and I was driven away.

We arrived back at Fort Saint Angelo and my captor parked the car. He opened the door and lifted the box out — onto the ground. He then opened the grill, releasing me there and then. Not only was I still feeling a little drowsy from my operation, I was now in total shock. I had not only earlier in the day been dragged away from my mother, but I had lost my siblings too. It looked as if things were going to get even worse. Was that possible I wondered.

My captor bent down as I unsteadily walked out of the cat box. He then stroked me gently behind the ears. What a strange and pleasurable feeling that was. I had never experienced that before. You see, I had barely ever allowed a stranger to touch me before. That was of course before the operation. What a difference a day was making.

I was still feeling confused and out of sorts and could barely take in what was being said to me. Something about *"You'll be ok. Just give it a day or two and you will be as right as rain"* Then my liberator was gone and I was sitting alone near his old car, as he marched away whistling to himself.

I looked to my surroundings and all I could see were several massive yachts moored by the quayside. Behind me soared the impenetrable limestone walls surrounding Fort Saint Angelo.

I felt I was at my lowest ebb in any part of my short life. Though I was unfamiliar with this exact spot, I knew I must return into the fort and locate the dungeon and my mother. She would undoubtedly now be frantic with worry about the three of us. I had to get back there and tell all that had happened these past few hours. It was really more than a few hours since we had been captured, as the sun was casting afternoon shadows in my direction. Probably around 4.00 pm I thought.

Looking back on it now, that afternoon and evening have become blurred in my memory. I was wholly unfamiliar with my new surroundings, never having been out beyond the vast walls of Fort St Angelo. Now I found myself peering up at what could only be described as a vast fortress, with impenetrable walls and from what I could see, no entry points.

I walked across the rough terrain and along the perimeter walls right to the sea covered rocks, where I could go no further. I retraced my steps until I eventually came to a small bridge. As I crossed over this bridge, my instinct told me that this must be the only entrance to the fort. I kept going and before long I had passed under several large entrances and climbed many ancient steps, and all of this time, I was still none the wiser about where

I was taking myself. I had not seen anything that reminded me of my previous life hereabouts.

Although the drowsiness from my visit to the vet was passing, I still felt weak and sore down below. I stopped on numerous occasions and just sat down and started to cry. Whether my crying and occasional moans of despair were simple sorrow or a vain hope that my mother would hear and rush to me, I do not know. Whatever the truth, my efforts served no good purpose. No one would find me. Not even my mother.

It must have been about midnight when I felt I could go on no further. Finding another set of limestone steps, I hid and curled myself up and fell into a fitful sleep.

This must have lasted until about 6 a.m. when the sun started to cast a few shards of light into the corner where I was sleeping. The light awakened me and I took a little time to emerge from sleep and remember where I was. I pulled myself up and then started to walk further up and into the fort. Not long afterwards, I found myself emerging into open air, offering stunning views of the Grand Harbour. However, these views were only partly familiar. I could see the entrance to the Grand Harbour but not the facing facade of Malta's capital city Valletta that used to greet me each morning - a greeting which prompted me to skip and play with my brother and sister under the watchful eye of our mother.

I began to realise I was at the back of the fort. I needed to follow a route along the top of the fort until I reached the harbour area. I deduced that once I reached this land mark, it would be a fairly simple task to work my way downward, to my prison cell home and my mother.

Although my logic seemed sound, it still took some four hours of meanderings in back alleys before I felt I was nearing my goal.

During all of this time I did not encounter a single human being, let alone another cat. It felt as if I had the whole of this strange place to myself. I now had a full view of Valletta before me, separated only by the Grand Harbour, but I was still too high up. The vista was not as I remembered it. I needed to keep moving down.

I found some stairs which led me down through dark passages. Turning a corner, I saw a beacon of light at the end of this tunnel and followed my nose. The circle of brightness grew larger and finally I emerged next to my old home.

My heart raced as I ran forward. There was a bowl of food just near the entrance. Although I had not eaten in ages, my one and only thought was to be reunited with my mother. I padded my way cautiously into the dungeon giving several meows that only my mother would recognise. There was no response, as I peered around in the darkness of the dungeon.

I turned and left this gloomy place and sat outside in the warm. I waited for some time as my mother would have to pass this spot on her return home. Finally, hunger and thirst overwhelmed me and I walked over to the bowl of food near the entrance of my former home.

I found the normal food station but the food portion left by a human earlier that morning was slight. That raised alarm bells. There was sufficient food for my mother, but not enough for her children. Maybe our benevolent feeder understood we three would not be returning here. However why had mother not eaten anything? The food appeared undisturbed.

I remained at the family home for maybe three or four days in the hope that mother would return and we would finally be reunited. It was not to be. In my mind I suspected my mother had gone searching for us in vain after we were captured. She would still be searching for us now in a senseless random way not even suspecting any of us would have returned. A useless exercise, even if she did find my brother and sister, as the old lady would simply shoo her away.

Eventually I gave up when I realised that mother would not think of returning here. I would have to leave this place and try my own search and trust to fate.

I spent my last night in the dungeon and left when the sun shone through the next morning. I found myself loitering below the fort next to Vittoriosa quayside. I was not to realise it then, but this would become my 'home' as a quayside stray for the next two months; two months of loneliness, constant anxiety and forever mourning the loss of my beloved mother, brother and sister. The daily search for them was unending, but was not helped by my being fearful of leaving the quayside. I was being fed daily it is fair to say, but this created such a dependency, I could not stray far. In time things started to improve and memories diminished just a little. Maybe things would only get better.

CHAPTER 9

Our short canter up and into Birgu Square awakened memories as I recalled events from past explorations of these houses and alleys. Journeys I had made daily after I first found myself on the Marina. Initially, I had to steel myself before daring to venture out from the Marina and onwards and upwards to the Square. As fear receded, I would explore the darker hinterland of alleys and back streets. Emboldened - seeking the house where my brother and sister had last been seen. After so many forays into these areas, I had eventually given up. Each search was nevertheless a fearful one. I was terrified of losing myself in these mazes. Trapped and never to find my way back to the Marina.

I remembered my first days at the Marina quayside. There, I was being fed by an English couple who lived in a floating house that gyrated with the wind and the tide. They had started to adopt me I think, as at morning and evening times, bowls of meat or fish would appear next to the bowl of water; all on this quayside — next to their yacht. I did not realise then that my choice of owner and their home would become one of the luckiest chances in my vagrant life.

As we strolled cautiously into Birgu Square, I could see that little had changed since I was last there. So many years had passed.

The old café on the top corner of the square, with tables and chairs outside, looked more prosperous now. Tourists with cameras were taking coffee and cold drinks. Coaches were arriving and offloading different looking people. One woman ran over to us and bent down as she pressed the button on her camera. 'Pretty puss,' she exclaimed but we shied from her outstretched hand. We ran sideways and found a new bar had opened where an old house had been. I recognised the door. The cat flap was still there. People were drinking coffee and tea and seemed content to rest awhile before they continued with their own journeys. We must be all searchers for something in life I thought.

I continued following Mouser until we came to the original café, where he turned to me and came to a halt.

'Now Licky follow me, we must go up this alley and then take the first squab on our right. Plenty of bowls of tit bits there. This is where I sense I have seen your brother and sister. However that means nothing now as things keep changing. I usually saw them much earlier in the morning and we are late today. We spoke too long at St Lawrence church and I am sorry for that.' He looked saddened as he said this and I felt I was to blame in spending too much time telling him all the details of my own sad story.

'Follow me.' I did. A couple of tourists uttered friendly oohs and such like as we walked past their tables. Mouser looked wearily in their direction.

One of the tourists had put her hand out and ran it along my back and up my tail as I passed, which I found very nice. Mouser looked back fleetingly with a disproving glare on his face.

I realised that Mouser had never been stroked by a human being. Forgetting the dreadful trip to the vet, I had from then since always enjoyed my fur being stroked together with tickles under my chin. Especially once I had been adopted. I learned to live for strokes and tickles behind my ears too. Clearly Mouser had missed those affectionate moments in his life. Mouser had never visited the vet of course. Oddly, that had made life with humans very easy for me to bear. Why that was so was a mystery to me. However a human lap to sit on and a gentle stroke was a great happiness and I felt sorry that Mouser saw this as a threat.

So it was that we strolled up the alley and into the square on the right, where we came across a line of small bowls left close to the doorsteps. Two cats were feeding themselves as Mouser bristled and hastened his pace. Both cats looked back at his menacing approach. They froze with their tails raised in the air. Mouser strode towards them and finally they backed away arching their backs and hissing quietly. They were annoyed. But not annoyed enough to risk a fight with a heavyweight and a lighter weight in tow.

I was unused to sparring contests and they stopped me in my tracks. Danger stalked this path. I had always avoided alley cats and their territories; mean, feral and vicious. Scratch me to death if they could. My sedentary nature may have been created in the vet's surgery but thus far it had held me safe from stupid arguments. I avoided confrontation. That was my protection and it worked. Running away was instinctive now and I nearly ran. Then Mouser suddenly turned towards me.

'Come on Licky, what are you waiting for? I think it's left over spaghetti with bolognaise sauce. A nice meaty sauce I'll be bound. Ignore the tomato sauce. Just eat around it. Come on, tuck in.'

I did as I was told - under the watchful eye of Mouser who continued to glare at the two cats retreating up the alley. This would be my first meal since the day before. Though very hungry, I did manage to ignore the spaghetti but the sauce was divine. I spent several happy minutes gorging myself on these remnants of some family's dinner. Then I recovered my composure as I realised I had consumed everything and Mouser had eaten nothing. My manners had been lost as speedily as those two cats, by now nowhere to be seen.

'Mouser I do apologise for starting without you. I don't know what came over me.' Maybe I was no longer used to dining in the presence of another cat. The last time I did that was with my brother and sister. That memory added greatly to this sudden feeling of guilt and selfishness.

'Oh think nothing of it Licky. Anyway, I am not very hungry as I had a light breakfast in the museum before joining you. And there are further treats up this alley and the next one and the others. We may be spoiled for choice as human generosity here knows no bounds.'

Mouser sat down and looked at me before continuing. I had finished eating.

'It was in any of these alleys that I last saw your brother and sister. Not every day to be sure. Now that is odd and I might add, interesting.' Mouser paused and looked away deep in thought, looking for an answer. 'I do think they are your siblings and I would bet my whiskers on that fact.' Mouser paused again. These pregnant pauses were becoming annoying but I bit my lip. 'Yes an interesting thing.' I looked at him once more with my head half cocked.

'Well go on then. What is this interesting thing?' He looked up as if coming out of a temporary trance and then mercifully continued.

'Yes well you see, your brother and sister must have been newcomers here in recent months. I have roamed these pathways over the years but only recently have I seen them. You say that they were adopted by an old lady near here after you had all been to the vet. Am I correct?' Mouser gave one of those fulsome luscious licks of his lips to emphasise the gravity of his question. He gave me no time to reply. 'If your memory is correct and not sullied by time then my question is this. Why have they become alley cats? They should be living at home unless another misfortune has afflicted them. That may make some sense as adopted cats never stray from gardens into streets. It is not safe.'

I had to agree. Mouser could think deeply when the challenge was strong. So his question became my own and with that came the worry. No one chooses to become an alley cat. Alley cats are born, live and finally die in the streets. No fault in that, as they have no choice. They are born out of cat wedlock and then have to fend for themselves, just as I had to do. I began to understand how a visit to the vet could untangle this very never ending circle of sadness. After that you would still be an alley cat as I had been, unless of course you became adopted by an old lady with a walking stick. Then you would become a home cat learning new ways. In my case I was not adopted straight away. I had lost my alley cat ways but I still had to survive amongst some very spiteful companions, until my adoption. Since then, I too had reverted to an alley cat life as had my brother and sister - if Mouser was telling me the truth. I was now on the streets but with no street skills because I had accidentally lost the security of my home and a life of luxury, and all in less than 24 hours. My thoughts returned to Mouser's last comments.

'Do you think my brother and sister misbehaved and got thrown out by the old lady?' It seemed unlikely as their manners were faultless. We did scratch at wooden things but no cat lover would abandon us for that. Scold maybe.

'Naw. That never happens. Once a cat is adopted they are a human's pet for life. Your brother and sister have clearly been well looked after. Mind you they were looking a little bit ragged when I last laid eyes on them. Still that's street life for you. I guess it makes us less attentive to the grooming part of life as we struggle to find the next meal. Then the safest refuge for a night's sleep.'

I became agitated as Mouser uttered these last words, and he sensed this right away.

'Now, now Licky, come on. Things are going to turn out just fine. I'm sorry about my thoughtlessness regarding the food and the sleeping. Remember your keepers will be back on their yacht any time now. We must think positively. There is an old human song I have heard here which starts *Always look on the bright side of life.* And that makes everyone smile and feel better when things are hard to understand.'

Mouser then went on to sing the same line three or four times. He obviously did not know the rest of the words but his sudden burst into song tickled me and I did feel better. I warmed to it instantly and listened and learned the line. Yes that is what I must do, as the words echoed in my ears. *Always look on the bright side of life.*

Mouser finished singing and then fed me an extra bit of news. 'I must say both of them have been well cared for and both had a collar and tag round their necks. Bells rang as they scampered away.' This was news to me and indeed good news.

'So Mouser do you know their names? Mother never got round to giving us names.' Mouser looked quite bemused by this question. 'No you must be joking. I have never been up that close to them to read their name tags.

67

They are very weary when they see me and they keep their distance. It is the usual mistrust between homely cats and the likes of me. Still it never bothers me. Live and let live is what I say. Prejudice prevails but I can live with that.'

I looked at Mouser and could not help but smile. What he had said was quite true.

The divide between Mouser and me could not be denied. He roamed the streets and alleyways by day and then took his job up in the evenings at the Maritime Museum. This of course really only made him half feral. He kept up his appearances and was well groomed, despite his nomadic existence. Besides he had good manners and was a kind cat. Anyone looking at the two of us would say we were the best of friends. Whilst I felt this union was improbable, it was forged from an adversity that onlookers would not easily see. So at this point in time I had everything to be grateful for, thanks to Mouser. All in all, he had proved quite the gentleman.

Mouser suddenly interrupted my thoughts. 'Licky, do you think you could remember the house where your brother and sister were dropped off, all those years ago? You see, cats, if they have been happy somewhere, always return to that place. Memories of good times can take them home.'

I pondered the question thoughtfully before giving my answer.

'It was near a large building off the main square, a building that a lot of tourists seemed to visit. Obviously I cannot be certain as it was a long time ago, and I was very young.'

Mouser looked very pleased with my answer and was quick to reply.

'The place I fancy you are referring to is the Inquisitor's Palace, just up the road from the main square. It's in Main Gate Street. And if I am right, I think I now know the very house where your brother and sister once lived.'

My heart raced with the news. Was there anything Mouser did not know, I wondered.

'Do you want me to take you there Licky? We might strike lucky and bump into your long lost brother and sister.'

My reply was a resounding yes.

'Now if I am right then the news may not be so good.'

Why Mouser always tempered good news with bad was becoming an agitation to me.

'I will not say anymore. Better we go there and check it out.'

And with these contradictory words ringing in my ears, we set forth towards Main Gate Street.

CHAPTER 10

I do listen well and hesitate to interrupt. Just as well, as Mouser turned to historical musing about the place we were walking towards. He started by telling me he had been a secret visitor to the Inquisitor's Palace these past two years. He would slip in through the main entrance, concealed by the throng of tourist legs and wheelchairs. Then, with care, could stalk those guides an entire day, listening to their rehearsed prose, exemplified with additional wild gesticulations and stretched shouts illuminating the limitless historical artefacts hidden behind glass cabinets, or hanging on limestone walls.

As we wandered through the alleys leading to the Inquisitor's Palace, Mouser enthused about the power of the Inquisitors who controlled this place between 1571 and 1978. Sixty-two Papal legates, as the Inquisitors were called, lived in succession at the Vittoriosa Palace. Twenty-four were elected Cardinals with three Bishops and two Pontiffs in tow. Alexander VII and Innocent XII. He spoke of the main hall of the Palace where the Court of the Inquisition met. Beyond were the Chancellory walls, decorated with the coat of arms of the Inquisitors. Below these grand rooms lay dungeons and a gruesome execution courtyard. I learned people were tortured here and my hairs bristled as Mouser repeated old stories of these barbaric times.

One of the prison cells held a legendary death well where unspeakable horrors were encouraged. The Palace had its own chapel, residential rooms and its "Piano Nobile". Mouser recalled the old Norman cloister which was much older and had been incorporated into the local court building that the Inquisitors called the "Castellania".

I felt mentally exhausted as we neared what had become a museum. Mouser's ability to retain such facts and figures from these occasional visits was commendable. He let me know again that he had listened intently to the English tour guides at each visit. He had also come across several other tour guides who proved incomprehensible, and he suspected some were speaking Japanese by their diminutive stature. Others he believed were German tourists as the strength of the guides' speech was strong and matched the height and girth of the listeners.

He reinforced his historical knowledge later on by picking up snippets of conversation from tourists as they sat at what was then, the Café de Brazil, discussing their experiences at the museum. He amused me by saying how annoying it was when he heard facts turn into fantasy, as happens when humans are over stimulated by too many sights and sounds, all at once. How frustrating it was not to set records straight. Listening to Mouser made me start to realise just how unworldly I was. Everything was new to me and I learned there was always something more to learn.

As we came alongside the museum, Mouser pointed me past the entrance and marched ahead some one hundred cat paces before halting. He sat down and looked up at a pair of large front doors facing the street.

'Licky does this house ring a bell with you?'

I edged closer to Mouser and peered up at an enormous pair of dark green doors. I remembered someone saying that cats are colour-blind. We see colours differently it is true and are always attracted to the sheer pitch of colour. These doors were alarmingly vivid in my memory and instantly recognisable. It was like yesterday. There were those same two polished leaping cat door knockers hung centrally to each door. Sunlight emblazoned the brass and it became golden; a squinting and uncomfortable colour. These must be those same knockers that our captor used all those years ago. Bang, Bang, Bang. The old lady had shouted something as she shuffled towards us. "Not so much noise. I am coming. Give me time for the sake of Santa Maria.'

My memory assured me that Mouser had brought me to the right place, just where I lost contact with my brother and sister. I felt strangely weak and terrified and I had to sit down. Mouser turned and looked at me.

'What do you think Licky?'

71

I reflected again on what I was seeing. Was this an illusion? Memory is a fickle thing at the best of times. No. This was real enough.

'Yes Mouser, this is the house. I recognise the door and those bright knockers. Why have my brother and sister been living so near to me all this time, yet I never could relocate these doors? Thank you for your help.'

I was amazed that Mouser knew much more than me and could deduce such an understanding from my sad tale of misery. He was truly a crime investigator like the ones I had seen on the television aboard the yacht. Mr Poirot himself. I wanted to ask him about the bad news he had mentioned but that would come later. I needed time to recover from this latest shock. I simply asked him how he had brought me here.

Mouser was as ever, pleased with himself. He had excelled once more as a cat of the world; an all seeing cat.

'I listened and used cat logic to untangle all that you told me. I must now come back to the bad news.'

My heart sank. I did not want to hear any more. However I had to listen.

'The old lady who lived here, died about four weeks ago - a sudden death in her home, sometime at night. There she lay on the ground floor between the drawing room and kitchen, so I heard. She had not been seen for so many days, and neighbours could hear a lot of meowing from behind the front door. Your brother and sister I believe. So, police came along and eventually got in. Later, I saw her body being brought out. I just happened to be there among the throng of spectators as I listened and learned more. I saw two cats dart out of the front door as it was forced open. They raced away in terror, down the street towards the square. I heard their bells tinkle as their collars swung from side to side. I think they were confused by the noise and the lack of food and drink. And there is more to tell.' Mouser gave a half yawn and then moistened his lips.

I stayed motionless, saying nothing to interrupt this flow of information.

'From what I heard, from snippets of street chatter, the old lady did not have any immediate family or known relatives. She was quite if not very wealthy and supported cat charities as well as the Church. She lived alone in that big old house, all alone, and kept herself to herself. She had a maid who came in twice a week to clean and dust, but that was about it. The old lady used to do her own shopping each day at the corner shop.'

Mouser paused for thought, turned and looked me directly in the eye, before continuing.

'So, returning back to the present, the house remains locked up and has been sealed. I wonder what will happen now? Her own relatives if any will surely be traced as will your own Licky. So we know why your brother and sister are back on the streets. They fled this scene in terror and became homeless again.' He paused. 'Does this make any sense to you?'

As I sat in the street blinking in reflective sunlight, I knew no sense at all. I was tired by it all. I felt confused and needed to withdraw and reflect. I was exhausted by the horrible story I had been told. It was surely a miracle that anyone had survived in that house over those many heated days. I needed a solitary moment of contemplation, with no more shocks from Mouser. Still, Mouser deserved a reply and a thank you for his clever detective work. My brother and sister had escaped from this hot house and could be found. Mouser' suspicions were so far correct. Those vividly blinding polished door knockers were my own Jerusalem; surely on to find my brother and sister. Would I recognise them after all this time? Would they remember me?

'Mouser I would like to thank your very much for all you have done for me today. I don't know how I would have coped without your help and advice. You really have been marvellous, and I mean that from the bottom of my heart.'

Mouser looked at me with an expression of delight. He smiled which meant a lot as cats cannot normally smile as humans do. The Cheshire cat I knew could smile but he was a human invention. I tried to smile too but it was too much of a struggle. Mouser gave me a purr and lowered his chin as his smile changed. A determined look emerged which told me the search was going to get much more serious.

'Think nothing of it Licky. It's been my pleasure. Now I am by nature a loner. I survive that way. But a loner is a lonely thing with little to share. My world is full of feral cats who step aside as I approach. I fight when I must. Domesticated cats I rarely see but they too run away. Fearful of what I am - frightened of my great power and my fighting spirit. Surely though I am not a bad cat? Misunderstood maybe but I always try to help when I am able. Am I making sense?'

I looked at Mouser and wanted to cry. I lowered my head and nodded approvingly and said nothing. Words meant little at this moment in time, so I purred instinctively to show I cared and I understood. I slowly composed myself and gathered my thoughts.

'I am beginning to understand how different our lives have been. I have been sheltered from the horrors of life while living on the yacht - pampered with every stroke of my fur. You have been left adrift to cope. I am truly grateful for your great insights which will steel me as we continue the search. Please tell me more whenever you will so I can learn and grow to love those secrets you hold so close to your heart.'

I had a sudden feeling my emotions might be stirring more revelations that I could manage right now. I had to adapt to these changed circumstances it was true. Gradually please. I was homeless and I needed to know how to survive. Mouser sensed my worry and turned his attention to the hunt instead. He suggested we return to Birgu Square and start our search for my brother and sister from there.

'It is now mid-afternoon and most cats would be sleeping in the shade. So it is those shady nooks we should investigate now — even though it is hot.'

So we padded our way back along the way we had come until Mouser deviated from Triq Il Mina into Triq Alessandru Vil, where I had taken a light snack earlier that day. We took a slow walk down this ancient street. Not one sign of any other cat and no sound of any collar bell. I was deep in thought as we meandered. What if we did discover my brother and sister and even maybe my mother too? How could I help them? I started thinking selfish thoughts. Maybe they had found another home. Maybe they could help me. Take me home with them. Leaving Mouser to fend for himself.

Stupid thoughts, as I was homeless and they might be in the same sad state. Where could they be living now? Perhaps they could render *me* some slight assistance, at least for the time being. Food and lodging was in the front of my selfish mind. I had to be more positive. Like Mouser. Surely my owners would soon sail back into the marina. Then dark thoughts engaged me. I was just kidding myself. They were gone for a very long time — perhaps forever. What if they returned finding me with my reunited family? Would they want three cats on their boat? If not, what would I do then? I could not be parted from them a second time by leaving them on the quayside. More foreboding thoughts clouded my mind.

Mouser then brought me to my senses.

'Licky, we are having no luck so far and I must get back to the Maritime Museum where duty awaits. What do you say?'

I was jolted back to reality in a moment. I realised I would be alone for the night in a place without safety. No sanctuary — only fear. Mouser must have sensed my worry and spoke quietly to me.

'I think you should return with me and stay on guard by the quayside - under that nice picture of you on the lamp post, with your name and the telephone number of your owners.' Mouser paused and said, 'you never know, they might be back there right now with their yacht, or at least soon to arrive.'

His tone sounded hollow - almost mournful. Maybe such a sudden deliverance was not what he truly wanted. Now I might have misread his tone, but I sensed that Mouser was starting to enjoy this situation too much for his or my own good. Perhaps for once in his life he had touched on a hidden emotion. His sense of isolation was dwindling. If that was true, then I would tread with great care. I would let Mouser know that if my owners did return, I would always value his friendship and that it could continue but in a different way. I would not be roaming around Birgu Square every day and all foraging would stop. He could come and sit on the quayside, whilst I roamed around the yacht, and we could talk. The thought of ever leaving the yacht again, if I was lucky enough to get back onto it, was fanciful. If fate should make it happen, I would leave the gang plank and sit with Mouser from time to time. That would be the limit of our friendship as evening and early morning forays would have to stop. No more curious adventures around closed gates and doors.

'Yes Mouser that is a good idea. Let's get back down to Vittoriosa Marina and take things from there. What time have you got to be back at the Museum?'

'Oh not for about an hour and a half at least and so long as I am back there just before five o'clock when the last of the tourists leave, everything shall be fine. We can spend some time on the quayside opposite if you like and see out the remains of the day together.'

It was decided. We took a leisurely stroll across Birgu Square but my eyes did roam into passing alleyways for any sight of my brother and sister. I saw nothing of interest apart from a few tourists and their cameras, soaking in the remains of this hot and humid day. They paid us little regard as we crossed the square, for which I was thankful. I was not in the mood for passing affection and Mouser becoming agitated.

We approached the quayside as the St Lawrence church bell chimed four times.

Mouser led me to the lamp post where my picture was still firmly in place above our heads. That was now my only connection to my recent past as there was no sight of my beloved floating home. The berth remained eerily empty. Mouser was the first to sit down and as he did, he spoke.

'Oh well Licky, they are not back yet, but don't despair. Maybe this evening they will return. It is still early.' His words seemed empty, although he was doing his best to keep me cheerful. 'So what are you going to do this evening? You'll be in need of a bit of supper later on.' Mouser hesitated for a moment and then continued.

'I mean that is if your owners don't make it back tonight. You'll be in need of a little something. Not a problem around here. These restaurants become busier as the sun sets and the moon appears. Many tit bits to be found under the tables, I am sure. That should be no problem, as you will meet cat lovers who will happily share their fish platter with you. Stroking human legs with my tail gives me no great pleasure but you are a natural. The real sharers at these restaurants are those who instinctively stretch out and touch. You are used to human beings stroking you, so you should do well. You won't have to catch them off their guard and do what I do - restaurant lifting.'

Mouser stopped and licked his lips, remembering no doubt those many opportunistic raids he had undertaken on the spur of the moment. 'Mind you my way gets bigger portions but is far riskier and has not always been too successful.'

I felt fearful going across to those restaurants and deceitfully playing on good intentions, whilst being on a begging mission. I was shocked to learn from Mouser that his way 'gets bigger portions'. To remember that he would at times jump onto tables whilst unsuspecting customers were distracted. Then seize a steak or a piece of lobster. That I could not do. I would prefer to starve to death. My life could not collapse into a slime soaked lake of thieving deceit.

'Oh goodness Mouser I could never do something like that. You commend daylight robbery. What if you or I got caught? It would be an open and shut case. Where would we end up? We would most certainly be barred from ever returning or worse.'

Mouser looked at me sheepishly. He felt he had said too much I sensed.

'That was a long time ago Licky. Before they gave me my job at the Museum and fed me. Before these happier times, every day was a day of survival. I have become a very different Mouser from those days. I was skin and bone where the fittest only could survive. Mmmm, yes I am glad those days are over.' Mouser gave me a curious up and down look. 'Licky, if the worst did come to the worst and your owners could not return, you will need to plan a new life, just as I had to do when I left the streets for the Museum. I can help you from my own experiences and show you how to adapt to this changing world.'

What Mouser was saying made perfect sense. I could not stay long in this alley cat world as I would finally starve myself to death. I thought Mouser had ended his own survival history to me but more would follow - prompted by my look of despair perhaps.

We continued to sit under the lamp post supporting my *wanted poster*. He pointed towards the second of the five restaurants bunched together near to the museum. He said this had been a particular favourite of his. It specialised in fish but offered steaks as well. The catch of the day was truly that as he had seen the vans arrive early each morning to unload the seasonal fish. Once customers sat down, they would be handed a menu. Before turning a page, their waiter would announce the arrival of a large stainless steel platter, filled with the uncooked morning catch. The monologue would start before any suggestion of a drink was made. Fresh fish it seemed was the holy - grail — to be treated with greater respect than a bottle of Dom Perignon.

Mouser expanded and shared secrets about profit and loss with me. The catch of the day was the real profit. The 'fish of the day' had to be fresh to be profitable. Some fish could weather the storm overnight in refrigerators packed with ice. Others would have to be wasted. That was the loss but thrown away fish was more than edible to cats. It all became a question of getting into the waste bins or charming the cook into leaving it aside on a plate by the back door.

Restaurant staff found themselves under strict orders to press perishable fish onto the plates of compliant customers through a litany of well- rehearsed phrases, as if reading from a hymn sheet.

Fresh fish was rarely priced, Mouser noted. Most customers on holiday would be reluctant to even raise this cruel embarrassment in front of family and friends. Those few that did were introduced to the brass and cast iron kitchen scales where the chosen bounty was forcibly and reluctantly sized for cost.

Mouser continued with his tales. He had learned these waiter scripts over the years and was pleased to pass on his knowledge. Lampuka, a dorado fish, he declared was the Maltese Islands favourite. The mainstay of the poor, as cod had been in Northern Europe so long ago. How he knew about cod and Northern Europe I had not a clue. The fish, lampuka had beautiful silver and golden colour and it only came to Malta from September to early December. It could not be compared with those expensive platter fish. However it was always readily available during these few months as a cheap local option. Mouser told me he was always saddened come the end of November when his favourite dish disappeared from menus. By then swordfish and tuna would start to arrive with great abundance as the spring to autumn periods approached.

Mouser told me a story he had witnessed while a waitress was working to perfect her own tale of fresh fish in this restaurant. She was explaining how just one fish could be shared amongst one large family tribe. Her focus was completely on the tale and she was losing her balance. The fish platter in her hand was tilting precariously towards floor level.

Mouser had placed himself under the gingham table cloth moments before this family group had arrived. He liked to anticipate things. The waitress led into the fish description part of the script, using direct eye contact to stimulate a salivating interest from her audience. She was truly succeeding. The very odd addition of the huge lampuka to the fish platter cocktail may have been its very last straw. Then over it went! The lovely whole lampuka slid from the tray and straight to the floor and under the table where it skidded into the welcoming paws of Mouser. The shocked waitress quickly regained her composure. She brushed herself down as she would be right back. She placed the tray with other tempting fishes on an adjacent empty table and scurried off.

Mouser exploited the chaos and with stealth and cunning, moved the lampuka slowly towards the quayside of the table. He grabbed the fish in his mouth and held it stoically as his freed paws gained traction. He moved more quickly now and escaped under cover of the confusion and into the open air. All eyes remained transfixed on the retreating waitress as he ran as fast as possible — away from the scene of the abduction. Not one person spotted the theft and no hue and cry ensued.

Mouser chuckled as he told me this tale and he pondered what the returning waitress would have made of the disappearing lampuka. Surely these tourists had not secreted it in that large shopping bag lying on the spare chair? She viewed it suspiciously but had not the courage to investigate it further. Besides, what would tourists want with an uncooked, smelly lampuka? These days no one of wealth really touched the fish and she wondered why the chef had thought to unleash it on foreigners. Mouser suspected she intended nevertheless to scoop up the soiled fish and return it to chef. He would supervise the washing under a cold tap; the lifting of surface grit and its subsequent reincarnation as a truly fresh but dead lampuka. Perhaps Mouser had done all other diners a favour that day. To my mind, I could not see that Mouser had done anything incredibly naughty. In those days, before joining the museum, he had to fend for himself and live. However his next tale would prove much more disturbing.

One night, Mouser had been studying a particularly boisterous set of diners who were paying more attention to their alcoholic drinks than their food. Laughter there was, as stories were told about car crashes and other great escapes. They had already made their choices from the fresh fish of the day display with no quibble. Largesse was their order as glasses never emptied. The very attentive waiter had been tasked to ensure no drought would ever occur at this particular table.

Mouser explained that he had not eaten properly for some days, and the very sight and thought of a piece of tuna had made him divinely ravenous. Eventually after many empty wine bottles had been stowed in the green bin, all six diners were served their fish dishes. All fish had been filleted and each came on its own silver salver.

At the magic moment — each cover was raised and a great shout of approval erupted, alarming the other diners on much more slender means.

The revellers gorged on the fish and the vegetables that appeared in unison but the show was pretence. The food was just a disguise for the drinking. Mouser felt there would be much useful waste coming from this event. The joking and laughing became ever more determined and of course irritating to the other diners. By now everyone was becoming sated on their second bottle of wine. Each!

Suddenly there was distraction from Senglea, across the water front, as a display of fireworks streamed into the warm night air. Everyone stopped what they were doing and allowed their lukewarm food to cool further. They topped up their glasses to celebrate the start of a fireworks display. The first rocket had already left the distant shore and the exploding noise drowned out all conversation.

One man was seated at the end of the table — close to Mouser who took great care to stay motionless. The man was seated away from Senglea but his wits guided him to an abrupt u turn and watch the forthcoming fireworks display. He dropped his knife and fork and spun round to absorb the exhibition. He then stood up and with camera in hand started filming. Mouser immediately took his chances, and edged up to the end of this table. With all customers' eyes transfixed over the water by the luminosity in the sky, he leapt up onto the table and grabbed the biggest portion of tuna his mouth could manage. No easy feat as tuna is inclined to be moist and crumbly. A grilled lampuka was a far easier catch to handle he told me. Nevertheless, with his mouth stuffed, he managed within a cat's whisker, to leap back off the table and race alongside the restaurant perimeter and into the relative safety of the arches leading to the museum. Mouser knew this had been a very close shave. Had he had been seen by at least one of the party? One child only had seen him and visibly frightened by the blasts, was crying. He was the only one to have spotted the actual theft but his family were alerted when he cried out and started to follow Mouser away from the restaurant. They all ran to rescue the baby and gave Mouser not a second thought. The evidence was therefore of scant consequence as the revelries continued. The petards exploded and the confusion aided Mouser's great escape - with a substantial piece of tuna steak.

I did not know whether I should praise or cajole Mouser about these past antics. I reacted cautiously considering that in those days, Mouser was on his own, uncared for by anyone and he was no doubt desperate. With Mouser now almost out of breath from these two story tales, I felt it was my turn to pose just one question.

'Mouser, what would have happened if you had been recognised - even worse caught? The consequences could have been dire!'

Mouser looked at me and chuckled. 'Well Licky if I had been recognised, no wanted posters, dead or alive, would have appeared. What could they do? Put me in a cat police line up? We cats enjoy protection from humans. They call it cat nature and we cannot be blamed for following our natural instincts. Only ever shooed away or chased. We enjoy rights that humans do not have. In any case, they would have had to catch me first and by that time the tourists would have been long gone from the island. There would have been no witnesses available to attend say a *police line-up*. Only the child but they do not count for much. If I had been caught and captured on the spot however I might have been hurt by the restaurant people, through summary justice or worse.' He looked suddenly very serious.

'What sort of justice?' I innocently asked.

'Some cats have been strung up and tortured for stealing or for much less. Sometimes strangled or shot by cat haters. You might call it instant street justice behind a courtyard door with the body thrown into a skip for collection the next day.' My jaw dropped.

Mouser was not concerned by what he had said.

'Anyway Licky, in those days I was very, very unhappy. To be quite truthful I was very much on the edge of my existence, and life really had no meaning for me. I suppose I was a lost soul and was close to leaving this world anyway. The idea of leaving here for a cat heaven, if it exists, was attractive. That is all in the past now. I am coping much better now due to the Museum.'

Mouser looked around for a moment and then at me. 'You know Licky, I will have to be off to work in a few minutes. I feel awful having to leave you here. What will you do tonight?'

For the first time today, my worries about my own welfare, paled into insignificance, as I grasped Mouser's thoughts about unhappiness and despair. Giving up life altogether was a troublesome thought. I turned and looked Mouser straight into his emerald green eyes. I noticed for the first time his eyes were not centric. A boss eyed, large jet black cat employed at the Maritime museum to catch mice? It made an odd sort of sense in this odd world I was now living in.

'Mouser I will stay here, under the poster and see what happens. You have been very kind to me all day, and I do not want you to worry about me. I shall be fine here.' I was not sure how to put the next question, but I needed an answer, one way or the other. 'Will I see you again?'

Mouser grinned like that Cheshire cat I had seen in a book. He cocked his head towards me as the grin turned into one enormous smile. 'Well only if you would like to Licky.' He knew the answer just as I did, but it was worth reinforcing. 'I would very much like to Mouser.'

Mouser clearly needed no further encouragement. 'Well that's that then. Shall we say meet here at just after 9am, the moment I get off work and out of the museum?'

It was agreed and Mouser raised himself up and looked at me for a moment. Then he raised his nose proudly just for a split second and pressed it against my nose and then he was off, skipping across the narrow road to the museum entrance. He then stopped, turned and gave one big meow in my direction. In an instant he darted inside and was lost to me for the night.

Now I was alone with all protection lost. I wanted the night to fall quickly and the sunrise to race to my rescue. I felt no hunger and no temptation to risk the wrath of the restaurant people. I was safer by far to stay here. I curled up under the lamp post, hoping that sleep would come quickly and be with me until I felt the first rays of the dawn sun on my furry tail.

CHAPTER 11

This was my first homeless night and it would be eventful. I curled up into an inconspicuous ball hoping sleep would quell my thoughts of fear and destitution. A series of cat naps followed with odd dreams of phantoms stalking me whose threats would frighten me back to the real world. Maltese people and tourists alike ambled along the quayside, taking the early evening breeze and talking in a mix of languages. Some were lightly spoken. Others shouted as though their companions were walking streets away. I stayed wary of this noise and bustle. This early evening throng passing on its way to quayside restaurants ready and waiting with menus open over tables neatly covered with white linen. I slept with one eye open for much of the evening. My slumbers would be interrupted by fear which made me peek around the lamp post to check for danger. Also to stare at the vacant berth in case my owners' yacht had miraculously reappeared while I had been dozing.

All of a sudden, I was wakened by a couple standing no more than a yard from where I was curled.

'Well hey, look at this Ma! Well blow me down. Have a look. Here at this poster. Blimey! I think it's Eric and Daisy's cat. Here she is. Look.' I sat bolt upright. 'Oh yes, Tel so I think it is. She looks exactly like the poster. She's got a collar on. Call her name and try and have a look at the collar tag.' They peered down and I allowed them to look. He bent down and gave me a stroke and at the same time raised the tag. 'Yes that's it Ma. This is their cat alright. Blow me down with a feather. Dear me. Well we had better try giving them a call on their mobile.' A minute or two later he closed his mobile phone while Ma kept my attention with loving strokes to my head and neck. 'No there is no signal. They are well out of reach by now. Heavens only knows when they shall be close to land again.' Apart from the feeling of comfort I was receiving I sensed the outlook was bleak and worse would follow.

'Well what shall we do Terry? We can't look after her. Dodger would give her a heart attack or eat her alive!'

Oh yes, I knew very well who they were referring to. Dodger was their ferocious pit bull terrier, who lived with them on their yacht- the *Up Yours*, moored a couple of berths past the *Sun in Splendour*. I had once or twice taken a stroll past their yacht and received a most unwelcome greeting from their dog. A greeting full of growling and gnashing of teeth, only to be silenced by the owners tugs on his lead and that hasty and forced dispatch to the cabins below. He was never allowed off the yacht unaccompanied by that lead and no cat would venture anywhere near this monster. I could certainly never live there and I hoped that Dodger would never pass this lamp post at night. Especially while I was sleeping and my guard was down.

'We will have to get the cat some food. We can get a bowl and leave it here. Plus some water. What do you think Tel?' At least Ma was making helpful suggestions for my welfare while her husband was trying to find my owners.

'Yes well I suppose we have no choice. Blimey Ma, this could be a long drawn out thing. How long did they reckon they might be away for? I reckon a couple of months at least, from what I recall.'

This was all I needed to hear. This news was bad. I jumped up trying to emphasise my shock but the motion was not understood. I was being affectionate, they thought. I was of course but I wanted them to feel my pain. I felt faint, the shock was so great. A couple of months at least! In a second my future had been mapped out. Times ahead looked grim and life would not be easy. Still I had been lost and in a fashion I was at least found. There was comfort in knowing I would be fed. It appeared they were going to leave out some food each day as long as I was here to receive it. This in itself was a kindness. I would need to use every ounce of my charm on them to ensure their charity would continue.

'Right then Tel, let's get back and I will fetch something for the cat. What's her name again, Miss Licky? Strange name indeed! Oh and there's a reward offered on the notice. Well that can go towards feeding the cat I suppose. We will probably need to go and buy some cheap cat food tomorrow. Let them know we found her. What's tomorrow, Tuesday? Oh that's alright, it's Birgu market day tomorrow. We can pick up a few cheap tins from the *hawkers*.'

With that they were gone. Before I could settle down again to sleep, Margaret returned. She placed a plastic container on the ground with some food I imagined her dog normally enjoyed, with another plastic container full of water. I responded with affection giving a gentle meow as I brushed myself up against one of her of legs to show my appreciation. I was laying foundations. She stayed awhile and spoke to me in childish tones and then she left. Smiling and waving as her mottled dress blew carelessly up and ahead of her.

Of course Terry and Margaret were known to me from their infrequent visits to the yacht.

I knew a little more about them too from that fateful first visit. They had been invited by Daisy and Eric onto the *Sun in Splendour* a month or so back, and they had stayed for more than a few drinks. I do not think they even recognised me that evening, as I stayed curled up in the spare bedrooms with the door wide open. I was always an avid listener of everything going on around me. Nothing could go unnoticed or unheard on a small yacht, so it was not a case of eaves dropping or being nosey.

I discovered Tel was an abbreviation for Terry or Terrance, and Ma an abbreviation of Margaret who was also called Marge from her schooldays, when she was a weighty girl who liked lashings of lard, margarine and butter on her bread. Dripping too was ever high on the refrigerator shelf which her mother replenished after each Sunday roast.

This pair had a nice lottery win in England the year before. They ticked the publicity box in error, or so they claimed, and wondered about the extra burden of begging letters their postman was forced to carry.

Things became so bad that special delivery arrangements had to be made to protect the health of this long suffering postman. Then the queues of people at the door, many wanting to know when their begging letters would be answered.

These worries, combined with an increasing gloom about the British weather, persuaded them to take police advice and make a run for the sun.

I overheard Terry speak about how *gutted* they were when they realised one Sunday morning, that all their six numbers had come up as had three other people's. They had to share the jackpot in a four way split. The total jackpot was £4,537,228 and their personal take was therefore only £1,134,307. I remember both Margaret and Terry muttering begrudgingly it was at least better than a kick in the teeth.

'The internet', Terry exclaimed with glee. That would be their salvation. A brazier was installed in the outhouse to manage the sheer volume of post. Margaret was complaining about her days being spent separating begging letters from utility bills and birthday cards. 'All quite simple,' Terry had declared. 'We shall use internet banking and direct debits. I'll get this sorted. We tell family and friends only to communicate by email. Then we can burn the whole dammed lot.'

These changes eased their escape to Malta by sheer chance. No need for a presence in England now these financial arrangements were in place. So one fine day, Margaret stoked the brazier with every box load of correspondence. By this time occasional puffs of smoke were seen rising above the house. The dust and smoke sullied windows and benefitted the window cleaner whose rounds were growing by the day. *'See — he has bought himself a new Mercedes CLK'*, one man exclaimed at the residents meeting. He passed around a photograph of the cleaner beside his new car. With his own van just in view showing *Jacks Window Rounds* emblazoned on the door with telephone number and web site address. All paid for by them no doubt! Besides not one of them had had a reply to their own begging letters now languishing in Margaret's funeral pyre. With all that money they should *surely* have responded to the vicar's roof appeal to replace the lead stolen by those gypsy people in the dead of night three months past. Of course it could have been any band of thieves armed with long ladders. 'It could have been Jack the window cleaner. He's got long ladders,' one member exclaimed but as he was British the very thought was catcalled.

The Committee passed the vote unanimously. To alert the Health Authorities and use the Clean Air Act to stop the carnage of Her Majesty's Royal Mail. Before proceedings could start, Terry and Margaret had wisely completed their escape plan. The ferry was booked. The luggage packed. All that needed to be done was to superglue the letter box, and dampen down the brazier. An error of glue application held Terry's hand to the brass letter box. Margaret managed to separate the two with a kitchen knife. Tel grimaced but gritted his teeth as his right hand was freed. 'I still have the scars.' Terry gave a hearty laugh but Eric and Daisy had trouble sounding relieved. Or feeling anything at all as it was late as the distant church bell struck.

So the story continued a while longer as Terry continued to help himself to more wine. Letting lots of cats out of many bags I thought. Terry had been an underground tube driver most of life and his wife Margaret was the housewife. They arrived in Malta where they had ordered a yacht for collection here. They had bought this brand new, for something like $400,000, but they had no previous sailing experience. It duly arrived, and they took delivery of it here in Vittoriosa Harbour. Terry and his wife enrolled in navigational courses in Malta and made minimal but sufficient progress to take their yacht out for occasional crossings to the small island of Commino and sometimes to Gozo. That was the extent of their sailing programme. They now lived on their yacht and their two grown up children from the UK would be visiting whenever they could entice them over. Terry looked down and mumbled something like 'not often'. I picked that up but then my ears are very, very sensitive to bass mutterings and mumblings.

Terry and Margaret were clearly the talkers and givers of information and my owners - the recipients who could only interject with polite laughter and the regular hidden yawn. The evening droned on and Terry and Margaret quaffed copious glasses of chardonnay, with Daisy and Eric quietly sipping at their pinot grigio, listening with great circumspection. I saw the chasm quietly widening. Eric's singular contribution to this diatribe was his reply when Terry asked him about his work back home. 'Engineering,' was his curt reply. Eric was totally at ease with the earth. Blunt. Not surprising as he was Yorkshire born and bred. Daisy complimented their union in life - both discrete by nature. Facebook was an invention of the devil. Television reserved for visitors. *The lantern of the imbecile* Eric would exclaim whenever his rare gaze fell on a documentary extolling the rights of the idle to limitless welfare funding. 'Difficult to draw much water from their well of life,' he would mumble. He would share facts about his past when pressed, and at present he did feel *pressed*. He would answer the question.

I knew far more of their life's experience. Eric had been to university, worked hard from nothing, and had eventually set up his own engineering company, producing metal implants or such like for women's bras, which included an expandable metal cup that would take a 42 to a 44 with ease – aluminium, lightweight and washing machine proof. That patent alone would make him a tidy sum. His patent was developed until such items as bullet proof vests became standard items within police forces and the military around the world. His cabinet was emblazoned with awards for his engineering achievements.

The glass shelf above with lalique statuettes also confirmed his status in the racing world. A clumsy visitor once dropped one such rare piece as they studied the intricacy of the maiden's stretched hand. Eric brushed it off and in time affixed the broken head to the body with superglue. He and Daisy liked taking racing cars around the world and putting them through their paces at down key meetings. He had now handed over his business to one of his sons and they were both staunchly retired. Eric gave some little detail of his career to this couple but neglected details regarding patents. The business was in good hands and discretion was everything for Eric. 'Tell someone one thing' he would say 'and the mole hill would turn into a mountain of treachery and deceit'.

That evening dragged on when finally Terry and his wife staggered onto the quayside as distant birds chat heralded the dawn. It was a godsend for them that they only had a few more yards to stagger to board their craft. Eric and Daisy spoke softly of their visitors. They would lower their profile and avoid much future contact. That lottery win had unhinged the two of them, Eric felt, probably somewhere around Dagenham in Essex where odd expressions were fashioned. Calling their boat the *Up Yours*, he mused, with a British flag on it. A red ensign too! Colour came to his cheeks and Daisy brought him a glass of water, to calm his nerves.

In my three years on the yacht with Eric and Daisy, I learned about yacht life and yacht neighbourliness. You cannot choose your neighbours. No, your next door neighbours can change from one day to the next. People will hire a berth for the long term but will then up and go on their travels, with little ado and at short notice. Then you experience a new rover. Not like living in a house or a flat, as we did occasionally in St Angelo Mansions. Here the neighbours rarely changed although a few of those who lived there constantly would prove to be the most unstable of people. 'No pets in the flats, by order of the management.' Notices would suddenly appear without real authority. 'No picnics on the rocks.' Pets and humans were quietly being displaced by containers of plants. Bedecking sea fronting terraces were growing like topsy. Cacti with prickly spines set there to discourage young local boys from diving into the sea, or even approaching this new civilised society.

This was in a territory that had always been the preserve of the locals. Fisherman and children listening to tales passed on through the generations, enraptured by the drama, whilst enjoying local ageing folk singing ancient songs while strumming their mandolins. The danger of seaside living and the ever threat of invading Turks had long since gone.

91

So the council agreed to drill into the rocks and put permanent signs up. This consisted of rounded signals showing red strokes through dogs, cats, fishing rods, barbecues and finally horses. No horse would ever again be cleansed here in these transparent waters. The local Maltese took exception to all these new rules and regulations, but sought to avoid the wrath of George Kafke who ran the Residents Association with the constancy of a Grand Master of Malta. A retired teacher, he deliberately avoided television or radio lest the slightest sound of a child above in shoes should be lost to his delicate hearing. He kept the mansion blocks safe from intrusion. From his outside terrace facing the sea, he would bawl at any child who dared to assert his historic right to a seat on those rocks and most certainly abuse families who might in all innocence organise a family picnic. Over time those signs would be bent and torn by local people whose resentment of this dictator was starting to know no bounds.

Most neighbours became immune to this terror. Other cats would appear on other balconies. Mr Kafke's hearing was insufficient to hear a cat paw though he could detect a miaow. Soon the cats learned to keep quiet lest an offensive letter was posted under their owner's door, threatening legal action should a second miaow ever be heard.

Once, the owners next door let their apartment on a two month let while they returned to the UK. The renters were a Maltese couple, with two young children, and they lived most of the time in Asia. He was a Maltese pilot employed by an Asian airline. He had a two month holiday break and therefore always returned to Malta, where his relatives lived, in the opposite facing bay of Kalkara. Those relatives had young children, and the apartment became the focus for daily family get-togethers. There would be laughter and merriment from morning, noon till night. Letters were pushed repeatedly under the front door threatening them with police visitations. They took no notice and continued as before. Oddly the police never came and Eric thought these protestations were being treated, quite rightly, as the act of a lunatic. 'Better things to do with our time than chide children for laughing, walking, existing,' said the police sergeant. 'Keep a note but focus on the HSBC bank robbery at Paola. They need all the help we can give.' He strolled back to his office and reflected on the trivialities of life that could overwhelm all of his officers if he ever let them.

People buy yachts for their own pleasure, but then numerous problems can arise. Where to moor it? Malta is now one of the safest and cheapest places to moor yachts and the advantageous fuel prices add to the attraction. At one the time marine diesel was free of VAT so Eric said. It was also something of a tax haven he felt which was why he and Daisy had elected for residents status here. The royalties he received from his inventions were tax free. As long as he paid the Maltese Government a nominal sum each year. 'Why should I pay taxes in the UK when they fund generations of idle people whose idea of a wage is a trip to the Social Security for a dammed cheque.' He would fume and his face would redden each time he was asked the question. Eric and Daisy told friends on countless occasions how lucky they were to secure their berth at comparative short notice. Nowadays there is a sizeable waiting list. People who doubtless prefer to spend their funds on the needy but never the idle.

Eric would frequently comment on the virtues of living aboard a yacht.

There is also the sea faring spirit yacht owners share. A quick readiness to lend a helping hand when mooring up and catching a rope while securing the vessel when winds pick up and spaces are tight. This is transitory however and may not compare with the same neighbour friendliness of a land bound community. Community spirit is as effervescent as the foam on the waves thrashing over boats in stormy weather. It can be as fragile on land but in Malta there are stout anchors to hold things together; the extended family which knots generations together, with faith which is universally shared by grandparents, parents and children.

In the yachting world I have seen envy between one yacht owner and another. Mutterings about size, design, colour. The larger yacht owners would pass their lesser brethren with a cursory nod or none at all.

My mind returned to the present and I remembered the kindness of Terry and Margaret discovering me and feeding me. Maybe they would make further attempts to call Eric and Daisy in the morning. At least to let them know I was still alive.

Tiredness overcame me around one in the morning. The quayside and restaurants were deserted as all restaurants had closed or were finally lowering their shutters. Just the odd car went past, delivering patrons to the Casino di Venetia to take their chances and collecting those others whose smiles or grimaces told their own tale of their fortunes this night. I fell into a deep sleep.

CHAPTER 12

I stirred from a rested sleep as the sun's rays were waking the skies over Valletta. I felt chilly. I noticed a slight ache in my neck as I had lain too long on concrete.

I sat up, raised myself on all fours and then stretched my legs. I looked at the casino then down towards Fort St Angelo. Everything remained deathly quiet.

I trotted off down to the casino lying in total darkness, apart from a low light flickering from under the door of the small security office to the side of the casino. The guard was probably dozing at this bewitching hour of the morning. I hoped so as I knew some of them were not cat lovers.

The Casino walls guarded all within and gave no hint of a hiding place. The outside flower pots were hard to climb without creating a fuss and possibly alerting the guard to my presence. However the building site next door offered a host of possibilities for entry and exit where privacy was assured. I could attend to my own needs and quietly scratch back the earth and hide all signs of my presence. Nature would do the rest.

I noticed things were happening fast here. I wondered what this new construction site would be, placed between the Casino and other century old buildings. Mouser would know of course and in time I would ask him. I slinked in under the wire gated fencing and took a casual walk around the site. There were plenty of discrete places and no guards on site to protect the bull dozers and concrete slabs. No need as only cats could enter and why should we threaten the enterprise by stealing bags of cement or marble tile slabs?

I took advantage of this solitude and then tidied things up before making the way back to my new home on the quayside – under this same lamp post on the public walkway.

The air was by now quite still with no humans, cars or lorries to disturb me. A good opportunity I felt to take stock of my current situation. I had been 'absent without leave' off the *Sun in Splendour* for more than twenty four hours. I had imprisoned myself in the Maritime Museum where I learned some things about myself. Climbing curtains to such great heights had been a new experience for me. Surviving dangers and discovering historic dangers in the past that had imperilled people and their beliefs. Through all this I had survived and oddly became pleasurably acquainted with a feral cat. An empathetic cat named Mouser who appeared to understand me and took pity on my plight and wanted to help.

Of course, I never wanted another *museum experience* but the learning taught me that adversity is often our greatest friend. I realised how grateful I now was, to have met Mouser. He had the sense to show me the way and possibly find my lost family or some of them if I followed his guidance. He had not seen our mother I sensed. Perhaps I should ask him more questions. I did not want to overload Mouser with new problems to solve. Finding my brother and sister alone would be enough. Finding our mother too would be short of miraculous.

I returned to my lamp post home and sat under the already slightly sun bleached reward notice scarcely held by tape as strong sunlight dissolved its ability to adhere. A sure sign that nothing lasts forever and time is the real enemy. Still, some progress had been achieved and this gave me optimism that in time I would be reunited with my human companions. Only wind and tide separated us now. The odd couple – Terry and Margaret were making time and effort to reunite us. Their perseverance would hopefully continue. I was certain they would keep trying to telephone Daisy and Eric. After all there was a reward on offer and that might be the icing on the cake of a lottery winner's good fortune!

I suddenly remembered, why I cannot imagine, the embroidered gift they had given Eric and Daisy which Eric immediately placed in the wheelhouse. *"A thrifty man is a happy man"* had been carefully embroidered decades ago. It sat in a framed small oil painting of a gaunt looking man wearing an oversized bed gown sitting at a table, his young and slender son by his side. Two plates of bread sat alone by a glimmering glass jar full to brim of golden coins. Underneath lay further embroidered words *"Slothful youth be woe your fate. Toil instead will make you great."*

Yes my situation was not totally hopeless and toil might bring its reward. Thinking back to the picture of the old man and his son, they still did not look overtly happy with their lot in life.

I had heard Terry and Margaret say my companions would not return for several months. The thought of staying alive for so long began to daunt my endeavour.

I reigned in my thoughts and started to think better of the future. Thinking ahead would be about each day, I realised.

The church clock chimed six times and movement along the harbour had begun. A man and woman in their late twenties, dressed in almost matching white shorts and sweat shirts jogged towards me. I sensed they had come from the direction of Fort St Angelo and they might have been crew members on a luxury yacht - he perhaps the captain and she the cook or housekeeper. I had learned that many yachts were run by married couples who would work briefly to move yachts from one port to another. Returning to their sedentary existence at home – waiting for the next contract to arrive.

A man approached with a labrador on a lead. I was grateful they paid me no attention and kept their distance. Nothing else was happening that attracted my interest or my curiosity.

I looked forward to the museum opening and being reunited with Mouser. With him by my side I knew there would be no nonsense from any other cats. The search would intensify for my brother and sister.

I had a little time on my paws and personal grooming became key to the day ahead. Eric would always say that 'cleanliness was next to godliness'. Daisy would remark on the boat about how clean I smelt. Eric would say 'an example to us all Daisy, especially on the high seas with no doctors aboard. No ambulances. No Hospitals. The cat leads by example and we should follow her example.' Then off to have a shower – inspired by the lesson I had accidentally given them. Followed shortly after by Daisy who seemed to take longer than Eric. 'Cut your hair shorter Daisy. We only carry so much water and your hair is absorbing half the supply. Besides it keeps the nits away and cuts the cost of these expensive hair lotions you insist on using. Soap and water, that's the answer, my girl.'

Cleanliness was an issue for me. Being homeless on the streets, the opportunities to keep up appearances were now severely handicapped. Too much time spent on survival, the next meal, avoiding scuffles and having somewhere safe to sleep at night. Hoping the lamp post has not been commandeered by others seeking sanctuary.

Many people, who take pity on the homeless, see the situation for what it is. They do not ask why you are living on the streets. Instead they stop and offer words of comfort and make an offering from what they have. I had experienced kindness of this before in my early days on the streets and also unkindness, being shunned with contemptuous looks and the occasional kick. Then, I would become depressed and think it was my fault. I was living as I was and had no way of explaining why I was seeking the kindness of strangers and more often their indifference.

Homeless I was but standards of personal hygiene would not drop. We inherit traits from our parents. My mother was fastidious. Cleanliness meant godliness and nothing else. Not in her book. I no longer had the luxury of lying on beds in cabins, or out on the deck, preening myself all day. Now I had to cope with the outdoor life, including searing heat and dust.

I spent some time sprucing myself into shape while observing the comings and goings along the waterfront. The place was starting to come alive as vehicles made their way down to make deliveries to those super yachts berthed beyond my gaze. Several large tankers rolled past, on their way to refuel vessels. Vehicles coming the other way would stop and start, reverse into narrow gaps to give these much larger vehicles of the road their preference. This road had just been reduced to a single file lane. The pedestrian area had been expanded to encourage more pedestrian tourism but it came at a cost. Not helped by those other lorries delivering concrete and clay into the building site. Who had planned this scheme I did not know but they had shown their dark but humorous side. Clever engineering which created an environment of tension. Arguments became regular occurrences, with expletives and clenched fists. Between the weak and the strong to get to where they hoped to be going, on time. They had tight schedules to meet and this delivery point had no doubt become the bane of their working lives.

I received a pleasant surprise as two welcome visitors came into view. Terry and Margaret suddenly came up the plank way leading from the jetty. 'Oh Miss Licky, I see you have been out all night again - you poor thing.' As Margaret said this she put down a new plastic container of food. 'Ah there you are and now we are off to the Birgu market to get some things and we will see what there is for you.' She then told me again that I was a poor thing, which gave me little comfort.

I barely had time to run myself against her leg as a way of thanking her before they were off. I did hear Terry say he really would try and call Eric again to let him know about me.

Good news had arrived to bolster my resolve. I was relieved to know they were still helping me as best they could and I was not forgotten on their list of 'things to do'. Breakfast on the quayside was never as palatable as breakfast at home. Still, open air dining can be pleasurable if intrusions are kept at bay. Better to eat fast and quickly before any marauding cats detected me and scared me away. As a domesticated and vetted cat, I was still vulnerable to any horrible threatening noises telling me to run for my life.

Shortly after the church clock chimed nine times, low and behold, there was Mouser. He raced across the service road and was beside me in an instant. 'Good morning Licky. Are you OK?' As he said this, he brushed up against me.

He was clearly as pleased to see me as I was him. I told him of my night stay here and how Tel and Ma had discovered me and were seeking to call my owners again. He lowered his eyes and looked away. Maybe he was worried I would be found. What then? I sought to reassure him. I felt the wait would be a long one. Plans change. Maybe they could not return here at all. Mouser raised his eyes but kindly responded saying he felt the reunion would come, sooner or later. He kept reminding me that it was not the end of the world. Patience was needed in a situation like this. I cannot say I felt more hopeful but it did make sense. Mouser showed genuine delight when he heard I had been given my breakfast. He had been fed in the museum and told me that he had been given a small lampuka fish as a special treat. He had delivered the mouse he had caught during the night at the reception desk as a proof of his diligence. I faked interest, although there was too much detail regarding the chase and the kill. I kept my thoughts to myself but wondered if this was the same mouse that I witnessed the night before, running for its life. I felt saddened but reflected we were now both well fed and better able to focus on the day ahead.

Mouser had the day well planned. We would visit the streets neighbouring Birgu Square, and search street by street, alley by alley, squab by squab for my siblings. I asked Mouser about the building site next to the casino. I was not surprised to discover that Mouser knew all. This would become a five star hotel lapping in those luxuries that well off tourists craved. It would blend in with the adjoining buildings in height and length. Maltese limestone would be the building blocks for the façade.

The two large buildings to the left, which had formally been Palazzios, would be incorporated into the new hotel and blend with this new and old build. Once open the hotel would bolster flagging sales locally. Mouser lectured me on the laws of supply and demand. The price of fish he said was set by the volume of fish caught. Also the number of customers prepared to pay for it. This would amount to a Battle Royal between the fishermen and the chefs who would be at the Marsaxlokk quayside by five in the morning to choose their wares and bid intensely for them. So too here, wealthy tourists would be drawn here to battle for the best rooms, the choicest restaurants, thereby bidding up prices as demand exceeded supply.

Visitor numbers to the museum would grow. Admission costs would rise. His status would become inflated as he dealt with the museum mice population.

I was not entirely convinced, but if correct, more visitors meant more peering eyes, and without his efforts, more complaints by visitors seeing vermin here. Any slackness on his part would surely lead to a severe reprimand for Mouser and even possibly dismissal and the return to a dismal life foraging for food. No extra fish tit bits in the morning - or ever.

He mused about a full time assistant and gave me a piercing look. Was he thinking that I should be that lieutenant to herd the vermin to their place of execution? I shuddered at the thought. I avoided his gaze and hoped the question would never again be raised.

What was I thinking about? I began to smile, diffusing the odd thoughts plaguing our own separate minds. Tears flowed as the smiles turned to laughter. I had to sit down.

'Well what's so funny Licky? I mean you and I could make a great team.' Mouser looked grave. His plan was a generous one and would guarantee my future safety should nothing come of this seeking and searching for my owners. I would park his proposal for now and focus on the tasks in hand.

Mouser came to his senses as he sensed my own feral side was far too weak to take on murderous activities. He started chuckling as he saw the absurdity of his plan. The thought of him and I chasing mice at night brought another howl of laughter to both of us. I had never caught a fly let alone a mouse. I certainly had no intention of starting now. Besides I would eventually be reunited with my loving owners who would not be impressed having a changeling abroad. A cat who had learned cruel ways and would prefer to be a scavenger of rodents, rather than a lover of laps, where purrs would ease the burdens of the day as gin and tonics were sipped by my owners.

Why Mouser saw me as a potential ally in the darkness of the night in this grim nocturnal museum was strange. I imagined I knew the answer of course. It was the company he sought. Spending night after night on your own in a dark museum for fifteen hours, surrounded by artefacts and relics was probably becoming wearing and he was finding it that much harder to endure. Well this was the life that Mouser had chosen and for better and for worse, he would have to stay with it, alone. Anyway, since when had Mouser been recruited to a position of *hiring* and *firing*?

We made our way into the square. I was grateful to Mouser for having momentarily lifted my spirits. Nothing had made me smile so much since the departure of my owners. That Mouser had lifted my spirits maybe by accident, was a source of some celebration to me.

I would broach the subject of my missing mother, but Mouser knew nothing. From the moment we were captured that fateful morning, high up in Fort St Angelo, the writing had to be on the wall. My brother and sister had been adopted later that day by the old lady, and taken away from the outside world. No one could find them, least of all their mother. I had of course been left below Fort St Angelo alone, the innocent victim of a lottery decision. My mother had certainly been searching for all three of us - never to return. If *only* she had returned to the dungeon, she would have at least been reunited with me. .

Mouser rehearsed his plans for the day with me. We should concentrate on what we knew and extend the search. He was showing great determination to reunite me with my long lost brother and sister. He *knew* the two cats he had frequently spotted over the past weeks were my next of kin. It was simply a question of spotting them again.

For this the second day running we patrolled the alley ways adjacent to the main square, but with no success. Mouser, true to form, kept my spirits lifted. 'Don't worry Licky, if not today, certainly in the next few days we'll come across them. Hmm, mind you that's when our real problems start. What to do with them then. I'm going to have my hands full, make no mistake. Still, we'll cross that bridge when we come to it.' With these concerns out of the way, Mouser sat down, back in the main square.

Mouser was amazing me still. Suddenly he was looking ahead. Seeing what we could all do together. He saw himself as our guardian who would guide us along the road once we were united. I wondered where this guidance would end. I drew comfort from knowing Mouser was in charge. He was a worldly cat who had intervened to create an unlikely union between him and my family. Without his support, I would have been driven mad. I wondered if there were places for deranged cats where they could be re-habilitated once the anguish of loss and closure had been securely managed. I could now be in an institution for neurotic creatures dreaming dark thoughts and feeding on memories of terrifying fantasies.

Mouser froze these morbid thoughts in a moment as he spoke.

'Now Licky, Lady Luck has deserted us this day and she has left no real clues about your brother and sister. I suggest we come up here tomorrow as usual. If we have no joy - and that is a very big *if*, I think we should make our way down to Marsaxlokk for the day. Have you ever been there?'

The name rang a bell. My owners used to mention the place as the home of fishing. Every time they went there leaving me to survey and protect their yacht, they would return smelling fishy with a plastic box for me. A little reward I always felt, for my diligence in chasing away nasty things and hissing at people who came too close to the yacht in their absence. The only times I ever became belligerent were when those foreigners crossed the line. Climbed over the gate and approached while the security man was absent. Cats and dogs then supplied some little security from idiots whose curiosity equalled my own. They would retreat and leave things alone. Whether the owners of barking and meowing creatures ever knew how much effort we took to uphold the sanctity of their lives I could not tell. However the reward of a tasty meal suggested to me that my owners at least appreciated what I was doing.

Once when Eric and Daisy returned on a Sunday, they met a fellow mariner who spoke of some youths that had tried to climb the gangplank. He spoke of my hissing which alerted him to climb the steps from his own cabin and shoo the brigands away. Swearing and noise. The portly security man had returned to his post and took charge, driving ruffians off with the help of this neighbour. Without his help, I could never have prevented these three persons coming aboard and creating havoc. The neighbour said that without my pleas for help, the yacht could have been trashed. I was the only one there to raise an alarm. Maybe Eric should pull the gangplank back up when they left. 'Miss Licky can only do so much' he advised. From then on, Eric devised a rope and tackle mechanism that would allow the gangplank to be withdrawn. His engineering skills were tested but he resolved the problem by creating a rope attached to the mooring point which could be lifted on their return.

I certainly felt the safer for it. I am not skilful in the ways of the police though on board I would be ever watchful. After all, this was my sanctuary too and I would do what I might to safeguard what by now was mine.

'No of course I have never been there Mouser. But my owners visit there quite frequently.' I told him about my fish experiences after those Marsaxlokk visits.

'Spot on Licky. That's where all the fresh fish gets landed daily. That's what Marsaxlokk is famous for, fresh fish and loads of it.' Mouser gave a decisive sweep of his lips with his tongue. 'I bet your owners only go there on a Sunday to get fish.'

I had to think about this one for a moment, and it came as no surprise, Mouser was right again. 'I do believe it is always on Sunday's that they go there. How did you know that?'

'Easy-peasy Licky. On Sundays all the fish stays at Marsaxlokk and is on sale from there. On other days, it is taken up to the capital early in the morning and is sold from the fish market in Valletta. Tomorrow is Sunday, which is why I am thinking we pop down there for a fish lunch. There's much to choose from. Phew, you won't be disappointed.' Mouser almost appeared to be dribbling from his lips at the very thought of this vast fish menu awaiting us.

'Well how long will it take for us to walk there? Is it very far?' Mouser I suspected, possessed more stamina than the average male cat, probably aided by his nightly acrobatics in the museum.

'Don't be daft Licky! Walk? No we'll take the bus. Walk! Over my dead body! It's a good four or five kilometres from here. If you walked there, the exercise might be good for you, but walking back after a full Sunday fish lunch! We'd never make it. Well we would but I could be late for work and that that would never do.'

An obvious question sprung to mind and I did not hesitate to ask it. 'Are you serious Mouser? We take a bus to this place! I have never been on a bus, and I am sure cats are not allowed on buses. How would they pay the fare? Is there a special rate for cats and dogs?

'Oooh Licky, you are such a doubting Thomas, and that's no mistake. Just trust in me. Believe me, when it comes to us cats, I am king of the road. I've been everywhere man, I've been everywhere.' Mouser's voice became lyrical. I rested my case, since wonders would never cease when it came to Mouser.

'Licky, we need to make this trip sooner than later. From July, bus trips for the likes of you and me will be a thing of the past, from what I am hearing. Out of the window! Oh yes, mark my words.'

Mouser showed remarkable knowledge of the Maltese bus service, reciting things he had heard and been told on one of his many bus trips. In July, new buses, all the way from England, but made in China, would replace the present Maltese bus service. Buses that had been operating for fifty or even sixty years would overnight become redundant. Those dodgy doors that remained forever open would be a thing of the past. The new buses could not move if the automatic doors were not fully closed. The Maltese buses that burnt old cooking oil would go to the bus grave yard, wherever that would be.

Some would go to a new museum. Some might be adapted for tourism so the doors would actually close and the slightest hint of cooking oil in their bodies would cause a lockdown. Malta was now in the EU and the country had to conform to new rules. The old buses were a Maltese national heritage. They were vintage, a huge tourist attraction, featured on post cards but rarely road worthy; rickety and with belching death defying exhaust gases. Driven by drivers who never carried change and who would regularly overcharge foreigners. The Maltese had learned over the generations, never to approach a bus without the right fare, or risk time delaying altercations as they protested their rights as the drivers protested their own in *not* giving back change.

Mouser told me more about the changes that were afoot. The new bus service was a radical change. Until now, all buses were owned and run by private individuals. The owner of the bus was usually the driver. There was no consistency in the service from one bus to another. Jumping onto a bus was a *wild west* moment.

Mouser had learned that the new bus service would be run by an English company named ARRIVA. All employees would be uniformed, fully trained, adhere to company rules, work tight rotas and most importantly no longer be allowed to be *themselves*. The Maltese way of doing things was going to be knocked out of them. No room for cavalier behaviour. A new dawn heralded.

Mouser made it clear. Bad times were ahead and free travel would be lost forever. Gratuitous cat passes for the likes of him would soon be a thing of the past. So we must make hay whilst the sun still shone.

The next day, I would be taking my very first bus ride, my very first Sunday fish lunch in the lovely village of Marsaxlokk and another day and a step closer I hoped, to finding my brother and sister.

CHAPTER 13

We spent the rest of the afternoon around Birgu Square then crossed to Freedom Square. We observed the ferry man and his *luzzu*, enticing tourists for short and expansive trips around the marina. Some chatter about the history of the place, these words coming from the mouth of this very ancient mariner. Only five feet tall, he wore weather beaten shorts and a vest of similar description. On his feet were sandals. Sacred items, held together by ships glue. These gripped the wood of his luzzu when blustery winds drove briny rain into his craft. His face had been crafted by his years working at the shipyards after the British left. He kept a picture of his shipmates on an English frigate in his top pocket. A faded black and white photograph of happier times he knew when the British guarded Birgu and found employment for him and his family. Everyone was so equal then. *Where the Royal Navy was involved,* he would say.

The Luzzu man laid up his oars and a small engine burst into life to cross safely to wherever these foreigners felt like going. Up to them he thought. No quibbling about the cost today. Smile, be happy and use his precious but limited English to lighten the mood. Lighten their purses a little once the tips tin was passed around, to end a memorable day with enduring sights captured on these visitor's cameras.

Mouser bade me farewell shortly before five o'clock to start his important shift at the museum. I watched him leave and felt sadness taking his place. I began to own up to my own feelings. These forty eight hours had brought a kindred spirit into my life and this had made a much bigger impression on me than I had cared to admit. We were both lonely souls.

Mouser had been able to build on my trust and help me to deal with my misery these past two days. He would turn worry into hope and distract me from the darkness of my fears. He had given me hope when all I could see was destitution and desperation. He had raised my spirits high when all I thought I could see was a well of loneliness. He had become my protector. Mouser had so shortly, become my one and only friend on the planet. I should learn not to take his concern for granted. Not to lose his support. Selfish maybe but maybe I was giving him something he was missing.

I reflected with sadness on my life from the time of my birth. I would never know who my father was. Cats are fickle and loyalty is only in the here and now. I managed to lose my brother, sister and mother all in one day. But had I perhaps lost the desire to truly reunite? My life had been transformed after my forced visit to the vet. He had with one quick cut turned me into a domestic animal. I had turned to human company. Maybe that had dulled my quest to search for my own family. Could I have tried harder? Had the enthusiasm faltered? So maybe it was me who was the selfish one.

As was my custom, I occupied my space under the lamp post and waited. Sure enough Margaret appeared with a small foiled tray and an opened tin of cat food. Keeping the fork in place as its handle peered above the tin.

'Well Miss Licky. So you are back after us.' She lowered her head and shoulders and began whispering as though a great and private confidence would be shared. "I must tell you that my husband Tel has tried getting in contact with your owners, but still no joy there. Obviously they are still out of reach of any land and signal masts. All at sea somewhere far away I guess.' She paused as she threw her head upwards and let out a coarse but apologetic laugh. 'Oh dear me, I don't know why I tell you all this, you silly thing. You can't understand a word I'm saying. Hmm, well never mind, as promised we bought some tins of cat food up the market. Dirt cheap, but a tad out of date! What's it called? Let me see.' She looked at the label. 'Rokus. Meat chunks with fish trozos de pesscado, whatever that means. Oh my gaud, there I go again, talking to myself. Well here we go.' She put the foil tray on the ground and then filled it with a generous but possibly hazardous portion of *rokus*. I smelt the contents but all seemed well and anyway my hunger would not be deterred by a *passed* sell by date on a label.

I did my usual thing by way of thank you, brushing myself up against her legs several times, with a few low meows thrown in.

'I see you have enough water in the other bowl to last until the morning. Good, see you at breakfast tomorrow.' Off she waddled down the jetty, with half a tin full of cat food in one hand and the empty foil tray from this morning's meal.

So communication and contact with my owners had failed again. I suspected even if and when contact was made, the likelihood of them abandoning their trip and turning round to race back to Malta to be reunited with me was unlikely. I remembered the event of a year before when all three of us went away together for around seven weeks. That was an adventure and a half. I would tell Mouser about that someday. He would be impressed by the dangers we faced and how adversity turned us into the bravest of sea farers. However, even comradeship could falter and dim with the passage of time. Maybe it was their time to forget me.

Mouser, from what I could tell, had never travelled far from his birthplace. He was a Maltese cat born and bred and might not fare well beyond these shores. He had a good memory and used his powerful memory to retain much of what he heard, which seemed a useful skill that probably supplanted his actual lack of travels abroad.

I nibbled the food and found it was quite edible even though my choice would have been for a bowl of Whiskas. I had been spoilt on the yacht where caviar was often preferred to lump fish and champagne to prosecco. I had tasted caviar there and learned to love its salty flavour. I ate all of my rokus before any other stray cat could approach and frighten me away. None were to be seen and I felt safe enough to lie down and sleep fitfully as the noises of the night interrupted my security. By midnight cars and people were gone and quiet returned to the quayside.

In the morning Margaret arrived as regular as clockwork. The clock chimed eight times as she lay the foil tray next to me. Full once more with rokus. She was not so talkative today but I was pleased to see her. She was in a routine now that was dependable and that gave me cause for comfort - considerable comfort for me, in my present situation.

'There you are Miss Licky. Breakfast is served! And see you this evening. Ooh my goodness, Tel is getting on my nerves this morning!'

With that, she hurried back to the yacht. I was curious to know what had happened between them. Still it was none of my business. Breakfast was my priority. I needed to stoke up on a good breakfast before going on this promised bus journey to the place Mouser called Marsaxlokk.

Time flew by and before I knew it the clock struck nine times. Then Mouser appeared, crossing the road and approached. He gave me a slight lick on my nose and I turned away. He was full of life and the joys of spring. It could be that he had caught another mouse or two during the night, giving the extra spring to his step. I was being ungracious. Whatever the reason, Mouser would explain all no doubt. I would not pry. Mouse catching and I were poles apart and I think Mouser was by now aware of that. He made no mention of any clandestine attacks on the rodents within the Museum for which I was grateful.

'So was everything alright last night? No unwelcome visitors I hope. And you've had breakfast I see. That's good. So shall we go?'

So off we set at a brisk pace up to Birgu Square and our usual hunting ground. We spent about fifteen minutes there, but to no avail. There were a number of feral cats around but no sight of my brother or sister. 'So what we shall do is pop back here later this afternoon after our return from Marsaxlokk. We are going to find them sooner than later.'

Mouser's continuous assurance kept my spirits up. At times I felt guilty leaving this area, as Mouser had remained constant in his belief that this was where my brother and sister would be found. However it would not have been fair to keep Mouser hanging around all day on the off chance of a discovery. Certainly I knew I could not hang around on my own in this place. Not with all these feral cats around. I would be a lamb to the slaughter. If even one of them squared up to me for a cat fight I could only run and hope my pace was faster than their own.

'So let's go off to the bus terminal, which is just below where the weekly Birgu market is held every Tuesday. Let's hope that Tal-Patann is driving today. He should be as he rarely has a day off.'

'Who or what is Tal-Patann, may I ask?' No doubt another revelation was about to befall me from Mouser and his wisdom.

'Tal-Patann? He's the driver of course.' Mouser for a second seemed to be puzzled by my question. 'Oh yes, sorry Miss Licky, for a moment I forgot your understanding of Maltese is so slight.' Ooops, here we go again, I thought to myself. Mouser and his know it all retorts. Never mind, I was more interested in the answer.

'Tai-Patann is his nickname. It means *chubby* in Maltese. Believe me he is! Everyone calls him by his nickname. I haven't a clue what his real name is.'

'Well that's an eye opener for me Mouser, I have to say. It strikes me as a bit rude to have *chubby* as a nick name don't you think?'

I should have known better than to ask. I received a lecture about nicknames in Malta and by the time we reached the bus terminus, which took about ten minutes, I felt I had been awarded an honours degree in the subject.

Mouser told me that in the villages of Malta and Gozo, each family has its own nickname, and family members often had their own separate nicknames. In general nicknames would be rather innocuous. When they referred to some weakness they were usually good-humoured. However some could be rude if not crude. He informed me that most nicknames were preceded by the preposition ''ta'' meaning ''of''. These two words stood after the Christian name.

'Can you give me a few examples Mouser?' I actually found myself listening quite intently to what he was

111

saying. This was becoming a lesson about human behaviour and their language.

'Oh yes easy. Now there is Toni who lumbers around Birgu Square. You must have seen him about - a giant of a fellow, so his nickname is Toni tal-Ggant. Giant you see in Maltese. And then there are the nicknames that refer to peoples occupations. For instance "tas-Surmast" – school principal, "tas-Saqqafi" – roofer, "tal-Melh" – salt vendor, "tar-Rizzi" – hawker of sea-urchins, and here's another one, "tas-Siggijiet" – a man in charge of chairs in churches.' Mouser paused for a moment. 'Oh yes the list is endless and you hear these nicknames all the time. They tell me who does what and where in two simple words as a rule around Vittoriosa and the Three Cities.'

Mouser finished his lesson by telling me that many nicknames came from names of animals. These were in limited supply on such a small Island and hence were prized in the main. Every year blessings for farm animals were held in the village of Zejtun around the church where stabling was provided with straw beds for them to lie on. 'So for example, "ta' Gelluxa" means young bull or the person who looks after the calves. "Tal-flieles" means the person who tends their chickens.

Mouser informed me that a local priest from hereabouts was nicknamed "il-Gurdien" meaning rat! Mouser of course had his own view how this had happened. He learned that parishioners, mainly young men and women, were occasionally going to confession and confessing far too much! Sometimes, in the case of young men, petty crimes and in the case of some females, a frailty of morality. Anyway the outcome appeared, or so word had it, that the local police were kept busy spying on some of these young men soon after their visit to the confessional box. Consequently the local village received an award from the Police Commissioner for achieving a 100 per cent success rate solving all crime in the area, for the fifth year running. In the meantime, other family members learned about clandestine affairs where another form of Justice could be applied far away from the eye of the local Police Station. That kept the ambulance service busy – especially after feast days when

112

extra confessionals might take place during the festive day inside the Parish Church.

'And what does the local priest have to say about his nickname the *rat?* Did people suspect his integrity and his discretion?' I was intrigued by this use of a nickname to spread the word, that of his duplicity.

'Oh he just shrugs it off from what I know. He takes a theological position explaining some of his flock are Doubting Thomases. His nickname is the staff he bears when seeking out prodigal lost sheep. Return them to the safe path away from the crags and crevices of original sin. One thing I have heard from time to time is that the *cat* is now out of the bag and less people are seeking his absolution. Already incidences of bag snatching are on the rise and another parish should get next year's crime 'clear up' award. I suppose some people may go to 'confession' in other towns and villages. Where being anonymous is more of a virtue than a vice and where the priest respects the sanctity of the confessional box.'

I was enthralled by Mouser's knowledge of the Maltese and their fascination and fixation on nicknames. I had learnt about the perils of confessing all. I would take care with my words in future less case they became misunderstood. Mouser last story brought to mind another tale I had heard on the yacht.

My owners were entertaining two of their English friends on board. The story they were telling my owners was filled with indignation and outrage as it unfolded. Their son, Daniel, attended a minor Catholic private boarding school somewhere in England. The college also had a seminary attached to it. A breeding ground for capturing pupils they said when they neared eighteen years old, to train for the catholic priesthood.

Daniel was twelve and a diligent student. Mathematics was his great passion scoring astonishing grades in his class all the time. Volumes of truncated cones would be calculated in a trice. More accurately than the text books as he would take the Greek letter 'pi' to its absolute conclusion. Into infinity they said. Such devotion was easily transposed into his religious beliefs and his piety at home was starting to worry his parents.

Euclid and the Church of Rome had joined forces to take him away they felt certain.

So he would return for the holidays and rise each morning at a punishing hour to attend early mass in the small village church. He became entrusted with the polishing of solid silver candle sticks and other silver and brass artefacts and had been given keys to the front door and the vestibule where the valuables would be placed with the cloths and the silver cleaner. On Sundays, it would be mass in the morning and benediction in the evening. That was disrupting family days out which had always been kept back for Sundays.

The fact was, his mother was Catholic and his father Protestant, who favoured plain panelling and plainer glass in plain rectangular windows. Gothic arches were a distraction from the word of god. The silver! Did not Christ throw the money lenders out of the temple, he shouted as his fist hit the table. 'That Church looked like a setting for the Antiques Road Show,' he shouted. By now the blood was rising and his face was preparing to explode. He calmed down and his wife explained that when they married, the children would be brought up as Catholic. So they were allowed to marry in a Catholic church.

As Daniel entered his final term at the prep school, and sat the final exams to determine his academic skills for the senior college, his best friend Andrew, sought his help.

He asked Daniel if he could help with his mathematics exam. Daniel was not told that it was vital for Andrew to achieve a grade no less than a C in the maths test, to gain certain entrance to a superior boarding school much closer to his parents in the North of England.

Daniel and Andrew decided to arrive early in the examination room so they could sit together at the back of the room. As far away from the vigilator's probing eye as possible. Daniel of course raced through the questions, providing both answers and structural explanations of the methodology used. Reference to sine and cosine formulae were hastily scribbled to show the examiner his thought processes - vital to push the scores into the 'A' bracket. Answers alone were never enough he had discovered when examining model answers from previous tests. He then laid each completed sheet of paper on the floor and in full view for his friend to crib every answer. Andrew may have been wise to have ignored the detail and simply provide the answers with a minimum of explanation. Nevertheless the deception seemed to be going well. The invigilator seemed a little bored by his role in the examination room and rarely raised himself to patrol and look for any sign of deceit.

The exam ended. However Daniel's conscience was bothering him. To wash away his sins, he attended confession that very evening. He confessed to the priest hiding behind the screen of the confessional box. Shrouded in low light; whispering, trembling. The priest encouraged greater disclosure but Daniel had said enough. The priest gave up and granted him absolution. While deciding further investigations could and should be made, he gave him penance of three decades of the rosary and five of Our Father Who art in Heaven.

Daniel completed the task set and prayed his sin was by now washed away and nothing further would happen. Why should it? No discovery of the deception had been made in the exam hall and no names had been given to the priest. His conscience was clear. The softly spoken priest taking the confession had however been the headmaster of the prep school and the head mathematics teacher, whose star pupil was of course Daniel. He left the confessional; gathered up the test answers from his locker and spent several hours comparing and contrasting the pages of mathematical data before him. 'At last – a correlation', he exclaimed.

Andrew was called to the headmaster's study in his pyjamas late that evening. He was shown the answer sheets of Daniel and the carbon copy sheet he had created. The only real difference was in the hand writing. The game was up. The boy confessed there and then explaining his parents had pressured him into doing everything he could to gain entry to another and more superior school. His early admission coupled with the disgraceful and traitorous behaviour of his parents,

115

controlled the headmaster's wrath. He received a mere six of the best from the headmaster's treasured miniature cricket bat, reserved for special occasions. It had his name engraved, as a token of appreciation from the days when he was the captain of the first eleven cricket team, at this same school.

The headmaster wrote a very stiff letter to the parents who realised their game was up with him. So Andrew was withdrawn. No doubt he could attend a 'crammer' school to get him over the mathematics hurdle, and Daniel lost his best friend. Daniel felt betrayed. The headmaster met up briefly with Andrew's parents at departure time. He allowed his indignation and fury to be broadcast far and wide. The diatribe continued – even as Andrew and his parents scrambled into their car. They screeched away at high speed with the headmaster in hot pursuit uttering expletives that the younger boys could not understand. Such language normally would enter their vocabulary much later in life.

The story ended happily for Daniel's parents at least. Daniel went on to the senior college where his delusion with the church grew stronger. He had learnt the dangers of the confessional box and intolerance and his fascination with the church dwindled. No more polishing silver on a Sunday and outings could now be planned and completed. Sundays returned as the days of rest as they were supposed to be. Daniel's interests turned to politics instead once he graduated to Hull University. There he would exchange church service for impromptu Marxist lectures in the economics of capitalism. 'It contains the seeds of its own destruction', he would tell his father. His father muttered and spluttered. He would never get along with, or even want to understand Trotsky's ideas about the permanent arms economy. How the armaments industry creates the wars that keep consumption going. However, better this he felt than indoctrination into a church he could have no sympathy with. He kept silent and would nod his head as the second glass of wine was poured. Daniel will grow out of it he thought and the smile returned to his face.

We arrived at the bus terminus, to find a few people standing in a patient queue. There were six people, mainly Maltese but two were speaking in French.

'It shouldn't be long now, Licky. When the bus arrives, just let the people go first and then we can hop on, and bob's your uncle, we will be in Marsaxlokk in no time. Have you decided what fish you fancy for lunch today?' Mouser finished off his question with a smack of his lips. 'Lampuka is well in season at present, and that would likely be my first choice.'

'Is there a choice Mouser? I mean surely in our situation, it is really a case of beggars cannot be choosers. Or can we?' Mouser was momentarily offended but offered this advice.

'Well of course there is a choice. Sunday is *fish day* in Marsaxlokk. And yes you are right, beggars cannot be choosers but we are not beggars. We are merely being enterprising and entertaining. Watch the people *try* and stroke us as we brush tails with their legs! A million miles from begging! Why look a gift horse in the mouth? That is what I say! And mark my words, on a Sunday is truly our gift horse. You'll see.' Mouser turned his head away. 'Ah here she comes. That's our bus. Yes that's Chubby alright. He's one of the best. No mistaking him and his bus or the way he drives it.'

I saw the bus that must have been fifty years old, chugging its way up the hill and leaving a black cloud of exhaust fumes in its wake. The driver appeared not to have a care in the world. He had his right elbow sticking out of the driver's window, with one hand on the wheel. In his other, he was holding a mobile phone to his ear as a cigarette dangled between his moving lips.

The bus swerved around the roundabout before halting abruptly where we all stood. Passengers on board looked alarmed. I have never had the chance to be a bus *fancier or bus spotter* so I could not tell one bus from another. There was something elegant about this machine that overshadowed the state of the exhaust system that made people gasp. Not so much from the fumes, more the design. It was made by Bedford an English company, and had a shiny chrome grill to its front, and was painted in two colours, bright orange and yellow. It looked a brute of a machine and this was going to transport Mouser and me down to Marsaxlokk. What a fascinating adventure this would be.

'Right here we go Licky. Follow me.' Mouser raced up the three steps as the last passenger mounted, with me close behind. I was worried the door would close but I discovered later these doors never closed, whether by accident or design.

'Well blow me down, if it isn't Mouser. Where have you been hiding all this time? I haven't seen you for weeks. I was asking the museum caretaker about you only a few days ago.'

I caught my first real glimpse of Chubby behind the steering wheel. My first impression was not chubbiness but sheer obesity. His stomach was crushed against the steering wheel. Perhaps he acquired his nickname Chubby years ago, when he was merely that, and the nickname remained.

He looked past Mouser and then raised his eyebrows. 'And what have we got here Mouser and who is your new friend? Not like you to be stepping out with anyone, I'll be sure. Look, best you both hop up here on the dash board, as we are quite full today. Make yourself at home. Better view all round here anyway.'

With that he reached down and grappled with a large mettle stick with a nob on the top, and created that grinding noise which told everyone to hold tight and brace themselves as the bus would soon be hurtling forward.

'Ladies and gentleman and tourists alike, Chubby's the name and driving's my game. Any questions, don't be afraid to ask. We're destined for Marsaxlokk and few places on route, so give a shout when you want to get off, as the pull cord bell doesn't work. Hey!' He gave out an enormous bellow of a laugh, then answered his ringing mobile phone with his left hand and reverted into a Maltese conversation. His right hand remained outside the window, rarely to enter the coach and touch the steering wheel. Somehow his stomach and that wheel were conjoined and the one would turn the other. His right hand was simply a back- up whenever sharp and immediate turns had to be made, with no loss of speed.

'He's picking up his lunch on the way,' Mouser informed me. 'I think it's his grandma on the phone, asking where he is now. He says he's about five minutes away. She'll be out in the roadway about a mile before we hit.'

I looked forward to seeing her with the lunchbox and wondered whether he would slow down. Would she just throw it through the open door? We rumbled on with someone talking of white knuckle rides. At Zabbar, some ashen people left the bus and their fingers were indeed white in places. Other suspecting and unsuspecting people joined us to take their place. That grating noise returned and the initiated grabbed whatever anchorage they could before the race to Marsaxlokk began.

Some passengers looked oddly at Mouser and me, hanging on for dear life. The piece of cloth stuck on to the dashboard held firm as our claws instinctively drilled into the fabric. We swung and swayed with every passing roundabout bedecked with flowers that looked freshly planted.

Only Chubby's jovial ways kept the passengers thoughts to themselves. Should they jump from the open door as traffic lights changed to red? No good, he just drives straight through and touches the statuette of the Madonna swinging from the rear view mirror. One old lady did come up the steps and on seeing us said how lovely we looked sitting there. That was nice to hear. She changed her tune when she patted Mouser on the head. He drew his claws from the cotton and gave her a swipe back. 'Nasty cat', she muttered and made her escape into the safety of the carriage.

Leaving Zabbar, I saw how pretty the landscape was. I had never seen this side of Malta before. We were passing through neatly kept farm land with neat dry stone walls. I saw men carefully repairing a section, chipping at the stones and matching them one by one. They were creating an elegant separation between road and vines. No concrete here and the wall would last a thousand years. The sign, *Marsovin* kept on appearing

119

behind more and more limestone walls which protected the vines now overflowing with fresh fruit.

We slowly came to a halt in the middle of this countryside, next to an old lady standing outside a small gate leading to a house that stood on its own.

'Ooh lovely jubbley. Oh she's a good old stick my grandma. Never lets me go hungry. Not in all these years.' Whether he was speaking to Mouser and I, or whether his comments were for general consumption, I do not know but it did not matter.

Chubby, with some effort, hauled his considerable self out of the driving seat, and eased himself past us and down the steps. He was handed a nicely wrapped parcel from his grandma. A few words were spoken, she got a peck on the cheek from her grandson, and then we were on our way again.

I looked around the interior of the bus and noticed how personal it was to Chubby. Apart from the small Madonna statue hanging from the mirror, there was a picture of the Madonna propped on the dashboard directly above his instruments. Next to this was a faded colour photograph of him and his bus. Yes in that photograph, taken quite some years ago, I could see how he had been given his nickname. Luckily nicknames stick in Malta from childhood so no one would ever call him fatty. There was also a sticker posted as far away from these two Madonnas as possible. It said simply I LOVE SEXY GIRLS. I wondered if Chubby was married. If so, I also wondered whether his wife ever travelled on her husband's bus. Maybe his wife had given him this. Knowing no harm would come of it. That would have been a true test of faith if it had ever happened this way.

We arrived in Marsaxlokk by 10.30am. The village was heaving with people and I became nervous. I had never seen such a throng before. We ground to a halt behind a large brightly painted red open topped double decker bus in front of us. It was a tourist bus and dozens of different nationalities were leaving and assembling close by. I could smell the fish and sensed they could too.

'Right here we go. Marsaxlokk it is. Please remember that my last bus out of Marsaxlokk will be at 3pm today.'

Chubby told Mouser and I to wait until all the passengers had alighted. He then looked at my cat collar tag. 'Miss Licky eh. Well I don't know how you have landed up on my bus with old Mouser, but I bet there is a tale to tell there. Yes something there to be told to be sure. Maybe I'll read about you some day in the papers. Two cats go to Gretna Green on Chubby's bus.' He chortled and told us to meet up with him later, for our free ride home.

Mouser gave a large meow to thank Chubby and I followed suit with a much softer purr. Then we jumped down and headed into the market place teeming with stall holders and tourists alike. Everything was on display from Gozo lace and Maltese trinkets, to handmade Luzzis in miniature with the eye of Osiris at the front. What a fascinating place Mouser had brought me to.

CHAPTER 14

Mouser led with his explanations of Marsaxlokk as we roamed the market place. Marsaxlokk came from Mersa, an Arabic word meaning harbour and Xlokk meaning the south eastern wind of the Mediterranean. So here we had it, "the harbour on the South-East." He spoke about fishing and how the fish were taken from the sea. Nets would trap them but they would become torn and frayed. The woman over there sitting on the stool was mending one of these nets making it ready for the next day's trip. Most fish was landed here.

'The fish market opens early each Sunday on this open quay. The fish is landed and everyone can see how fresh it is. So the catch is sold out very quickly and the early bird arrivals have the best choice. Lampuka, tuna, swordfish, you name it.' Mouser's lips as usual started to moisten at the thought. 'For our lunch today we could try for a mixed platter and share it. How does that sound?'

I assumed he knew just how that would be. No money, just feline ways to tempt well- wishers to share the bounty. Or did Mouser have other ways in mind? I hoped theft was not on his mind. Leaping on tables; grabbing fish tails and making a run for it. I simply nodded and looked around to take in my new surroundings. Across from the quayside, I could see a large number of restaurants, already starting to open up and setting out tables and chairs for fresh air dining.

I had yet to see anyone selling fish. Vegetables, clothes, footwear, lace and tourist souvenirs were in abundance. A lot of Gozitan lace was displayed from table clothes, bed spreads and napkins. An old lady was wearing traditional lace clothing with people asking her questions as they felt the textures. Then the sale! The folding and the bagging and the exchange of notes and coins commenced, with final smiles and the invitation to come back. Better still visit Gozo itself.

Mouser pointed to the brightly painted luzzu boats, bobbing lazily up and down in the water. These boats I was soon to learn were of ancient origin and many had parts of their own origin, lovingly restored generation after generation. Planking replaced as it aged and painted to hide its newness. Some were brand new but made from these ancient skills that were still being handed down from father to son. For the many the means of survival in times gone by when food was short and only the sea's harvest could forestall hunger and misery.

Shiny reds, yellows, blues and greens reflected their colour over the azure waters. These colours were the memories of centuries long past and told tales of violent storms, heroic rescues and miraculous rescues. Seamanship allied with superstition. I asked him why every luzzu sported a pair of eyes on it's bow. He of course knew about these "Eyes of Osiris." They guided these boats through gale and rain back to safe harbour.

The tourists were keen to include the boats, colours, and harbour line as backdrops for family and friends, carefully positioned as the centrepiece of an impending photo. 'No Amanda. Come in next to your mother. John, next to your father please. Oh Caroline dear, take the baby out of the pram and hold it....... That's better, much better.' She raised her head and growled. 'John, I saw you pinch your sister. Leave her alone.' She returned to the pose mode, satisfied order had been restored. Caroline tapped her son on the head. 'Now smile please.'

The path was blocked to other tourists and locals as the stage was being set. No one dared cross the line between this intrepid photographer and her brood. Finally, the shutter clicked; the family disassembled and the path was re-opened. No one seemed to mind at all and some were even smiling at this imposition. People can be very strange I thought. Even Mouser would be hard pressed to hold back a dozen stranger cats for a single moment or for any reason at all.

We approached the town square where I saw the statue of St. Andrew, the patron saint of these fishermen of Marsaxlokk. The statue was overlooking the village and gazing out to sea. Another lighthouse of protection was situated above Marsaxlokk church. The Virgin Mary was in her own luzzu ready to row her way out to help those in peril on these seas.

Mouser saw my interest and said he had once strolled into this church while the main doors were open. The Marsaxlokk Parish Church was dedicated to Our Lady of the Rosary, the Madonna of Pompeii. He had seen many sacred things including the statue of Madonna and child imported from Lecce in Italy over one hundred years ago.

Walking further along the landscape changed. The fresh air became perfumed with the unmistakable smell of fresh fish. Soon we came to rows of stalls displaying nothing but fish. A paradise for cats had been created but the stall holders were eagle eyed and watched our approach with apprehension. Little chance of an act of theft here and I was relieved.

Mouser announced that we should walk down to the end of these stalls and choose where we would dine. He would find a quiet spot away from the suspicious glances of fish wives and noisy tourists' children.

'This is a good spot I think Licky. It's shaded here and we won't have to share our spot with anyone else. Let alone other cats.' He told me to wait here a minute, and then he disappeared. I sat there wondering where on earth he had gone. He reappeared moments later behind me. He was grasping two paper plates in his mouth, which he placed by my side.

'There we are. I came across them just up near the small public bin. They are hardly used. I want to make this something a bit special today Licky as this is the first time I have had company for Sunday lunch here in Marsaxlokk.' He paused for a second. 'In fact the first time I think I have ever had any company for lunch. Indeed, any meal in my life.' He seemed for a moment to drift in and out of his thoughts on what he had just said. Then he was back to his old self.

'We'll stick to the first few stalls nearest us and up this end. We will split ourselves up between one stall each, and play the game we cats are world famous for. Then we will bring back each offering and load up the two plates. Shouldn't take long, and then the feast will be ours. How does that sound?' Mouser looked at me as though I understood. What game I wondered?

'Pardon me Mouser, but what on earth is the game we are to play that cats are world famous for?' I felt myself frowning as I said this. I hoped he did not mean a game of distraction and theft!

'I refer to the game of looking lonely, hungry, helpless and meek *of course*. The game where you prey on human's sympathy and get them to give you what you want. In this case a selection of different fish. That is the game!'

'Oh Mouser, I don't think I am going to be much of a team player here. Better I just stick next to you at a stall and let you *play the game*. You can play it for two, can't you? I won't interfere. I can just watch and learn, if that's alright with you?'

'Dear dear me, Licky. The whole idea about today's *special* lunch was that we would go for a platter of sea food. A variety of fish we could share.' Mouser paused for a moment and looked most solemn. 'Just you and me.'

He said this so touchingly that I found myself speechless. So I half agreed to do as he proposed, and we set off to the two end stalls next to each other but run by two different hawkers. Not brothers nor even relatives I felt sure, as one was short and fat and the other tall and slim.

Mouser took to sitting at the end of the second stall, close to where a fish bucket lay at the feet of the stall holder. Every few moments a fish head or tail or something as appealing would get tossed into this bucket. Mouser had already started to meow quietly so as not to annoy. Instead of throwing the next fish head into the bucket, he smiled and tossed it gently towards Mouser.

As quick as a flash, Mouser had it between his lips and came scurrying past me towards our *dining area*.

Whilst Mouser had been playing the cats game and had won the first round, I had done nothing yet to contribute to this embarrassing charade. I had actually half hidden myself from the view of my stall holder and had tried not to be seen. I was just too shy to sing for my supper. I could not bring myself to go along with it.

So the very best I did was scamper off behind Mouser and back to our somewhat bare plates.

'Well Licky, this is not going to work out as planned. Not to worry, onto Plan B.' Mouser was unconcerned by my lack of enterprise, which put me a little more at ease. 'What we can do is put you in charge of dining and protecting the table from other hungry cats. Set up the table as I bring back the food. This place setting is not ideal.' Mouser looked over further to our right and his eyes lit up. 'Look over there. Maybe you could move things over so we could dine in better comfort.'

He was looking at a small unoccupied stone table with two circle stone stools. It was shaded and out of the way. Placed there as an afterthought to fill this unused and quiet area. 'Now you Licky can take our plates over there and set them up, whilst I go and fetch the seafood of the day. Does that make sense?'

It made great sense to me, as I was a domestic cat and could make this place quite homely. I would play my part with no need to beg and risk censure and maybe even retribution.

'Right see you in a bit and no tucking in whilst I am away.' With that advice and a wink, Mouser trotted off at a sharp pace back to the end of the fish market.

I made my plan and moved the fish head from the plate to the table. Then I bit on the two plates and carried them over. I separated the plates, laying out the one fish head to make it look as attractive as I could. A moment later Mouser was back with a much finer delicacy. He jumped up on the table and deposited a piece of tuna on the second plate but was off before I dared ask where this had come from. Fish heads is one thing but tuna steaks? Further fish heads turned up on his third and fourth trip but on the fifth, a couple of large sardines, totally intact!

'Ooh Mouser, surely those have not been tossed in the bucket. They are whole sardines.'

Mouser gave a toothy grin. 'Don't you worry your cotton socks about that Licky. There was a bit of a distraction going on between one hawker and another, so I took advantage and popped up on the side of the stall and helped myself. Completely unnoticed, I might add.' My look of disapproval did *not* go unnoticed.

'Licky it's all about opportunities that present themselves in life. You must act on them, there and then; otherwise you will always be a loser. Never look a gift horse in the mouth. Those two hawkers were doing much more harm to each other than I could ever do, and besides people say that God looks after those who look after themselves.'

I knew humans had odd beliefs and behaved in odd ways. Was it true that their God approved of theft? I was confused and pondered Mouser's words of wisdom as he took stock of our food situation.

'Yes we are almost there. We have tuna, sardines, lampuka. A bit of sword fish should round it off nicely. Back soon!' This would be his final exploration and I feared for it. What would be our last dish of the day?

Mouser returned with 2 large prawns in his mouth. I had never seen such huge prawns. Not even on the yacht. Now this must certainly have been theft on a grand scale, but as I was still pondering the alleged virtue of self reliance I said nothing to disrupt the moment.

While Mouser was away I too had been busy. He placed one prawn on each plate and noticed the table decorations had changed.

'Oh you have done well Licky. Where did you get them from?' He was looking at the small posy of wild flowers that I had managed to up root from about ten yards away. I had found a discarded paper cup from the same place that Mouser had obtained the paper plates. Somehow I had managed to push the flowers into the cup and turn it up. There was a slight breeze and I feared the cup would tumble. It wobbled a little but held its ground. 'Seek and you shall find Mouser,' I said with some pleasure.

'Well done Licky. Now before we start lunch, just bear with me a moment.' Mouser was away again, but in a different direction. He scampered off across the main

127

road and onto the opposite pavement, where there were a number of restaurants, all with tables set outside.

He returned maybe three or four minutes later, but this time with a large wedge of lemon in his mouth. He plonked it onto one of the plates. 'Phew that was a bit of luck. Ooh my eyes are all watering, having that lemon in my mouth. I was nearly spotted getting that off the customer's plate but he was playing with his camera and did not notice me.' Mouser looked pleased with himself. 'Before you say anything Licky, the customer had finished his meal, and the lemon wedge was untouched, so there was no robbery there, unless of course the restaurant planned to reuse it. If so then the restaurant would have been the robber. Not me. So maybe I have buried temptation which is a good thing to do.'

Mouser's way of thinking would never cease to amaze me. He could always justify his actions. In all fairness, I had to admire him. Mouser's train of thought and explanation led him to *exactly* where he wanted the listener to be, and it worked.

'Now tuck in Licky and *bon appetite*. Fresh fish without a squeeze of lemon is just not the same.' With that, he lent over the table, grabbed the lemon rind between his teeth and squeezed a gentle drizzle of lemon juice over my fish. This was a whole new experience for me - fresh lemon juice on fresh fish. It tasted odd but I was hungry by now and soon learned to tolerate if not like this additive. This whole dining experience was new to me. Who would have thought even a few days ago, that I would be dining here, in Marsasloxx, sitting at a table in the fresh air with a big black Mouser, watching brightly painted boats on a blue sea?

If this dining experience was not already something extraordinary, more was to come. We were attracting unwanted attention. Tourists noticed us and started filming. Some used flash cameras to counteract the glare of the sun. Some of these tourists sought to stroke, which I did not mind. Mouser was less sure. However he restrained himself for once and no hand was bitten. In fact one couple bought us squid from the stall and placed it on our plate. That caused another flurry of picture taking. We were becoming celebrities but still hoped the interest would stop and we would return to the privacy we enjoyed before. I had seen stories on the yacht TV about Hollywood red carpets events and now understood how difficult it was to have a public and a private life.

We had both been hungrier than I thought and we ate far more than was good for us. It was not helped when a young English couple returned. Earlier they too had photographed us in various poses. Indeed Mouser was becoming even more adept at sitting, lying down and even standing on both hind legs for a moment or two. Just enough time to let the light into their camera. He is a contortionist I though. Maybe all those narrow escapes he had climbing up walls and through narrow spaces had taught him these tricks. Mouser realised his antics had worked when the lady pulled out a white plastic bag hidden behind her.

'A surprise' she exclaimed as she settled one whole lampuka fish onto each of our plates. Mouser did learn something from this. Never bite the hand that feeds you and instead he rolled on his back, exposing his tummy. He even let the lady stroke him. A new experience for him and perhaps for the lady too. Fortunately for her, his temper had not been aroused and her hands remained intact. No need for accident and emergency treatment this time!

The lady stood back and joined her male companion. And then another photo shoot, as Mouser and I tackled a whole lampuka each! By now our hunger was sated but we felt obliged to show our appreciation. We ate the lot.

Mouser commented on how truly fresh the lampuka was. 'Fish is fresh when the eyes are clear and bulging. The gills are red or pink - never grey, the scales are intact, there is no evidence of missing scales or patches, the skin is shiny, wet and slightly slimy and the tail is stiff. Fish meat is stiff but elastic and has a pleasant smell of seaweed and sea. Look here Licky.' Mouser pressed his paw on the flesh. 'See Licky, the meat is stiff but elastic, so I have left no mark when pressing it with my paw.'

I listened as patiently as I could and maybe something of this lesson would stick in my mind. However, I thought, fish is fish and if it smells right then that should be enough. Too much knowledge could be a dangerous thing.

Mouser and I spoke of fine dining and he recalled coming across two famous actors who were filming on the Island. Everyone was taking their photographs every time they were In Valletta but they seemed to enjoy it all. Just like us he thought. I was not sure I would want to be photographed every day. Once was really enough. There was a price to pay for fame. I felt it better to shy away from this lime light. Not having to act a part to be fed. Mouser took a different view. The feeding and the fame were two sides of the same coin. Hiding from the public was not helpful. His public had fed us both with minimal disturbance he suggested.

He thought these two actors who he believed were married, had to put up with this same coin all the time. That would have to include visits to restaurants. Mouser then drew an analogy with our experiences of the day, with the tourists clicking away, touching and stroking us. The only thing missing I thought might be an ink pad. Our paws pressed down and the imprint transferred to an autograph book.

Mouser paused briefly in his thoughts. 'I imagine they choose carefully which restaurants they visit, to avoid the paparazzi and other nuisances. I mean you would not want to have your picture being taken continuously while eating – would you. It cannot be dignified.' I smiled. Was that not precisely what had been happening to us? Maybe he thought cats need not have such delicate thoughts. The problem was, I did...

'I am sure you are right Mouser. However, I did not see you objecting today. And let's face it; dividends were brought to us – dividends by way of a whole Lampuka each. I mean that must have cost something. She had a whole bag of fish in her hand.'

'Oh yes, they bought it from that second stall, and I guess it would have been a kilo of Lampuka, which would have been five euros for the lot. You get about five or six pieces per kilo. It works out at around roughly one euro per fish. Do you know what they charge in a restaurant? They rarely price it up on the menu because it is priced by weight. Phew, a license to print money, 'cause you won't get a piece of lampuka for much under at least eight euros in a restaurant.'

'Is that so, as much as that?' I was quite taken back. That's about eight tins of Whiskas!'

'Mind you, there will be an accompanying small side salad with it and that's your lot. Let me tell you more about the actors while I remember. I was up in Valletta a few weeks ago and popped into Da Pippo and there he was, in two photographs that had already been framed.'

I was confused. 'What is Da Pippo and who had been framed?'

'That famous actor Brad Pitt of course. There were two photographs of him, standing in the middle of the two brothers, who had their arms around him. They are the owners of Da Pippo, a very fine and well established restaurant in the heart of Malta. Much favoured from what I can tell, by lawyers, members of parliament and their peers. I have often sat outside, watching them all come and go. The restaurant is only open for lunch.'

'Well how on earth did you manage to get inside the restaurant and see these two photographs? Don't tell me you were a guest of Brad Pitt? The truth please if you don't mind Mouser.'

Mouser gave me a mischievous smile and I guess he did then tell me the truth.

He told me he had *visited* this same restaurant a week or two before, purely by chance. He enjoyed taking the bus up to Valletta and just wandering around and soaking up the atmosphere. He had happened to chance upon Da Pippo by accident early in the morning. The main front door had been open. A delivery was taking place and no one else was around it seemed. He slipped in down the stone steps and looked around. The walls were adorned with memories of past and present diners.

This array of photographs targeted celebrity visitors and leading political figures who had become regular patrons of the place, Mouser surmised. He spotted a fresh fish and meat display that was slowly being filled as the delivery van was being unloaded. Temptation over took him. He looked around and for the moment, the coast was clear. He crawled towards the tilted display cabinet, chose his target and then leapt into action. Three finely sliced strips of sirloin steak disappeared from the ice bedded tray.

'Ooh they were so tender. Prime cuts and no mistake, and I was out in a flash, straight down Triq Melita, and no one was the wiser. Oh and there were no pictures of Brad Pitt to be seen then.'

'Was he the actor you had seen in Valletta?' I asked. Mouser liked my conclusion which showed I had been listening. 'So you would return again I think. Not a good idea as you must have put everyone on alert.' I had no intention of chastising him about his criminal behaviour as I was learning not to teach old cats new tricks.

'Oh yes, I was back there a couple of weeks ago in the morning. My luck was in again, with the comings and goings of some delivery or another. I blended in and took my chances. It was easier this time as I knew where to go. However something had changed with the walls. Two new framed pictures of Brad Pitt caught my eye. They had not been there before.'

'Well I have to give it to you Mouser. You certainly have an eye for detail, even at moments of great peril.' The sarcasm in my voice seemed to go over Mouser's head.

'Remember that I had seen all the madness going on around the streets of Valletta with Brad Pitt during the past week. The film was taking over whole streets of the capital which was all good business for anyone who lived or worked there. Whole streets cordoned off. New signs erected in a foreign language. Of course compensation was paid to shop owners whose business would halt as customers were held back. Film company canteens arrived which encouraged more generosity as nice tit bits were thrown in my direction. Welcome back Brad Pitt to Malta any day, that's what we cats say.'

'Back to the subject of Da Pippo, was your second visit fruitful?' I really did not want to know and yet I asked the question. I would no doubt feel uneasy when I heard the answer.'

'Oh I should say so. I managed to help myself to two enormous fresh king size prawns, from a display resting on a bed of crushed ice. Well nearly fresh.' Mouser grimaced before continuing. 'You don't actually get fresh prawns here in Malta. They are all imported, so you cannot say they are part of the fresh catch of the day. But not everyone would know that, so who cares. The fact was they were delicious, once I had tackled the shell parts. Yes Da Pippo is a cut above your average restaurant and the customers come back time and again, which includes me.' He smiled and brought his paw to his mouth to hide a smirk. I would not be amused he knew, though I did want to smile. 'I'll take you up there one day. I presume you have not been to Valletta, Licky?'

'No I cannot say I have Mouser. After all I had never really been out of Vittoriosa until I met you. Except when I sailed on the yacht and then that was sometimes to other countries. Yes I would like you to show me Valletta, but perhaps not the restaurant Da Pippo, if you don't mind.'

Mouser seemed happy with my response realising another adventure could be planned shortly. He would be the tour guide and leader of course.

Having finished our sumptuous Sunday lunch, we sat where we were, taking in the early afternoon atmosphere. We took in the sights of parents with their children parading to and fro. The breeze had not brought down the potted flowers which glistened still in the gentle rays of the sun. Mouser reminded me of those eager photographers and their gifts and all felt well with me. Kindness – the gilding on the pictures – these visitors would soon be pressing into memory albums.

Mouser wondered if other photographers capturing celebrities like Brad Pitt would then offer him tokens of steak or fish as thanks. Humans were odd at times but I wondered whether they would do such things. 'I hardly think so,' I exclaimed. 'I mean can you imagine that happening. An actor finishing his food between camera flashes and finding another plate of food arriving. On the yacht, many pictures were taken of me, but I never saw a piece of steak appearing as a *thank you*.'

'Well Licky, it certainly happened to us today, though you may be right. I have never seen the same happen with human beings despite my times around the restaurants of Malta.'

With that and conscious of the time, Mouser suggested we take a walk up towards where our bus would arrive in around one hour's time. We strolled towards the high end of Marsalokk near the church square. Mouser suggested we sit down on the pavement, by an empty table, supporting a small umbrella.

'Now this is Gerald's restaurant and named after the old man who set it up years ago. Basically he is retired now, but his son Anthony now runs the show. And believe me there is quite a show to watch. You just look and listen.'

I did. From my pavement seat, I could see a number of taxi drivers sitting inside at the small bar. Mouser informed me that they would be waiting for customers they had brought to the restaurant. For that service they did get a present of food from the restaurant's proprietor, Anthony, plus a free drink or two, even though they were not celebrities. More strange human behaviour I thought.

'Anthony has a good restaurant operation going with this place, I can tell you Licky. He has them all organised. The taxi and minibus drivers know clients tip well after a good meal, as long as it is good. The view from the restaurant upstairs window is stunning. The cruise liner tourists have a few hours to spare but they too come and enjoy the food and the scenery. Drivers offer them a special price to escort them around the island to points of interest. Then they bring them here for lunch. *Voila*. Everyone benefits and everyone is in pocket. Maybe not every tourist, whose appearance suggested they might have done better just jumping on Chubby's bus for ninety cents. Look there's Anthony now.'

I saw this large, portly man appear in the doorway of the restaurant, leading directly onto the pavement. He looked both ways, up and down the street, and then saw what he was looking for. He stepped down onto the pavement, just as three tourists were about to pass by.

'Good afternoon, and are you English? Are you looking for somewhere nice to eat and at very competitive prices? Where do you come from in England? Oh really, I have a brother who lives there. In Manchester you say. So does he! We both support Manchester United. Now I have a lovely table by the window upstairs. Come inside.' They did. 'Maria, give these fine customers the window seat,' he shouted up the stairs as he pointed them to where they had to go.

Over the course of the next half hour, I saw Anthony' *modus operandi* repeated countless times, with every tourist passing by, being assailed with the gift of many tongues. He seemed to have a brother in every major town or hamlet in England. Italian tourists from Perugia were surprised to learn his nephew went to University there. Pleased to be hailed in fluent Italian. Rome, Milan, Naples and even Sicily were home to his nephews, nieces and aunts. Brothers too should the need dictate. Although his German was not so fluent, he still spoke of fresh fish in their language.

One thing that puzzled me was the way he promoted that singular but alluring window table. From where I was sitting I strained my neck to see anything more than this one position which surely could seat four to six at best.

Mouser satisfied my curiosity. 'It's quite simple. He herds them in and up the steep steps into the restaurant. The *lovely table by the window* has just been taken he discovers and if pressed will apologise for his mistake.'

"*Never mind*" he would say as he thrusts the platter of the daily catch under their noses. "*Our fish is the finest in Malta and for you I will give a special price.*"

That sorted, he leaves his staff to take over as he must be back on the street, filling the next table nearest to that elusive window table. What the heck. Once he has them in and up that steep staircase, the capture is normally complete. Few people lured into the restaurant, are going to then back out just because they don't have that coveted table. After all Anthony will quickly usher them to whatever table is spare. When he is busy – that means the rear end tables where only very tall diners ever catch a glimpse of the sea. There are no other windows there as far as I know. He might have paintings of the harbour on the wall to hint of a missing view. I cannot be certain for I have never dared go upstairs. I know cats who have, but this is the only escape route out and he stands guard like a hawk.'

I was intrigued by this street theatre I had witnessed. Anthony, if nothing else, was very enterprising. From tourists to taxi drivers, his limits knew no bounds.

I was suddenly feeling quite thirsty, which was not surprising. Not a drop to drink since I had left Birgu. 'Any chance of us getting a drink round here Mouser? I am really parched.'

'That sounds like an excellent idea. So am I. Come on, follow me, I know just the place. It's good that we are a pair, as otherwise we couldn't get a drop.' Mouser got up and I followed, as I pondered what this joint effort would mean.

It soon became clear, when Mouser stopped near the church square, under a drinking water fountain. 'Oh good there's no one around so jump up Licky.' With that, Mouser leapt up onto the stone basin, and I immediately followed. 'Ok you go first Licky, whilst I press the button to release the water. Here we go.'

Well, it came as no surprise that on the first attempt, the moment Mouser pressed the button, I got doused from head to toe, causing Mouser to fall about in a fit of laughter. I think he had done it on purpose, but I saw the funny side, despite my hatred of getting wet. The second attempt was better as Mouser's paw carefully pressed the button and water trickled down. I stayed on the edge of the bowl and stretched my neck. My lips lapped up the cool liquid and when thirst had gone we changed places.

'You see Licky, you need two cats to operate this thing. One of you on your own is useless. Mind you I have in the past, sat up on the bowl and waited until a human being has passed by and seen my plight. Then they might press the button for me.'

We were both now well fed and watered and it was time to stroll back over to where our bus would soon arrive. Sure enough, some fifteen minutes later, the old bone shaker appeared, belching its way down the Marsaxlokk main street and grinding to a screeching halt half way past the queue of thirty people biding their time.

My exciting day out in Marsaxlokk was coming to a close, and I would soon be back in my own familiar territory of Vittoriosa and Birgu. I hoped Mouser would suggest we check out Birgu Square and its back streets before retiring to Vittoriosa Marina. Just in case my brother and sister made an appearance.

If I was never going to be re united with my owners, then at least I held out the greatest hope of finding my siblings, and never losing them again.

Before I knew it, everyone had boarded Chubby's bus and we were the last to hop aboard.

'Hey hey hey! Mouser and Miss Licky. Welcome aboard. Oh I've got a surprise for you two. Jump up on the dash board, as we are pretty full behind.' And with Chubby's beckoning, we took our positions and indeed the fun did begin.

CHAPTER 15

'I've got a cracking cassette tape. Full of all the golden oldies which I put together on one tape. I call it my *travelling music*. This will get them all going. Hey hey!'

And with that, Chubby slammed a grubby tape into an ancient cassette recorder, held down by two straps stuck onto the dash board. As he leant towards me, a familiar odour of strong drink wafted towards my nose. Whisky was spilt onto the carpet under the dining table on the yacht where I was lying. That stayed there and the memory of this odd smell stayed as well.

Chubby adjusted his stomach and posture, to accommodate the movement of the steering wheel. He had probably had a very good lunch which was perhaps more liquid than solids. Strangely at this point I was not worried about his driving ability. That was to come later. Indeed I hoped the drink would calm him down and slow his erratic turns at traffic lights and roundabouts. Things surely, could only get better after we left Marsaxlokk . Chubby was in good *spirit*.

The songs rolled out and before I knew it, both Mouser and I were moving to the rhythm and having a whale of a time. Mind you, moving to the music was hardly avoidable, perched as we were on the cloth panel glued to the dash board; hanging on for dear life as Chubby took some of those bends in the road. The drink had not wearied him at all!

King of the road...

Trailer for sale or rent, rooms to let 50 cents
No phone, no pool, no pets, I ain't got no cigarettes

'Come on, let's be hearing you all up there in the back of my limousine,' Chubby bellowed as he waved his left hand up in the air, still clutching a cigarette between his

138

stubby fingers. He knew all the words and sang like a walrus.

Last Train To San Fernando
Last Train To San Fernando
Last Train to San Fernando
If you miss this one, you'll never get another one
Di Di Bum Bum
San Fernando

'Whoopee. Good old Johnny Duncan and his Bluegrass Boys.' Just then a violent swerve was felt. A few screams could be heard from the back. Mouser and I lost our grip in sheer terror. We slid the whole length of the dash board and clean onto the cushioning of Chubby's stomach.

'Whoa, he got a bit close.' Chubby had missed a *parked* car by a fraction. Another coat of paint and we would have had an accident. 'Bad parking by an idiot,' he mumbled. He immediately took off from where he had left off singing.

Twenty Four Hours from Tulsa
Dearest, Darling, I had to write to you to say
I won't be home
I was only twenty four hours from Tulsa
Only one day away from your arms
I hate to do this to you.......
I can never, never, never go home again

The tourists and indeed the few Maltese, who had been singing along with great enthusiasm, went very, very quiet. Several of them sought to grip hand rails in front of them. These were not secure and twisted and turned as the gyrating bus loosened already very loose screws. One hand rail came off altogether which encouraged an elderly lady to scream. Then put her hands to her face. Was she making a direct appeal to God or was she experiencing a sense of guilt for dismembering a part of the bus? I could not be sure. In any event, the

139

incident provoked a further period of silence and probably silent prayer.

Chubby's spirits were not dampened. If anything the drama seemed to empower him even more. His singing got louder and his driving was worse than before and even Mouser was having his doubts. He looked as worried as any cat can. Chubby was drunk. Mouser had seen these signs before. Normally at night time – outside of Band Clubs he whispered. His sing songs he felt were brought on by the drink rather than a simple desire to cheer everybody up.

He nearly clean whistled past a bus stop, as an elderly lady struggled to get to her feet and stop the bus. Of course we knew the bell would not ring no matter how hard she hit it. She tried her parasol. Nothing happened and her bus stop raced backwards into the distance. She took her life into her hands as she leapt to the front of the bus where a bash of that parasol on the rail above his head, brought Chubby back to his senses.

'Stop the bus,' she screamed. 'Stop the bus.' He ground the wheels to a sudden halt and she was almost catapulted over his shoulders. She went to disembark uttering dark oaths I felt certain. Suddenly she looked at Mouser and crossed herself. 'A black cat of all things. Whatever next, she exclaimed and crossed herself again. She looked at the pair of us. Though Maltese she spoke in English. 'Cats! Cats on a bus? A black cat crossing my path. Whatever next. You driver are turning your bus into a zoo. Never again. Never, never again.' Just as she neared the pavement, Chubby let the brake slip and the sudden movement made her fall backwards onto the steps. The lady managed unaided to get back onto her unsteady feet, with her parasol still in hand, but said nothing. The driver was in league with the devil she probably thought and those two cats… better to get home and put on the kettle.

Chubby reeled off something in Maltese at her, revved the engine and made the bus grind forwards.

'What did Chubby just say to her as she left the bus,' I asked Mouser.

140

'He told her if she didn't like cats on his bus, then she could go and *sling her hook.'*

The last part of our journey was uneventful, except to say that I found myself crying to myself, and Mouser spotted it. The Vittoriosa Marina had just come into view over the brow of the hill. It was not the view that upset me, just the final piece of music that accompanied the sight of all those yachts. Some of the tourists had started to sing again – but more cautiously and with less enthusiasm than before. I imagined they knew they were nearing the end of their journey, hopefully safe and sound. As usual Chubby was leading the chorus. 'Come on I can't hear you at the back. Sing up!'

I am sailing, I am sailing
Home again cross the sea
I am sailing, stormy waters
To be near you, to be free

The song made my eyes water and it only got worse. The more I listened the more I felt sorry for myself, and the watering of my eyes turned into a full scale flood of tears, even dripping onto the ancient vinyl dash board.

Can you hear me, can you hear me
Thro' the dark night, far away
I am dying, forever trying
To be with you, who can say

As Chubby brought the bus to a halt, he wailed out the last final lines of the song.

Oh lord, to be near you, to be free
Oh lord, to be near you, to be free

'Now now Licky. Look at you. You have come over all emotional. Oh dear me. I know what has brought all this on. That last song was a bit too close for comfort. It is only a song Licky.' Mouser stopped in his tracks for a moment. 'Or maybe not, since maybe that song is a good omen for you! Yes, that's the way to think about it, a sign that your yacht may be fast approaching.'

Mouser was as ever on the right track. Yes it was only a song, but *maybe*, it was trying to tell me something. I saw in my mind's eye two people singing below billowing sails, smiling as they played with the ropes, forcing every ounce of strength from the wind as it caught the fabric. Driving the yacht homeward to be with me – *I am dying, forever trying, to be with you, who can say. Oh Lord, to be near you, to be free.*

Mouser paused to let me take in his own thoughts and assemble mine. He turned towards me and gently brushed his left paw across both my lower eye lids. 'Now that's better Licky. No more tears. It's all a question of looking on the bright side of life. My motto in life is that things can only get better. Do you know that song, *Things Can Only Get Better*? No you probably don't. Humans like to dance to the tune. At places they call discos. Well I'll remind you of it when I next hear it, which might be on Chubby's bus.' That thought worried me greatly as I have never been a dare devil cat and I wondered how much longer it, the bus, could stay on the road. It would either collapse of its own accord or be demolished in a roundabout accident. Either way I hoped to be as far from it as possible.

I had no idea what a disco was although I had seen Eric and Daisy embrace each other and step in time around the clutter of the decking on the yacht, with music playing. Maybe that was dancing. I said nothing in case my understanding was wrong. I was in no mood for ridicule.

'So Mouser what shall we do now?' The last of the passengers were alighting, and all made friendly gestures as they passed us perched up on the dash board. With the last passengers making their way down the bus steps, Chubby turned to us.

'Now you two, remember to be on time later in the week if you want a lift up to Valletta - around ten o'clock or thereabouts. But skip Tuesdays, as it's market day here in Birgu and is far too busy for my liking, but any other weekday. Mouser will tell you Miss Licky. He's done the journey enough times with me. Haven't you Mouser?' I was beginning to believe Chubby thought we could understand him. We could of course and now he believed it too.

With that we were off the bus, having paid our respects to Chubby with polite and sincere meows of thanks. 'See you cats and don't do anything I wouldn't do. Hey!' Chubby flung the gear lever upward, creating that fearful grinding of gears and the bus lurched forward, no doubt propelled by that vast belch of black and choking smoke emitted from the exhaust. We leapt backwards to evade its putrid smell.

'So Licky it's nearly four o'clock, so shall we do the usual check just off Birgu Square and see if there is any sign of your brother and sister?'

I needed no encouragement and nodded before following Mouser who did not wait for my answer. We crossed the two roads, using the zebra crossing as a precaution.

'I always recommend extra precautions when on the roads on a Sunday here in Malta. A good lunch with lots to drink can make some of the younger Maltese drivers a bit too over confident for their own good.'

Heeding Mouser's advice, I looked left and right and did not put too much faith on being protected by a mere zebra crossing. The white markings had faded with time and scant effort seemed to have been made to restore their vitality. Mouser informed me they were mainly ignored anyway, especially by young men in sports cars. These marks were there to signal points on the racing compass when impromptu racers joined each other. Pumping up the accelerator and turning roads into race tracks. Many Maltese people avoided zebra crossings for this very reason and safer by far to cross elsewhere. Unwary tourists soon learnt this lesson. Pedestrians were a nuisance to the racers. Scaring them off the roads freed up the race track and reduced the risk of damage to their precious customised cars.

We made our way under the scaffolding surrounding the restoration of the archway leading down to Birgu Square. We came across that house which had almost certainly been my brother and sister's home for the past few years. It looked sad and uninhabited. Green paint was flaking from the window sills revealing grey and brown shades of times gone by. I peered up at the two brass leaping cat knockers, now tinged with green, pitted in places, neglected and slowly tarnishing. There was no doubt in my mind. This was the very knocker the man had used to summons the old lady to the door, the last time I ever saw my brother or sister.

We made our way up the usual alley ways behind the square. There were a couple of cats sitting quietly on doorsteps, in their own territory, patiently waiting to be let into *their* homes. I thought how lucky they were to have a home. They would not have to wait long for their tea and the comfort of a warm room for the night. I wondered where my siblings might be spending their nights. Maybe they had been re adopted and now lived miles away. This thought should have comforted me but it was distressing. If they had been re-homed then I would never see them again. I realised I was being selfish and better to stop these thoughts and listen to what Mouser had to say.

Mouser as ever, brought me out of my gloomy thoughts. 'Now Licky, it does not look as if we are going to be in luck today, and my thinking goes like this. We are leaving it too late in the day to be searching for them.' Mouser was now seated half way up the alley. He looked both ways. The alley remained very quiet. 'You see we are not hitting this area at prime feeding time. The old ladies who devote themselves selflessly to leaving food out for stray cats and the like, do it early in the morning. We have been getting up here shortly after nine o'clock, and that is no good.'

'But Mouser, what you are saying does not make sense, since you claimed to have seen them several times, and you do not get out of the museum until just after nine o'clock most mornings.'

'Ah but Licky, that was some weeks ago when I spotted them. In those days they would have been in new surroundings and it takes time to adjust. Now a little time has elapsed, and they have learned how best to survive

144

on the streets. Feeding time would have been their first lesson to learn and that being early in the morning. After that they would make themselves scarce, keeping out of harms way. They might come out early in the evening to see if there was any other food on offer. Or they might hide until breakfast time. It is all very difficult to say, in my opinion.' Mouser gave me a quizzical look, his head slightly lilted. 'Well that's my suspicion which would certainly explain their absences during the day.'

'Mouser, what if they have been adopted by someone else and are now locked away in some other house, maybe a house not even here in Birgu?' I couldn't help but ask the question.

'Highly unlikely and I am sure, too early for that to have happened. They would not warm to anyone easily in the early days here. Not after what has happened to them before. They would need to find a garden to *adopt* and gain the trust of the owner over time. Remember, there are two of them looking for a home, not just one. So that creates a new problem. They would not want to find themselves being split up after all these years. Oh dear me no. You may be right of course. Life can be cruel.'

'Oh Mouser please do stop.' He was agreeing they could be separated. 'What a terrible thought.' I became tearful again and felt desolate. Mouser was shocked.

'Licky now calm down for goodness sake. Oh don't cry. Now come on, dry those tears and let's work this out together. We *are* going to find your siblings. But sometimes you have to give things time.' Mouser once again wiped my tears away, in between my wet sniffles.

'I do not want to relive the past Mouser. Finding my brother and sister and even maybe my mother too is all I ask. Not split up. Not anything else.'

'So it should be. I did not mean anything else, but to succeed we must be clever. Turn over every possibility. Listen. Ask around. Change our tactics from time to time.' Mouser wiped away the last of my tears.

'Mouser I know you meant no harm. The thing is you might be right. Perhaps they have already been split up.'

'No not a chance. As I said, it would be too early in the day for them to have found a home. One thing for a start is that few of these houses here in Birgu have gardens. Most of them have backyards and that is all. That obstacle is enough to lessen the chance they have been adopted. They would not go far if food was readily available and I know that it is. Cats are driven by hunger. Only that makes them migrate. They are still around and homeless. It's only time before we find them Licky. Trust in me.'

I did. Mouser outlined a plan of action starting from tomorrow. As we walked back to Vittoriosa Marina, I knew what had to be done, and I found myself with an optimistic spring in my step and no more tears. Well not for this day anyway.

CHAPTER 16

We settled down at my home, the lamppost on the Marina waterfront, as the clock struck four times. Mouser rehearsed our plan for tomorrow making sure I understood what we would be doing.

'I want you to be in the same alley we were in this afternoon by seven in the morning at the latest. You will be alone but keep roaming around until I catch up with you shortly after the Museum opens. I feel guilty about this but it will be impossible for me to be there before a little after nine o'clock.'

'It's fine Mouser, I will be ok.' I paused for a moment worrying about those other cats. 'As long as you can come straight up there and join me. Two hours alone will be fine.' Two hours alone would be terrifying I knew but if I was *left* alone I would cope. 'Yes I will be fine Mouser. Honestly.'

'Of course I will be right there.' He paused for a moment then looked me in the eye. 'I will be there for you the moment I am out of the museum. I would never let you down Licky. Not for the world. You do know that, don't you?'

Mouser I knew would be true to his word. I sensed his commitment to time was hiding a greater commitment to me. My spirits were lifted and my heart missed a beat. Adversity was drawing us closer together but who could tell where this would end. In disappointment I felt. I said nothing to dampen his enthusiasm and felt a sense of guilt overwhelm me. I hid that with the slightest of smiles and looked away, towards Birgu.

'Of course I know. Where would I have been this past week without you?'

Mouser was pleased and began to smile again. 'Probably forever sitting under your lamp post, moping and feeling sorry for yourself I fancy,' he said with a grin. 'Anyway, tomorrow keep a low profile and ignore the

147

alley cats. Just pretend not to notice them. Look straight ahead as though you are going somewhere else. Just in and out of their territory. Do not linger. Do not trespass on their food. You are not up there for breakfast. That is what they are all there for around that time, but not you. Your task is simply to spot your brother and sister and make contact. If you succeed, try to keep them there until I arrive. Perhaps go with them to wherever they are staying. Try to remember the trail. Now, they may not remember you! So tell them things about your mother and the vet. Anything to reassure them you are who you are.'

With these words ringing in my ears, Mouser was off, bidding me a goodnight's sleep and assuring me once more that he would be joining me tomorrow morning. His senses would take him to wherever I was taken.

A short time later I received quite a surprise. As ever, I lay behind the lamp post passively, to avoid contact with passing strollers and those other alley cats who would bully me if I was seen. Fortunately they normally avoided this area – as the kicks of waiters shooing them away could be hurtful. They liked the smaller alleyways where they could make their presence felt. No people walking their dogs. No sullen waiters looking for a target. The Marina was a favoured spot for exercising dog, often lead less and bounding after cats for sport.

I was minding my own business quietly grooming myself when I heard a familiar voice.

'Ooh there you are Miss Licky, and have I got news for you!'

It was Margaret. I stood up facing her and gave myself a short stretch. Margaret was wearing multi coloured striped shorts which accentuated her fortress like hips. She had become a giant in my gaze. Her pink blouse by contrast was skimpy and whispery. It was almost translucent and drifting around her tummy as she turned and bent, thereby amplifying her middle and adding to the new sense of volume I was sensing. She had become newly proportioned and just a little more frightening to me. However, she looked so pleased with herself that I sensed she was bursting to tell me something helpful.

'Just guess what Miss Licky. You are just so lucky. Oh what a lucky Licky you are.' She was peering down at me and shaking her hips. 'Yes a truly Miss Licky lucky, if you don't mind me saying.' She stopped shaking her hips for a moment, shook her head from left to right, looking at her empty hands. 'Oh silly me I forgot your plate of food.' With that she laughed, threw her head up in the air, turned round and wobbled back to the boat. Which left me standing, watching her sway onto the gangway, and wondering what was to come.

I was none the wiser even though my luck had apparently changed, but for what I thought - for better or for worse? I could try to guess what she meant but that would be futile. I reflected on the lucky and luckless days past - meeting Mouser, being found and fed daily, being trapped, becoming a vagrant and living under a lamp post at night. These recollections passed as I saw Margaret return. Her shorts were different, much looser and those stripes had disappeared. Wobbling no longer she strode towards me with a confidence that only loose fitting garments could give. She was carrying a plate of food in one hand and a piece of paper in the other.

'That's better Licky. Thank goodness the stiches broke after I got back to the yacht. Why Tel thought those shorts suited me I'll never know - a dreadful birthday present.' I could only agree, as Margaret's appearance was now much less staggering to my eyes.

'Well now this is something to be going on with.' She leant over with a new found confidence and put the plate on the floor. 'Oh look. You have hardly touched your food.' Of course it was the huge quantity of food I had eaten that day that put hunger to bed. Margaret could not know that of course. She looked concerned as though perhaps her odd behaviour had made me ill.

'Now I have taken down all of those other *Missing* posters from the lamp posts around the quayside. After all, we can't have any old Tom, Dick or Harry claiming the reward. They might take you away. Let's face it, we found you. I've been keeping you in breakfasts and dinners and will continue to do so until your mummy and daddy return.' I looked up at her, still perplexed.

'I've brought a nice marker pen with me. I thought it best to leave this poster up here on this lamp post, so you know where your home is until *your* ship comes in.' She let out one of her raucous laughs, head flung in the air. 'Now let me see. Yes I've got it.' She then produced a red marker pen from her pocket and crossed out the large word *Missing*. Under it she wrote in Capital letters FOUND AND IN FOSTER CARE UNTIL OWNERS RETURN.REWARD CLAIMED. 'That will keep anyone from catching you and holding you ransom,' she said as she stooped down to tickle my neck. I rolled over and she stroked my tummy - anything to get her to move onto why I was in luck.

Margaret took a pace backward, looked at the poster and her handiwork, and then turned towards me, flushed with success.

'Oh my goodness Miss Licky, I am just wondering. Have I told you that we spoke with your owners around midday today on the mobile? Oh my goodness gracious me, what a silly mare I am! I don't think I told you, did I? They are coming home early. Yes they are cutting short their trip and have promised to be back by the end of July or even earlier. And I told them you are safe and well and living nearby and we are looking after you.'

This was at last some very good news. Eric and Daisy were cutting short their trip and returning earlier and I had not been forgotten. They knew I was safe though I wondered whether any mention had been made of my lamp post existence, on the quayside, night by endless night. I suspected the poster above with her odd scribble would be lost before my owners returned. I doubted whether a missing child, found homeless would be left on a doorstep, being fed by neighbours from time to time until his or her parents turned up with reward money in hand. No matter. They were coming home and my home was coming home. I felt happy enough to stroke Margaret's ankles letting my tail brush against her calves.

'Yes Miss Licky, you understand what I have just told you. I can see it in your reaction. You are a clever thing. I swear to God that you really do know what I am saying.

That is why I have brought you this. I am going to stick it here down near the bottom of the lamp post. See?'

Margaret produced a small one sheet of a calendar, showing the month of June and July and she stuck it to the post with adhesive tape.

'There we are. Now I have ticked off today's date here in June. Sunday twenty six of June. We can tick off every day when I feed you in the evenings. Then you will know where you are.' She deserved another swish of my tail and she got one.

I peered up at Margaret and fixed my gaze on her eyes. She blinked. What more could I do? Some low meows; purring and the final rub of my tail against her legs.

Her calendar idea had merit as I was losing track of time. I wondered if she really knew I could understand English. Maybe she just wanted to think it. People do talk to cats so they must suspect we know more than we let on. Better they only suspect and can never really know.

'Oh Licky, you really are a *great pretender*. At times you half convince me that you understand everything I say. Then I get real, and realise that us human beings would love that to be so. If Tel heard me talking to you like this he would put me in the mad house. You cats know how to entrance us with your tails and eyes. Never biting the feeding hand, Tel says. Ooh yes I know your game, but you are lovely. A pity Tel adores that barking and biting dog of ours so much. I can't tell him that. If you lived with us you would die with us as we can't keep it locked away all the time.' With that she bent down and tickled me behind both ears. 'And remember, no straying away for good, because there is that reward for your safe return. And that belongs to me and Tel.' She gave an enormous chuckle and then she was off marching with new dignity back to the boat.

I watched her go down the walk way and then grasp the railings and haul herself on to the boat. A few loud barking noises then all remained quiet. I took to looking at the calendar. Even if Eric and Daisy did not make it back here to Malta until the end of July, it would be no more than thirty odd days at worst.

Settling down for the night, praying I would have no unwanted visitors, I drifted in and out of sleep wishing to make two dreams come true. I would soon be rescued from my present sleeping quarters and reunited with my owners. In the meantime, I would be back with my long lost brother and sister. Mouser had set out the plan for tomorrow, and I was going to do my best. Nothing would stop me. Come hell or high water, I *would* find my lost family. At this moment, I felt that nothing else mattered, and to fail would make life more pointless. Sleep came and went, but I slept well enough to gather the strength to fight another day.

CHAPTER 17

Uncurling myself from my fitful nights' sleep, I slowly stood and stretched myself full length. I then sat and looked towards the east where the sun was waiting to rise. The sky was clear and turning more blue as a tinge of redness painted the horizon. In the distance, a church clock struck six times. It was time to get myself ready. I needed to look my best as I strolled into Birgu Square looking as confident as I could.

My toilet as usual was conducted in the privacy of the building site next to the Casino de Venetia. At this time of the morning, no workers had arrived. The work force was one hour away and I was safe from prying eyes. I spent a few minutes walking around the skeletal rooms on the first floor. The hotel, when complete, should augment the waterfront as it joined the old parts with complimentary limestone and hid for all time the hideous bomb site from the Second World War.

I crossed the first floor from the front to the back, then back to the front and onto a new limestone balcony. This was certainly where the finest bedrooms would be – looking directly onto the Marina and across to Senglea and Valletta beyond. The half- finished bedrooms at the back would lack much natural day light. They would buttress a high rock face which supported houses above. I wondered how local people there felt, as they slowly lost their view of the harbour. Yes, a bedroom and a balcony at the front would bring wealthy people into the area, perhaps encouraging even more new restaurants and generally more business for the area as a whole.

The day dreaming came to a halt. The half past the hour chime was struck and then with a slight pause, two more chimes. It was six thirty in the morning and time to get my skates on. I retreated from the balcony, across the concrete floor and through a half completed doorway – a slight wrong turn. I was in a bathroom, with pipes

153

protruding and basins, taps and other things stacked in a corner and all ready to be fitted. There was a mirror standing on the floor, wrapping still around the edges. I went over and checked my appearance. All was as it should be. I spent a few moments combing my face and hair with my paw and adjusting my whiskers. Looking like a domestic cat and the collar adding credence to my claim. Feral cats were less likely to attack a domestic cat as we had no interest in territories. Or so I hoped. Appearances were everything. I quickly left this bathroom area and moved down the staircase to the ground floor.

It took a few minutes to pass by the Marina water front and up into Birgu. The square was almost completely deserted. I had never seen it like this before but then I had never been here so early. I walked across the square and up towards the first alley, apprehensively.

I left the square by the corner of *Café Brazil* which was open and readying itself for its first customers of the day. I walked up the alley way and took the first right turn I came to. I entered with upmost caution. There was some activity. An elderly grey haired lady, dressed in a green housecoat with slippers still on her feet, was bending down and putting plastic containers on her doorstep. She looked around, no doubt expecting to see the first of her own furry customers arrive for breakfast. Then she went inside – leaving the door slightly ajar. I looked at the contents but nothing appealed to me. I had no appetite. My mind was set on much greater things. I passed by lest any feral cat suspected I was here to gobble the first pickings. I was very nervous by now and I felt my heart pumping as the adrenalin soared through my veins. I would keep a distance from this harvest and hide behind that large planter just ahead that was bedecked with hanging plants that surrounded the tall cactus in its middle.

I sat behind the pot where I could clearly see the alley in both directions. I was well hidden for the moment at least and three large, ragged feral cats passed me by, more interested in their food than me. I was given a cursory look and ignored. I did have two escape routes should trouble start as the pot stood unimpeded out from the doorstep.

My ears suddenly pricked up. I could hear a few plaintiff meows coming from the end of the alleyway to my right. The old lady came out again with a final container and welcomed these three strays that were already tucking in. I turned again to peer up the alley hoping to see what was creating this distant sound. The light was still weak and shadows confused my sight. I could just make out a couple of young cats as they ran towards me. One wore a mottled grey coat and the other was completely ginger. They were shabby and seemed very ill- suited to this kind of life. I sensed they had never experienced human love, let alone the comfort of a proper home. I felt sorry for them as I could easily have gone that way. Indeed I might go that way if my owners did not return, or if tragedy struck their voyage home.

These were definitely not my siblings. The colours were completely wrong and I had no sense of seeing either of them before. They had no domestic traits at all and I felt had never been caught and taken to the vet. I felt saddened by their desperate state where only the kindness of this old woman was keeping them from death's door. Perseverance and luck too. As pretty, unkempt babies they had a chance someone would have taken them in. However the ravages of such a short time on earth guaranteed them no respite from the life they were now forced to live. Who would ever adopt these two I wondered. The short answer was – nobody.

Humans treat each other the same way I have noticed. Good looks and charm are admired. However I have seen plump, old gentleman walking hand in hand with young, attractive and well-dressed ladies sporting bracelets and chains glistening gold and bright light. Sometimes I suspected these elderly but wealthy gentlemen were being escorted from those large Super Yachts in the harbour. One of them I had seen on more than one occasion sat in a chair with wheels on. So, something else was at play there. Humans want more and the more they get the more they want. Elderly but wealthy men seem to be able to give these presents freely – despite ailing health and looks. Their money keeps away the young and the active men who would otherwise claim the prize that was theirs. I imagined that the kindness of wealth could create a fondness with time that sublimated passion. Money could create some sort of happiness that could mask the fragility of it all.

I thought about myself and Mouser. He had no wealth because in the cat life it meant nothing. However Mouser had knowledge and wisdom and boundless intuition and more valuable to me than a bell on my collar. Indeed noisy trinkets were dangerous annoyances and I was grateful my owners had never put one on my collar. Alerting all to my presence so that I would stand out in any crowd would not have served me well and especially not in the dire times. Mouser had become my own quiet wealth which protected me as surely as the yacht owner protected his own human property. I could only imagine what retribution would befall anyone who tried to tie a bell around his neck!

Eric and Daisy sometimes spoke of human women who fall in love with mature men, for their intellect and consideration. Not for wealth but for stimulation. They had friends back home who had no interest in fashion, gadgets and bangles. I felt I was more akin with these humans in my feelings for Mouser. If anyone dared place a bell around his neck then murder would have been done I was certain.

Is this the same, for older women with much younger men, I wondered. I had never seen such a thing - certainly not around Vittoriosa. I remembered our trip on the yacht to Agadir in Morocco where Eric and Daisy questioned why so many elderly women were on holiday there. 'Parties of these old women everywhere,' Eric would exclaim. 'They should know better, arm in arm with those young Moroccan men. They would not carry on like that in Scarborough!' Daisy would mutter. 'They are way past their prime and out of shape too. Money has a lot to answer for!' she would add. I sometimes wondered whether so much antagonism hid another side to Daisy, perhaps letting off steam against something that appealed deep down, but something not to be confessed.

I overheard similar commentaries when we moored in the harbour of Monte Carlo for a three day stay. Eric and Daisy paid for a day's membership at the lido of the Hotel Hermitage. They arrived later than they wished, just before midday. They had found the pool sun lounges fully occupied by very elderly but wealthy looking women, accompanied by their companions. 'A Greek God to be sure' said Daisy. 'I wonder if Adonis was his real name.' Eric ignored her comment. However they agreed on one thing. Something was afoot and the waiter seemed unconcerned whenever Adonis escorted any elderly lady back to their suite. 'Maybe the hotel used Adonis to steady them,' said Eric. 'I suppose any accident between pool and room could lead to ambulance chasers suing the hotel!' Eric laughed aloud. 'Don't be so daft Eric. Adonis was on a sex conveyor belt and you know it. I bet his bank account could tell the tale better than anything we saw!' Daisy joined in with the laughter and soon the tears were streaming down both of their eyes. 'Kleenex, Kleenex,' sobbed Daisy as the pack was thrown across the table. Once calm was restored, Eric told Daisy they would not be returning. 'Not really our kind of place,' he said.

I reined in my thoughts and returned to the task in hand. I noticed two stray cats had now arrived at the feeding place. Their stay would be brief.

From round the corner at the top of the alley, strode a cat with a real attitude problem. I came to know him as the *cat with attitude* but his adopted name was Top Cat, I discovered later. His strident walk, exuded confidence, menace and authority. He also looked very dapper. His coat was an all over light pearl grey and immaculately maintained and over his left eye lay an imitable butterfly quiff. It seemed to replicate the quiff Mouser sported. He quickened his pace towards the two hungry cats. They spotted him and moved backwards – ever so slowly – away from the two food containers. They retreated a little further but held a little ground on the other side of the alley, in the shadows.

Top Cat merely gave them a distant stare. They lowered their heads in submission. I imagined they had

157

learnt never to trifle with Top Cat. He sat where they had sat and ate at a leisurely pace. Several minutes later, he stopped. Then he raised himself, turned and glanced in my direction. I sensed he had seen me before but food had been his priority. Now he was going to turn his attention to me!

He looked at me with an air of indifference. No threatening hisses. No sudden movement in my direction. I felt calmer. He then resumed eating for a further minute or so before licking his lips and standing up, arching his back sufficiently to make himself look as big as possible. He turned towards the two strays who had not taken their eyes away from him. They now lowered their eyes to the ground which seemed appropriate.

'Right, help yourselves chaps and have a nice day.' Top Cat wandered back up the alley from the same direction that he appeared. He gave me a secondary and curious glance. *"No threat here,"* he must have thought, seeing the collar around my neck. He then disappeared round the corner.

The two strays went running back across the alley and continued with their deferred breakfast. Occasionally they looked back up the alley, perhaps in case Top Cat was playing games with them. They ignored me – apart from a second glance. If Top Cat had left me alone, then maybe they felt they should do likewise. After all – maybe he knew me. Anyway I was wearing a collar which I sensed was becoming my own passport of safe haven through this troubled landscape of unpredictable cats.

These two strays were so very different in their coloured coats of mottled grey and ginger. After several minutes finishing the ample portion left for them by Top Cat, they moved to the large water bowl. Here they drank their fill before moving back up the alley, where they sat down together.

I thought of leaving this alley for another as nothing of interest had materialised. No point staying here and feeling safe if my quest was waiting for me elsewhere. Many other food deposits lay in these parallel alleys even though Mouser had assured me that his sightings of my siblings had always been here. Things change. Maybe there was too much competition for food at this one spot.

An inner instinct told me to hold my ground and wait a little longer. Mouser's intuition lay here and he had always seen my brother and sister here – but later in the day. Besides I was fearful of getting lost among this maze of alleys without someone to guide me. My navigation skills had become dulled by domesticity. They were defective. My travels with Mouser made him the driver and me the mere passenger- a passenger who sits back for the ride, and mentally takes in little or none of the detail. Besides, this was the alley where Mouser had expected to meet if nothing lured me away. If I got lost then I suppose Mouser would track me down but I would prefer not to become the object of a search and rescue mission. I had my pride to consider.

I spent time peering at the doorways to my left and right, looking at the different name plaques for each house. Every house appeared to be competing with the next for attention. There was *MIKEELLEN, MARYJOSEPH, RICHARD HOUSE*, and other conjoined names of the principal inhabitants. Some were named differently. *BLUE DANUBE, HACIENDA* and THE VISTA. Very few numbers were on view which must have confused new post people who could not equate VILLA ROMANA with number forty seven. No doubt wrongly delivered post would simply be reposted back into the correct post box. Every local knew where THE VISTA was after all. Several of the houses had no letterboxes at all that I could see. However gaps under the doors were just wide enough to allow delivery of most items. Evidence enough of this at one house that had a plethora of junk mail forced into the gap. Signifying an absence, a holiday or a hospitalisation or even death maybe? I could not understand why people would put more mail on old mail. Better to call the police to find out why the collection of post had ground to a final halt. A Malta post person's lot was not always a happy one.

Something suddenly brought my attention back to my reason for being here. A faint sound - a sound of tinkling bells became audible and heading in my direction. I was

159

not the only one to have heard it. The two stray cats sat upright and looked to the end of the alley. I followed their gaze. The sound of tinkling bells suddenly stopped.

Two furry faces appeared, one above the other, peeking round the corner and looking straight towards me. They held their gaze for about twenty seconds. The pair then cautiously crept round the corner and walked slowly together. The bells were almost still but an occasional tinkle could be heard. Both cats wore almost identical fur coats – white with some light ginger markings to add extra colour appeal. Similar to my own coat! The only other memory I have of this first moment is the sagging of their fur coats, as though they were oversized for the contents within. They had evidently being going through hard times and had lost some weight. Left on their own, they would continue to do so.

I looked mesmerised. They came closer and would meet those near empty food bowls before they would reach me and the cactus. They were watching the other two cats as they approached the bowls. Not me. They passed them with no trouble and were allowed to visit the near empty bowls unhindered.

I cannot say when my observations turned to the realisation that my dreams were coming true. The tinkling of bells had raised my expectations greatly. Was it when I first saw those two fury faces peer round the corner of the top of the alley? Was it when they began their walk and I could see the patterns and colours of their coats? Whatever, I was certain once they were within clear sight that my brother and sister had *finally* come home. Home to *what* was another matter, but one step at a time. Mouser would know what to do after.

I stayed observing as these cats licked what was left of these platters clean. The old lady appeared at the door as she had seen the goings on around the steps. She took pity on them and managed to find a little more food from a tin. She moved forward quietly but the cats took a step back and stared at her. Slowly she spooned out the remnants and then retired inside, knowing they would not eat if she stood over them. However she was ready to shoo away those other two greedy cats if they dared approach once more. She made sure her eyes stayed directed at them through the slight gap between door and wall. She remained at her post as my siblings ate and licked every remnant from the bowl. I was relieved someone else was now taking the trouble to make sure they were being fed.

They raised themselves up and turned towards me. Their energy was by now much the greater and the bells tinkled with renewed vibrancy. They passed me without a glance. I began to follow, ever so slowly so as not to startle them. I did not want to risk a race and I worried they would not even recognise me after all this time. They reached the top of the alley and disappeared round the corner. I was close behind but not close enough. I broke my pace into a run and reached, then turned the corner. The sound of my padded feet on the paving stones, made them stop in their tracks, several yards ahead. They looked back at me and were visibly alarmed to see me. For a moment, I was lost for words.

'Is it true?' Those were the first three words I found myself saying to a brother and sister whom I had not seen in more than three years. In cat terms I had learnt this was the equal of twenty human years. A lot happens over such a long time.

William and Mary became puzzled. They became inquisitive. I found myself saying the same thing over again. 'Is it true?' They looked at me and then at each other. They examined my fur with their eyes. They listened to my words. I would speak again. 'Have I found you after all these years? It has been so long.'

William and Mary looked again at each other and then at me. Mary spoke first. 'Are you our lost sister?' I had no chance to reply.

'Are you our sister?' asked William.

I paused for a moment as though I might be mistaken. I would not want any of us to be in error about who we were.

Finally I found my tongue. 'Yes,' I replied. 'I am sure of it .You two must be my long, long lost brother and sister.' Tears followed as the gravity of our discovery sank in and with it the consequences we would only now begin to understand.

CHAPTER 18

We were overcome with emotion and questions. Why had we been parted? What had we done that was so wrong? We had been happy living with our mother but she too had lost us. Where was she now? None of us knew.

I remembered seeing news programmes sitting on Daisy's lap when she would cry and wipe her eyes. Switch channels when things became too terrible to watch. Families separated by wars. Sometimes killed and lost forever or hidden in remote graves. People trapped beneath buildings toppled by earthquakes, or victims of tsunamis, never to be found. Sometimes family members did find their way back home to confront even worse questions than we were facing now - terrible injuries, physical and mental, as they coped with the loss of loved ones. At least we were all intact with no bones broken. However, we would still need to talk about our times apart and how we coped with this brutal and uninvited separation. Understand the anguish and soothe the lingering fears that burdened our hearts. Help find hope and make that our anchor. A secure and happier future would surely be ours if we could try.

Mouser would be here soon and I hoped he could help me bring things together. He could confront those questions I worried about. Suggest ways we could stay together – in safety, hidden from the view of those who might separate us again. He knew about strategies for survival.

I quickly learnt that my brother and sister had given up hope of ever seeing me again, or their mother. I told them that if one reunion was possible then a second was just as likely. We should all persevere as I had been doing these past days. I mentioned a story I had heard where a family of children had been separated for many years but were then suddenly reunited. They were now looking for their mother as we should be doing. We were not alone. I would return to this story later but in the meantime, William and Mary were reassured all was not lost and indeed much was yet to be found.

Both William and Mary ran forward and spontaneously leapt on me and gave hugs, kisses and licks. I worried this display might attract attention but it said more than words. So I responded and a new bond was made between us. Suddenly we three had not a care in the world – at least for this moment in time. As the hugs and kisses subsided we looked at each other. We all spoke at once. William was by far the most vocal leaving Mary quiet but listening with great intent.

'William! Not so many questions all at once. There is plenty of time. You will wear yourself out.' Mary sought to assert herself.

The first thing I did was to explain my name, Miss Licky. Mary and William discovered I had earned the title by licking my owner's necks – whenever they sat back on the couch, watching television or reading a book. Such unusual behaviour everyone would say. I thought it quite natural and my owners grew used to it.

William and Mary looked perplexed and wondered whether they would need to learn new tricks like this. 'Not normally I think. But there are other things you need to know about humans, especially Eric and Daisy who you will probably meet in the weeks to come.'

I explained that Daisy was always talking to me especially when Eric was aloft – tending to the ropes and sails. I would always look and stay still at these times. Besides Eric was poor company when ropes tangled and sails twisted as a sudden gust of wind threatened to undo his work. Painstaking he was. The wind was fine when sailing. Not when the preparations were underway.

Eric thought Daisy's chats with me were both unnecessary and unnerving. An occasional stroke with his hand was all the communication he would entertain. Women often like talking to cats, he said. They like talking more than men who seemed to find other things to do when dialogue threatened their peace of mind - like tending to those ropes. I expanded on my life with Eric and Daisy over the past three years, hoping to give these two novices an insight into survival ploys, away from the streets.

I reflected on those earlier and hurtful times when we were all separated. However I did not want to dwell too much on the past. Rather paint a brighter picture of my times on the yacht. They understood why I could not be around looking for them while I was at sea and in far distant lands. There was no acrimony. Rather envy I suspected, as they learned about the world that lay far beyond their own horizons.

I was by now desperate to discover how they had fared after being taken into the house by the old lady - past those brass knockers and into a new environment. At first things went well. Their patron was a wealthy woman and born into a *noble Maltese* family. She was mildly eccentric and preferred their company to that of fellow humans. She avoided ever answering the door – unless the caller had booked an appointment over the telephone.

She spent a lot of time stroking William and Mary, probably bolstering her lonely sense of security in this enormous palazzo. Plenty of rooms to explore and the cat flap extended their reach into the large walled garden that kept humans and other cats at bay. They soon learned not to climb the walls. Jagged pieces of glass had been inset into the concrete at the top – spaced too close for the comfort of their paws. They were curious to discover what lay beyond but that was never to be.

The only regular visitor to the house was a maid who came in twice a week, every Monday and Friday. Precisely as the Church bells rang nine times. There was another visitor, a gardener who often called on a Saturday. But he had the key to the garden door and the shed so he had no need to enter the house.

Mouser had suspected William and Mary lost their home when the old lady died suddenly, over a month ago. I learned she had collapsed on a Monday, shortly after the maid had finished her cleaning duties and left. William paused and looked at Mary who lowered her head. The air became filled with a sense of sadness and foreboding. A sense too much had been said.

'So what happened next? Please tell me.' I felt their anguish.

'Should we say William?' Mary peered at our brother intently. 'I think we should tell all we know. Licky is family and will keep our secret. It need go no further.'

Before William could say another word we heard sounds of cats arguing around the corner – between the two alley ways. We all turned and Top Cat appeared with a young bedraggled cat at his side.

'When you see me, show more respect in future. Now walk on the other side of the alley. Then nod when passing me. Look away and move away.' Top Cat was determined to put this cat in its place. Respect and good manners, these cost nothing and without them trouble would arise. A little fear was needed because without it, life had no meaning. No sense at all. Top Cat had learned these lessons from others who in turn had passed on this knowledge. Between them simple survival had become an art and that artfulness gave zest and meaning to life on the street. That cat would learn. He would learn. Top Cat gave a curt nod to the passing cat who looked away and then slinked slowly forward.

Was Top Cat *out of salts* this morning I wondered? He was definitely wearing his leader's hat full tilt today. We nodded as he expected.

'I've earned respect over the years' he said – anticipating any question we might impertinently raise. 'From you I hope and everyone else round these allies.' His comments were addressed as much to that slinking cat as they were to us. 'Not so fast. Just remember this.' The scraggy cat stopped in his tracks. He turned back in Top Cats' direction, with eyes lowered to the ground. 'You may think you are the new kid on the block- come from heaven knows where. You are in my territory now and remember to behave. Or leave. I want no trouble here between you cats and certainly not with the humans living here. They feed us and look after us – as long as we all behave. Then Birgu will remain a safer, well ordered place for everyone.'

166

I was sitting in the middle with my brother to my left and Mary to the right, listening to Top Cats' continuing lecture to the unkempt cat. He was not quite finished.

'Remember that come tea time, you keep well away from the bowls of food until I have dined. Everyone knows the rules, but just a gentle reminder. You may *look* but not eat.'

Scraggy looked like a frightened school child and he nodded again. He responded with a barely audible question. 'When will I know that you are ready, sir?'

Top Cat looked at him with astonishment. Was he being impertinent or just stupid, he wondered. Top Cat decided on the latter and so his tone of voice changed. It became softer as he felt it made more sense to advise rather than scold.

'You will know when I am ready because when I am full, I will leave the feeding place. Make sure you wait for me before eating. Then we will have no need for any more arguments.' Top Cat licked his ample lips. 'I presume you have had breakfast?' Scraggy looked up at him and gave a nervous nod of the head as a yes.

'Good now get along.' Scraggy, eyes again lowered to the ground, started to walk away. 'Oh and one thing more less I forget.' Top Cat was off again. Scraggy stopped in his tracks and looked back in Top Cats' direction.

'Make sure young man that you smarten yourself up before I see you again. There is no excuse for looking unkempt. God gave you paws to clean and preen yourself. Use them. If you drag yourself backward through a hedge that is no concern of mine. However get rid of the leaves and earth after. No excuses. No tales of a homeless orphaned life please. I have heard it all before. You make the best of what you have from now on. As I do. However….' He paused. 'If you have any problem, then you may share that problem with us when we meet, as the clock strikes seven each evening in Birgu Square. I lead, but you tell and then listen to what I have to say. You can also have your say if you have something helpful for the other cats with problems. Troubles shared are problems solved and that includes day to day things like eating enough.'

167

Top Cat lifted his paw, and so tweeted his butterfly quiff above his left eye. 'Now, be off with you my lad and have a good day.' Scraggy slithered away down the upper alleyway, and probably did not hear Top Cat's final words on the matter. 'Oh the youth of today, what is the world coming to?'

I looked left and right for William and Marys' reaction. Both merely raised their eye brows and shrugged.

Top Cat slowly turned and looked down at the three of us. A frown appeared on his forehead as he took in the sight of his observers.

'What have got here? You look like the three wise monkeys. No evil around you three.' Top Cat chuckled while we felt nervous. What an odd cat this was.

'Good morning Top Cat.' William spoke first as he bowed his head slightly in deference. Mary spoke next. 'Good morning Top Cat.' She gave the same nod which seemed instinctive. Unsure of what to do, I did not move.

'Aha, so it's Mary and William I do believe. I thought I saw you a bit earlier this morning.' He moved his gaze directly in my direction.

'Who is this piggy in the middle?' he enquired. No answer was demanded as he continued talking. 'I know you from somewhere. Now let me see. Ah yes, I have seen you strolling around with old Mouser from the museum. That's it. Why are you sitting in between William and Mary? The more I look the more my eyes are seeing in triplicate.'

Top Cat shook his head for a moment from side to side, as if trying to work things out. 'Now that was not very clever of me. What I mean is you all look one and the same. But there are three of you! What is going on and I do not have all day to wait for an answer!'

Top Cat did pause this time and William spoke first. 'Top Cat, may I humbly introduce you to our long loss sister, Miss Licky. We found her this morning. Rather, she found us.' William now paused for effect. 'After three years of separation.'

'After *three* years? Phew well that was some search. You must have all been searching up blind alleys for years. There are enough of those round here in the Three

168

Cities.' Top Cat gave out a deep chuckle. I was surprised to hear both William and Mary join in. Muted laughs but laughs they were and enough to please Top Cat.

'What is your name again middle cat?' Fortunately he answered his own question which seemed to be his way. 'Miss Licky did I hear? Well knock me down with a slice of wet tuna. That's a funny name if ever there was one. Still it is different.'

Top Cat paused for a second. He strained his eyes in my direction, peering at something. 'Oh I see you have a collar and name tag to. A bit like your brother and sister, except they have those noisy bells that give them away whenever they move, which is not so clever. I did toy with the idea once, so the other cats would hear me coming and behave accordingly. Give them the chance to compose themselves. No surprises and less unpleasantness. I much prefer cats behaving well before I need to interfere. Before the 'capo' arrives. However, only a human could attach such a bell and I would never trust any of them with my neck.'

I wondered what other wisdom Top Cat was preparing to share with us as the shadows were shortening and the sun was gently rising. I was resenting the intrusion as I wanted to hear more about the old lady's sudden death, but I knew enough not to make an enemy so I remained calm.

Top Cat gave a rather gross yawn, licked his lips, and then cocked his head 'Now who is this coming along now?' We all turned to look behind us. 'Ah yes, it's old Mouser.'

Sure enough Mouser was trotting along the alley, his eyes firmly fixed on me and my siblings. I had lost all track of time and had not realised it was now just after nine. He stopped just short of where we were sitting, immediately acknowledging Top Cat's presence, with a quick flick of his paw to his own butterfly quiff. Top Cat did the same.

'Good morning Mouser. We have quite a little party here.' Top Cat never really seemed to pause for thought. 'I need to take stock and decide just how many more waifs and strays I can take into my territory. Anyway we can talk about that another time. I will leave these three here in your care while I do my rounds. Make sure they behave themselves.' With this parting advice, Top Cat raced away and out of view.

I introduced Mouser to my brother and sister and told them how we had met and planned this reunion. My siblings took time to understand how and why Mouser and I had formed this attachment. We seemed like chalk and cheese to them. He was so obviously feral and had never seen the insides of a house let alone a vet's surgery. They were sure of that. However they soon mellowed once they learnt how painstaking Mouser had been, bringing us together. Without his guidance, we would not all be sitting here together. Mouser was becoming a champion in their wide eyes.

'Could I say on behalf of us all how grateful we are to you Mouser. We cannot thank you enough, and shall always be indebted to you.' It was Mary who spoke these sincere words.

The expression on Mouser's face lit up the world as surely as the rising sun was driving the shadows out of the alley. 'Oh think nothing of it. It's been my entire pleasure for sure. I would do anything for Miss Licky and I promised her to do the same for you, once found.'

William and Mary were starting to look uneasy. William spoke up. 'Would you mind if we could all go somewhere else to talk? Mary and I do not feel safe here.'

Mouser looked puzzled. 'Not safe here? You haven't got anything to worry about while I am here.' Nevertheless he looked around – just to be on the safe side. 'Top Cat knows you are with me, so there is no threat there. In fact I sense you seem to have made quite an impression on him. He doesn't give many cats too much time of his day. I suspect he sees it as a weakness, lest he says or does anything which would threaten his position. Being aloof is his way of fending off trouble from ambitious cats that might be a little jealous of him.'

'No you see it's not like that. It's not Top Cat or any other cat that poses a threat to us. There is this man...' Mary's tone was full of fear and she paused for breath.

'What man?' Mouser was intrigued to learn that a human could incite such fright.

'Oh please can we go somewhere else and we will tell you all about it.' William's voice echoed his sister's. It was full of fear.

'That's fine by me and I shall lead. Follow me.' We left with Mouser at our head walking close together down the alley and then into Birgu Square. Already a band of tourists were milling around the square following a raised flag, held by a guide pointing out places of execution and other historical sites. We worried we would be observed as another party of sightseers, but without a flag but with Mouser as our own guide. A photo opportunity we were in no mood to accommodate. We were right to worry. Cameras started clicking but there was no time to stop and pose. With those sibling bells tinkling behind, I kept close to Mouser at the front.

Mouser took us down a different route to Vittoriosa Marina, a route that I for one, had never known before. Away from tourists, it went down a steep set of steel steps built between the new block of St Angelo Mansion flats and the old Palace walls. They led right down to the harbour. This pathway was steep but ingenious - a hidden short cut to and from Birgu Square, for anyone living at this end of the marina.

Once we had caught our breath and were seated on the marina, Mouser was the first to speak.

'Well this had better be worth the rush young William. I'm all out of breath and beginning to sense a maniac is nearby. What an imagination I have.' Mouser composed himself, gave us all a big smile, and then urged William and Mary to tell us everything.

The tale they had to tell was sinister and intriguing. At the end of the telling, it came as no surprise to me, that Mouser would unravel it and put some meat on the bones.

CHAPTER 19

William looked away as he collected his thoughts. He cleared his throat and began his tale. I would wait patiently until he came to the old lady and what passed after her death. I sensed this had triggered events which were placing us all in some peril.

Once they were placed in their new home, they realised their new owner not only loved cats. She had a heart of gold and always asked infrequent guests how they were doing. She had some money parked under her mattress for real emergencies. If anyone needed help she would walk to her bedroom. Close the door, and forage for notes. Her failing eye sight would not betray her sense of touch as she counted the value of the currency in her hand. Then she would walk back – slowly - with her walking stick in one hand and the money in the other. She was fiercely independent. Many times the maid offered to come in more often to 'do' for the *Marchioness* but these suggestions would be brushed aside. 'Later maybe. When I get old…' she would say. 'Put the kettle on dear and I will make the Earl Grey today. If you could pluck a lemon from the tree then I can cut it up. No sugar for me.' She chuckled – realising sugar was not going to make much difference. She was dying she knew so why not a drop of sugar? Yes maybe half a spoon.' She smiled again at this reckless thought as she looked down at William, his tail swaying between her ankles.

On rare occasions a tall thin unsmiling man would call, a fedora worn on his head. A black suit complimented his highly polished black shoes and he wore a less sober red bow tie around his neck. He carried bundles of papers and when the knock came, the old lady knew. Seven taps were his code for gaining entry. She would turn and wait. A further seven ominous taps. The maid most times would let him in.

172

She called him *Notary*. Only once or twice did she ever address him by name, Mr Stick. 'Notary, how kind of you to come,' she would say but her meaning was quite the opposite. He sensed this but nevertheless would always tell her how well she looked. He would bow, removing his fedora as a token of respect and speak. 'May I say as always I am enchanted to see you again. Has the walking stick helped?' She remembered his gift and it had helped and she told him so. She had for once broken her rule of independence by accepting this small gift. The maid was usually present when he visited and if need be would attend to extra cleaning duties at the request of her mistress.

William and Mary told me how they would observe these uncomfortable meetings with slight amusement. However any sense of *slight* amusement vanished when, looking for attention, they moved under the table cloth where the Notary and the Marchioness were sitting, facing each other. They both brushed against his suit covered legs. He kicked out with viscous intent. The Marchioness did not see the blow strike Mary but she was also startled. 'Do you have a problem with your leg?' she enquired. 'No, just a bit of cramp,' he replied but would not elaborate any further. William and Mary began howling under the table. They ran from beneath the table cloth and out of the room completely. He assured her that her cats must have been startled by something. 'Maybe a rat?' he surmised. The Marchioness felt there was only one rat in this room but she would not dwell on the thought. Better to get this over with and better still – get him out of the door. She added the caveat 'cat hater' to her list of his defects but ignored the cramped leg as it was, she was certain, a convenient fiction.

The Notary would return two times more. On his penultimate visit, William and Mary kept out of the way. The last time that leg had lashed out once it had only scored one direct hit. This time, it might do more damage. They listened by the stairs beside the lounge door that was open. Just close enough to hear enough. 'Marchioness are you sure this is your express wish?' and

'Well I hesitate to offer advice on the matter but I do think you are being hasty.'

'My mind is made up and that is final. Please get these matters drafted.' Her spoken words sounded firm and concise.

He was obliged to leave the drawing room and he bid the Marchioness farewell. She should not get up he said. He would see himself out. 'I shall have the papers drawn up and returned here next week for signing. Good day Marchioness.' She forced herself up and grabbed her stick. He noticed and turned to wait as his escort showed him the door. He did not notice the Marchioness hide the gold chain she was clutching. Squeezing the two golden cats her jeweller had sculpted for her. He did not see her pain as she bent down and hid the ornament under the blanket chest. Low enough to the floor never to be disturbed by the vigorous sweep of the maid's broom. She looked cautiously towards the notary's back. Then at us and she winked but said nothing.

'He saw the pair of us sitting very quietly across the hall way and he glared. Hisss. Horrible cats he muttered which was quite audible to us but lost on the Marchioness as she grappled with her walking stick. He soon vanished as he pulled the door behind him. Slamming it shut.

'We had done nothing to provoke him.' Mary remained perplexed by this odd man who seemed to hate cats.

'That's true Mary. Maybe it was just a bad day for him. If you remember, on his next and very last visit that very Monday, the day she died, he was a transformed man.'

William and Mary reflected over that last visit on the Monday. He had met with the Marchioness but this time the lounge doors were firmly closed.

Some many minutes later the Marchioness emerged. It seemed a witness was now needed and her maid would suffice. There were papers to be signed. The maid entered and did not close the doors.

The Notary told the maid she must sign a document, as the witness. It was the Marchioness' Will. When the maid asked to know what she was signing, the Notary face grimaced. 'All you need know is that on this day you witnessed your mistress' signature on that very document and nothing more. Your signature is enough!' Sensing the dark moment ahead and the fury all around, she signed. She was then dismissed by the Notary who instructed her to close the doors behind her. The kind old lady whispered as she departed, that she would be well provided for, and the maid sensed she had been the witness to a last Will and Testament.

Mary and William had managed to hear something the Notary had said to the Marchioness. 'Better never to let people know about the contents of a will. Better they know after you are dead.' He placed great emphasis on the word 'dead.' As if it had happened now and in this house. 'Things can and do happen.' He explained. 'Once a Will is made public, people react. Do things they need not do. Plan things they should not plan. Arrange things …. You understand my concerns? I shall in time furnish you with a copy and I will keep this, the original, under lock and key in my office, for safety's sake.'

'I know what he was suggesting,' Mouser interrupted. 'But never mind. Please carry on.'

So the Notary took his leave, recovering his fedora and placing it on his head. He spotted William and Mary sitting beside the staircase. He paused and placed his thin brief case on the flag stones. Then promptly raised his *fedora* and half bowed. 'Good afternoon my sweeties, and what a delight it is to see you both, young William and Mary. Now you take care.' Confusion followed. Why was he being so nice now? He slowly walked backwards, as though William and Mary were now royalty. He then bowed towards them and left.

Once outside the maid appeared from a side door for a word. William had jumped onto the window ledge and he witnessed this odd encounter. He heard her tell the Notary that the Marchioness was getting frailer and she wondered whether he might have a word with her. She would be happy to call in each day to make sure all was well and cook and clean as ever.

The Notary brushed her aside in a trice. 'Fit as a fiddle that woman. I know your game. Make extra money out of her. She gives as good as she gets. Besides she has her cats to look after her - her blasted evil cats.' He brushed the maid aside and she returned back into the house. He turned back and saw William at the window. He waved and smiled. Then turned away and cursed.

'Well what a turn of events,' I said. Mary and William looked at me expressionless. 'I mean how odd that he should so suddenly be nice to you. Well to your face at least.'

'Licky, let them carry on. I am getting more and more intrigued.' Mouser gave me a quick stroke with his paw.

'Then it happened. No time for games now with the Notary. A terrible thing and it was all my fault.' William looked close to tears.

'No William! Not your fault.' Mary was alarmed. 'No one's fault really. It was visited on us all by accident.'

'What happened?' I sensed a greater drama would unfold with nn awful climax to this tale.

'The church bells chimed six times.' William paused and Mary nodded. William's voice was faltering. He looked around in case he was being overheard. He began to whisper and Mouser and I were straining to hear his words. 'Six was our feeding time and the French clock on the mantelpiece always rang moments after the church bells. The Marchioness would probe the passage into the hallway with her walking stick. Gently tapping to let us know she was coming. Then to the kitchen to replenish the feeding bowl and add water to the other. On her way to the kitchen we would become excited and run around her feet, legs and walking stick. We would usually then lead the way to the parlour, with the Marchioness following slowly behind. It was time for our tea.'

'However she never reached the parlour that evening. Did she William?' Mary was looking nowhere in particular as she spoke. She was in a trance, looking over the water.

'She fell over with a cry and hit her head on the floor. Blood mingled with the orange and green hues of those ancient ceramic tiles. The colours blended together so patiently that it was hard to see that a deadly accident was reforming their textures. She lay perfectly still, and as we approached she took her last breath. It was just so terrible.' Tears slowly started streaming down Mary's face. Many drops followed her whiskers to their end and dropped silently into a small watery pool beside her feet.

'Oh Mary, she did not just fall over. I tripped her up. *She* tripped up.' William looked terrified.

'William we were both responsible. It could have been either of us. Who knows? We were both running around her feet and in between her walking cane. We had done it a thousand times before with no mishap. It's too awful to think about!'

'If I might just put in a little word here, by saying it was clearly an accident.'

Good old Mouser, always one to find a positive where no one else could. I felt very sorry for my brother and sister, but they could not blame themselves.

'Well accident it was, but it was preventable. In a court of law maybe manslaughter would have been the verdict. I just do not know what to think.' William looked absolutely pitiful as he said this. 'Remember this.' William said. 'We fled the scene after Mary scooped the necklace from its hiding place and pushed it over my neck, so here was also robbery and violence combined that fateful day.

'Now you are taking this all far too personally.' Mouser wanted to pour oil on these troubled waters. 'Now you are probably right when you say that it was possibly a preventable accident. But let's face it; neither of you nor the Marchioness was governed by health and safety rules. This all happened in a private dwelling. Now if this had happened in a sea food factory that might have been a whole different kettle of fish.' Mouser stopped and licked his lips. Fish always affected him this way. He resumed. 'If a factory cat did startle a worker by running around his ankles and he had an accident, maybe there would be blame. Against the factory owner that is, not the cat. The same would be true with the Marchioness. She chose to let you stay – knowing the risks. Of course, the notary might try and make more of it but I sense he was content to see her off and get his own reward for administering her estate. Besides he knew nothing of the necklace with those two golden cats from what you are saying, so that is ever hidden from him.' Mouser paused. 'Whatever became of that necklace? ' he enquired, as disarmingly as he could.

His question was not answered as the three of us remained saddened by this sudden death of the benefactor. Mary's tears had now stopped but she looked shaken while William seemed senseless to it all. Despite Mouser's legal opinion, guilt remained and with it the larger question. Could William and Mary have prevented this catastrophe? Should they have been more circumspect with their meanderings around this old lady's legs? They knew where the two golden cats now lay hidden. That was to be their secret and as the notary had said – 'trust no one.' For the moment, they could rely on the gravity of the situation to keep this question at bay. However not for very long they feared. Mouser was just too inquisitive.

I felt sure that Mouser had no intention of upsetting my brother and sister and I wondered why he wanted to know where the golden cats had gone. He retraced his comments and became much more reassuring.

'Mary and William, I was only trying to put things into perspective. What happened will be seen as an accident I am certain. The Notary will imagine you ran away after the old lady fell. With no food and water that would have been natural. He would never imagine any thievery was involved. Would he? Everything remained in its place – as far as he knew. He would simply report facts as they were. Maybe be grateful you two were gone and out of his hair.'

Mouser reflected further. 'Cats are not like dogs. They may scratch a little but are never taken to court. Now biting dogs are another matter. I know that dogs can turn bad. Bite people and babies. Now that can lead to a death sentence. I heard of a pit bull terrier that was sentenced to death because of its violent behaviour. You are not in that category at all!'

We all sat there looking at Mouser. Heaven knew what other reassuring facts he would acquaint us with. We did not have to wait long.

'Maltese people are great animal lovers. We are lucky that we are protected so well here. However, there have been isolated cases of animal cruelty in recent times. There was the man from Vittoriosa, who was fined twenty thousand euros and given a nine month jail sentence for tying up his boxer dog. Then putting him into a black garbage bag and leaving it to die in a skip. That was just a few weeks ago. However we cats are always looked after, always fed. Water left in bowls along the alleys in the height of summer when temperatures climb. No one reports unfinished buildings whose owners neglect to secure doors and windows. Our homes when wintery times arrive. We have the people on our side and they protect us from the law. We may be gypsies but we are welcome.'

Mouser looked at us and continued with his stories of health and safety at the Maritime Museum. 'That's why you find me out of the museum during the day. They prefer it that way.'

'Who prefers it that way?' I asked.

'Well the management of the museum of course,' Mouser exclaimed. 'That is another story but one I shall keep for another time. I would like to hear more about what happened after your owner's fateful fall.'

I had to agree. 'Me too, I'm dying to know.' My intervention prompted William and Mary to give us a little more detail about their most recent movements.

'We had been trapped in the house with no food or water and our owner dead. Eventually the maid arrived. She discovered the body and panicked. She phoned Mr Stick immediately. He advised her to stay put. He would be over immediately. Mr Stick arrived very shortly afterwards. A dark shadow fell across us and we could not move. The fear was so great. He surveyed the scene and scowled at us. The maid was inconsolable and sobbing.

"The Marchioness is dead I am sure Mr Stick."

He reached for her wrist but it was lifeless. 'No pulse' he exclaimed.

He turned towards the maid and tried to calm her. She may know more he thought and now was the time to find that out.

'Now, before the police come tell me more about these past few weeks. Did the Marchioness seem in any ways strange? Saying odd things? Doing odd things?"

'No the Marchioness was always the same and I saw nothing to predict her sudden death. How could I?' She wiped away her tears. 'Oh Mr Stick, I do hope you do not think badly of me.'

'Come, my dear. The Marchioness was very old and she never said anything bad to me about you. Should the police ask questions you have nothing to hide I am sure.'

The maid had nothing else to say. Mr Stick rose to call an ambulance.

'You stay here my dear and I will let the police know about the accident. The ambulance will be here shortly and you can tell them about your discovery. I need to go now and make arrangements.'

'The moment Mr Stick opened the front door, we were out like a shot. He noticed the glitter of the gold around my neck.' William looked downward as he said this.

'Stop thieves he screamed but we were out of sight as he entered the street. Please don't get me wrong. We were not intentionally leaving the scene of the crime. We had been without food or water for several days. We were frantic. Starvation makes you mad and stupid. At the time we felt trapped. On hindsight we made a stupid move. We should have stayed there. The maid would have come to our rescue. Mr Stick called us thieves! Maybe he has told the police about the two golden cats.' William paused for a moment, allowing Mary to have a say.

'Yes well that was how we landed up in the unfamiliar back streets of Birgu, homeless and with two heavy golden cats jingling from a chain around the neck of my brother. There was worse to come, wasn't there William?'

'Indeed there was. The next day, Saturday morning, we discovered where we could get the odd bite to eat around the alleyways. Then we encountered Mr Stick. We could not believe it. He was pacing up and down the different alleys, calling our names, dressed as ever in black and wearing that odd fedora. He was carrying a big butterfly net which had surely never trapped a single butterfly!' William shuddered as he spoke. 'He was definitely after us, wasn't he Mary?'

'Certainly but we did not know why. He is still after us, or after those golden cats. We have seen him at least half a dozen times during these past weeks. Fortunately we have seen him first and have managed to escape. Finally we had to hide the golden cat necklace. They were becoming too heavy for William to carry and we thought they were attracting Mr Stick's attention. They made an odd jangling sound each time he appeared and we feared the noise was known to him. A signature tune he was using to find us. We worried whether the maid had noticed our departure with the golden cats. Maybe she had told Mr Stick and he wanted them for himself. We imagined there was a reward out for our arrest because of the Marchioness death.' Mary seemed sure this was so.

'Hmm, let me get this quite clear.' Mouser was looking very serious. 'So Mr Stick, the Notary, is now actively searching for you. For his own purposes so I doubt the police know anything of his antics. You are innocent of any crimes so something else is afoot.' Mouser gave one of his lovely pauses, causing us all to become extra alert. 'There is much more to this than meets the eye. You, William and Mary may be worth more than your weight in gold, and certainly more than a few ounces of a golden necklace.' With that Mouser licked his lips. 'Do any of you know where this is leading me?'

I was clueless and so were Mary and William, looking at their faces.

'It's simple. I reckon that you two cats meant more to the Marchioness than you realised. Did she not hide the golden necklace for your eyes only? As a keepsake in case her plans failed? I think you may own everything she owned. She signed her Will hours before she met her fate and now this Notary has had to cast her wishes in stone.'

'Ooh Mouser, how have you come to that conclusion?' I couldn't contain myself. The thought of my brother and sister being the new owners of the Marchioness' house with all of her wealth seemed ridiculous. Or was it?

Mouser slowly stood up. 'Let me suggest we take a walk along the Marina, and I shall tell you more. Licky, you for one have not had any breakfast yet and that is waiting for you by your lamp post. I saw it on my way to meeting you this morning. You need to go and help yourselves to what you may before other strays steal what is yours.'

I felt we had spoken enough of stealing for one day but we nevertheless followed Mouser back to the marina. As we went he added more embroidery to his theory that we had suddenly become cats of substance in this City.

CHAPTER 20

The marina was coming alive as we walked between the growing throng of people. The adults paid scant regard to us and stepped aside as we passed by. The children however wanted to play and join us in our march. They looked kindly down at us as their parents pulled them back. Well away from Mouser's claws which would react instinctively to any approaching hand. Mouser still remained a cat not for stroking.

Everyone was here to enjoy the coolness of the day as the sun played its mischievous dance over the yellow limestone of Senglea, one of the Three Cities on the other side of the harbour.

We arrived at the lamp post where fresh food and water had been placed, just as Mouser had earlier stated.

Mouser rehearsed his theory again by reminding us of those visits by Mr Stick to the Marchioness and his apparent intense dislike of cats which changed in a moment as suddenly they were his best friends. He had even doffed his fedora in William and Mary's direction. Such deference! After all and not so long ago had not Mr Stick urged the Marchioness to re-think things? Why was the maid a signatory to a will? Mouser needed to explain to us what a human will was.

'A will' he paused and thought. 'A will is something you leave behind before you die.'

'Did the Marchioness know her days were numbered?' William asked.

Mouser thought for a moment. 'Sometimes people know. Sometimes their age tells them. We cats often know when we must leave. A sense moves us. Then we find a quiet place to lie down and leave. None of us know where we are going. We only know the time is right. So we make plans. The Marchioness made her own plans I am sure.'

Mouser also reminded me about that thin man in the alleyways of Birgu. We too had seen Mr Stick on the prowl. The Notary! We three shivered but Mouser was not perplexed.

'Phew. I enjoyed this snack. Anyone else want a drink?' William and Mary both politely declined. 'Oh I will if you don't mind Licky. This thinking is thirsty work and there is more to do.' Mouser lapped up the remains of the water and then sat between us. He looked around before he spoke again.

'What shall we do next?' Mouser gave no pause for an answer as he continued. 'We need to tackle the issue head on. It is clearly not safe for the pair of you to be running around those alleyways on your own with Mr Stick on patrol at odd times of the day. He could catch you napping. That butterfly net is a worry. I suppose it might be quite innocent, but why then does he carry it when calling out your names? I fancy you two are the butterflies he is out to capture for his own selfish ends.'

We agreed that William and Mary would be protected during the day when Mouser had the time to act with me as their body guards. We would escort them back and forth from Birgu Square, morning and late afternoon, until we had formulated the long term plan. Should Mr Stick surface we could distract him while William and Mary escaped into back alleys and old buildings. We could always meet up later at this lamp post when the coast was clear.

I was determined that William, Mary and I would never be parted again. So for the interim, they could continue to stay at night in the old deserted house they had found at the back of Birgu Square. We would all meet there once the museum was open and scour the alleys of Birgu for food. This plan would work until the yacht returned when we would need to plot and scheme our longer term futures together. That settled, the plan was put into place and Mouser and I escorted William and Mary back home. We returned to the Marina where Mouser left me under the lamp post to start work at the museum.

We met as planned the next day, carefully padding our way up to the old house and keeping a careful watch for Mr Stick. He was not to be seen and so we joined William and Mary and managed to scavenge food and water from the various doorsteps leading back to the marina. Back at the lamp post we talked about past adventures, catching up on those long periods of separation. Margaret and Terry suddenly appeared – laden with shopping bags. They came across looking surprised to see they now had four cats whereas before there had only been me.

Mouser appeared uneasy and ushered William and Mary to the next lamp post.

'Well Miss Licky, who on earth were those three other cats? I hope you have not been sharing your breakfast with all and sundry. I looked for you this morning but you were nowhere to be seen. I hope you are not becoming an alley cat!' Margaret laughed and that became a wail of laughter, louder now and quite enough to worry Mouser who wondered who this mad woman was. 'Odd company your sister keeps,' he whispered as he barred the way between these two lamp posts. He just hoped she would go. She picked up the bags and signalled to Terry they needed to go. Get the food into the fridge. She stroked me briefly and turned towards the boat with Terry trailing behind.

Mouser, William and Mary returned, and our conversations continued. Mouser reminded us about his brush with health and safety in the workplace, in the museum's small coffee shop to be exact. A favourite haunt for Mouser until the Inspector arrived about a year ago.

There had been an unexpected food and hygiene inspection of the coffee shop. Mouser had been ushered away by the museum doorman as soon as he saw that black briefcase and the dark suit approaching. A sure sign trouble was brewing as this moustached man had the bearing of a sergeant major. With Mouser hidden away, the inspection began.

'There, right there!' The Inspector spoke directly to the mild mannered manageress who needed to find her glasses, to see what he was talking about. 'Mice droppings,' he exclaimed as he drew his handkerchief from his pocket and sneezed, almost adding drama to his discovery. The manageress peered into the corner of the room. She spotted a hole in the skirting board and outside, several bits of detritus but only just visible to her own eyes but glaringly obvious to the Inspector. 'What do you make of those mouse droppings?' he shouted. The manageress sighed. 'Oh well, that is better news,' she said. The Inspector was appalled. 'Better news! Better news!' He awaited her response. 'I mean where there are mice there are never any rats.' The Inspector was speechless. 'Get that sorted and I will be back to check again. Maybe you need to get a cat to catch these mice, before I close you down.' The Inspector marched out and the doorman gave him an instinctive salute, just In case he was ex-army, or similar.

Mouser suddenly became the museum's treasured possession. Extra fish pieces guaranteed and promised if he rid the place of this vermin. The doorman was instructed to make it happen and he was given funds to reward Mouser for his efforts. This would frequently entail fresh fish at the start of the day. It all depended on the tally count of deceased mice the next morning. The coffee shop manageress had also become steeled to the task. Her manners had been sharpened by the threatening visitor and she wanted no more trouble. So Mouser was told to treble his efforts and the lampuka would be there for the taking. 'Gather them up here behind the desk. She wants the evidence and she will be counting!' Those were the doorman's instructions.

Mouser became adept at tackling the problem. His hearing suddenly improved. Scampering sounds boomed from hidden corners. Small holes were magnified into great portals where mice might linger. The mouse count rose in a trice and the manageress was impressed. 'More lampuka!' she exclaimed and the doorman duly obliged as another five euro note was thrust into his palm. The inspector returned a couple of weeks later and gave the establishment a clean bill of health. All seemed well until another incident happened a few weeks later that so nearly brought Mouser into direct contact with the Inspector.

Mouser spent much of his day time hours mooching around the museum, in between frequent periodic visits to the coffee shop and always looking *keen* whenever the manageress caught his eye. She was much fonder of him now. After all, he had helped save the coffee bar from a likely closure. However she had learned never to stroke Mouser as apart from the risks to her tender hands she needed him to stay feral.

Mouser was especially drawn to the fresh warm *pastices* served there. There were always tourists who would break off a piece and give it to him under the table. However some of these cat loving tourists would try their luck and try to be over friendly. The manageress would warn against too much familiarity in a friendly way. Familiarity bred contempt she knew. That only ever led to trouble.

An unguarded moment arose when a French tourist took a shine to Mouser the moment she saw him. She had just entered the coffee shop when she spotted Mouser. She bent over to stroke him. He became agitated. His back arched and he hissed. Then he lashed out, and caught her on the back of her bare leg. A nasty scratch appeared. The manageress ran for the first aid box and on stooped knee, applied neat iodine to the scratch. 'Get lost Mouser!' she exclaimed as she stemmed the rush of blood. The tourist screamed as the iodine penetrated the wound. The blood continued its passage and the manageress pondered a call to the ambulance service. However, such an incident might attract press coverage she thought. Better to apply a large plaster to the wound and hope for the best.

A first aid bandage was taken from the box and applied. But still the wound was oozing with blood. The time came to call for an ambulance. Maybe Mouser had touched a vein or artery. The tourist would be taken to the new Mater Dei hospital where stitches would be needed to hold things together. The manageress now in somewhat of a panic, offered the tourist a goodwill gesture - a souvenir of her visit from the small souvenir counter. For all the tourist might know, this was a wild feral cat that had strolled in from outside unannounced - nothing to do with the museum who would remain an innocent party to a spiteful event. Besides, the tourist molested the cat! The tourist however did manage to hobble over to the souvenir counter where her selection began. Not one item. Oh no. She had four children and five grandchildren to consider. She would take her time. "The Cats of Malta" calendar went into her capacious bag, followed by "Colourful Maltese Roundabouts in Spring." and "The History of the Last Days of Hompesche and the French Invasion." Finally a DVD collection about the Maltese people and their heroic efforts during the Second World War, plus four booklets depicting the ancient bus transport of Malta, all in colour. She continued filling her bag with other trinkets right up to the time the ambulance people arrived. Museum souvenir pencils, pens, leather wallets, key rings and just about everything else she could lay her hands on. She appeared more intent on her present purpose of a *Supermarket Sweep* than that of attending the hospital for a few stitches.

Mouser had observed all of these events unfolding from his position hiding behind a pillar in the main entrance hall.

She muttered some thanks to the manageress and said she would not sue. This surely had been a wayward alley cat but maybe the museum should take more care to keep these rabid animals out. Put up nets. Close doors and windows. Put down pest poisons.

The museum was saved from litigation and another visit from the Inspector. Safety was his other remit and he would take no nonsense when the health of tourists was concerned. 'Vital to our economy' he would say whenever he mentored his colleagues about their importance to uphold health and safety for the sake of Maltese society and *tourism*.

It was decided Mouser should only be allowed in to the museum *after* the public were all out. So Mouser's daytime visits to the coffee room were suspended. He would have to chase mice alone in those quarters late at night and thereby lose access to titbits proffered by unsuspecting tourists. Mouser accepted his change of fortune with alacrity. He would do the night shift.

'Every cloud has a silver lining,' Mouser said. 'I was bored spending twenty four hours of every day in the museum. Apart from the mice chasing period when my talents were sorely needed, there was not much else to do. Once the coffee shop had lost the attention of the Inspector, things would go back to their old ways. My real job came into play at night when all was quiet. Undisturbed by the noise of strangers and their chatter, I could hear those mice. See them in the gloom. I even caught a rat as it clambered up a broken pipe from the sewers below! The noise was clear and I found the break.' Mouser paused for thought. 'Daytimes were better spent outside, in the sun, visiting new places and meeting people like Chubby and exploring towns and villages on his route.'

Mouser looked at William and Mary who were strangely quiet and maybe subdued by these daring tales they could and no doubt would never wish to replicate.

'You seem to have done so much in life Mouser. Doesn't he Mary?'

'Indeed you have done so many things. You have been up against Inspectors and tourists alike, whilst trapping vermin, travelling everywhere and always seeing new things.' Mary gave a sigh. 'Our lives have been sheltered living with the Marchioness. She would never let us out. It would have been lovely to have visited new places but there was never the chance.'

'Now you have that chance. We can plan where to go. Chubby will take us I know. Visiting different places in the south, where fish come ashore almost by magic and where boats are painted blue and green and orange too and where painted eyes guide the way. Church bells peel in a different way and people love to see cats. There are some truly magical places to be found in the south of the island, simple and kind. Licky knows. Licky has been there with me already.'

I had indeed and felt we could all explore the south together and the fishing ports of Marsaxlokk and towns where we could blend and avoid detection from Mr Stick.

Out in the morning and back before sunset. Mouser would organise things I knew. We just needed to be at the bus stop at the right time. Going there but also coming back. Mouser could tell time by looking at the sun. However he would also listen to the chimes of church bells and know his estimations were sound.

I remembered with dread Mouser's tales on his trips to Valletta - chiefly his unannounced visits to that restaurant Da Pippo. I certainly had no intention of introducing my brother and sister to criminal antics such as stealing fish during the morning hours, or any other hours for that matter. I sensed the people of Valletta were less tolerant of fish napping and Mouser had evaded capture by the skin of his teeth. A little 'wastage' around the fish markets of the south would be more likely overlooked. William and Mary from all accounts had barely escaped charges of manslaughter and theft of their elderly owner. I would keep them away from the fish pots of Valletta as long as I could.

'If we are sensible and if Chubby agrees, then maybe we can travel south. For now we must plan each day at a time and keep our wits about us. Sooner or later, Mr Stick will learn more about us and plan his schemes with greater precision. People talk. With four of us prowling around we could become a focus of interest. Tales will be told.' There, I had said my piece and I hoped Mouser would take everything on board.

'You worry too much Licky. We will stick to our plan for the next few days and if that works Mr Stick should lose interest. Then we can travel further afield. Indeed keeping away from Birgu during the day should thwart his evil intentions. While we are out enjoying life, he will be searching dark corners with his net. Sooner or later, people will wonder what he is up to. Prying eyes at windows with nets drawn back will spot him. Someone will call the police, sensing him to be someone up to no good. We can give him the rope to hang himself – if we make ourselves scarce.'

I warmed to this idea. Mouser was right as ever. How long can a man with a butterfly net stalk the streets of Birgu without eventually drawing attention to himself?

Safer by far for us to be miles away when the police car arrives to hear his story of bring an avid butterfly collector. Where is your collection?

So we agreed. Better to move around more. Not be trapped by complacency and keep Mr Stick guessing. 'Mouser, we must avoid trouble at all times. I agree we should take care to visit safe places during the day keeping well away from nets and other hazards.'

William and Mary were looking at me with concern. Clearly they saw Mouser as their champion and of course they wanted some adventure to uplift them. Mouser could be impetuous which was at times good. Not so good when others face the consequences as he flees the scene. He was a better Scarlet Pimpernel than we three who simply had no knowledge of survival in the raw. He would need to teach us more and in the meantime we might join his adventures but at a safe distance.

'Mouser, perhaps we can go on outings but let's not rush things. Perhaps it would be safer to leave this for a few days so we learn how to cope in the environment we at least know.'

'Oh super idea Licky. I knew you would come round to my way of thinking. I value your thoughts. You are quite right, things should not be rushed. So let's say the day after tomorrow. It's too soon to go back to and anyway it is really only on a Sunday that we want to be there. Perhaps next Sunday for that, as you two would love it there.'

Mouser looked at William and Mary as he made this suggestion. 'The day after tomorrow would be best left for a visit to Valletta, especially as you Licky have never been there. A treat in store for all three of you I am certain. We need to make this a special day out. Chubby will be on time and he will drive us there. A great day for your reunion and you can dance in the square around the fountains with the children. As the music flows across to excite the waters as they race up and up, into the air.'

The last place I wanted to go but I said nothing. We would take the chance and hope we could hide safely within the crowds. Not dancing with the children and not drawing attention to ourselves - somewhere in a quiet

191

corner away from sunlight. That was my wish. However I feared Mouser's exuberance might place us in harm's way. It was fine with just the two of us. However with four cats in a potential danger zone, I was much less sure. I saw in William and Marys' faces that sudden look of expectation and excitement. I could not deny them their right to their own adventure. I would say nothing and with heavy but hidden heart, agree to this latest plan.

'Yes, well a visit to Valletta the day after tomorrow seems reasonable enough, providing that suits William and Mary.' I did not have to wait long for a reply.

'Hoorah, that sounds fantastic. Oh yes we would love to come, wouldn't we Mary.' William appeared over the moon at the very prospect.

'Oh yes, that would be a trip of our life time. After all, my brother and sister have never been anywhere in our lives, except here in Birgu. Thank you so much Mouser and Licky. We promise to be on our best behaviour and do everything you say Mouser.'

I needed to urge caution at this point. 'Yes but can we avoid visits to restaurants where you are likely known Mouser. Bad enough for one cat to steal their fish but If they spot you with us they may take some revenge. On us all! I mean that Da Pippo restaurant Mouser!' I gave him a stern look, only to be greeted with a mixed smirk and grin on his face.

'Oh Licky, you can be prudish at times. Forget Da Pippo, there are plenty of other interesting places to visit.' Maybe I had been a little harsh. Maybe Mouser had other safer tricks for us to play. Visits to museums and especially higher end cafes and restaurants where we could be hidden from view, by the legs of endless tourists and linen tablecloths.

'There is a lovely restaurant we can visit in safety. With an outside area that will suit our needs. Very discrete with a sheltered corner area where we could never be disturbed. The four of us can easily sit there discreetly.'

Mouser knew everything of course. He had managed to ignore my own worries about this trip to Valletta and instead turn it into a reason for going! His reasoning so he would have me believe was of course to keep away from Mr Stick. I would have to watch things closely on the day. With two lively relations and a vibrant tour guide in our charge, my paws were looking very full. We would avoid direct involvement with theft. I might not be able to stop Mouser poaching but I was determined the rest of us would play no part. The problem was separating the deed from the response. What if Mouser presented us with a fresh salmon to eat? It would be churlish to refuse. However, simply ignoring the offering was no easy option. Hunger has its ways of making hypocrites of all of us. I feared hypocrisy could turn into the main fare of that coming day. I suspected that Mouser's tunnel vision would affect us all. See a fish? Grab it. Rush away. Eat it. Lessons easily learned but so much harder to forget.

Mouser returned to earth for a moment and reflected on the hours ahead. I was grateful as the clock had just chimed four.

'We must get your brother and sister back safely to their temporary home.' Mouser became the here and now planner stating we should all return to Birgu Square.

'Licky, if you wish, you too can stay with them overnight.' Mouser tuned his head sideways, looking me directly in the eye. An ear drooped slightly. Something I had not seen before.

I thought for a moment. 'I would love to do that but if I disappeared then Terry and Margaret would know something was wrong. Turning up with food and with no one to feed at the same lamp post where they saw us all today. They are in contact with my owners, and I would not want them to think I have disappeared. A wrong message might be sent. My owners could change their plans and give me and Malta up for lost...'

'Hmm, yes you are right.' Mouser gave my brother and sister a glance, and clearly noticed their look of despondency. 'Don't worry you two, we shall soon get everything together. It just takes time. Shortly, all three of you shall be together permanently, day and night but for now – no risks!'

193

Mouser paused and gave a slight frown. Something was troubling him, and it showed. He lowered his guard and his words became mumbled. 'I do not know where that will leave me.' The sadness overwhelmed us all. The pathos was too much to bear. Mouser's heart was on his paw and we saw it. Tears welled up. He realised a chink in his armour had become blatantly exposed and quickly sought to compose himself. 'It is just a matter of logistics, planning and timing. Yes I will come up with something soon enough.' The optimistic bounce in his voice was not yet recovered but it was enough for him to regain his ground. 'Move,' he said gently.

We slowly made our way back to Birgu Square. This time I walked alongside Mouser, with William and Mary walking in unison behind us. 'Mouser, you spoke of my brother, sister and I being together in the future but nothing of yourself. Remember?' Mouser continued looking straight forward, and gave no reply. 'You know what I am talking about Mouser. I said we should never be parted but I cannot guarantee the future. Anything might and probably will happen. I have been thinking. We must plan for the longer term to stay together. Don't you think so? After all life is too short and every day must be seized the moment we awake.'

Mouser slowed his pace somewhat and gave me one of his quizzical looks. 'If only life was so simple Licky. If only. Soon your owners are going to sail back into harbour, and many of your troubles will be over. You shall return on board as the long lost daughter. However the problem of William and Mary will surface. Can they go with you? That will be the trickiest hurdle to overcome.' Mouser paused for a moment and then regained his momentum. 'As for me, well that is a different matter. I am not family. I know I am an ageing feral cat and my resting place will be in the museum. That is my lot in life. You three have your years ahead of you. Focus on that and not on me. We shall be soon parted and you will be reunited on the yacht, all three of you. My future alas does not lay there.'

'Oh Mouser, come on. We have agreed that life is what you make of it. You are so full of life. Things can and must get better for us all. Something will turn up. Something did. That famous English author Charles Dickens said so. Mr Micawber always told friends that something would turn up.'

'Did it with this Mr whoever? Did something turn up?' Mouser had a slight smile on his face.

'Well to be quite truthful Mouser, I cannot tell you, since I only ever heard bits and pieces of the novel being played on an old cassette machine on the yacht. I think it had a happy ending. It must have had a happy ending, because everyone likes a happy ending on the yacht. We too will have such an ending.'

'I hope you are right Licky. I hope your owners might take to what we see as a happy ending but I cannot be sure. Not sure at all. Still, we can never predict in life what is round the corner. Maybe there would be room for all three of you but I have to be the *joker* of the pack. I would be the square peg attempting to fit the round hole, which in all probability might sum up my life to date.' Mouser sounded just so doleful that I was lost for words. I chose to give no reply, whilst choking back a tear and just looked ahead of me.

We had just entered the square when we heard Mouser's name being called. Halted in our tracks, Mouser looked across to his right towards his name caller..

'Oh blimey, it's *Seven*. Stay here, I'll be right back.' Mouser raced towards the figure of a young man who called his name again. Mouser ran between Seven's legs, stroking himself against his Levi jeans. A torn garment, holed at the knees and frayed at the seams. Had Mouser attacked him before with his claws I wondered or was this merely the latest clothes fashion?

Seven was now talking to Mouser who sat at his feet. Moments later, Mouser scurried back while Seven sauntered away across the square.

'Sorry about that but I haven't seen Seven in quite a while. He's not been driving the family bus much these past months since he gained employment as a plasterer. Anyway he's back driving again now, and he is on the Valletta route and will pick us up the day after tomorrow.'

195

'Well you do know some curious people Mouser, but useful people too. Why do you call him Seven?' We three settled and listened to his answer, overcome by another curious emotion.

'Because everyone knows him as Seven in Birgu. He has six brothers and he was the seventh. So the only nickname he could ever have been given was Seven.'

The mystery was solved and we perked up and continued our walk up the alley way and onward. William and Mary led us to their home about three or four minutes from the two alleyways that I had become accustomed to and far enough from the main street to be safe.

William and Mary arrived at a shell of two properties. Part finished in limestone blocks but lacking doors and windows. There were two entrances, one for each property. The excuses for doors were simply plywood sheets held only half in place by obo nails and flimsy locks.

'Here we are. I can offer no apologies for the state of our new abode. I feel quite ashamed, but it was all we could find at short notice.' Mary looked down at the ground as she uttered these words. 'It is certainly not a place for entertaining but it protects from wind and rain.'

Nobody said anything for a moment, and during the silence I found myself looking up at the unfinished building and reflecting on life's changes over the past few weeks. Like these houses - full of promise and then laid bare by neglect. I was now living at the bottom of a lamp post on Vittoriosa Harbour, and my siblings were housed in a most forlorn unfinished housing project.

Mouser was the first to break the silence. 'Aw think nothing of it. It is only a temporary state of affairs. I know this place from a few years ago. There had been an old derelict house here on the corner. It got sold to a youngish Maltese guy who had it knocked down and then crammed this monstrosity into the land and he got too greedy if you ask me, trying to put two dwellings into one small site. They won't sell you know. Look at them. Open to all elements and turning black with mould, with plants feeding on the mortar and opening the joints. It would need more than Seven's skills as a plasterer to set things right. A bulldozer I reckon. Take care where you walk inside, as I have spotted needles here.'

'Do you mean drug addicts Mouser?! What on earth are you talking about?' I could not contain the alarm in my voice.

'Oh don't panic Licky. I am just being cautious and warning your brother and sister to take care where they are stepping. They need to be aware of any sharp needles and avoid getting infected. I was just saying take care because I have seen odd looking people staggering in and out late at night to find their own kind of sanctuary. This was before my museum days.'

William and Mary had noticed one discarded syringe the past week or so, but had carefully stepped over it. They recalled being awoken by someone entering in the dark downstairs. They were sleeping on the top of the concrete staircase at the time. They were huddled together, and at first wondered whether Mr Stick had found their hiding place. Whoever the intruder was, he stayed no more than a few minutes. Made a gasping noise and then coughed. Then they heard footsteps leaving the place.

I became very worried about this hiding place. Quiet and off the beaten track it might be, but that in itself created new problems. Dangerous people could lurk here, hidden in the gloom and others might join them, using these needles. I decided a new place of safety was needed – the sooner, the better. Events would soon overtake us all and then drastic action would be taken. However that was yet to emerge as another danger in my line of sight.

Meanwhile Mouser spoke of some last minute practical details for the morning to come. His intuition was causing both of his ears to twitter. Mr Stick was on his mind. Something was coming of that he was certain. Mr Stick was close by and planning to go to the ends of the world to capture William and Mary. Surely to fulfil his artful quest to *look after these lovely cats,* and thereby control the late old lady's Will.

Mouser felt William and Mary should leave their current lodgings early in the morning on their own, at sunrise. They should leave for the alleyway and take an early breakfast. Food was always set out nice and early hereabouts. Then return to this hiding place and wait for our arrival. I should wait for Mouser at my lamp post. We would then come straight up shortly after nine and collect William and Mary. Mouser felt it safer if I stayed where I always did this night. His concerns added greatly to all of our fears – not helped by those quivering ears. I wondered whether he was simply under the weather. Bidding William and Mary my fondest goodnights, Mouser and I made our way back to the marina slowly and in the meantime Mouser's ears lost their twitch.

As Mouser settled me by my lamp post, he bade me good night with a brief peck on my right whiskers. 'I am so happy for this day Licky, where you have been reunited after all these years, with your brother and sister. Sleep tight and I shall see you just after nine. God bless.' Then he was gone. He skipped over the road and made his way into the unlocked museum doors and was greeted by Peg leg with a bowl of fish.

'Mother's special,' he said.

CHAPTER 21

The moment Mouser departed, I began to gather my thoughts. So much had happened today with tales of intrigue. That thin man lurking behind lamp posts. I imagined sometime later that evening that I saw such a man further down the quayside, hiding in the shadow of a post. I shuddered and realised this was no person. A ghostly apparition maybe made of light and dark and all of my own imagination. I looked away and thought of better things. We four were united in a God given purpose. To stay together and plan adventures together. Plot the longer term when things might go very wrong. Avoid conflict with strangers who could destroy us. Be careful about all these rewards on offer and what they might mean for us. My own of course seemed fairly straight forward but maybe others were in the offing. If Mr Stick was so determined, he might well start posting his own and other signs, new and cleverer traps to displace his own useless net.

I felt the presence of St. Francis close by. He tended to the poor and the sick and loved all animals. We were fortunate indeed to have come together as we had. Surely he was here in spirit and would protect us in the days ahead. So far, we had made great progress and much more would follow, if we remained alert and resolute. God helps those that help themselves. So it was written in the wheelhouse of the yacht where a small statue of St Francis himself lay above the wheel. A simple prayer hung encased in glass by the door.

Lord make me an instrument of your peace
Where there is hatred let me sow love
Where there is injury, pardon
Where there is doubt, faith
Where there is despair, hope
Where there is darkness, light
Where there is sadness, joy

Maybe this was the start of a miracle for the four of us. We would be elevated from the despair of the alley into a new world where all our needs were cared for. People were already noticing us as a band of brothers. However, too much notice now would be a bad thing. Better not to become conceited. Pride and arrogance were dangers we must avoid. Mouser must not let us get ahead of ourselves, as complacency remained our biggest enemy and we must stay alert. Find out more about these plots and schemes that had entered Mouser's head. Act accordingly but certainly together as far as we were able.

I suddenly remembered that chain with the two sculptured golden cats. Where was it? Mouser had asked questions but he had appeared to have forgotten to ask William and Mary anymore on the subject. In any event that must stay hidden and lost for the moment. Signs of ostentation dangling and jangling around William's neck would never do. We could find ourselves being targeted by thieves. I made a note to myself to mention this tomorrow. Maybe William could say the thing had indeed been lost if and when Mouser asked further questions. Lying to Mouser would be a real challenge though. He had a sixth sense about him and would probe further. I hoped he had forgotten and that the chain was hidden. Out of sight and well out of mind.

I wondered whether our recent stories would even become known to the world and whether St. Francis himself would appear within these memories. Terry and Margaret might be keeping a diary and therefore maybe by now, the four of us were appearing in it. A simple brief sighting might spur them enough to see another profit from these tales. They did have the reward of course but sometimes people want more. Turn our story into a revelation. Publish it and make us famous. The miracle of the reunion... I shuddered to think. Maybe they too had their own scheming ways which would be yet another thing to worry about.

I had allowed myself to slip into a world of fantasy but such things do happen when you find yourself alone and homeless under a lamp post, and especially when there are no distractions save the singular one of survival. For which an alert ear and eye played their vital parts. I sought to reign in my darker imaginings and seek to settle my mind for the prospect of some light sleep.

'Licky, I can see you. There you are. I don't know, but you seem to be awfully absent these days. Where have you been *all* day? Up to no good, I'll be bound.' With that, Margaret threw back her head, her long peroxide hair flapping in the breeze and let out a raucous laugh. 'Running around with every Tom, Dick and Harry in Malta, I bet. Who are those other three cats? Two of them look very much like you. I will bring my camera down and put your picture in my album, with some notes about you all.' She smiled as she looked down at me. I feared my suspicions about her and Terry were coming true. Photos, albums *and* notes sounded sinister to me. Better to keep William and Mary away from here for a while I sensed. Or else it might be the newspapers next!

'Anyway here you are. A lovely dinner of part tuna, two fish heads, left over from our lunch and a dollop of tinned Princess cat food.'

I looked up at Margaret, pleased as always to see her and being careful to show no hint of doubt. She and her husband were my only links to my floating home and the missing Daisy and Eric. On her top half, she was wearing a figure hugging tee shirt, with the word *BEST OF* written right across it. I raised myself and went over and stroked myself against her bare legs as my normal gesture of thanks which says everything and almost nothing too. I detected a faint whiff of their dreadful dog on her. I would delay eating until she was well away, taking that smell away with her.

'And what do you think Miss Licky? The eyebrows eh – come on take a peek. I had them tattooed in Sliema this morning. Smashing I thought, all said and done.'

I really had no idea what she was talking about but she was peering closely at me now and I could not evade that manic gaze. I had never ever noticed she had *lost* her eyebrows.

Now we cats never lose our eyebrows. We do not really have any to worry about which makes some sense. Worse though our whiskers. To lose even one whisker is irksome. How could we crawl through narrow gaps in times of trouble if we lost them all? Navigate around in choppy seas while sensing when we are too close to table legs? Pencilling in replacement whiskers would make no sense. Whiskas give us an extra sense of touch. Pencils and tattoos do not.

I looked more closely at her eyebrows as they began to rise above me. They did give some perspective to her face and showed me where her eyes were. Like a picture frame. Very nice I wanted to say though these thoughts were tinged with questions about usefulness. Oops, there she went again. Still bending down and looking at me, she brought her eyebrows almost together, in a frown.

'See Miss Licky, that's me looking serious and giving you one of my puzzled looks, as I might well do what with you so often on the missing list, with those other cats. Ooh I am so pleased with them.' Was she talking about William, Mary and Mouser - obviously not as she stroked her tattooed eyebrows. She stood up erect and looked down towards the marina. 'Mind you Tel thinks it's a load of cobblers and a complete waste of money. But I ask you, what would he know anyway about women and their eyebrows? Now he did use to admire the footballer George Best's good looks, with his bushy black eyebrows. But he never mentioned my eyebrows in the days when I had any. They are just a part of our facial beauty. If Tel had any sense he would have his bloody one's clipped and trimmed. They are far too bushy and going grey. Not attractive.' Margaret was still peering down at me, with me looking up directly into her eyes. 'Tel reckons that in hot weather out here in Malta, his extra bushy eyebrows are a god send. They are eye protectors, stopping salty perspiration flowing down from his forehead into his eyes and causing irritation. Hmm well I suppose that makes a little bit of sense. Still they need cutting. They do him no favours with his looks, but then let's face it; he's past the age to worry about such matters!' With that she gave out a whelp of laughter.

I had no understanding or knowledge of eyebrows or indeed English footballers, and let alone this George Best. I imagined however there to be some connection between this footballer and the word *BEST OF* emblazoned on the front of her tee shirt.

I was grateful Margaret spent these magic moments with me, sharing her thoughts about eyebrows. A distraction I felt but I wondered how Terry coped on the boat? Maybe she only shares these thoughts with me. She has learned over time to stick to talk of football matches and rope knots. Perhaps I was her confident. I understood everything she was saying, and more besides and I sensed she knew. Maybe knowing or at least guessing was enough. Any confidences she shared with me could go no further. Not in her world at least. However, of some interest to me if I needed to know more about what these two were up to. I ran my tail around he legs and she smiled.

'Oh and I nearly forgot Licky, I have a bit of good news for you. A bit of good news for all of us I suppose. Guess what?' Margaret turned her head slightly to the left, adding further compliment to her *up in the air* question. 'I spoke to Daisy and Eric just a half an hour ago. They phoned us and they will be back in just ten days. You will be at home and we will be in pocket! With the reward they offered on the posters for anyone finding you. That's ours for sure. I wonder how much?' Margaret was not looking at me at all as she said this. Just merrily talking out loud and peering up to the sky. 'Mind you, it is a little bit of a tetchy subject this. What with us knowing them and being neighbours and all. However we are hardly close neighbours. They keep themselves to themselves.' Margaret looked in my direction. 'I find them a bit snooty at times if you ask me. Still it makes it easier to take the reward from them.'

She suddenly raised her new eyebrows. 'Oops did I say *take* the reward. I meant of course to say, *accept* the reward. Well if I get a new hat out of it that will be something, if nothing else.' She used both hands to lightly flip her long hair back. As if she was wearing that new hat already and giving herself a last once over check in the mirror.

'Now Miss Licky, I cannot spend all evening chatting to you. I had best get back to the boat and see what old grumpy is up to. If Tel has anything more detrimental to say about my new eyebrows, he'll be sent to Coventry for the night. That always sets him straight. He likes his late night snack and when in Coventry he goes without!' Another high pitched laughter and then she gave me one last look. 'Breakfast about eight tomorrow morning Licky and make sure you are around.' She was not quite finished. 'Oh and let me just tick off the date on your calendar.' She produced a marker pen clipped to the top of her blouse, bent down and drew a line through today's date. 'There we are, just so you know what day of the year and month it is and counting the days for Eric and Daisy returning.'

With that, Margaret turned around and started walking back towards the yacht. I was left with the waddling view of an ample backside clutching tight fitting white shorts. There was a small colourful flag of the Union Jack emblazoned on the left buttock, with the word *British* underneath it and on the right buttock the word *Beef*. I wondered for a moment what that was all about, and then remembered the front of her tee shirt and the large word written in black *Best OF*. Not the footballer George Best after all.

I enjoyed my evening meal whilst thinking about tomorrow. I drifted in and out of sleep as ever, all the time willing the night to fall quickly and pass. To wake as dawn arrived. My dreamy thoughts that night were peppered with thoughts of *ten days* and the 10th of July. Oh what joy that day would bring. I would be rescued and then be home and dry. Nagging doubts would cloud my dreams, as I wrestled with the challenge ahead, that of keeping us all together. The real problem was Mouser. He was right about his age. Would anyone want a scratchy old cat on board their boat? Menacing the decking and furniture? I kept reminding myself that tomorrow was another day, and I gently hummed myself back into sleep as an old song, *Que Sera Sera*, stirred me. Any nightmares would surely be turned into dreams as I slumbered:

When I was just a little girl
I asked my mother, what shall I be,
Will I be pretty, will I be rich
Here's what she said to me

Que Sera, Sera
Whatever will be, will be
The future not ours, to see
Que Sera, era
What will be, will be

CHAPTER 22

I awoke as ever, well before the sun had the opportunity to wake me. The night had been uneventful, though I remembered drunken crew revellers returning to their yachts. Chanting sea shanties about boats cast in stormy seas. These would be young people I imagined who had the chance to do what they wished as the yacht owners themselves were often absent. They would follow their own orders for the next day. Hose the decks. Prepare the cabins. The owners will be here midday and food must be bought. No need for worry now.

I had learnt about absentee owners of super yachts, moored at the end of the Vittoriosa Marina, closest to Fort St Angelo. Some with small submarines that could sail below the seas and others with helicopters whose blades were hidden in bays. To be assembled only when the owners instructed. These toys were not for the entertainment of the crew. The owner might just ignore a little leakage from the wine cellar. As long as the yacht was in great order, linen clean and starched and fine food was on the table, minor sins would be forgiven.

So latitude towards the staff and their activities was allowed within strict limits. While the cat was away, the mice were allowed a little play. As long as one or two responsible people stayed on board, they could take it in turns to go ashore and make whoopee. They were young and knew about fun. Shore leave would always be short. Time would be short. Make hay they would say. Tomorrow we are marooned here, maybe for months at a time and much more fun than being at sea.

This shore time leave posed no threat to the bar owners of Birgu. It had encouraged new and expensive restaurants catering for this new influx. That in turn attracted tourists to these newly revamped areas but also discerning Maltese patrons, tired of older haunts and now attracted to this whole new vision of these luxurious yachts and their mainly industrious crew.

I awoke to see this company of revellers peering down at me. Wanting to stroke me and wondering why I was there while I wondered if they would ever go away. Strong hints of crème de menthe attracted my nose towards the younger woman who was being held up by her friends. She spoke to me in a language I dared not understand. Her companions made nothing of these ramblings, appearing more intent on staying upright themselves I thought. The anchor man had wisely grabbed onto the lamp post above me. The rest swayed around him, grasping his stomach for support. They wore the same white tee shirts, with the name of the yacht sewn into the left breast pocket – *Jackpot Lucky*.

I jumped up, and before I knew it, I was being stroked by several of these revellers. I really could have done without such unwanted attention at this hour of the morning. However I knew they meant no harm, so I acquiesced. 'Oh look. She's got a name tag on. It says Miss Licky. What a name I ask you.' That came from the female mint flavoured member of the group.

As quickly as they had appeared they were off, swaying away, rolling together, arm in arm, drifting down the quayside. Singing a new song as their tangled arms and hands knotted them together, away from the unguarded waters lapping inches down from unsteady feet. Everything was safe and I heard no splashing sounds suggesting otherwise. Just that discordant singing noise.

Show me the way to go home,
I'm tired and I want to go to bed
I had a little drink about an hour ago
And it went right to my head
Wherever I may roam
On land or sea or foam
You will always hear me singing this song
Show me the way to go home

Silence slowly returned but this disturbance kept me awake. The words of this song worried me and reminded me my own home might not find its own way home to where I lay.

Frustrated by this intrusion, I wandered over to the hotel building site and cleaned myself from a bucket of water that stood next to a new pile of sand. Nothing stirred now along the Vittoriosa water front. Just the sound of creaking timbers from the high masts of sailing yachts, as they rocked gently back and forth.

I left the building site feeling better now, invigorated by the coldness of fresh water against my fur and enlivened and readier now for the day ahead. I would use the time to ponder my situation and work harder on our plans so we would make no mistake. I returned to my lamp post and imagined things that might happen to us all and things to do to evade capture. Escape routes needed to be plotted for every place we visited. Mouser would join me later of course and then I could share my ideas. These thoughts kept me awake until the clock struck seven times and the sun was now rising over the marina.

Once I had finalised these ideas, my thoughts turned to times gone by on the yacht. I had a further two hours to kill during this lonely vigil. I remembered the Eastern Mediterranean Yacht rally we joined twenty years after the first flotilla was assembled. Then, the idea had been to fill empty Turkish Marinas and promote these destinations to wealthy yacht owners. The strategy had paid off and Eric and Daisy would now contribute their own efforts to those of past mariners. They had planned the trip for months.

Eric and Daisy had reservations about taking on board that English married couple they had befriended at the Marina. They had their own small yacht which rarely sailed further than Gozo. Eric said that Betty and Bert had little spirit of adventure and besides they had no navigation skills to speak of. Indeed he thought their lack of skill made them dangerous on the high seas. They could not read a map and if their engine failed they had no understanding of how a screwdriver worked. He had seen Bert twist a screw the wrong way once with such frustrating force that the offending head had been shorn away from its body. He had to bring the drill over and bore the shank out taking great care not to shear the screw thread! 'What an idiot Daisy! We should steer clear of these two.' Daisy ignored this advice as she felt Eric could manage any problem that might befall them. Flattered by her confidence, he relented. They were invited into this adventure.

Daisy reckoned the extra crew would lighten the work load of the trip. Help with the ropes, hold the wheel tight when complex turns were made and assist in sails being shifted to catch the wind. After all, this was a sailing race and she and Eric needed to focus on the sails. Their companions could do the basic stuff. Like keeping the yacht away from jagged reefs poorly mapped on aging charts. This thinking would prove a disappointment.

The rally started *proper* at Istanbul. Betty and Bert arrived on board with two slender cases of clothes and toiletries. Betty was clad in a skimpy brown v necked over shirt, with buttons missing, and hanging tautly over her upper torso. Eric whispered to Daisy. 'That leaves nothing to the imagination,' and he smiled. Daisy was not amused. Not sailing gear she thought. Provocation she saw ahead of her and maybe even a temptress on the yacht. Bert thought nothing of it, she noticed. Betty said nothing as Daisy sought the comfort of her sewing basket. 'These tight fitting dresses barely hold the buttons together' she said. 'Not to worry, I have some buttons and thread to hand and if you pass that over I can repair it in a jiffy.' Betty sensed compliance was in order and in a second the garment was off as Daisy was threading the needle. 'Yes dear, these brown buttons match and should do nicely'. The job was done and Daisy smiled at her handiwork and passed the garment back. Betty returned later to confess she had quite forgotten to pack any underwear. Daisy's suspicions deepened but she maintained her smile. After all it was she who had pressed the issue of extra hands on a reluctant Eric. She popped into her room and grabbed several pairs of nautical knickers, robust elastic and reinforced cotton webbing, right down to the knees. To keep the wind out Daisy explained although other things too she may have been thinking. She smiled as she passed the garments

209

over but Betty looked at these Victorian relics with apprehension. Hard to tell front from back she mused.

It took us twenty days to cover the nine hundred and fifty nautical miles to Istanbul as the weather worsened. We had left Malta in the afternoon and sailed the one hundred odd nautical miles to Syracusa in Sicily. Eric battled with the sails as the wind threatened to part them from their masts. We arrived late in the afternoon under an ugly sky weeping rain that burnt the skin at every touch. The entry into the harbour was hazardous. The engines had been engaged to control the path of the yacht. Even then it took a further eight hours of tacking before safe haven was reached. The English couple were exhausted, trying to identify where we were on the maps whilst holding a wheel which at times seemed to have a life of it' own. All they felt they could see was nothing ahead but swells which concealed treacherous rocks beneath. They finally decided a watery grave was more the likely outcome and so retired to their berths, with two glasses, a gin bottle and some tonic. Whilst muttering something about needing something to calm their jagged nerves. No one else slept at all. I certainly could not. All my efforts were taken up holding onto a floor rug with my paws. Fortunately that had been screwed to the floor and would act as my own anchor.

We stayed in Syracusa until the following day hoping the weather would improve. I enjoyed sitting in the harbour on deck, watching a number of cats slink past. Eyeing me, I fancied with envy but not daring to approach. We avoided eye contact. We did not try to speak as I heard their chatter in a language I could not understand. Later I learned they were Italian cats but I of course speak only English.

There was a moment when a large dark grey male cat strolled past and spotted me. Strangely he had a definitive quiff, just like Mouser, above his left eye. He stopped for a moment, stared at me in a challenging way before flipping his quiff with his paw and walking away. This I can now appreciate was probably a capo cat. Like Top Cat or Mouser. However, he came from a cat mafia family here, Sicilian born and bred and with his own territory along Syracusa, in the marina where the fishing vessels came in each day to unload their catch. He would control *soldier* cats who would steal fish as it was being landed, loaded, transported and delivered. Those cats would have his protection from other predators who likely had their own masters to obey.

We left Syracusa early the next morning, setting off for the Greek island of Zakinthos, near the main land of Greece. The weather had improved and less choppy seas bade us farewell from the harbour. We passed the tip of Italy and into the Aegean sea. This journey lasted three hundred nautical miles and two full days to complete. Our progress was slowed as the seas attracted bolts of lightning and thunder strikes of deafening intensity. I stayed well below deck gripping the carpet with all my strength. Betty and Bert became terrified once more and were no doubt grateful they had sacrificed clothing for strong bottles of drink in their cases.

Much to Eric and Daisy annoyance, they made their excuses yet again. Sea sickness they muttered but I sensed the strong gin was the greater player in their misfortune. Daisy retrieved an empty gin bottle from the dustbin and clawed her way onto deck. Clutching the bottle in one hand and holding the rail, she shouted to Eric. 'Look what I have found!' she exclaimed. Eric wiped the brine from his reddened eyes and spotted the bottle. 'I thought they were pissed yesterday he shouted'. Daisy nodded and returned to the wheelhouse.

Eric joined her and decided the electrical strikes were by now so severe that the navigational instruments should be turned off, until the storms subsided. The yacht was sailing blind but Eric knew the waters were deep. Bob around he thought and sail with the wind. The safest thing was to ride out the storm. Leave that daft pair asleep downstairs. Away from the wheel!

Many hours later, the storm subsided and the navigation equipment was re-activated. Then the slow progress to the harbour began. We eventually entered, in blinding rain, and I managed to poke my nose up on the deck area. As a way of support, I joined Eric and Daisy on deck. Needless to say the other pair chose to remain

211

below and keep dry. However as the seas calmed Betty called up from the kitchen. 'OK if we open this bottle of Bacardi in the fridge?' she enquired.

We stayed in harbour that day and night, due to the bad weather before departing the following morning on the short trip to Patras on the main land of Greece. This journey was much less eventful. However we were now on the mainland where the two friends could easily jump ship – and they did just that! They left in a moment once the gang plank had been lowered. Bags packed. Betty thanked Daisy for the loan of the underwear but left it behind. 'You need it more than me' she said as she noticed the state of Betty's drenched life jacket. 'Good Luck.'

They had spotted a taxi by the quayside and fled in it back to Athens Airport. The next day they arrived back in Malta, hardly the worse for wear. Eric asked Daisy for a nice Bacardi and Coke but was disappointed. 'They've nicked the bottle' she told him, so he settled for a glass of Grappa instead.

Arguments began as Eric and Daisy debated what sins had provoked the visitation of those two friends on their yacht. Eric had always treated this place as their own sanctuary and of course wondered how his inertia had allowed the walls to be breached. Never again he kept exclaiming, as Daisy tried to apologise for her own spontaneous invite. 'We're better off with each other!' he exclaimed and the icy dialogue was broken, with a smile. The couple embraced and shortly after, the hugs and kisses followed and not just between them. Between them and me! I responded. At least I had kept awake and had popped upstairs from time to time. 'Licky kept us safe and sound,' Eric said. Daisy hugged me and burst into tears. 'She is our good omen,' she said as she reached for the tissue box and blew her nose. Peace was restored and the arguments stopped. I slept on Daisy's lap and Eric stroked my ears. All was well again.

The following day, we sailed off to Corinth about sixty eight nautical miles away. This trip was uneventful and Daisy whispered in my ear. 'There, there. Those horrid people are gone. You are with us and the sun is shining.

Eric was right. Just the three of us….' She gave me a stroke and I licked her hand as a show of affection. Hoping we three would never be parted. Hoping I would forever be the only stray on this boat.

We all went to sleep and everything seemed calm. However in the early hours I was, so I thought at the time, pushed from the bench and awoke with a start. What had pushed me off I wondered. For a moment I worried that the English couple had returned but no one was there. I jumped back on to the bench and peered up through the porthole. The room was tilted. The cabin window was closer to the mooring than I remembered. Everything was oddly angular. Pictures had moved and my sense of balance was wrong. Water was lapping around the porthole window.

Had the tide gone out? Had the yacht fallen over? Surely Eric would have known about these things and made sure the berth was secure. I began to worry the events of these past days had affected his judgement.

I skipped down to the salon floor and went immediately to the master bedroom which was firmly closed. Eric had no time for cats in bedrooms. When I first arrived on the yacht, Daisy would pander to my fears of loneliness and let me in so I might sleep on the eiderdown. I would be easily awakened in those days and sound an alarm. I raised many false alarms in those days. 'Daisy, enough is enough. The cat sleeps outside. Waking me up each time a dog barks. We close that blasted door at night and every night!'

I understood Eric's viewpoint. I tried to be quiet but it never lasted long. After an hour or so I would get restless and start shifting about on the bed, which would wake Eric from his snoring slumbers. In truth it was his terrible noise that would often awaken me. Make me move about. Humans cannot hear themselves snoring. If they wake up, something has caused it. That cause was always to be me. So I would be picked up and placed outside, with the door firmly closed behind me. How Daisy slept through it I could not understand. Even the closed door could not muffle the venom of Eric's piercing snores.

213

Today was very different. Danger lurked and something had to be done quickly. I ran to the bedroom door and began to scratch furiously at the wooden panel. I also broadcast an alarm with my mouth. Assertive meows echoed against the door I was agitating with my paws. Banging noises added to the commotion as the door brushed its frame. I knew any normal sounds from me would be totally ignored. The sounds had to be different. No waking and sleeping responses. No - 'Oh my god it's Miss Licky. Just ignore her.'

After several minutes of madness – scratching, scraping, moaning and banging, I had a response. That came with a grunt from Eric and then an enormous thud.

'Good grief Eric! Are you alright? Whatever has happened?' Daisy was awake and her voice carried alarm.

'What do you mean? Am I alright? Of course I am not alright. I have fallen out of bloody bed. What on earth is going on?'

Then I heard a large scream coming from Daisy followed by another thud. 'Oh Eric, what is happening?' She too had rolled clean out of bed and found herself on top of Eric. 'I think we are capsized. Call the coast guard.' she suggested.

'Don't be so silly woman. Get yourself off me. Let me out. I know exactly what has happened. Pull yourself together.' Seconds later, the bedroom door flung open, and Eric, appeared. A Dickensian figure in pyjamas with a night cap on his head. He jumped over me and raced down the hallway.

Fortunately none of us were injured during these frolics though Eric's language was tinged with blue. He checked the moorings and the outside of the yacht. 'Nothing more to be done now,' he sighed.

He returned downstairs to greet Daisy who was standing at an odd angle, afraid to even fill a kettle for a restorative cup of tea. 'Nothing to do but be patient and wait for the tide to come back in.' He said. Daisy managed to stand at an angle and fill the kettle. Placing clothes around it she then switched it on and eventually it boiled. Then she cautiously placed the mugs on the sink;

dropped two tea bags in and made the tea. That was sipped as the in- coming tide slowly righted the boat. By half past six everything was righted and we were standing up with no fear of a tilt. 'Let's get out of here,' suggested Eric, who felt we had been lucky this time but he would take no further chances in an odd bay not suited to deeper craft where silt and sand displaced water. We were gone by eight o'clock.

Soon we were sailing through the Corinth Canal where our speed slowed to a walking pace for safety reasons. The gorge was narrow and occasional rocks and stones would fall towards us - dislodged by the cruise liner ahead which was creating a slight swell. Enough to undermine the fragile walls, inches away from its sides and creating fresh dangers for all sailing in its wake.

Finally we emerged and arrived in Piraeus harbour for the night. The next day on to Laviron, known as the Olympic Marina, built in 2004 for the Greek Olympics. I could see bars and restaurants along the quay side. Flickering lights becoming brighter as the sun lowered towards the horizon. Expensive looking motor cars were being parked here as we reversed into our allotted berth for the night. Eric and Daisy went ashore for the evening and left me here to keep the night watch and do what I could to keep things safe. The weather had improved for the moment at least and I could sit aloft without getting wet. I watched the world pass by.

Bad weather returned during the early hours of the morning and that held us in Piraeus for two days before we could chance sailing to Limnos, a full day's distance. I liked this pretty island with its port full of tourists. So many cats I saw. I was alarmed to spot a wild cat walking up and down the quayside with a paint lid stuck to his left side. Blue paint had oozed from it where he had lain. Congealing and matting his coat and gluing the lid to the fur. Eric noticed this and blamed the careless yacht owner who must have left the lid off the paint in the first place. He recognised the name on the tin lid and it was most certainly a boat paint he stressed.

The cat remained attached to the lid when we departed the next day for the Dardnelles. The poor pussy seemed unworried by this addition to its fur, as it lay near a post connecting electricity to static boats. We arrived in Istanbul uneventfully and found our place for the night. Many yachts were larger than ours sporting unusual names, new registration places like Delaware, USA and different flags, fluttering and dancing in the strong wind.

We continued our journey to Israel and seven more yachts joined us on the way, creating a flotilla. We berthed next to each other and noticed another cat lying on the deck of the yacht next to us which flew the Red Ensign. I thought we might become friends and share stories of our adventures. However this cat had a serious problem. It would leap from yacht to yacht, spraying on each to mark out its extending territory! I discovered this weakness when Eric and Daisy blamed me for soiling the moveable cushions they had placed on the bench on the main deck. I was perplexed. I had never done such a thing and surely I would have known if I had. I kept a close watch on this other cat and soon spotted its nightly meanderings. Soon everybody was complaining of a rancid smell on their cushions too. It took no time before the culprit was spotted and the owners were urged to keep the cat down below. Eric and Daisy did apologise to me for their precipitous accusation and took the precaution of bringing the cushions downstairs each night.

I did not see much of the cat after this and I wondered whether it had ever visited the vet to make it more sociable. It certainly avoided contact with me for which I was grateful. If it was a domesticated cat then it had a defect I had no interest in trying to correct.

I was happy to note how carefully Eric chose future berths to keep as far away from the unsociable cat as possible. Eric would hold back and deliberately sail well clear of that Red Ensign and indeed clear of any other yacht the cat could use as its launch pad. We visited many new places of interest, though the Marina in the Gaza strip was suddenly closed to us. We berthed elsewhere and then sailed back to Malta without stopping. What an adventure for a cat and it was a shame I dared not share my experiences with the other cat. I would however be content to tell my brother, sister and Mouser too, in due course. That would be some time when we were safely together away from the forever *searching* Mr Stick.

Time had raced by now and the Marina was slowly starting to come alive. It was not quite eight when a hawker's fruit and vegetable lorry drove past to stock up one of the large yacht's pantries. Then a fish mongers van raced by determined to gain the right of way down this single lane roadway.

I was feeling hungry and was relieved when I saw Margaret prancing along the jetty towards me. A dance or an exercise routine, I could not be sure. Few people were around to worry about her deportment or question what she was carrying in that foil bowl, or more likely query her odd sense of dress. She was wearing a tee shirt emblazoned with words I could not decipher. Hiding the top of her translucent mini skirt where rainbow coloured patterns hiding vital parts of her anatomy. Certainly it was never designed for the *larger* lady. Not a stock item in the ladies section of T & A as she preferred to call Tall and Ample, an abbreviation which hid as much as T & A's product range would allow. Vertical stripes with subdued colours too, which would never accentuate a client's obvious problem.

Margaret's girth risked a structural disaster to the skirt as the stitching stretched. Carefully elasticated I hoped to hold things together. Long enough for her to deliver my food and not rush back for needle and cotton. Those large yellow and pink platform shoes did not make things any easier for her. They were making her calves twist and testing this garment to its limits. Not at all comfortable I thought.

Margaret stopped to twist her mini skirt into a more comfortable position. She grimaced as she pulled on the waist band and turned to raise it ever higher. She moved towards me with a newly formed smile. Her gyrations had calmed the agitation in her skirt for the moment at least.

'I see you are actually here for a change Miss Licky. Not gone off on one of your early wanderings with other friends. Now here's your breakfast, and jolly nice too I might add. It's tuna you lucky puss. I got it up the weekly Birgu Market last Tuesday. The stall was selling loads of tins of this and that at *well* under half price. They were all a bit past their sell by date as stamped on the tins. Only by a year or two but then anything tinned keeps for *ages*. Whoops, I think I've got a problem here.'

I was peering up at Margaret, whilst still visually trying to adjust my eyes to this dazzling wet suited miniskirt. Silver glitter had been woven into the fabric I noticed because the sun was making it sparkle all along the seams. She was now attempting to bend down to place the bowl of out of date tuna at the base of the lamp post.

'Oh fiddle sticks, I don't think this is going to work. I can't bend down in this outfit. If I do, I fear the worst. I would have passed it on to my daughter but her hips haven't been too kind to her either. I don't think I can bend down without something giving. It is so figure hugging. Heavens knows who they make these outfits for.'

I smiled to myself wondering if anybody else would be seen in this skirt. I too was becoming worried. Margaret was starting to attract unwelcome attention. People were looking at her and me. Mouser would be here shortly and the last thing we wanted was publicity.

'Now let me take this slowly. I'm not going to lean forward. That would be wrong. I'm going to lean only *slightly* forward on my feet and then slowly slip down into a squat position. And here we go.' So with some grunting and groaning she descended on the soles of her feet and put the bowl of tuna on the ground, and then she froze.

'Oh my giddy aunt, I think I am stuck.' She placed the fingers tips of both hands just touching the ground, and then pushed down for lift off. She started to raise herself, suddenly accompanied by the sound of seams splitting. 'Oh sugar, looks what's happened. And brand new on today too.' The fish hawker was returning now and slowed his van to take a closer look. Ma was eyeing a thin split directly to the left had side of the mini skirt, running downward a good six inches. So was the hawker. Half of the length of the skirt was in turmoil. 'That Miss Licky is shoddy workmanship I'll be bound. All knocked up for a shilling in places like China and with no real attention to detail. And if Tel knew what I really paid for this, he'd blow a fuse!'

'Need a hand love?' asked the hawker who by now had stopped his van. He rushed to leave his cabin and help. Any way he could. Ma sensed he might not be the Good Samaritan he pretended to be. His hands were large and rough. His nails a little dirty she thought. Been in places where common decencies were out of view. Would she let him help her to her feet? 'The devil's in the driving seat' she muttered. She agreed to take his hand and allow herself to be pulled up. The hawker involuntarily grabbed her waist to steady her but Ma reacted in a moment. She slapped his face and made it clear she had met men like him before. She did not say where! He backed away and ran to his van and raced out of the marina, as quickly as he had raced in.

Ma was peering at the split with a look of worry on her forehead. Lines were deepening as her newly tattooed eyebrows frowned in the direction of the fault line. 'Hmm well it's not that bad actually. I can get that seamstress up in the village to do some invisible mending.'

I wondered whether an extra yard of material might suffice to hold things together for the future. However I suspected this garment had become surplus to requirements. Attracting the interests of other men as it had. Maybe Ma was actually courting the attention, unknowingly perhaps, but doing it just the same. 'Kind to do what he did and I shouldn't have hit him.' She smiled to herself.

'Anyway Tel will be happy to know the skirt has had it. He was not happy to see me leave our cabin this morning. He told me not to be so ridiculous. Of course I just ignored his silly remark. Men get jealous.' She smiled again. 'Tel has no taste. He cannot see *glamour* when it is under his nose. Fortunately not all men are like Tel. I won't go into any of that. After all you are only a pussy cat.' She let out her loud laugh; swung her head up with pride; stroked her hair backwards and then declared she was off. 'Back with dinner about six this evening. I hope you eat it all and with no ill effects. If so then I may feed Tel a tin of it for his supper!'

With that final utterance she was off and negotiating the jetty on her yellow and pink platforms as if on a catwalk. I smelt the foil bowl with suspicion. I would wait until Mouser arrived and be guided by his sense of taste before indulging myself.

I was fairly certain Margaret would not poison her husband with this dish. There was ample water in the bowl next to the breakfast. Besides, enough food was left over from the day before to keep me going. I took a few sips of water to dispel the taste of olive oil lingering in yesterday's offering. Then I sat down and waited for the museum to open when Mouser should appear. I began to feel excited at the very thought of soon seeing my brother and sister again in the next hour or so. I began to wonder what Mouser might have planned for us today. He had organised our trip to Valletta the following day which continued to worry me. I would not tolerate any monkey business from Mouser, such as leading us all astray in restaurants before they were even open. Uninvited, and having a free for all at the restaurant's unknowing expense. William and Mary would not learn bad habits, thereby leaving me the task of unlearning them!

I suddenly spied Mouser making his appearance under the arches of the museum. He raced across the service road and was beside me in an instant. As always, he was happy to see me, and vice versa. This night had been very long indeed. He gave me a small pat on the head with his right paw. 'How are you this morning Licky? Did you have a good night's sleep?'

I explained the interruptions and the singing and how I was left pondering our futures. I pointed my paw towards the foil bowl and invited him to eat. Mouser sniffed it and then devoured most of it. 'Scrumptious' he said. I ate the rest with great confidence and knew Tel would survive the feast Ma was preparing for him. I was keen for us to leave for the Square and collect my brother and sister from their nocturnal slumbering. We left.

CHAPTER 23

We strolled in single file up to Birgu Square, taking care not to be noticed, halting from time to time behind a tree or a pot. Keeping close guard lest we were being followed. Mouser felt I was being too careful but he understood my worrying and played along. During these moments I spoke of my earlier day dreams, of my travels on the yacht. He seemed distracted, as though other thoughts were occupying his mind.

'Mouser, you seem on edge today.' He kept looking ahead and walking now that much faster.

'I don't know Licky. I just suddenly feel that something is not right. I cannot put my paw on it, but I feel a chill in my bones. Don't ask me why, but something is troubling me and I just wish I knew what it was.'

We had now arrived at Birgu and Mouser continued walking at a brisk pace. There were a few locals taking a coffee at the Café Brazil. We passed by and on to the first alleyway on the right.

'Not this one, we will take the next and then down to the end and up to the back of Birgu where your brother and sister are staying.' There was a sobering edge to Mouser's voice – nothing I could define, but it was there.

We had just passed this alley, when everything happened. Top Cat raced around the corner towards us, almost crashing into the pair of us.

'Mouser, thank God you are here! Quick we haven't a moment to loose. He's got them!'

'Got who Top Cat?' Mouser knew. The look of horror and fear was apparent. It was mirrored on Top Cat's face.

'Miss Licky's brother and sister have been *netted*! Mr Stick trapped them a few minutes ago. I need your help now if we have any chance of rescuing them.' Top Cat did not pause for breath. 'Look he's up this alley. You Mouser go down to the first alley and come into the second alley and come up from behind and surprise him.

I'll approach him head on and keep him distracted. Licky, be prepared to rush him if all else fails!'

'And what then shall I do?' Mouser was poised to go but was still trying to collect his thoughts. I remained rigid, almost frozen to the spot I stood on. What could I do, *if* all else failed?

'Just do what I say and distract him! Bite or scratch his legs. Anything! I need a moment to get that net off them. You Miss Licky follow me but just stay by the entrance to the alley. Go Mouser, now!'

With that Mouser was off like a shot down the alley we were in and then flying out of view into the first alley. Top Cat instantly ran forward up to the entrance of the second alley, with me in pursuit.

The first sight of Mr Stick and his prey sickened me. I could not believe what I was witnessing. The adrenalin rushed.

'Now you horrible, time wasting cats, you are now all mine. I've got you at long last, and you shall not be going anywhere from now.' Mr Stick was peering down at my brother and sister, who were wriggling and screaming under that horrible butterfly net, attached to a long pole. He was holding it as if his own life pulsed within it. He grasped it with such fury, the blood draining from his hands, turning them white. His expectations were within the mesh. His hold was certain. But he smelt of fear. Fear of a mistake. He hissed at the contents like a snake. 'Your fun and games are up now,' he snarled. 'And my fortunes will rise as yours surely die. I always hated cats. You two I scorn.' He hissed at them again to turn discomfort into foreboding, whilst make them shake and squirm as he had, enduring the torments of the Marchioness and her blessed cats. 'Cursed cats' he muttered as the blood rose from his hands to his cheeks in an awful mixture of grey and red.' 'I'm not done with you yet,' he screamed. 'There is more to be done! Oh yes, much more to be done, with the pair of you.'

I ran forwards to the middle of the alley. To do what I did not know, but I had to do something. I had to be near this scene to play my part. Wait for the script to come. Top Cat would be my prompter.

223

'Miss Licky, don't move. Stay here and leave it to me and Mouser. I don't want to find we must rescue you as well.' Top Cat's fur coat was standing on end, as was mine. I was shivering with fear. 'Look, Mouser is coming.'

Neighbours came out to find the source of this annoyance. An old lady shook her fist. 'Leave those cats alone! Are you a vet? Are they ill? I will tend them. They can stay here with me.' She looked across the street and Mr Stick looked perplexed. Other neighbours were being drawn in, from doorways with bowls of food for cats like these. The old people called themselves their guardians. They were weary of strangers who came and went as they pleased.

Mr Stick lost his composure as the residents approached, his grip loosing on the net. He held a folded parchment in his other hand, something to be protected at all costs. An old man brandished a heavy stick and his wife cheered him on. Others joined in. Mr Stick was momentarily caught off guard. He dropped the net. That gave Top Cat the chance he was waiting for. He raced over and pulled the net away, and all of a sudden Mouser was there too. He pelted down the alley and leapt on Mr Stick. I saw Mouser take off and fly. A short flight maybe but he was air born. A massive leap and he flew over Mr Stick's raised right arm, and snatched the rolled up document between his teeth and out of the evil man's hand. People cheered. Why, they did not know but cheer they did. 'Run!' they cried 'run.'

At the very same time, Top Cat leapt up and clawed himself onto Mr Stick's lapel. Firmly anchored, he swiped Mr Stick clean across his cheek. Blood trickled down his face. A hand was raised and that too received a scratch from Top Cat before he released himself from Mr Stick' jacket lapel.

William and Mary were free of the net.

Top Cat instantly signalled me to lead my brother and sister to safety. Head towards Fort St Angelo he barked. Mouser and he would meet us there in due course. I did as instructed and we three fled down the alley, allowing the uproar to subside and for the old lady to find a

224

bandage for Mr Stick's damaged hand and scratched face. He was in shock and had given up the fight, for today at least.

Mr Stick realised valuable documents had been stolen. 'You come back here with those papers right now. Thieves, thieves, I'll call the police.' Mr Stick was holding his left cheek where Top Cat had made his mark. 'I'll have your guts for garters, you mark my words.' The old lady felt he needed an ambulance. His brain was addled she said. Cats do not steal papers, she exclaimed and her neighbours laughed. True he had been brandishing something and threatening cats with it. Maybe it was a parchment, or nothing more than a rolled up copy of the Times of Malta. Mr Stick tried to give chase but the residents would have none of it. 'You need a nice cup of strong tea' said the old lady. All agreed and he was helped against his will into her home. She put the kettle on while her husband seated him in the lounge. 'Have a drop of my home grown Grappa,' he suggested. 'Just to settle your nerves before the ambulance arrives.'

The neighbours had dispersed and Mr Stick composed himself. Suddenly he leapt up and raced from the house. He needed no ambulance. What he needed was those papers. He spotted Mouser at the end of the alley beyond his damaged net which lay lifeless in the street.

Meanwhile I had hidden William and Mary around the corner when I saw Top Cat return, in the company of dozens of other cats recruited to stave off Mr Stick and safeguard our retreat. 'Licky get them away quickly and we will hold Mr Stick back.'

William and Mary needed to be prompted. They were excited by all that had happened and wanted to see what would happen next. I tried to move them on, but to little avail.

I peeped around this corner and saw Mr Stick running back down the alley in our direction. He grabbed the net and saw my face. 'Get back here now you two.' 'Now come on my lovelies, don't be afraid. You know I mean you no harm, only a good and a happy home for you both.' The change in his voice and the words he was uttering had been tempered as some neighbours were still keeping him under surveillance. Wondering what on earth he was really up to. We retreated a full ten or more yards away from the dreaded net and Mr Stick.

Top Cat ran towards us. "Right Miss Licky, move yourself and your brother and sister out of here now! Get them well away from Birgu Square. Down to the Vittoriosa Marina is the best bet or up to Fort St Angelo. I'll catch up with Mouser and let him know you are safe. In the meantime I'll keep this mad man at bay. Now go!' Top Cat turned towards Mr Stick who was inching forward, net in one hand and his other hand holding his scratched cheek. Top Cat let out the most menacing hiss in his direction, which appeared to set off all the other feral cats nearby. The last I saw of Mr Stick that day was his slow retreat backwards.

'Follow me!' I raced back down the alley with William and Mary in hot pursuit. They had seen enough and realised their own danger. We reached the square in a matter of moments, and hurtled to the other side. A dozen or more tourists were now standing in the middle of the Birgu Square and were startled to see this commotion. I had no chance to look at them but no doubt we were an odd sight to behold on their historical tour. As we rounded the church of St Lawrence, I was able to slow my pace to a trot, allowing my brother and sister to catch up and walk more calmly now.

'Phew! What a close shave. Whatever happened? How did you get trapped by Mr Stick? I thought the house was safe.' I was still in disbelief and I felt betrayed that our plans had come apart so easily.

'Oh Licky, we are so sorry. We'll tell you everything in a moment.' William was breathless and in shock. 'Where are we going?'

'We are going back to where I live, under the lamp post opposite the Maritime Museum. We will be safe there. Mouser will know where to find us.' I started to feel calmer - the more distance we put between us and that Mr Stick, the better. He would not dare wiggle his net down there. There were too many people on the marina and besides his confrontation with the local people ought to have taught him a lesson. However that could only mean greater circumspection as he sought us out.

We arrived back at the lamp post where ample water lay in the bowl for us all to share. We drank like fishes, replenishing the water we had perspired away during our flight to safety. It was not long before we had company. Mouser came trotting along, the rolled paper document still in his mouth. He hopped up onto the curb side and joined us. He placed the document at his feet.

Mouser spoke of our escape. 'You see Licky, I sensed *evil* in Birgu today. I may have a sixth sense and if that is so, it has kept me alive so many times. That sense will safeguard us all I hope.'

Top Cat arrived moments later as Mouser sought to explain how he had sensed trouble before he and I arrived at the scene of the crime in motion. The explanation brought no more clarity to the matter except that Mouser had an early premonition of evil at hand.

Top Cat added his own concerns to our plight. 'A day light attempted kidnapping of two cats under my protection. Outrageous and never to happen again! My authority in these streets was nearly compromised.'

It was my turn to speak. 'Top Cat we are indebted to you for our lives. What if you were not there? I would have lost my brother and sister for a *second* time in my life.' I simply burst into tears and that burst other dams of emotion. William and Mary began to howl and finally we were all weeping tears of fear and joy.

Mouser moved closer and placed his paw on my neck. 'Come on there, no need for this. All is well that ends well. Top Cat saved the day and we arrived just in time'. I sensed I would need to learn more of Mouser's psychic gift. Not walk unwittingly into danger. If only I had felt his premonition of something bad to come, the day before. That would have made me put William and Mary into a safer haven. Perhaps in the half built hotel.

'Well you are all safe and sound now. We must be realistic about the immediate future. It is not safe for any of you three to come anywhere near those alleys, day or night. Mr Stick is up to no good and he will be back again. Mark my words. I would also like to know how on

227

earth did that Mr Stick so nearly capture the pair of you?'
Top Cat was full of questions.

'I agree. What happened this morning?' Mouser was
back in the picture. 'After all, we agreed yesterday that
you should keep away from the alleys until we came to
pick you up this morning. We said you could take an
early breakfast, but not after nine when danger might
lurk.' Mouser was now wearing his *policeman's hat.*

'It was my fault. ' William looked apologetic. 'I over
slept and did not wake up until just before nine.' He
looked at Mary. 'Well we both overslept. Didn't we
Mary?'

'Yes it's true. We were up so late last night talking of
our excitement about being reunited with our long lost
sister. We did not go to sleep until very late.' Mary looked
down at the ground. 'In the morning, we felt very hungry
and ventured out to eat, even though we knew the
church bell had already struck nine times.'

'We had only been in the second alley for three of four
minutes. All seemed safe. No one was around apart from
some alley cats. We saw plates of leftovers half way down
the alley.' William voice was lowered. 'So we moved
there and started to eat.'

Top Cat knew precisely where the two had eaten. The
old lady had held a party for her grandchildren the day
before and tables had been set in that alley, filled with
chicken, meats and fish. Some rabbit too. 'It was a very
fine spread,' said Top Cat licking his lips. Later, he had
gathered up his followers who fed on some of the left
overs before he in turn went to sleep and ready for an
early start.

'Don't mind me asking Top Cat, but what did the
grandchildren have to do with it?' Mouser slightly
lowered his head in Top Cat's direction, and gave a quick
deft touch of his quiff with his right paw.

Top Cat yawned. 'Come on Mouser, work it out for
yourself. Grandchildren mean visits to their grandmother
and that sometimes means parties. She has many
grandchildren and they bring their friends from school.
The street was awash with children yesterday afternoon.
One of her grandchildren had a birthday cake with eight

candles on and I spotted the boy blow them all out, with just one puff!'

'So how do you know so much about these human parties Top Cat?' I was curious. Top Cat cocked his head and pondered.

'I've known that grandson from when he was a toddler. Seen him come and go with his mummy. She is always visiting and bringing her son with her. Her mum often used to look after him during the day, when he was younger. Not so much now while he is at school. His mum and her sister do cleaning jobs down at those fancy apartments on the Vittoriosa waterfront.'

Top cat explained why cakes had candles on them. Why the grandmother had tied eight balloons outside her front door. The figure 8 was written on each one, with a love heart. The boy was eight and the grandmother held him as he blew out the candles.

Top Cat was pleased with his answer. 'It will be a few more months until the next party I am sure. These cost money but fortunately time passes before the next birthday and money can be collected, to pay for it all - family, friends and neighbours, pooling what little they have to create a lot.' Top Cat paused. 'I always know in advance because I see new balloons outside porches, signalling the next celebration. Then I can pass on the news to the other cats so they are close by. The leftovers remain after the revellers have gone. We are always welcome there and if we did not come and parade for a while, the magic would be lost. We are thrown tit bits during the merriment and we know the platters will be filled later on, as night falls and all is quiet again. There is more to follow around six in the morning as Grandmother likes to spread her charity with care.' Top Cat smacked his lips and wiped them with his paw.

Top Cat was an old and a wise cat. Both had been around for quite some time and had grown up with human children who they had learned to understand. Mouser though would have seen less than Top Cat when it came to street parties and the like, as he was always away in the museum at night, working.

Top Cat brought us back to the present. 'So what *did* happen this morning?'

'It all happened so suddenly.' William gave a little shudder. 'Mary and I were eating from the same bowl. There were some lovely chicken bones, with quite a bit of meat left on them, marinated in a lovely barbecue sauce but which Mary did not like. I licked that off and we both ate the chicken, together with scraps of ham too and on another plate with prawn heads.'

Top Cat suddenly frowned. This food was an unintended trap he could see and had placed the two off guard. He said nothing so he could learn more.

'There might have been cheese and chicken too, but we never got the chance to find out, did we William?' Mary looked and whispered.

'It l happened so fast. One moment we were enjoying our breakfast and then, whoosh. We saw the net fall and it was too late. William and I tried to run but our claws became entangled in the mesh. The more we struggled, the more we stretched our paws until the pain was too great. We were ensnared feet away from where we had been eating. After that came the rescue and the people all shouting at Mr Stick, probably wondering why he was there and interfering with their tradition of feeding cats. I understand now Top Cat, why they were so angry. Thank you for telling us of these tales, regarding children, their birthday parties and cats.'

Mouser spoke next. 'Once our feral nature is taken from us we cannot steel ourselves against misfortune. You and yours are no longer protected as Top Cat and I.'

Top Cat added to this gloomy assessment. 'Domestic cats cannot live long outside. Mouser is right. Maybe for a few days but your defences are weak. You will quickly forget the dangers you are in. We feral cats always guard ourselves, day and night. Something you three must learn and learn very quickly.'

I sensed I might be expected to be the tutor here and hold constant guard against threats to come.

Suddenly Mouser spoke of other things. 'Whatever happened to that gold chain? The one with the two jangling cats hanging?'

I looked at William and Mary who sensed they should be cautious. 'We hid it in a pot around the corner from the Marchioness' house when we fled the place.' Mouser asked if they could remember the location. 'It was close by but there were many pots with plants in them. I scratched a hole and William threw it in.' Mouser expressed his thoughts. He might try searching the area. Top Cat thought he too might take a look.

I sought to move the conversation away to more topical things. That chain surely linked William and Mary to the Marchioness late Will. I would speak privately to William and Mary later.

I asked Top Cat and Mouser what simple things we could do to help ourselves.

'Top Cat is quite correct in what he says.' Mouser gave a moment's pause then met Top Cat's gaze, before making his point. 'You must remember who you *were* and what you must do *now* when dangers surfaced. We two are always highly alert to all hints of danger.'

'Unfortunately you are right Mouser'. I sighed with worry. How could we three cope? These two would have heard Mr Stick coming a mile off and they would run. William and Mary had to be made more *street alert*. How to make that point and how then to make them more cautious?

I asked Top Cat if wild cats could be captured when they have all of their wits about them.

'Oh no,' Top Cat was crystal clear. 'That only happens to kittens. They have learnt nothing and can be trapped with ease, with a little food and then the dreaded net. Then off to the vet. If they are lucky, then back to a home to live the life you three have all known.' He pondered for a moment. 'If not then a more tragic outcome shall likely be the case, that of living this street life with little or no protection. Thinking everything and everybody is their friend, since that visit to the vet, but discovering the world is changed and never really learning anything at all. That is why you *must* take the lead Miss Licky and help lead the way. We can help but you must learn quickly and teach them what they need to know.'

This made sense but I had to ask why Mouser and Top Cat had survived away from human company. No contact with vets.

Mouser felt he had been fortunate though he understood human companionship had its attractions, offering a warm home with plenty of food and affection. Top Cat appeared less sure, suggesting an attitude with a hallmark of better to stand alone and stand proud and within a community of cats *he* could control. Top Cat could keep a distance but without losing sight of his responsibilities. Did he ever seek or attract any affection in life I wondered. Perhaps that came through loyalty he showed to all those other Birgu cats.

Top Cat continued. 'Where would you two be today, if there hadn't been a couple of un-neutered cats around to help you? Two kidnapped cats you would have been today! Word on the streets would have reached me that you were taken in my territory. It probably would have remained a mystery unsolved. Fortunately we stopped that, though Mr Stick's part in this remains a mystery. That is strange and we must discover more. I cannot allow outsiders to threaten the sanctity and peace on my turf. We tackled him this time and my followers saw us act. Not completely coherently as I might have liked, but successfully nonetheless. Mouser and I held our reputations together. Just. However we live under constant threats from other domineering cats. You three are causing me trouble. Forget the past and follow the rules in future.' Top Cat was sounding very serious indeed.

I started to feel prickly as I heard the name Mr Stick once more. Time to move forward I felt. 'Well Mouser and Top Cat, where do we go from here? I mean my brother and sister will not be safe living near that alley, where Mr Stick could return at any time.' Top Cat agreed immediately.

'You are absolutely right Licky. I have a large enough area to cover and so cannot be in all places at once. The cats of Birgu expect to see me doing my rounds at least twice a day. They pay their dues and show me the respect I deserve. I in turn give them peace of mind by protecting their territory and keeping law and order.' He looked over at Mouser, who nodded in agreement, with a quick tweet of his quiff in Top Cat's direction.

'Top Cat is quite right' Mouser said. Ever deferential to him I noticed. 'It will be better if you three stay down here, by the marina, until we get something more permanent sorted out.' Mouser looked at the three of us and we all nodded.

'Oh I say, does that mean we can stay here with our sister?' Mary was overcome and William lost his timidity. He spoke next. 'We have no ties with Birgu now and would be much happier living in the Marina.' So it was settled.

William suddenly looked perplexed. 'There are two little things I need from Birgu.' He tried to look as disarming as possible, whilst Mary suddenly looked alarmed.

'Oh for goodness sake William, you don't think we are going back for *that*.'

William looked extremely down hearted. 'Yes but I have had it almost all my life. Our owner bought it for me. I will miss it.' I wondered what he was talking about and could see Top Cat yawning again. *No lessons learned here today* he was probably thinking. I asked William about these things he was missing. 'The necklace,' he volunteered. 'What else?' I asked staying calm.

William looked sheepishly at the ground and said nothing. It was left to Mary to shed some light on the matter. 'Oh it's Timmy. He won't go anywhere without him as a rule. They are quite inseparable, him and Timmy. Odd but he keeps my brother happy, and that's all that counts.'

'Who is this Timmy, and where is he now?' asked Mouser. He hoped it was not another cat in need of protection from Mr Stick. Top Cat mirrored his angst in his face but kept silent. 'Is this Timmy all alone?'

'Oh don't worry.' Mary seemed amused by the concern. 'Timmy is only a mouse.'

Mouser's eyes lit up and became the size of saucers. Top Cat's ears suddenly pricked up.

'Timmy is *only* a mouse?' Mouser could not contain himself. 'What on earth young man, are you doing befriending a mouse. As your best friend too! William! I cannot believe what I am hearing.' Neither could Top Cat from all accounts. His ears portrayed signs of irritation as they remained erect. Top Cat was clearly on edge.

'Oh no, It's nothing like that.' William looked at us in turn, more sheepish than ever. 'Timmy is my pet mouse. Not a real mouse – I mean not alive. He is just a furry stuffed toy that the Marchioness bought at a pet shop. I named him Timmy at the time and I cuddle him at night. I must have him near or else I cannot sleep. He is my imaginary, furry friend. He keeps me safe at night and Mr Stick cannot come near when Timmy is next to me.'

'Well I can't imagine where he might be. This Timmy - he is hardly going to go off wandering in the night, is he?' Top Cat was shaking his head as he pondered what he had said. Was he losing his wits he wondered? Chasing lifeless mice in the dead of night!

'From what you say, Timmy is I imagine in your lodging house? If you are so fond of him, why did you leave him behind? Why not have grabbed him by his tail and brought him along with you for breakfast in the alley this very morning?' Top Cat appeared exasperated. Perhaps his view was that for a cat to have a mouse as a pet showed signs of decadence and moral depravity of the lowest order - maybe a losing cause by the second.

Top Cat's moral indignation made us smile. 'A priest among cats,' I muttered which made the smiling worse. Top Cat was not amused. His reputation was all and the hunt for an artificial mouse would simply attract derision. Enough to have these cats here, laughing at him, or even worse, should his *foot soldiers* join the merriment.

William did not laugh. He remained silent – wondering if his pet mouse and he might ever be reunited. After a minute or so we composed ourselves. Top Cat was still not in good salts. A young cat can pick up silly notions and ideas. Older cats should scold them. Talk to them. Educate them. Not indulge them with laughter and ridicule! Certainly not direct such rough humour at him!

'Come on William, cheer up. You look as if it is the end of the world. I'll sort it out.' It was Top Cat, perhaps as I had never seen him, doing a complete turn around and showing every bit of kindness in his words. Had Top Cat remembered that golden chain? Perhaps it was close to Timmy the mouse, in a pot maybe, in the derelict house? Had William and Mary told the truth about its whereabouts? One way or another he might wish to find out.

'There's a little job for you Mouser. You know where William and Mary were staying so you can take me there before you go to the Museum.' That might give Top Cat all night to dig into plant pots and time enough even to find a pet mouse. 'William, tell Mouser where you left the mouse please.'

Mouser's eyes had by now returned to their normal size. He took William to one side and they discussed locations and entry points. Mouser knew exactly where to look and would go with Top Cat to resurrect this fallen creature. Before Mr Stick could find it and cause more mental catastrophe. Mouser sensed the sooner it was found, the better for everyone.

Top Cat eyed the returning pair. 'Good. Mouser you know where to go? I will come with you but it is best you bring the pet mouse back. I have other things to do today. Mouser, you can return here to keep watch on things before you start work.'

Perhaps I was being too harsh with Top Cat. Was he thinking about that chain? Did he have a contact he trusted, with scales and testing equipment, to give a fair evaluation if indeed that chain and those hanging cats were pure gold. To exchange for what - boxes of tinned fish, sardines, salmon and tuna? Things he could hide and store. Barter them away and maintain his status with the other feral cats. Keep them under his control.

We all had a laugh about the mouse. Not the other search for the chain. We knew nothing of it. William thanked Top Cat for his fine suggestion. Mouser seemed happy to accompany Top Cat into Birgu and leave him to his searches. Mouser could soon be back and keep watch until late afternoon, stopping any further trouble in its tracks and also keeping Top Cat happy by agreeing with his plan. That was the way things were. Mouser knew his place in the order of things.

We made decisions about the new home arrangements. William and Mary would certainly stay with me beneath my lamp post and maybe for many days to come. Providing things stayed safe. We would play that by ear and move them around should danger lurk.

I worried about the planned trip to Valletta tomorrow. We would have to see how the night passed. I could speak with Mouser and cancel any trips that might imperil us all. I also worried about Margaret and Terry. Would they do anything rash once they realised a colony of cats was now beneath the lamp post? Call Eric and Daisy and alert them to an impending problem of looking after three, four or even five cats? Maybe Mr Stick was known to them. Would he offer them some bounty for the capture of my brother and sister? They certainly loved money and it might take little to get them on board with his scheming ways.

Top Cat had to return to his own territory to keep up appearances. 'I am always a little nervous about being down here on the Vittoriosa water front. You may have noticed me looking around when I arrived. You cannot be too careful. This is not my turf. I need to be careful of *Monti*, the Vittoriosa water front *capo*. He is really old now but he has his followers and loyalty is everything. Have you seen him Licky? He sleeps around the clock. Still you should take care.' I had never seen Monti. 'I know nothing of Monti,' I replied.

Top Cat's eyes diverted to the paper scroll lying near Mouser's feet on the quayside. He raised his eyebrows and at the same time slightly tilted his head to the left.

'What is the scroll that you have there? It looks important with the fancy red ribbon wrapped around it.' Top Cat was becoming inquisitive again and it concerned me. 'You did a good job there Mouser, distracting Mr Stick by grabbing it. It is definitely a document of sorts. Not the first time I have set eyes on it either. On each occasion I have seen that Mr Stick prowling my alleyways, he has been carrying it under his arm. Like a dagger. Will you open it?' Top Cat's curiosity was rising as he possibly sensed other opportunities ahead.

'We can do that later Top Cat, after you have done your rounds around Birgu. First things first! I could walk up there with you, on my way to fetch Timmy, if that would help.'

Top Cat gave Mouser a glance and then cocked his head to the right and gazed again at the red ribbon bound document. A frown revealed itself on his brow. As quickly as it had appeared, it vanished.

'Good idea' he said. 'Company is always welcome from you Mouser.' Top Cat began to look serious again.

'William and Mary will need sustenance whilst they are camping out here on the Vittoriosa water front. They shall need food and vitals. I am not wholly clear on your position here, Miss Licky. Can this Margaret and Terry be trusted to deliver?'

I quickly explained to Top Cat that the yacht neighbours brought me breakfast and dinner each day, and that I would share this with my brother and sister.

'Well that is all very well but maybe not well at all! We must sort out a better arrangement than that. A breakfast for one and a dinner for one can never equal the feeding of three. My goodness, if it is not one problem after another, but we shall muddle through and maybe this Margaret and Terry will help. Come on Mouser, let's make a move. Time is pressing.'

Mouser raised himself and looked briefly in my direction. He winked, glanced down at the rolled up document and winked again. The pair then sped away.

I pushed the scroll next to the lamp post, where we three hid it as best we could. It clearly held some importance and should not be blown away into the sea. Or worse be retrieved from us by Mr Stick or one his own devious followers. We rehearsed the events of the day so far. Whilst William and Mary remained somewhat uneasy, all was presently under control and the future looked a little brighter. I told them this while knowing the future was very uncertain. I said nothing of my own reservations, as that might create more alarm and despondency.

237

My optimism failed to displace new questions. What would happen to them, once my owners returned? Where would they fit into all of this? Mary was becoming more pessimistic than her brother. She saw separation looming on the horizon.

'Yes Licky, your owners will return, and welcome you back onto their yacht with open arms. What of us? They will simply take you away with a wave and leave us here alone, maybe forever.' Mary hid her eyes with a paw whilst weeping inwardly.

I had to put such fears to rest. William said little but the thought was becoming ingrained. I saw that immediately. He was subdued in silent thought.

'I have an idea!' I needed to change the subject. 'Let us look at this document that Mouser wrestled from the horrid Mr Stick. See if it is of interest to us. No problem taking a peek. I can read English but if it is written in Maltese we will be in trouble. What do you think?'

William perked up. 'Good idea Licky. If you undo the ribbon, I can hold the paper scroll down and stop it blowing away.' There was a slight breeze but we agreed we should do it now. William placed one paw on the document as I gently tugged at the ribbon, which began to unfold. 'Be careful William, as we must try and put it all back together as we found it. Mary, grab the ribbon with your paw and hold onto it like grim death. Later, Mouser may have to return it somewhere.'

The ribbon was off. William held the top end of the document with both paws, as I gently unravelled the parchment until it was fully extended. What I saw written in English was extraordinary. 'I just cannot believe it. I just cannot believe it.' Mary tried to lean over my shoulder to see what *I could not believe*. William was less fortunate, as holding the top end of the document down, he could only see everything upside down. In any event, neither appeared to be able to read proper English and I had to become their translator.

'Licky, what does it say. Oh tell me.' William was as excited as I was speechless. Mary continued to press against my right shoulder for a better view.

'This is the Last Will and Testament of the Marchioness.' I read slowly so they would understand everything. 'William and Mary, my adopted cats, are the sole beneficiaries of my estate. Of my funds I leave my maid thirty thousand euros. Also ten thousand euros to Mr Stick who will fulfil the obligations placed on him by this Will, administering the estate and ensuring the beneficiaries receive the proceeds. Failing which, Mr Stick will receive NOTHING' I paused.' She has left everything to you, the Palazzo, her other properties and her cash. Also some stocks and shares I see. Her jewellery too and it gives mention here of the gold chain with two gold cats attached. Mr Stick has to ensure you do benefit or he receives nothing. Small wonder he needs to find the two of you. Keep you somewhere safe until the Will is read.'

I paused for breath before reading on. The next section nearly took that breath away. The Marchioness recognised in the Will that William and Mary had a sister who she had not at the time felt she could adopt. Three cats would be a bit too much for her. She was now stating that if that other sister, *me* was ever to be found, I too must be reunited with my brother and sister and provided for under the inheritance. We must all three live together and be looked after for the rest of our natural days.

'William and Mary, your previous owner was indeed a very kind and thoughtful person. There can be no mistake about that. She even states here in the Will, that should any other cats befriend you, they too can be provided for. So surely who immediately springs to mind?'

William and Mary stared at me for one mere instance. 'Mouser' declared Mary. 'Or even Mouser *and* Top Cat!

'You are hot on the money Mary. And further on it makes it absolutely clear that Mr Stick can have no part in looking after us. His only part in all of this is to discharge the terms of the Will, which includes having us re-homed to someone who *really* loves cats.'

'But what good is all of this to us?' Mary looked dumfounded. 'How can we claim? We are only cats?'

239

'Shush. Let me read on. William, don't let go of the paper.' I read through the details as fast as I could to allow William and Mary to know more. Little else was stated in the Will, apart from the declaration that no living relative would receive one single euro cent. I continued to read out aloud. 'My ingrates who have constantly sought to deceive me will receive nothing. They have never aided me, but instead have simply defrauded me, borrowing money with no intent to pay back any funds owing.' She named them all to make absolutely sure there could be no confusion, including her two sons in particular, Horace and Horatio. "My two boys will from the date of my death stand on their own two feet. May they learn from their selfish indifference towards me and become better people once parted from my funds and make their own fortunes in their own way, just as their father had to." I let out a worried sigh, as here there was evidence of more humans to worry about. Surely they would be looking for this Will. I knew from tales told on the yacht of people who died intestate. Everything then went to the family. This Will was a time bomb and we were all sitting on its fuse.

'William, gently let it go and roll it up. We need to get the ribbon back on. This is dynamite and could cause us all terrible trouble.'

It took William and me, with a little help from Mary, a minute or so to have the document fully restored and back in the red ribbon. I spoke of what we had learned to make the situation crystal clear to William and Mary.

I explained again that William and Mary would inherit everything apart from the legacy made to the maid and a handsome fee for Mr Stick notary work. The house and the content were to be sold. The proceeds, together with all other savings, were to be put in trust, generating income to take care of William and Mary and basically a few more cats should the matter arise. Mr Stick would see to that apparently. On the death of William and Mary and any other cats that might by that time have appeared in the picture, the whole residue of the trust would pass to the Malta Animal Welfare Centre in Floriana.

'How can this all be put into place? As Mary has just said, we are only cats. We can't claim. Who is going to listen to a pair of cats?' William was confused.

'In the Will, it says, that whoever becomes your guardian must commit to your welfare using the benefits of the trust fund for that purpose. I rather fancy that Mr Stick might very well seek to take on that role. God forbid. Well he can't since the Marchioness has stated this quite plainly. Thank God!' I sought to give further explanations of the Will and the content. 'The late Marchioness stipulates that no expense must be spared. Your dietary needs shall include the highest quality fresh fish to be bought and cooked every day.' I paused for a moment before continuing. 'There was something written about fillet steak, calves livers, truffles and cheeses. A richer diet I could not imagine. It is all beyond belief. She must has have loved you two dearly.' William and Mary looked as if they had landed on another planet.

'Here lies the key to so many unanswered questions. You remember Mouser's suspicions about Mr Stick? Mouser was right.' As ever, I thought. 'He is a clever old *tom* that Mouser. He must be psychic.' I wondered if Mouser could see into the future. It was as though he had seen the Will before it was ever written! His misgivings early this morning that things were not right, simply added to my sense he was prophetic. 'We should all heed Mouser's observations with greater care,' I said. William and Mary stared wide eyed and nodded.

The three of us suddenly found ourselves looking into thin air. What my brother and sister were thinking, I could not be certain. They were no doubt taking in all the complexities as best they could. We looked at each other and mentally agreed on one thing. Mr Stick had to be avoided at all costs, since his whole being exuded danger and malevolence. He should never be allowed to set eyes on my brother and sister ever again. 'We must keep away from Mr Stick,' William under stated. So it was agreed, with the nodding of three heads

'We must sit tight and keep this document safe. Not let it out of our sight. Hide it.' I thought back to that chain with the two golden cats. Maybe take it there. Hide the two together. However Top Cat might find the chain and with it this document too! Maybe better to hide it elsewhere. We'll talk to Mouser. He will have an idea. There was not much else to say. By now we had become totally reliant on Mouser. He was a thinker. His survival was the testimony. We three were by now, innocents abroad in a land filled with a few ungenerous people.

'So we tell Mouser what is in this Will. Do you think that is wise?' Mary asked her question simply but with great purpose. She was thinking.

'Of course we must tell Mouser. Why not? After all without Mouser efforts we would not be in the possession of this important document in the first place. Alright Mouser was not to know just how valuable a document this would turn out to be, but that remains neither here nor there. Remember how reluctant he was to open the document in front of Top Cat? He gave me an odd wink as he left for the square. He was almost certainly suggesting we should look after the document whilst he was away. Take a look maybe, whilst no one else was near.'

We needed Mouser more than ever. Thoughts were fermenting in my mind, but I needed to share these with Mouser. For now, keeping William and Mary safe until the tenth of July had to be the priority. Once my owners sailed home, maybe they could become the new guardians. How to explain all of this to them, remained a question I would need to answer in the days ahead. For now, simple survival was the issue.

Mouser came into sight and I felt relieved. He trotted casually down the quayside with *Timmy* in his mouth. He dropped the toy mouse at William's feet. 'There you go. It's Timmy, and I think he's seen better days - a bit tatty and worn to say the least.' He sighed. 'Too much love over the years has taken its toll.' Then Mouser smiled and saw how simple things like the deliverance of a tatty mouse brought their own pleasures.

'Oh thank you Mouser. The best present in the world.' Clearly William was overjoyed by this reunion. Mary looked over wondering what the fuss was all about. I looked on and was touched by this act of kindness from

Mouser. It meant nothing maybe but everything at the same time.

'Mouser, you didn't see that Mr Stick again up in Birgu?' I still had that vision of him prowling around with his butterfly net.

'No not at all. I think he got the message that Birgu was unsafe for his constant meanderings. He may be laying low. However he will be back. He might widen his search. Maybe here, if he hears anything, from anybody! He has designs on William and Mary and time will tell what they may be. Birgu Square and its alleys must stay out of bounds for your brother and sister.'

It was as if Mouser had read the Will already! I was by now eager to share the news with him. Mouser looked at me directly. 'Licky, you look as if something is on your mind. You look tense.' I peered straight into his eyes. Were psychic powers at play here? Or was it me revealing myself by a simple look?

'It is this,' I said as I peered down at the scroll and red ribbon.

'Oh yes, we must have a look at what that is all about. Shall we open it?' Mouser sounded as keen as mustard - oblivious to the fact it had been already opened, read and resealed while he was away.

'I've done so already or should I say we have done so already. We opened it and have read it.' I looked to Mouser's reaction.

'Oh well you might have waited until I returned.' Mouser sounded miffed, as if he had been excluded. 'Well not that it matters but more to the point does it offer anything of interest?'

'The snatching of this document Mouser, which turns out to be a Will, was a very clever move. We now know what Mr Stick is up to!'

William could not contain his excitement and Mary became agitated. 'It's true, it's true,' they said in unison. Mouser looked perplexed. William suggested we three should miaow three times with gratitude - Mary began to clap with her two front paws and William added to the emotion. I could do nothing but sit looking embarrassed. Where had my brother and sister learned these street cat ways? What would a passer-by think of such a spectacle? They were drawing attention to us all. I looked to my left and right but no one was watching and I was grateful.

'Steady on there. Whatever has got into you two? I am lost by all of this affection, touching though it may be. You all obviously know something that I don't.' Mouser held a puzzled grin on his face. 'Come on then, tell me everything.'

Calm was restored as I passed on all I had learned about the Will. William and Mary listened again, lest they had missed something in the first telling. We were now in possession of this Will which left William and Mary in clover for life. Property and money were theirs for the rest of their lives! Mouser's jaw dropped as he discovered the magnitude of his discovery. I added more detail to my tale and Mouser would simply say unbelievable, every time I paused for breath.

'So would you like to look at it Mouser? Shall we unroll it again so you can see for yourself?' I went to lay my paw on the priceless document.

'No Licky, there is no need. You have explained things perfectly, and it is better not to risk damaging it by re-opening it.

Mouser had guessed what Mr Stick was about and now the Will had put the flesh onto the skeleton. Mouser felt pleasantly pleased with himself I could see. Then his attitude changed as the gravity of the detail began to bother him. He left no time sharing his worries with us all.

'Now listen. This document could be your gateway to heaven.' He paused. Perhaps a worrying choice of words, as there were people who might like to see these two dead he realised. Not allow them their days of wine and roses. He looked directly at William and Mary. 'We need take great care' he said sternly. 'No wandering from the path we must take. You are in some great danger and only the strictest discipline will protect you. Your sister-Licky – may be safer but I know how people can behave. Easier to eliminate anyone and everyone that stands between them and what they want. We must stand together united which means all for one and one for all. Am I making myself quite clear?'

William and Mary remained quiet. Then nodded together and looked at each other, no doubt making a secret vow to do everything expected of them.

'Oh Mouser, of course we must all remain allies together. There is no other way. You have saved us from Mr Stick and now we must be saved from any others who would harm us. Do you understand what Mouser has told us? No more wanderings. Curiosity will kill all of us cats. Be alert at all times. Do what Mouser says.' I really could not think of anything else to say, to make the point.

Mary spoke for William when she pledged to keep to our plan and thanked Mouser for his help during these past few frightening hours.

'Mary is right Mouser. What you have done for me and for my brother and sister shall never be forgotten. Our friendship is the bond that may never be broken. Whatever happens, united we stand, divided we fall. Isn't that so William and Mary?'

Mouser looked at each of us in a puzzled, disbelieving way. He looked upwards at the swallows circling the Marina, making their final flight before settling for the night.

'Your words have touched me and I value them. Thank you very much for those kind thoughts.' Mouser paused for a moment. He was thoughtful.

'I could take this document into the museum tonight and hide it where no one could ever find it.'

'Yes but what shall we do with it in due course Mouser?' I was asking the obvious question.

'We keep it safe until your owners arrive back here in Malta. Then I will retrieve it and pass it to you Licky. Then you take it to them for their eyes only. I suspect you would not want to pass it over to Terry and Margaret?' Of course not I thought. Mouser was right. He would hide it so that only the four of us would know it whereabouts.

'So that is settled.' Mouser was in the driving seat once more. 'I know exactly where I can hide the Will. No one will ever find it. I will tell no one. *Maybe* not even you three. In that way you can never be forced to reveal it, to anybody. On the tenth of July with your owners return we can recover this paper. Not many days away now. Tonight you need to keep a vigil, maybe two sleeping and one on guard. Then tomorrow – off to Valletta, to get well away from here and Mr Stick and his cronies. Are we all agreed?'

I asked Mouser if visiting Valletta was really such a good idea after everything that had happened today. It could be stressful for William and Mary, with their unworldly ways. I peered over at the pair of them. They looked very disappointed.

'Licky it would do them a world of good and take their minds off today. Keep you all safe. No sense in hanging around here tomorrow taking risks and doing nothing but hide. Better to live life to the full. We shall take a trip on the bus and then onto the sights of wonderful Valletta. Life is for living!'

That was decided and Valletta would be the hiding place for the day. Mouser would make his way here shortly after nine o'clock and be our escort. William and Mary were excited and wanted an adventure to take their minds off of things. They would sleep well tonight and I feared it would be me keeping the all- night vigil over them. Never mind.

Mouser reassured me that Top Cat would call in from time to time after Mouser was back in the Museum. He might be bringing something with him. That was a secret however and he would say no more. Mouser bid us farewell, took up the parchment and trotted back over to the museum to seek out this hiding place of his.

A little while later, Top Cat appeared. He was carrying a bag of assorted left-overs from that young mans' birthday party. We thanked Top Cat for his thoughtfulness, which he shrugged off with the customary flick of his quiff. He did not stay long. We explained that we would be off to Valletta in the morning and hoped to see him when we got back.

'Certainly,' he said. 'I plan to see Mouser before he returns to the museum tomorrow and if I see that Mr Stick I will tell you.' Top Cat looked around, raised himself up onto his paws, gave a slight stretch and then bid us a good night. 'Miss Licky, keep a close eye on these two.' He looked at both William and Mary and then gave them a quick wink. 'After all I cannot have another day like today. Upset my usual routine but no matter.'

With that Top Cat was gone, and we were left to an early supper. I had wondered whether Top Cat had found that golden bracelet. If he had he said nothing of it. I suspected we would be the last to know in any event. Never mind. Food was more important than gold at this moment and we shared the contents of the bag with relish. Later Margaret arrived with further offerings.

'Ooh you still have your two friends with you then. How very strange. Well I suppose they are company for you Miss Licky.' William and Mary had again chosen to sit slightly back from my position by the lamp post. They felt they would be less conspicuous. 'Mind you, don't you go sharing your dinner as cat food does not come cheap,' on that note she let out one of her laughs. 'And Tel is still going on about my eyebrows. Oh when he gets something into his head, he's impossible.' With that, she swirled away down the quayside, her silken shawl pulling at her hair, both hands gripping the ends as the wind fought mischievously to unseat her.

CHAPTER 24

The sun had set and already William and Mary were asleep. I kept watch but all was calm. By midnight most people had disappeared and the restaurants were clearing the debris from their floors. I eventually fell asleep until the first disturbances of the day. The jangling of bottles in plastic bags being thrown into the dust cart caused me to stir. I drifted back to sleep until that vegetable van raced by as the clock struck seven times.

I was surprised William and Mary slept through these strange noises. I worried they might have been disturbed, but felt reassured however that my senses were keener and I could have woken them at any time. I could manage this pattern of sleep in their company during the nights ahead. We would be safe. Our breakfast arrived earlier than usual accompanied by Margaret and Terry, just as the bells chimed eight times.

'See, I told you Tel. Miss Licky has got two new friends, and they look as if they are staying. Both of them have name tags, so they must belong to someone, but not here.' By this time William and Mary were awake. On this occasion they did not move away from the lamp post, showing any concerns they may have had for this pair were probably fading.

Terry stood there and wondered whether these two *extra* cats had been abandoned by other yacht owners. Perhaps more posters to be posted and more rewards to come - best to look after them as well maybe, by way of an investment. The cost of some extra out of date cat food tins from the market would do little harm.

'Well as long as they are not eating us out of house and home, that's all I can say Ma. Blimey more rewards might come our way. What you think Ma? At this rate we could make a living as bounty hunters! Come on let's move ourselves, before the big rush starts. Buy extra tins of that cheap cat food for this lot.'

Margaret placed the foil tin in front of me and stroked my neck before leaving. The couple moved off towards the weekly Birgu market, with empty shopping bags in hand. On Tuesdays an early breakfast meant market day, probably the biggest weekly market anywhere on the island. Mouser had explained this to me. The market attracted far too many people and held little attraction for him as many stallholders sold household goods of every description, but of little interest to cats. Apart from that, the dangers of being trampled to death were great. I hoped those shopping bags would be filled with the extra rations we needed to survive a little longer in this place.

Mouser was the next to arrive and I assured him the night went well. No intrusions and nothing to speak of. Mouser was happy but then became thoughtful.

'Licky, I think it better you three know where I have hidden the Will. I am getting older and if anything happened.' He paused. He cleared his throat. 'So I will tell you but you must keep this very secret. Even Top Cat need not know. Do you agree? I have pushed the Will up the leg of a Captain General of the Galleys. It is as safe as houses.' Mouser gave a hearty chuckle and he wondered if I knew the location. After all I had spent that terrible night in the Museum. I had no recollection at all.

'On the first floor,' Mouser whispered. 'Look for the glass case with two life size figures, dressed in eighteenth century naval uniforms and the accessories of the Order of St John.' Mouser described the Captain General of the Galleys, sporting a red open jacket with white lapels and seven brass buttons down each lapel. A white waist coat trimmed with gold braiding and two gold tassels, which lay on top of a red vest with a Maltese cross in white and a Maltese jewel cross. He wore black shoes with brass buckles, grey stockings and white breeches with three brass buttons to the left, just above the knees. 'I pushed the wooden flap open at the back and squeezed the parchment into the right leg and then pulled the flap back. No one goes in there – not even the cleaners.'

We thanked Mouser for sharing this secret with us and securing the Will in such a safe place. 'Let's go before it gets busy down here. Before the likes of Mr Stick arrives to broaden the search.' We followed Mouser to the bus terminal below the Birgu market. Life was

249

bustling and a little frightening. Even at this early hour. Mouser's confidence shone through, as we arrived beside the bus driven with Seven at the door, smoking a cigarette and checking his watch as he hurried late arrivals on board.

'Well stone me Mouser, you've got some friends today. Come on, hop in, there is plenty of room for you all, as the shoppers have left and few return to Valletta at this time of day.' Seven did not blink an eyelid as Mouser leapt up onto the old dashboard and summoned the three of us to join him. 'Better make the most of this trip Mouser. Only a few more days and this bus and all the others will be history. On the fourth of July we go over to the new Arriva buses, with stricter new rules and bus inspectors looking for infringements. Like live cats on dashboards! Electric doors will have to be closed at all times when the bus is moving. All buses shall have air conditioning too. Nothing shall be the same. No more mixing diesel with spent chip oil fat, to cut the costs of fuel. I call it re-cycling. They moan about carbon emissions, whatever they are.' He sighed as though his own world was being trampled to death, in the name of progress.

The journey to Valletta was uneventful apart from occasional skirmishes with roundabouts and tyres skimming kerb stone. Apart from these small distractions, Seven proved to be a careful driver, giving way to other vehicles and keeping his speed down. He owned his bus and no one would instruct him about timetable behaviour. Customers got on and off at will. "Let me off here Seven." He would slow and stop. His elderly clients would never be dumped at a bus stop, to walk distances back to their homes. He saw to that. A thoughtful smile was enough to stop his bus.

A Maltese family signalled with customary waves but not within a bus stop in sight, and still the bus would stop. All paused to stroke us though Mouser would hiss his disapproval. Let him be, they wisely thought. Cat lovers they were and seemed unperturbed by our presence. If Seven broke the rules regarding bus stops in their favour, then they would say nothing of free hitch hiking cats to inspectors.

Our slow drive to Valletta allowed us to see ever changing scenery. We saw and passed old houses of character together with ugly developments which marred the view, with washing fluttering from balconies of these plain built flats, simple but nevertheless functional. My brother and sister were immersed in everything that passed them by. By now we had stopped at the Valletta bus terminus and we were the first to alight. A farewell wave from Seven with a gentle reminder about the times we could return with him. Nothing as indelicate as a firm moment - he would flex the timetable as much as he could until passengers complained about the sweltering heat aboard this relic from the distant past. Windows had often buckled into their frames and would never be opened again. Then he had to go.

The terminus was in chaos, with so many old buses vying for spaces to park. The constant hooting of horns as frustrated drivers joined queues that never moved. More aggressive shouting and more use of those horns. Fortunately, passengers could leave if they chose because the faulty doors were never closed. At least the smoke from drivers' cigarettes had its own escape route. Still, the rising temperatures encouraged the able bodied to get out, whilst the going was good.

Mouser chose our moment, keeping close looking left and right should another bus suddenly seize its own moment to race past us on the inside. Cats were never seen at such times, often passengers too, as they made unprepared leaps into the unknown. Accidents were not unknown and these simply added to the madness, as and when they happened.

We leapt out into the relative safety of the pedestrian area leading into Valletta proper. Mouser told us about the history that was enveloping us as we moved forward. On our right a massive building project was gathering pace. 'That was where the old opera house stood in ruins for many years.'

The Germans, Mouser informed us, bombed it and it remained a wrecked site forever more. The Germans did apologise after the war and said they would restore it. Using German workers! The Maltese would have none of it. If it was to be re-built – they would do it themselves. No mood then to let hordes of Germans in.

'This whole site is being turned into something very modern. You can see the designs illustrated on the billboard over there, showing natural light walkways and a sense of natural space.' We looked where Mouser had directed and saw architectural plans on a large hoarding along the walkway.

'This is the start of Republic Street, the most important and best known street in Valletta.' Mouser was moving us on a bit. 'We will walk a little way down here and then we can relax.' We were now in a side street off Republic Street. Further down I saw a restaurant called Da Pippo. I remembered the name from somewhere even though I had never been here before in my life. William and Mary sat patiently looking around them in this small sloping street, with tall buildings in shadow from the burning sun. Suddenly I remembered why Da Pippo rang a bell with me.

'Mouser, is that the restaurant you have visited in the past, when doors were ajar and you could slide in unannounced? As the chilled display counter was being filled? ' Mouser licked his lips and let out a gentle smile. I became agitated. 'If it is, I do not want any funny business today. My brother and sister are here and they must know nothing of these incursions. Please, they look up to you. I do not want any adoptions of strange ways and least of all getting into trouble.' Mouser let out a chuckle and promised to be good.

'Licky, we will go somewhere safe to eat today, where temptations will be put aside. In the meantime, we have some sights to see, so let us walk back into Republic Street.'

So the four of us strolled back into Republic Street where tourist groups were being herded together. At each head, a flag waving tour guide, shepherding their flock with Napoleonic precision. Tourists adopting a marching walk and keeping up with their tour guide. Stopping and starting. Forming circles to hear what the guide had to say. Being careful not to push and shove each other. Allowing the more elderly forward to compensate for any hearing difficulties they might have. I had never seen humans behave with such consideration. Normally they would rush and race around each other, paying no heed to age or infirmity. Here there was a great sense of order.

Mouser explained that most of these tourists were from large cruise liners that had docked in the Grand Harbour for the day. They would be the very best people we could find, kind and considerate. The type who would buy an extra portion of fish for a cat they might adopt for the hour. Secretly feed it under a table, hiding it from over-zealous waiters who might otherwise kick us out and basically camouflaging cats like us from the piercing gaze of the owner who would much prefer us to be gone. All we needed to do was adopt a table discretely and then the rest would take care of itself. There would be no stealing or searching for fish heads in dank buckets.

Mouser showed us St John Co- Cathedral to our right. He had never been inside though he knew we might gain access by the side entrance. That was free but only devout Catholics were allowed to use it. Guards would patrol to make sure tourists were not circumventing the pay booths at the front entrance. However, cats could enter with great care he knew. Then view the paintings and the marble floors, sculpted into skeletal figures which would frighten the angels themselves. Certainly the devil!

I decided it was safer for us not to test the patience of anyone here in Valletta. Besides skeletal figures would be bad omens for William and Mary. Give them nightmares. Keep me awake at night too. No, better to leave that place to these tourists who had learned how to cope with such things.

Passing the cathedral, we looked up the steps of the law courts. There were people arriving with families. Mothers producing ties pre-knotted, to slip around waiting necks and pulled tight under collars, adjusted and making the wearer at least half presentable. Others were

253

well attired in suits, carrying documents and cases. Documents like the very same one we had hidden, with silken bows around them.

Many people were smoking and talking nervously to each other, sometimes almost whispering. Awaiting their call to enter this ancient building and discover what fate had in store. Mouser informed us these were people accused of crimes and now speaking with lawyers, rehearsing stories and getting things straight, before seeking justice.

'They say there are far too many lawyers and notaries in Malta. The Parliament Building is just as overcrowded, with too many Members of Parliament! Everyone works in the courts or the Parliament building, leaving no one left to grow potatoes!' How or where Mouser obtained his information from I did not know. Probably from Chubby and Seven as bus drivers and taxi drivers apparently know everything and seem to have strong opinions about the rest.

Mouser suggested we take a pre-lunch stroll down to Freedom Square, then into some side streets, to another Cathedral, an oddity in Malta. It was the first Anglican Church to be built here. We could enter and stroll around at will, he said. The ladies who kept watch were great animal lovers and encouraged everyone in to look around. It was cool and simple. There was nothing here to worry cats or people. The carpentry was simple. He spoke of people called puritans who preferred their churches plain. Not liking silver and gold. These people passed on their own beliefs to generations to come. They would abide by simplicity. The devil would be in the detail and for that, good eyesight was a must, to spot intricacy of carvings, the quality of the hardwoods and the *smell* of purity. A different insight into the way some humans chose to believe.

'The volunteer ladies hold court near the entrance door but they have never objected to me just popping in to keep cool and look around. Just follow me in.'

We did as we were told and entered through the large open doors, unchallenged. Yes there were two middle aged English women busy chatting to other visitors. If they noticed us they said and did nothing. This church was open to all they were saying and they were simply here to tell visitors more.

Mouser became our unofficial guide, as we strolled through the pews. We came across so many memorials to Navy, Army and Air Force people on the oak panels around the Sanctuary, with names of so many people who had died before their due time. We learnt that Queen Adelaide the widow of King William 1V, the 'Sailor King', laid the foundation stone on 20th March 1839. She paid for the building of the church herself which was finally completed in 1844. I thought she must have been as wealthy as the Marchioness herself, to have created such a quiet and peaceful place. A true sanctuary for cats and people with no stone unturned in the quest for quiet reflection midst a bustling metropolis.

'Well here we are Licky, William and Mary and enough exploring for the day. Let us stroll on to take lunch and join those tourists as hunger beckons them too. What do you think?'

'That sounds good to me Mouser. Thank you for bringing us here today, into this lovely building. We have never been in a church before I think.' William and Mary agreed. They had always been left behind on a Sunday when the Marchioness attended Mass. "*Not really a place for cats,*" she would say.

We left through the entrance where the two ladies would bid us adieu. We tried to stay as anonymous as we could. In case we were somehow in the wrong just being there. Mouser led towards the open doors. It was then that we caught the eye of one of the volunteers.

'Oh Mildred well just look at that. We have had four pussy cat visitors!'

'Well June that's surely a first. How sweet. They won't be leaving a donation in the box though, more's the pity.'

June bent down to stroke us as we left and Mary lingered just a moment. I looked back but all was safe. The lady stood up and Mary passed by. Our exit marked by one simple miaow.

Mouser did not quicken his pace, but simply turned his head in our direction as we followed close behind him and gave a wink. Was he winking at Mildred and June? Whatever that meant, we were out in the bright sunlight, on the pavement below the steps.

'Let us have a time check. It is nearing midday, so we really want to be up in the square for twelve o'clock, when we can have a refreshing drink and a cooling shower. What do you say, boys and girls?' None of us had a clue but the idea seemed good and of course we agreed. Mouser bade us follow him back the way we had come.

Five minutes later, we found ourselves in Palace Square. 'Take a look over there.' Mouser pointed his paw towards two guardsmen marching back and forth past each other. Between two narrow sentry boxes. At either side of an entrance to a very grand building they would stamp their feet and make a noise each time they turned. Tourists took photographs and smiled. They were as intrigued as we by this odd mechanical behaviour.

'Ooh, that is lovely to watch. What an unusual way to spend the day, marching back and forth and going nowhere.' Mary's attention had been captivated. 'Are those real rifles they are carrying? Do they shoot people who try to get inside? '

Mouser gave us a glance. 'I doubt it very much. It's for show, chiefly for the tourists, letting them know about the past, when buildings needed protection. ' Mouser gave pause for reflection. 'Everything has changed here in the past year or two. The whole square has been restored. It used to be a messy car park, with the floor stained with foul smelling diesel oil.

Mouser told us about the Grandmaster's Palace ahead of us. Here lived the Grandmaster of the Order of St. John from 1530, when King Charles 1 of Spain leased Malta to the Order. That ended when Napoleon captured the island in 1798. Hompesch, the only Grand Master to learn Maltese, was a kindly man but foolish too. He allowed Napoleon to re-supply his ships. They sailed in and simply invaded the island without a fight. However the French decided to auction off holy silver from the former capital of Malta, Medina on a Sunday. That started the rebellion which with British help drove the French away in 1802. After that Malta became a British

Crown Colony until 1964. During that period, the Palace became the home of each British-appointed Governor.

'Now it is Malta's own parliament where the President and the people meet. When parliament is not sitting, the public can visit the Palace for free. There are some lovely sights to see in there.' Mouser looked content with his explanation.

'So you have been in there and strolled around?' William looked quite incredulous. 'That is how you know so much! I envy you Mouser.' Mouser gloated just a little. 'Actually no I haven't been inside, but it is on my *bucket* list and I will.'

'Come on Mouser, let us into your secret. How do you know so much about this place?'

Mouser turned. 'It is quite simple Licky. People talk. Tourists share their modest understandings. I listen under tables over there where we are going for lunch, the lovely Malata restaurant.' Mouser looked to where tables were being laid out by a young waiter. There were already several seated customers. 'That is where the nicer tourists dine. They visit The Palace and then cross over to the Malata for lunch. They reflect and they chat and drop offerings to me on the floor.'

'It really is splendid how you have learnt so much by just listening Mouser. William and I have never gone anywhere and the little we know has come from the Marchioness and the maid. Our world was the garden. What do you think Licky?'

There was little I could add, though I had learnt more of the world on that yacht. I would listen to conversations about books and places we would visit. My brother and sister up to recently had only idle chatter to lean on within their isolated home.

'I think it is about time to freshen ourselves up and have a nice drink of water,' Mouser exclaimed. He was looking into the square as he stood and we followed his every move. Suddenly music appeared from nowhere and moments later, huge bursts of water leapt from the floor around us. Fountains growing ever higher whose spray would saturate us. Children ran towards it and soon everyone was drenched.

Tourists stopped to gawp; cameras started to click and more young children broke away from their parents to join in the fun. They started dodging in and out and between the rising and falling shoots of water. 'What do you make of this?' Mouser enquired.' All fun and games and somewhere to cool down and take a refreshing drink of cold water'' Mouser raised his eyes and blinked in the spray.

I kept my own eyes on my brother and sister as cats normally hate water. They were keeping well away.

'Mouser you are actually suggesting we get wet? We are pussy cats and I have never known any cat enjoying getting wet.' By this time, a small dog was bounding in and out of the streams of water, loving every moment. William and Mary presumed the dog was quite mad and preferred to keep their distance from it.

'Oh come on Licky, it's only water and it's the best way to shake off that dust from our fur. Besides, you can drink it. Watch me you three.' Mouser raced into the sodden throng of people and around the edges of the water jets and just close enough to experience a light shower, but not so close to be drenched. He paused and gathered water in his paw and started to drink. As he did so two tourists walked over from the restaurant and began taking pictures of him and the barking dog.

'What do you think Licky? Shall we give it a try?' Mary needed my reassurance before moving any further. I remained unsure. It seemed safe enough and surely Mouser would not court danger. Besides Mouser was a worldly cat who had brought us safely here – away from other likelier dangers. I relented. 'Come on you two, let's all give it try.'

With that, all three of us trotted towards Mouser who was some small distance from the prancing dog. That was my only great concern. Then we were alongside him and following his lead. In and out of the jets of water, catching light sprays on our backs and lifting our heads up to moisten our lips and then drink. The water was cold and refreshing. Mouser had at some time or somewhere along the line learned how to skip, side to side and up and down. We watched. Soon we were copying his dance

258

in a line. It seemed so natural placing one paw forward and then one paw backward. Soon we learned how to stop and turn as one. Back and forth we went. The dog approached as if he wanted to join us. However he stayed back fearing an alliance of cats might overwhelm him. 'Now swing those hips a bit,' said Mouser. We did, always keeping a close eye on Mouser to follow his trail and all those twists and turns.

In no time, our antics were attracting crowds of people taking pictures and recording this strangest of sights, a troupe of dancing cats. I worried we were making a spectacle of ourselves and drawing too much attention. Those doubts evaporated as children ran and followed us. Skipping and dancing in our wake. Everyone was having the time of their lives. Suddenly, Mouser broke formation and started a new dance. He could stand on his hind legs and wave his front legs. Then twist and turn followed by a skip to repeat the twirl. He then flipped himself backwards and over. I thought for a moment he had skidded and slipped and this was simply a freak accident. However I said nothing as the children squealed with delight. An eruption of applause from the crowd threatened to drown the music and its ability to keep this momentum going. What did Mouser do next? He managed again to skid and jump backwards, completing a full backward summersault once more and then faced the audience. He rose up on his hind paws and with his right front paw placed across his waist, he gave a bow. Further great applause and the music came to an end. A little clapping continued from a table of diners at The Malata, which did not go unnoticed by Mouser. He joined us. He had found the spot for our lunch, under or close to *their* table - the restaurant clappers. The last fountain of water subsided as we strolled over to our place of refuge. Away from any more cameras I hoped. We shook our fur until it was nearly dry posing no threat to those legs we might seek to brush against, with our bushy clean tails.

'Look, those four cats have all come over to see us. Oh how sweet and what a lovely combination they make with three of them so alike stalking the leader of the troupe. He is so different, what with his jet black fur. He really was born to stand out. What a break dancer he is! He must have learned it from the television.' It was a young woman, talking to her friend.

'We seem to have an audience here Mouser.' William was happy to have risked getting wet for his moment of fame. 'I think you've made stars of us all. I mean Mary and I have never done anything like this before.' William turned to his other sister. 'Have you ever done this before Licky?' 'No' I replied with great certainty. I imagined I would never do such a thing again. I just hoped we had not been seen by anybody from Birgu. I would not place us in further peril by even thinking of dancing around those alleyways, or along the harbour side.

'That I am certain was your first time *cat busking*, for your supper.' Mouser explained how human buskers worked for tips and we would now be reaping similar benefits here. The only difference with us was that there was no hat to pass around for tips. 'The reward for our sterling performance will be with us shortly, given I fancy by these early diners who saw us perform. We just play on that with our tails.'

Mouser turned his gaze to a large blackboard clipped to an easel headlined in chalk, 'THE SPECIALS OF THE DAY'.

'I fancy there are many things of interest for us, here today. There is certainly an extensive menu to choose from. Freshly cooked fish shall definitely get taken up by a customer or two at some considerable expense and hopefully a little extra and enough for us four troupers!' Mouser smiled as we moved beneath the table of our new fans, but out of sight and out of mind, to the waiting staff at least. The diners might toss down prawns or salmon pieces, octopus, or even slices of steak or chicken. Everything was possible.

'Well the Seared Fillets of Sea Bass with,' Marys' voiced trailed off.

'With *confit* tomatoes and caper *beurre noisette*,' Mouser helpfully added.

'The fish part sounds very nice.' Mary peered at the other words which made no sense.

'Ah well you see these are French words Mary. People must know a little French to understand menus like these. Otherwise they have to guess and never know what they are ordering.' Mary wondered why it was necessary to mix up English and French but was embarrassed to query this with Mouser.

Mouser had our full attention, which led me to ask the burning question. 'So you have learnt some French Mouser? How did that happen?'

'*Escusez- moi Licky? Moi?*' Mouser was trying to impress me I knew. '*Un petit peu, un petit peu, Madamoiselle.*' Mouser smiled. He was clearly enjoying the admiration and would pause before sharing his secret with us.

'It's very simple really. Over the years I have visited the finest restaurants in Valletta where both languages are used and where fish menus are common. By looking at these menus and listening to people order food, I have picked up enough French to understand what is written and what is spoken.' Mary plucked up the courage to ask why menus would be written in two languages. 'Customers think the food will be better. It is called a touch of class. It may justify higher prices too.'

'So what does confit tomatoes and caper beurre noisette really mean?' Mary enquired.

'I will tell you. Confit means nothing at all as far as I know. Confit means preserved but how can you preserve fresh tomatoes? You can dry them or preserve them in other ways. Put confit in front and charge more! And as for caper beurre noisette you might well ask. Hmm, well that is just capers, the immature flower buds of the caper bush, which grows out here in Malta. It's normally pickled and you would hate it. The beurre noisette, is butter ruined with vinegar or lemon juice. How people can eat the stuff amazes me.' Mouser paused for a moment, still looking up at the blackboard menu. 'Anyway people know cats like fish simply cooked and hopefully they will make some choices with us in mind.' The cooking lesson was over.

We would be in luck today. Our benefactors above were happy to keep us hidden while they secreted tit bits of prawns, chicken from the Paella, fillets of sea bass and

261

even rib eye steak under the low hanging white table cloth. Mouser was tossed a fine piece of his favourite duck breast. Mouser's manners were perfect as he gave us the first choice of all that was on offer. He waited while we ate. There would be plenty to follow – when Mouser could eat his fill. William was the greedy one and Mary told him off. She patted him on his nose and told him lady cats should come first if he wanted the manners of a Mr Mouser!

Beneath the table and hidden from the world by the tablecloth, legs and bags, we were in a seventh heaven. Secure and satiated. Periodically the redundant and clean ashtray placed by our sides was replenished as another helping of perrier water was discretely poured. We could observe all around us. The waiters were racing up and down stairs, taking orders and far too busy to notice us. A bell would ring from downstairs signalling the advent of another order. Time was precious, as dishes were served together with military precision.

The activity above stairs was commandeered by the owner Francesca with eyes of steel, directing operations at all times but still finding the time to talk to her customers. Her imperious English accent added weight to her skills and confidence to her customers. Francesca would always get it right, someone said. Whatever a customer desired, if at all possible, they would have it. Mixing starters together into a main course - extra mushrooms and no tomatoes in the salad please never created the slightest of problems. Nothing was too much trouble for Francesca. She had full command of all situations and complemented every scenario as it arose.

The two young ladies from an adjoining table suddenly left to take a walk. Or so we thought. They had been our co-conspirators throughout our meal. Cutting fish and meat and dropping it below. They left their coffees behind and while they were gone, two glasses of the liquor Averna arrived, served on ice. They went into a place opposite called Marks & Spencer and came out carrying a bag. The first lady was wearing a straw hat over her strawberry blond hair. Very tall and very slim. We thought we could smell fresh prawns but there were none to be seen. We sat up as she peered under the table, as if she had lost something. Mouser twitched his nose and looked uneasy as the lady's head came right up to us. She opened the large white paper bag, with the words Marks & Spencer displayed on its side. Out toppled ten fresh king size prawns. 'There you go my lovely pussies. Help yourselves and keep up the dancing!' She blew four kisses before sitting down to finish her coffee accompanied with the liquor.

We would surely never have such a feast again. Of that I was certain. Mouser was taken aback. This had truly been a lunch fit for royalty. A whole plate of fresh prawns all to ourselves!

We left our below table dining spot shortly after our friends above had bid their own farewells to the Malata, and to the four of us. The remnants of our meal then started to be cleared away. *'Messy eaters those English people'* a waiter muttered as he swept away the debris. We were hiding behind a planter before taking that slow walk up Republic Street. Our tummies were bloated and none of us wanted to play or dance. Simply get back to Seven's bus, safe and sound.

We arrived at the bus terminus and luck was with us. Seven was leaning against his bus – cigarette in hand – urging stragglers to take their seats. He saw us coming and beckoned us to be quick. We raced over as best we could and jumped up onto the dashboard. I heard children talking.' It's those dancing cats' said one. His three companions looked and agreed. They waved at us and we looked back. My worries returned. They might tell people about us. I just hoped they would not be alighting in Birgu.

Mouser had other concerns about William, Mary and me, which concerned the night ahead. I told him I still felt the lamp post was safe enough judging by last night's experiences. There were few options and anyway I wanted to keep watch over the empty berth of my owners. They might return any time now given a fair wind. I needed to be close by with my brother and sister and *even* Mouser, as the welcoming committee.

We left the bus in Birgu and fortunately those children had alighted earlier. Then down to the waterfront where Mouser bid us goodnight. Off to do his nocturnal work in the Museum. As he reached the other side he stopped and looked back. He paused for a moment, and I was certain that he had a tear in his eye. 'Licky, you take care until the morning when I will return as usual. Take care of yourself and your siblings.' He looked sad to be leaving, maybe even tearful. I wanted to cry. Enough of that I thought as I raised a paw of farewell.

I was certain Mouser had become more than a companion by now. I had become the centre of his world. No surprise really as Mouser never had another real friend he could trust. I had fractured his life of loneliness. I found my eyes moistening as I wondered what would become of that friendship, once my owners returned. In my own mind I knew I could never forsake Mouser and his kindness. Something more needed to be done.

'Licky you look upset. What's the matter?' William brought me to my senses.

'Oh it is nothing really. I was just thinking. Will my owners take all of us on board? It seems a lot to ask.' I was thinking out loud and both William and Mary became upset. I think they believed that would happen but now I had put questions in their minds. Questions better left for another day.

'Oh Licky, you won't leave us, will you? Oh please say you won't leave us when your owners return.' Mary was now openly crying and William followed suit.

'Mary and William, come on. Calm down. We shall never be parted again, not in a million years. We shall always be together, forever and ever.' My words, which were completely true, had the desired effect and moments later the tears receded and warm smiles returned to my siblings faces. 'I was thinking more about Mouser, and what happens to him. That is where the real problem lies. How do we keep him with us?'

A puzzled expression loomed on both Mary and William's faces. 'Mouser? Well he is not *family* and besides he has his work at the museum. Is there really a problem?' William's question startled me. It seemed so selfish. However I bit my tongue a little.

'William I am surprised to hear you say that! True, Mouser is not a part of our family in one sense. However he has become such a part over time. Just think of all the good things he has done for us. If it wasn't for him, we would never have been reunited after all these years. We would not all be sitting here together, as one happy family.'

William lowered his eyes to the ground, clearly remorseful for his remark.

'Licky is quite right. We have everything to be grateful for and it is all down to Mouser. Where would we be now without him? Captured and locked up by that dreadful Mr Stick. That's where we would be!' Mary paused for a moment before continuing. 'And there is more to this than meets the eye, if you have not noticed William. Mouser is very attached and protective towards our sister. I think he would do anything in the world for Licky. So he must be included in our future plans.'

William was now nodding in agreement and Mary had got it exactly right. Only time would tell but if you want something badly enough in life, you can make it happen. We would make it happen, one way or the other. If Mouser could deliver the parchment Will onto the returning yacht for our deliverance then maybe his own future with us might be assured. I would make this task my priority.

CHAPTER 25

Margaret suddenly appeared armed with a heavier bag than usual. She felt the weight and passed the bag from hand to hand as she approached. I sensed she had more food than normal. More food than we could possibly eat, given the banquet of the afternoon.

Today she was sporting a bright canary yellow outfit, the skimpy top barely concealing her stomach when she was erect. A sudden movement however would surely cause it to fly up, probably revealing a belly button surrounded by cushions of flesh, struggling to escape. The skimpy yellow shorts held together even though the top button had been stretched beyond its limits. It was gone and only the stout zip and an act of God were holding things together. I had not noticed those varicose veins before, behind her legs and bulging strangely as she walked.

'Well there you are Licky, and you are still with your two friends. Yes well my advance thinking told me that this would be the case, so I have made provision.'

She placed three large plastic bowls on the ground. Then she took out a litre bottle of water and poured it into the empty water bowl. All three of us looked up at her with smiling faces.

'Well you don't seem over impressed. Have you all lost your appetites? Don't tell me someone else has been feeding you! We will have to put a stop to that one. Can't have someone unknown trying to carry favours with you Miss Licky and then claiming the reward when your owners get back. Oh my goodness no, that shall certainly not do!' Margaret let out one of her curdling screeches of laughter as she threw her head backwards.

'The latest news for you Miss Licky is that we had another phone call from your owners this morning. They reckon they will be back midday onwards on Saturday the fourth of July. What do you say to that Miss Licky?'

Margaret took a breath and looked up in the air. 'What day are we now? Oh yes Wednesday. So in three days you will be back on board, all being well. Yes and keep that date in your pretty head. No disappearing now. I just haven't a clue where or what you get up to during the daytime. You are never around when we are.' She looked down in William and Mary's direction. 'Yes and I hope you two are not leading Miss Licky astray. Pretty as you may both look, I bet butter wouldn't melt in your mouth.'

She let out another gale of laughter before calming herself. 'It really is most uncanny. The two of you are the spitting image of Miss Licky. I must take a peek again at your name badges and take a note of the telephone number. I think you must be lost and if that is the case a reward may well be in the offering. I am sure of that. Now I must be off before my fish and chips get cold.' At that very moment a voice shouted out. 'Ma, your fish and chips are getting cold. Hurry up.' She turned towards the yachts. 'I am just coming Tel. See, just what I told you! Oh just a moment, let me tick your lamp post calendar off. Only three days to go after this.' She bent down, put a line through today's date and with that she was off, bouncing along the boardwalk unburdened by heavy bags and bowls, and without a care in the world.

We looked at each other and smiled as she left. What to do with all this food? We looked at each other. A day of plenty upon plenty we all thought. We all burst out laughing. Margaret was suspicious of our appetites. No rush to the bowls. We needed to take care. She needed to diet and maybe she might draw the same conclusion about us. *'Those cats are on a diet Tel,'* with Tel looking at her and saying *'follow their lead my dear. You could lose a few pounds yourself.'* I smiled imagining the scene. However every day would not be the same. I did not want her rationing food. Simply because she felt we were setting her an uncomfortable example!

We settled down to sleep later by our trusty lamp post contemplating the good news. My owners, Eric and Daisy would be back here in Malta on their yacht this very Saturday. I found myself already ticking off the minutes

267

and hours to that event. We would surely all be saved. Sleeping that night was not easy. Maybe too much food, though William and Mary had no problems at all. Purring away and stirring from time to time. Then back into a deep, deep sleep.

I was thinking about what was to happen when they returned, whilst also keeping an eye open for possible trouble. Once sleep finally did take over, it was intermittent and filled with dreams – fuelled by my own uncertainties. Most vividly Mouser was racing across the roadway separating the museum from our lamp post. That Will was firmly between his teeth. He was going far too fast, and flew past us and straight into the water. The parchment left his grasp, to float out into the Grand Harbour. Mouser was screaming. *"Help me Licky, I can't swim."* I woke up in a cold sweat and lay there a while. These dreams were just nightmares.

Daylight was peeping over the horizon, so I knew I would not return to sleep. William and Mary remained sound asleep and looked so peaceful. I arose and stretched myself. All was quiet. I could safely visit the hotel construction site and freshen up. Twenty minutes later when I returned, both Mary and William were awake but wondering what had happened to me.

'Where were you Licky? We thought Mr Stick had taken you!' William and Mary were clearly relieved to see me back.

'I just popped over to the building site to freshen up and carry out my ablutions. You and Mary were sound asleep so I decided not to disturb you.' They thought they would do the same and I showed them where to go, before the workmen started to arrive. On their return they were keen to know what our plans would be for today. I had no immediate plans but no doubt Mouser would have been plotting new adventures for us all, whilst he worked the night shift. I would have been happy to just stay here in relative safety, counting the hours until Eric and Daisy arrived home. My mind continued churning over more important things to worry about, once Eric and Daisy were back on land. Maybe better to put these worries to one side for the day and simply see where Mouser was taking us today.

We did eat everything eventually, forming a very hearty breakfast. I managed to persuade my brother and sister that it would look bad if the food went untouched when Margaret returned. She might stop calling and think we really had lost our appetites. That would never do. We could not guarantee a lavish lunch every day, and there were still two full days to go before my owners returned.

Margaret made her appearance along the boardwalk as usual. She was wearing a full length scarlet red Arabic looking kaftan. I sensed she was trying to hide as much of herself as possible from the world. Maybe she was thinking about a diet! Whatever it was, its flimsy looseness caused it to billow in the light breeze, rising up and down and partially exposing her knees.

She held two bowls, one in each hand, and a plastic bottle of water under her arm. 'There you are my petals and it's going to be another lovely day. I don't know what you three are up to today, but Tel and I are off in the yacht to Gozo. A good enough wind is blowing to let us use some sail.' She was correct if her dress was foretelling how the yacht sails would behave today. She carefully placed the two bowls on the ground and then undid the cap on the water bottle, refreshing our drinking bowl. 'So not long now Licky. Just get today and tomorrow over with and then you shall be home and dry.' She looked down at William and Mary. 'I think your two new friends will miss you. Still they will find a new friend soon enough.' I glanced over at my brother and sister who mirrored each others expression, saddened by what they were hearing.

'I know you cats are like nomads, using your charms. Guile your way into our lives. Wherever I lay may my hat, that's my home. Oh I feel a song coming on and only you three to hear it.' She looked around checking the coast was clear before bursting into song.

Wherever I lay my hat, that's my home
By the look in your eye I can tell you're going to cry

Is it over me?
If it is, save your tears for I'm not worth, you see
For I'm the type of girl who is always on the roam
Wherever I lay my hat that's my home

A pair of hands clapped from a nearby yacht. Margaret looked startled. She turned to face her admirer. An owner was out on deck, mop and bucket to hand. 'That was very nice too Margaret. Bravo.' She twisted her torso feeling the burning sense of an unexpected intrusion. Her face reddened. She saw those hands and that smiling face. She paused and composed herself. She saw Ray, a strong man with a ruddy but happy complexion. Margaret may have wondered how this tall and forceful man had looked as a young man.

'Thank you Roy darling. I just felt a song coming on and couldn't help myself.' Her racing pulse calmed as her face became whiter. She burst out laughing; her way of stamping embarrassment into its proper place. Forcing it back to where it belonged.

'Just keeping the pussy cats entertained Roy! You may be hearing more of my song until Eric and Daisy are back this Saturday. Then my cat rescue days with Miss Licky will be at an end. She seems to have adopted a growing tribe of followers herself. I am feeding them too now. It is a real never ending task!' She was laughing. 'Tel and I are off to Gozo for the day.'

Roy asked if she needed help with food provisions for the *cats*. Margaret thanked him and said no. She talked with Roy of a nuisance. The yacht nearest her had been let out again, to the same noisy youngsters who hired it last year.

'Yes they have it for a whole week, which means the usual partying on board all day and night. Hip Hop music they call it. Nothing we can do.' Margaret made her way down back along to the boardwalk exchanging occasional waves with Ray. There was a spring in her step which may have been brought about by her friendly exchanges with that Roy.

We sat there for a moment, pondering on the words of the song Margaret had just sung for us. It *was* a nice

270

song and the words were happy though not so appropriate for the three of us I sensed. William and Mary would soon be on the roam again if these words meant anything at all. Looking for food and shelter and maybe another permanent home found through *the kindness of new strangers.* I said nothing as I turned the songs words over in my mind. I wondered what William and Mary had made of them. They remained pensive.

'Come on you two, it was only a song and all a bit of fun and I wonder if she was really singing to us. Maybe to Roy and we became a pretence.' My words worked wonders as they came to believe that Margaret was also trying to find a new friend - using her words and song to attract a welcoming visitor to her flailing life, with a new affection perhaps. All remained well with us.

We had just finished breakfast when a surprise visitor headed towards us. Top Cat came trotting under the arch and ran over to where we were seated. He deftly flicked his immaculate quiff with his paw. We all give him that customary bow of our heads.

'Aha so you are here. Thank goodness for that. Mr Stick is prowling around and up to no good I am certain. I just spotted him ten minutes ago with his large net. Trawling for prey around *Triq Gilormy Cassar* and *Triq il Majjistral,* behind the *Café de Brazil,* so I thought I would pop down here to brief and check on your safety.' We were grateful to know we had our own security cat on patrol. We thanked him for his concern.

'So where is old Mouser then?' I explained he would be joining us shortly, the moment the museum opened. 'Oh well I will hang on a bit for his arrival.'

So we sat with Top Cat and filled him in on the latest events and the good news. My owners were returning from their travels, this Saturday. On hearing this, Top Cat gave us all a quizzical look and then addressed me. 'So what will happen then with your brother and sister? They will be back where they started, homeless again.'

'Oh no Top Cat. I will not let that happen. I am going to...' I found myself temporarily lost for words. 'We shall sort that out when it comes to it.' I really couldn't think of anything else to say.

271

'Well you will have to get your thinking cap on. You don't have much time.' Top Cat then titled his head to one side and gave me a long stare.

'But what about Mouser?' he enquired. I nearly found myself replying *so what about Mouser* but managed just in time to stop myself. 'I am also getting my head around that problem.' I really did not sound very convincing.

'Well, I know Mouser has become very fond of you Miss Licky. I have known him a long time and I can vouch that he has always been a loner and has never had a buddy or companion in his life.' Top Cat came to a halt for a fraction of a second. 'A bit like me.' Top Cat looked away. He looked sad. The veneer was peeling. The softer, lonelier side of him was exposed.

'A bit like you Top Cat?'

'A bit like me, never having a true friend in life. No matter. I am Top Cat in Birgu and that makes me the number one. Keeping everything calm, taking no sides. I am rather the judge and the jury which in itself can be a friendless thing to be.' He sighed.

Top Cat looked skywards as swallows flew above. Perhaps he wished sometimes he could fly. He gazed again in my direction. 'Mouser is a good old stick but he is *only* the museum mouse catcher. My duties reach far and wide around Birgu. I have to keep things under control. If things go wrong regarding your owner and their yacht, you just tell Mouser to come and see me. I can always take in a couple of new cats onto my territory. William and Mary would need to learn new tricks but I can teach them. Hide them from the likes of Mr Stick. Set up roadblocks. Make his life impossible with hissing cats leaping down to frighten him away.' He turned towards William and Mary. 'We need to find where you hid that golden bracelet – before someone else finds it. With all the activity in these Birgu streets it is just a matter of time before Mr Stick stumbles on your hiding place. Best to tell me where or take me there so we can get the thing back. Hide it properly.'

William and Mary looked alarmed. I was taken aback by this complete change of tack. Why the sudden interest in that necklace? What was Top Cat up to? However he was right. If everyone was searching for parchment Wills and inheriting cats then golden chains would soon be taken. I decided to change the subject back to Top Cat's earlier piece of thinking.

'That is very thoughtful of you Top Cat. Very sweet of you to think William and Mary could have a safe home with you here. I am determined we shall never be parted again however. They are my family, and families must always stick together.' Top Cat gave me a very thoughtful look.

'Oh well the offer is there. Did you say I was *sweet*? Well I have never been called that before. I rather like that.' His eyes became much wider and he smiled. 'Yes family – family always comes first, if of course it is there. No family for me though as I was abandoned after birth, with no memories even to recall. I say that things you cannot know you cannot miss.' Top Cat looked away. I sensed he had always wanted a family like mine but it was never to be. Perhaps he experienced fleeting moments of a memory lying deep and undisturbed, in his mind.

'Today, I am simply Top Cat. I shaped my life on my own and took my chances.' He stopped for breath. 'It can however be a lonely life.' He sighed again but moments later he was reinvigorated. 'The chain, that golden chain with the two golden cats - we must find the thing before it is too late!'

Would Top Cat simply take the chain and barter it for other things? Should we say nothing? Leave it for another day?

Top Cat would have nothing of it. 'We must seek out the chain! Tonight! It will prove ownership. With the Will safely hidden, the chain will add evidence that the Marchioness intended to leave everything to William and Mary. I must have that chain.' He corrected himself. 'They must have that chain,' he said, with resounding vigour.

I was alarmed by the intensity in his voice. Surely he was not seeking the chain for himself? I looked at William and Mary. A look I hoped that conveyed *say nothing*. I would do the talking. They sensed my look and kept quiet.

'You are right. The chain is important but we must be very careful. It could be a trap. Mr Stick may have found it already and could use it as a bait to ensnare us all.'

Top cat became very quiet. He was reflecting on the perils of the moment. Something else was bothering him. I said nothing to alarm him further. I thought better thoughts. How Top Cat and Mouser had fought to keep us safe, on the quayside and in the streets. I felt great guilt about that chain. Why would he want to steal it from us? Surely a ridiculous thought. Nagging doubts nevertheless remained. Top Cat was much cleverer than us. He could turn tables on anyone. Break his word. He had a much bigger audience to please. Turning a gold chain into great bounty would consolidate his rule in this place, with a guarantee of fresh fish for all Birgu cats.

Top Cat's gaze suddenly moved towards the Museum. He had spotted Mouser leaving as the main doors were being opened. Top Cat excused himself for a moment and walked over to meet Mouser. I reflected briefly on the dreadful separation we had endured these past three years but in our own different ways we had become acquainted with loving people who had taken good care of us. Despite the fragility of the Marchioness, she had kept evil away. On the yacht too, these elements had never endured. Storms and rain kept aloft, as I lived aboard in my own watertight, safe and happy environment. Top Cat and Mouser had never known such luck and we three should be grateful. Then the chain business came back into my thoughts. I felt we three should retrieve it on our own.

I spoke quietly with William and Mary. 'This chain, do you know precisely where you hid it?' William looked at Mary and then whispered. 'In a flower pot, in the alley and I know where that pot is. So does Mary.' I reflected for a moment before Top Cat returned. 'Listen carefully. We need to find that chain tonight, in the early hours when all is quiet. More importantly we say nothing to Mouser or Top Cat. Once we have hidden it here it will be safe. Top Cat is right. Mr Stick or anybody else could find it and claim it as theirs. We need to move fast. Do you agree?' William and Mary looked perplexed but finally agreed this was a good idea. They agreed to say nothing. I would answer any odd questions that might arise and be as evasive as a domestic cat could ever be, without causing offence.

'Oh here comes Mouser and Top Cat.' William looked in their direction as they moved swiftly along the pavement. I think we were all pleased to see Mouser at this point, who would raise our spirits.

'Good morning Mouser. Top Cat has told us about the evil Mr Stick and his meanderings around the streets of Birgu. With that or a new butterfly net. Hopefully he will not come here. He hopefully still thinks William and Mary live in those narrow Birgu streets and I hope that falsehood continues to confuse him. Let's hope he wears himself out going up and down those deep stone steps and finally gives up the search.'

Top Cat agreed. Best keep well away from Birgu. With no more words about golden chains and cats, he left. Hopefully, we could avoid any more questions from anybody. Meanwhile find that chain as proof of a greater entitlement!

We four then sat together for a time below the lamp post, discussing plans for the next few days. Everything rested on Saturday afternoon and the final outcome, for *all* our futures - a very prickly subject with a prickly uncertainty for us all. We needed to kill time and keep safe - until Eric and Daisy made their appearance.

'Well I thought we could pop down to St Thomas bay for lunch. How does that sound?' Without waiting for an answer, Mouser stood up. 'Good idea? We can usually bank on a good lunch down there with plenty of British tourists to cosset. A *lower* end of the tourist budget sector I know but well worth a visit. These people may be a bit poorer but they do not brush us away. When they see me down there, they do make a fuss and throw me bits and pieces. They are probably pining for their own cats back home, wondering how things are going there - probably worrying about their children having rave parties at home while pussy is hiding in a cupboard. Hoping the noise will end.' Mouser paused before continuing. 'Down at St Thomas bay I can tug on their heart strings and that suits me. Today we can put on a real show, with the four of us making a grand appearance!'

So the day was mapped out and yes, we were happy to leave for a place of greater safety. So it was we followed Mouser to the bus terminus. Mouser was uncertain who we might cadge a lift with but Mouser's luck was in. The driver, Seven, was sitting in his bus marked Marsascarla at its front.

'Well there's good news,' Mouser declared. 'He's driving a different route today.' With no hesitation, Mouser marched us up the steps of the bus and gave Seven a big smile.

'Oh Mouser what are you doing. I'm not going to Valletta this morning. I am back and forth on the Marsascarla run today.' Mouser continued to smile and we all followed suit and then leapt onto that gnarled dashboard. 'Oh well, as long as you know, then that's fine by me.' Seven waited a little longer for a few more passengers to board, and then off he set. He grinded the gears of his ancient bus as the engine responded. Churning fumes at the back which obscured his view. No matter. He was going forward. No need to see behind. The bus staggered on until it reached its own momentum. Picking up speed as the engine calmed down. The black fumes subsided for the moment at least. We skirted pretty roundabouts, newly planted with flowers of every colour. Not a wheel touched the borders and we could relax our grip. Cultivated fields of potatoes and vines passed us by. Vine leaves glistening in the sun, as they captured the energy as the nutrients of the red earth below entered their stems, fuelled by irrigation sprays that soothed the heat and saturated the land. We arrived some thirty minutes later in Marsascarla.

We followed Mouser from the bus stop and onto the pavement next to the sea. A host of small colourful lutzu boats lay at anchor bobbing up and down, whilst spraying the sea with reflected colours from their sides. Reds, greens and blues, mingled with sea spray and the natural hue of this watery azure. The odd textures encouraged tourists to reach for their cameras and capture what they were seeing. "*You don't see colours like that in Grimsby. Even on a fair summer's day.*" the lady said. No one demurred.

On the other side of the road small restaurants nestled together, some were serving breakfast, others only just preparing to open a little later for the lunch time trade.

'Now you understand this is not St Thomas' Bay. That is about a good ten minute walk up the hill. I thought you might like to see Marsascarla first. We do not want to get to St Thomas Bay too early. The Beach side restaurant does not start serving food until around eleven o'clock. Many people staying in the hotel next door have eaten breakfast so no need to offer more food to them before lunchtime.'

Mouser then led us on a slow walk around the harbour. Nothing much seemed to be happening. A few lutzu boat owners could be seen doing small odd jobs on their boats. Unravelling nets; polishing paddles and repainting the eye of Osiris. It appeared to be a sleepy village where people did what they always had to do - never too much, never too strenuous but enough to hold things together.

Mouser pointed to a couple of bars and discos in a side road, all closed and uninviting. 'That's for the younger crowd who come out at night. Friday and Saturday nights are always busy along here. The youngsters come from around here and Zejtun and thereabouts. It's *Ibiza* for those without *deep* pockets but becoming more popular so I have heard.'

'What are these places?' I asked. Mouser went on to tell us of Paceville. He explained it was the heart and soul of nightlife in Malta, in a place next to St Juliens, a long way away. It came alive at night with dozens of bars and discos catering for young people, Maltese, tourists and students from faraway places. He described the chaos of streets packed with revellers, going from one venue to another. Becoming more confused as the night wore on and drinking and smoking strange things. The more they fell over the more they laughed. Mouser could not explain why these things happened. All he would say was he had seen it and it was all true. I wondered whether he

277

was making up the story as I had never seen people walking, falling over and then laughing. They normally cried out in pain! Not the moment to ask further questions I thought.

'I visited Paceville years ago, before I became the Museum night cat. In those days I could escape into the night with ease, until that injury to the tourist. I had the nights to myself. So I could visit many places and see things differently as the moon shone down.'

'Did you go out alone Mouser to far distant places where people acted strangely? How far did you travel?' Mary looked genuinely curious.

'Ten kilometres from here I reckon.' Mouser paused for reflection before continuing. 'And yes, always on my own. Not my choice but then I really had no choice in the matter.' A deep furrow appeared on his furry brow. 'I was friendless.' His frown partially evaporated as he sought to make light of the matter. 'Mind you, if I had known you three, all three of you would have been welcome to accompany me.' The furrow on his brow reappeared. 'But I didn't know you then, mores the pity.' Mouser suddenly forced a smile. 'Anyway let us just regard that as spilt milk and water under the bridge. I do know you now and that is all that matters. Mind you thinking back, Paceville would not have been for you, with all those staggering feet in crowded streets, and occasional moments of aggression. After my second visit there and seeing the dangers and with little food ever offered, I vowed not to return. A place fuelled by young party people hell bent on having a good time, some even passing out and sleeping on benches. No, not a place for the likes of you or I and I will not take you there. Do not ever ask me to.'

Mouser became more upbeat as he led us side by side to the brow of the hill, along the road abutting the sea. To our right, lay substantial modern villas, all facing towards the sea. Everything seemed so quiet and still. We had left behind any sight of shops, bars or restaurants. We said little, simply enjoying each other's company, the sea on our left and lovely villas to our right, which we *could* have made our homes. I thought a little about

Saturday and what we needed to do to make the yacht our home, together, with the flat overlooking Kalkara. Mixing and matching twixt the two. Demons plagued my thoughts but there was a way. I would hone and sharpen it. That Will accompanied and complimented by the gold chain, could and should make all the difference!

So, William, Mary and Mouser would not be cast aside and I would find safe harbour for us all. If that proved impossible, then I would have to abandon my home and stay on shore with William and Mary. Togetherness was the only option and that we would achieve. I needed to outline my plans with Mouser later on but for this day I would say no more. Not cause any trouble or alarm as there was no reason to ruin the happiness of the hours to come with my own worrying thoughts.

'Well we are nearly there.' Mouser pointed his left paw towards a small sandy beach below. Twenty or so people were enjoying themselves and the numbers were growing with families carrying umbrellas, towels and large boxes, housing the food and drink for the day. Small stools too. Young children were running in and out of the water, under the watchful gaze of their parents. A child ran in laughing, with water wings strapped to his arms. He was running too fast and too far in. His father jumped to his feet and raced into the sea. He picked up the boy and twirled him around. No arguments, no shouting but just smiles. Later he would no doubt try to explain to his son that he must be careful in the water. Now was not the time. They played in the water and then returned onto the beach to drink chilled drinks and pat cream over their reddening bodies.

'Ooh just look at that William. We've never seen a beach before let alone sand. What a lovely sight to see all that lovely golden sand. Have you seen a beach and sand before Licky?' Mary seemed quite beside herself, with this new adventure. 'Mouser, can we go down there and walk on the sand?'

Mouser remained untouched by what he was seeing. I had seen many beaches around the shores of Europe on my travels in the yacht. I was not too impressed but of course I was not here to depress. I had to admit that I had never actually walked on a beach. That sand would surely make my paws sore and my coat matted. Still, if we had to go there we most certainly would.

'Of course you can go down on the beach but you will want to keep an eye on that pesky little poodle dog down there, running in and out of the water. If you really want to go down there, I must be with you to keep that dog away. He could get very excited at the sight of a couple of cats and chase you into the sea - a dangerous place for cats. Personally I do not care for the water and the sand makes trouble only a shower can cure.' After hearing Mouser's opinion, we agreed it might be safer to view the scene from afar. Mouser led us down off the pavement to steps that led down to a beach café set in concrete. Plastic chairs and tables, all supporting umbrellas, made an agreeable sight. We could stay there and well away from that abrasive sand.

'We can rest under this bench, away from the other visitors. No problems with moving later but I doubt we will be disturbed here as it is rarely used. In the sun, but the bench will protect us. We can rest and take in the sights below. Watch families enjoying a day out on the beach. Later, with luck, those families will want to share their good fortune with us. Time then to move about as food is being served.' Mouser had everything organised and I was content. A light breeze made things very agreeable as we sat underneath the bench. All was well.

We stayed watching the beach people play and laugh for an hour or so. Suddenly Mouser looked towards the causeway in front of the restaurant. 'We are in luck today.'

A large convertible light blue limousine had pulled up and two angular men emerged.

'Oh this is good news.' Mouser exclaimed. 'Giving me oddments, bits of fish. I do not know whether they would have enough for the four of us but it is a good start. I will wander over shortly so they know I am here.'

Mouser told us these benefactors were British and often drove here for a relaxing afternoon. Away from other beaches and lidos that attracted far too many people. They liked their privacy. They were always together. A little like Mouser and Top Cat. One of them liked to dust down the windscreen and shave off bird droppings from the paintwork, keep the car looking pristine. It was worth a lot of money and these small touches made them feel happy. After all, it was their status symbol.

'These two have no family as far as I can tell. A bit like me.' He paused. 'However they seem happy enough, watching other families down here having fun. I have heard some people say they may be gay'. William and Mary were keen to know more.

'What does "gay" mean?' asked William. I needed no explanation as my owners had a number of pleasant *gay* friends who would stay on the yacht. Cuddle me and make me feel happy. They never brought young children on board to pull me about. Twist my ears. Pull my tail. I liked them for what they were, cat lovers. Mouser for reasons of his own I can only imagine, ignored William's question.

'We can stay here a bit and let them get settled. They won't be ordering any food yet. They usually like to order a Cisk lager before ordering food. Then the owner will pop over and chat. Maybe take an order for food. If they see cats around they always order fish which means we need to be roaming around their table. After the lager glasses are presented.' Mouser stretched himself with an arching of his back and then resumed his sitting position.

Mouser's prediction was true. Two lagers arrived and some banter took place between these patrons and Bruce the owner. More people started to arrive and occupy tables. Maltese intermingling with mainly English tourists, though a little German and French could be heard. 'Time for us to reposition our good selves,' said Mouser.

A man in his early sixties approached the two males with the fancy car. He was reminding them who he was. He had been the Commissionaire at the British High Commission in Taxbiex, until he retired. A sensible moment for the four of us to approach the table and make friends I thought. Mouser saw the opportunity and led us over. We sat a yard or two away from their table,

281

thereby not being too intrusive but nevertheless hoping to be spotted once their conversation came to an end.

The former Commissioner spoke about very recent times. The tale was saddening by the moment. He had lost his wife after thirty years marriage, to cancer. Two weeks ago. She had been Maltese and he had met her as a British tourist. They had fallen in love. Now he was all alone learning how to cope. Learning new skills such as how to use an electric hoover, fill the steam iron with water, iron shirts and clean and wash around the household generally. He had now even mastered operating an ATM machine using a plastic card. Pressing keyboards with the same numbers his wife used to use. Each touch brought back memories of happier times when he would go to work. She meanwhile was keeping the house and the money in fine order. That was then.

Today was the first day since the funeral he had left the apartment. He had spent this time of mourning, learning to operate the washing machine, micro wave and dishwasher. He said he had always thought he would go first to his maker, if it was not for the pacemaker. Now he had to be positive, embracing new learnt skills, but never being able to forget his past happiness that had been cruelly taken. He was offered a drink but declined – better to leave. Tears were welling up and he would compose himself elsewhere. He bid his farewells and slowly made his way up the pathway and onto the promenade.

I felt saddened by the sight of this broken man, although at the same time encouraged, determined we four would stay together, in harmony with the yacht and the flat and with Eric and Daisy in command of us all. I would attend to the Will. Mouser would secrete that out of the Museum before the yacht berthed. Top Cat would deliver the golden chain onto the yacht, after Mouser had presented the Will. We three would retrieve that golden chain and hide it for this reunion. Maybe the Will mentioned that very chain. After all I had only quickly scanned the Will. The sight of it, coupled with the Will and possibly even mentioned in the Will, might sway Eric and Daisy to adopt us all as a *package deal*, or maybe not.

Never mind it had to be found and this very night. Be hidden away from Mr Stick who might use it for his own hidden purposes.

William and Mary stayed quiet, looking twixt the table and the sea, embracing the activities below on the beach. Several people had looked in our direction and pointed us out to their friends. We were an odd sight, sitting in a row, taking the sea air and admiring the view. Three white and ginger cats with that jet black cat.

'Ah the wafting smell of beautiful cooked bacon.' Mouser turned his back to the beach to face the dining table and several others close by. We made an immediate turn in perfect unison. 'I fancy a good old English breakfast is in order for everyone.'

Two ladies with two children had opted for this fare. 'Jason these are full breakfasts!' said the lady. 'Why order so much?' Her friend looked shocked at the huge pile of food on her plate. 'Much too much for me' she said. No good for my diet.' The children saw no harm in it. We saw opportunities lying beneath this table and were under it in a trice. We would not be disappointed.

We sat together under the table. Not too close to bruising feet, but close enough to be noticed. Our manners were impeccable. The two children, the older boy and his younger sister started to drop tit bits of bacon to the floor. The two ladies appeared at first to take no notice. However that soon changed in our favour and all for the better. They started to exchange encouraging cat loving comments to their children. 'Oh how sweet they are. Let them have what they want.' This lady wanted everything passed asunder. She pecked at her platter, determined not to succumb to temptation and keep those calories down. Nibbling on Maltese bread was all she wanted, graced with a little Balsamico oil.

My sister and brother moved towards this falling grace from heaven. Gulping it down as fast as it would fall. Those pieces of sausages were devoured in moments. I joined in the fray but it was a calmer affair. Enough here for all as the bacon rained down.

'William and Mary don't be too greedy.' I turned my head back to where Mouser was sitting. 'Come on

Mouser, it is your turn.' Mouser raised himself up and cautiously came over to join us again. He looked up at these four generous tourists and helped himself to a generous piece of bacon. The young boy and girl were now taking it in turns to stroke William, Mary and myself. All three of us were enjoying the physical contact immensely. Tickles behind each ear, strokes under each chin coupled with loving strokes of our fur from head to tail.

We responded as domesticated cats should do, purring all the time which in turn encouraged even more food to appear on the floor which also included buttered toast that we could lick. The generosity slowed and we realised their plates were now almost empty. Mouser had disappeared.

'Right that's enough now I think. Let's go back and join Mouser.' We all looked up at our kind hosts, and then retreated back to where a very observant, calm and sedate Mouser was now lying, under the table of the two English men.

'Mouser, you look quite distant. What are you thinking about?' I was asking too much I knew. I had betrayed my ambition to have a trouble free day by leaving difficult questions for later. Mouser said nothing for several moments. He was troubled by my enquiry. He looked at us all, slowly shifting his head. A frown on his forehead spoke volumes of speech. He fixed his gaze on me. Then all of a sudden the frown vanished and a half smile obliterated the worrying frown from his brow.

'Oh I was just thinking about ...... 'He came to a sudden halt as quickly as he continued. 'Oh just about how nice it was seeing you and your brother and sister enjoying life in general.' He paused for a moment. The frown flickered back briefly but disappeared, returning as a smile. 'I am glad you are enjoying this place. I thought you would like it.' Mouser curled down on the floor and to all intent and purposes appeared to return to his own private thoughts. We three followed his example.

I would have to have *that* private chat with Mouser very soon. Not today I decided, but maybe tomorrow and if not tomorrow, then certainly on Saturday morning.

That would be my last chance, as my owners were scheduled to return sometime later that day. I was lost in thought. It was just such a tricky subject. Anyway I could not do much until we had found the gold chain. That was the key to the door that Top Cat might well open. Climb through it and be on board. I knew in my heart that I had to steel myself and get these things settled.

I would have to recover that chain this very evening. Take William and Mary up to Birgu. There they could recover the golden cats and we could hide them. I would need to stay alert. Listen to the clock chiming twice. Then wake them up and announce our sudden expedition. Say nothing now. Keep this secret. Show nothing to imperil memories of this happy day.

CHAPTER 26

We returned to the Marina as the church clock chimed three times. We were safely back but from the safety of St Thomas Bay. Another night of worry lay ahead for me though William and Mary seemed happy enough. Jumping and skipping in tune with those bells. Mouser had been right about those two English men. One had ordered scampi and chips and the other battered cod and chips. Their appetites were sorely challenged by the food piles delivered on two plates, so much so that the bulk of the fish ended up below the table. It did not lie there for very long. They ordered a second bottle of Marsovin wine, seasoned with the Girgentina grape which is only found growing in these Islands. Sipping this blended wine stimulated greater generosity. Looking down at us feeding discretely below, they suddenly ordered another plate of scampi, with no chips or salad. 'It's for the cats,' he informed the waitress, who looked somewhat startled. 'Cats dislike chips and salad and we have eaten quite enough!'

She smiled when she learned these English people were on strict diets. 'No room for chocolate cake and ice cream before his gall bladder operation,' advised one. She demurred. Her father had to avoid eggs, cheese and rich chocolate before his operation. 'Six weeks it was. Mind you he did lose a lot of weight and after the surgery he kept away from pastizzis and other fatty, greasy foods. Good luck to you. My father has never been fitter!' she added, though the singular tear could not be hidden. She brushed that aside and walked away, whilst probably thanking God he was alive after surviving the searing pains that kept him awake – before he was told to change his own diet.

A whole plate of scampi arrived and the waitress laid it at their feet. They smiled, appreciating she understood the fish was really for us. So she would wait on us too.

Later she would receive a generous tip and the memory would linger. No more shooing away of cats that might bring good fortune to her tables. The kind waitress returned with a bowl of icy cold water. 'To wash down your fish supper,' she whispered. The kindness of strangers is never to be underestimated in the world of cats. *Kindness* keeps us alive, happy, fit and healthy. God bless them all, I thought. But not that *Mr Stick*! That reminded me of my plan for the night. When Mouser would be on museum duty and Top Cat was asleep. Once we three were together I would share everything with William and Mary. Awake them from their dreams and rescue the golden cats from their pot.

By now we were settled beneath the lamp post on the quayside. Mouser started to muse on what we might all do tomorrow. His thoughts seemed to drift as if his heart was not in it. 'Yes, well it's your last day tomorrow.' He said this slowly and with some trepidation. 'Come Saturday morning I can say that you will all be here, waiting for your ship to come in Licky.' I felt he really wanted to say - *without me*. I sensed terrible anguish and worry. Mouser was no past master when it came to disguising the undercurrents, remorse and pathos he might be going through. It reinforced my need to do something but to say absolutely nothing, until those final moments arrived. My plan would work but it could not all be shared with Mouser. He might resist. Timing was everything. Saturday would be the spur. In a second, thought would not count. In a flash it would be all for one, with no time for doubt. Action alone would finally challenge all these uncertainties.

I had to set the scene at least. 'Mouser, you are wrong. We will all be here. Even Top Cat if he chooses. You Mouser have a place in all of our hearts. We cannot abandon you and we have no intention of doing so. Never imagine otherwise.'

Mouser looked at me with his eyes wide open. I had surprised myself by sounding so forceful. I had to be assertive now for things to work for the common good. Any feelings of sadness should things go awry, I put aside.

287

'Thank you Licky. Thank you very much. Those words have brought music to my ears.' Mouser's eyes squinted as he said this, and then he looked at all three of us. 'Well *we* shall all have our work cut out for us come Saturday. For a start, I shall need to make sure that I bring the old lady's Will out of the museum that day. We've got to make sure your owners have possession of that as early as possible.' Mouser looked at William and Mary and gave them a big wink. 'That shall be your passport to a new life.'

Mouser sounded upbeat though I felt sure part of this was mere bravado. 'Mouser, you must take that Will on board. You must make sure as you race up the gangplank that it is handed to Eric. He is the one we must impress. Daisy would likely put it away for another day.' A part of my plan was now exposed but it was the simpler part. Something Mouser could fathom I hoped. Mouser thought and then agreed.

'Yes I can do that. All we need to do is hide the Will between the time I leave the Museum and the yacht arrives. Not difficult. I have a place in the building site next door, which shall certainly be safe enough for a few hours. There is no work and therefore no workmen on weekends.'

I looked at Mouser, and all I could see was a true friend. Someone who had shown me nothing but kindness, from the moment I had met him, forgetting entirely that hair-raising moment with me and that mouse hiding in the fabric of a museum curtain.

It was shortly before five o'clock, when Margaret and Terry appeared along the quayside, shopping bags in hand. 'See Tel, Miss Licky now has assembled a family of her own. She is never apart from these three other cats.' Terry looked down at all four of us. 'That's true Ma. I cannot argue with that. It's the Blackie's presence that I can't quite get my head round. He doesn't seem to fit in. No matter. Still – four cats now. Who would ever take four cats on board a yacht? I sense sad times ahead for all of them.'

Mouser turned his head slightly away ignoring Terry's observation. Probably true he felt. Time alone would tell.

'Oh Tel, get your mobile out.' She plonked her shopping down by her feet. 'I will try and see the telephone number and you call the owner of these two cats. Maybe they can be collected and that would solve a big part of the problem. With that, she stooped down directly in front of William and Mary, pulling a pair of glasses from her bag in order to better read the engravings.

Margaret started to stroke Mary taking care not to confuse or frighten her. She pulled gently at the brass tag and turned it over.

'Yes here it is Tel.' Reading out aloud the eight numbers in his direction, Terry punched them one by one into his mobile. She moved over to William and checked out his collar tag. 'Oh Tel, it's the same number. Tell the owner we have got their William and Mary down here at the Vittoriosa quayside. Don't forget to ask if there is a reward for having found them.'

'Yes well I would Ma, if I could get through. The line is dead. It's out of service I think. It must have been cut off. I will try again later though I think this is hopeless.' Terry snapped the phone shut and put it back into the top pocket of his shirt.

'Oh well that is that, Tel. A fine time to have a phone cut off. The owner goes to all the trouble of giving them name tags and a phone number. Now they are lost and the phone has gone dead!' Margaret was now standing up and looking down at us all. 'Well William and Mary, I guess you are truly lost.' With that she laughed in her own emotional way, her head thrown back and then forward as she picked up her shopping. 'Come on Tel, let's get all this indoors.' She looked at all four of us and then finally at me. 'Right then, I shall be back with your supper shortly.'

They headed back to their yacht, leaving their shoes at the top of the gangplank, ensuring the yacht floor surfaces remained clean. They would then no doubt grapple with their awful dog and give it many undeserved cuddles.

Mouser broke the silence, talking to no one in particular and starring forward at the departed couple. 'Well *we* all know why the phone has been cut off.'

'Oh Mouser, please don't say that.' Mary sounded so timid. 'Please don't remind us.'

Mouser gave a slight wince. 'Oh I didn't mean anything Mary. Now don't go upsetting yourself. These name tags may well prove useful themselves in times to come.' Oh dear. Mouser was on edge now. 'If you are taken on board the yacht I expect new tags will be made with a new telephone number that all three of you will share.' No mention of a fourth tag for Mouser. Nor would I say much more about that - not for now.

'No point in putting carts before horses. We've got some way to go before anyone gets new tags with new numbers. William and Mary have got to get themselves adopted on board the yacht. Well before.... ' I stopped there and it was as well that I did. I was not certain what next I might say.

'Indeed and quite right. Talking about carts and horses, that has given me an idea for tomorrow's outing. Yes, not a bad idea at all if you ask me.' Mouser would be no more candid. It was getting perilously close to the museum locking up time. 'I must love and leave you all and see you in the morning.' With that, Mouser gave me a gentle tap with his paw, smiled at William and Mary, and trotted over to the museum. As always, he stopped on the other side of the road. He turned to give us a last reassuring look, and then disappeared from sight.

CHAPTER 27

At last I could tell William and Mary of the plan ahead. I would keep guard this night until the clock chimed twice. Then we would move carefully into Birgu and find the gold chain in the pot, returning here to hide it in the building site. William asked why we were doing this. I explained we needed more proof of who they were. The Will, their name tags and an almost certainly valuable gold chain with two gold cats attached all gave extra credence to their pedigree. I also suggested Top Cat could be the one to present the chain to Eric on the yacht, immediately after Mouser raced over with the Will. In this way, both Mouser and Top Cat would be seen in a good light. Not be shooed away in future. Maybe invited to stay with us all.

Mary looked worried by my plan. 'What if they take the chain and do nothing with the Will?' she asked. I felt this highly unlikely but I could say nothing certain to reassure her. We could only offer prayers to St Francis of Assis that things might work out well for all of us. Not a word to anyone else must be said.

Margaret appeared at her scheduled time with a large bowl of food and a bottle of water. She was looking very tired and kept rubbing her eyes whilst yawning as she passed the food down to us.

'What an afternoon! No siesta for me today. The party people from last year arrived late this morning and have been singing and dancing ever since with that wretched music blaring and getting ever louder as the day wore on. Tel had a word but they just turned the music up I think. There is no point calling the police and we have five days more of this I fear. We may be camping out with you three tonight! At least I can barely hear the noise from here.' She looked pensive. A smile came back to her face and she left.

I realised having Margaret and Terry as our bedfellows might disturb our plan for the night but not surprisingly, they did stay on board the yacht. I dozed lightly and as the night wore on, the noise from the noisy yacht grew ever louder. Suddenly it stopped, just as the clock chimed twice. I woke William and Mary and said we should go. The coast was finally clear and better to get away and back while things were quiet.

We made our way into Birgu and followed William to the potted plant which we hoped had remained undisturbed. He jumped up as Mary and I kept guard. All was quiet. No people and no cats to be seen. Lamps were glowing in the dark which did not help our efforts to stay hidden. However, they made the recovery effort easier, as William scratched into the earth. Seconds later he had the chain in his mouth. He brushed away dirt from the two golden cats and leapt down. Mary said she could throw it around his neck but no. He could hold it in his mouth for the short journey back. Suddenly the lights were extinguished. All was in darkness. The lights were obviously on some council time device to save energy. We remained unseen and used the moment to escape this alley and return to our lamp post. No lights anywhere. Even our own lamp post was in darkness. Only the moon gave us direction as we crossed to the building site. A cracked pot had lain idle behind the entrance and this would be our new hiding place. I pointed this out to William, who jumped into it and dug a very deep hole. Earth scattered around us as he laid the chain in the hole. Then using his back paws he filled the hole in. Mary and I brushed away any fallen earth to hide every scrap of evidence from our visit. Then we returned to our lamp post. We could sleep again and no further noise was coming from that yacht. It would remain quiet until Margaret appeared in the morning.

The bells awakened me as Margaret appeared with our breakfast. 'Oh thank God we had a quiet night! We thought of coming over here to get away from those drunks fuelled by alcohol. Still they did stop fairly early. A pity that hotel is not open yet. We might have to move away if it gets any worse. Or stay with Eric and Daisy in their flat, although that would probably not be to their liking. Thank God they return tomorrow when you, Miss Licky, will be back in your own home, or with us all in that flat!' She was about to leave when she suddenly turned back.

'Now do you know what I haven't done for some time? I have bought a marker pen with me.' Margaret then bent down next to the lamp post and crossed out earlier days on the calendar sheet attached to the post. 'Well that leaves one day to go. See Miss Licky, tomorrow this piece of paper will be redundant. After of course I have shown it to Eric and Daisy so they know how thoughtful I have been to your interests.'

With that she turned and retraced her steps back to her yacht, muttering something under her breath about disruptive drunken tourists giving tourists a bad name. "No sense of dress! No sense of shame."

Shortly afterwards Top Cat gave us a surprise visit. We found ourselves giving him the proper salute with our right paws. He asked how we were and how the past day and night had gone. 'We all had a quiet and peaceful night,' I lied.

Top Cat had just seen Mr Stick again. He was prowling the familiar alleys of Birgu again with that large butterfly net in hand. 'He will tire of his exploits soon enough and give up I am sure. However, he seems determined to keep searching so you three must remain very careful.' Top Cat said he would stay with us until Mouser made his appearance in the minutes ahead.

Mouser walked leisurely across the road and seemed genuinely pleased to see Top Cat, giving him a full salute and Top Cat brushed his own snazzy full quiff of hair with his paw. I thanked Top Cat for all of his help and then he had a quiet word with Mouser.

'I have been doing quite a bit of thinking lately. I am not getting any younger Mouser and I need someone else I can trust, to keep these alleyways safe and secure.' Mouser listened intently. 'Yes I think you should become my *First* lieutenant. You can patrol this Marina of course but keep a watch on Birgu - when I need extra help. Some younger cats are already challenging me, though so far so good. A quick pat with my paw keeps them in line. However with you behind me, my job would become easier. We can share the spoils and help keep the peace. Otherwise everything could fall apart and that would spell trouble. Council officials could start appearing from the Pest Control division to curb our numbers and control the behaviour of some cats that have started to turn bad. Humans may be kind but they can be very mean if they sense nuisances in life. Anyway I could do with some company as I tour Birgu. What do you say to that Mouser?

'Well what can I say Top Cat. This is indeed an honour and quite unexpected. I am lost for words.'

'Oh think nothing of it. I know how responsible you can be and you have shown extreme kindness and care towards Miss Licky and her family which I might add has been above the call of duty. The combination of good sense and kindness will prove vital as we keep the peace and stop cat wars in their tracks. We could do with more souls like you in this world and surely we shall find them and nurture them. If you agree then you shall be my First lieutenant from this very day! Start work tomorrow as I know you four have plans for today which must be respected.'

Top Cat brushed his quiff in Mouser' direction and bowed his head. Mouser bowed in response and the union was settled. 'Less you think I have forgotten something, bear with me. We might be invited to join Miss Licky, William and Mary on board the yacht and become domesticated cats. In that case, even more vital we find other cats now who could take over from us, though time may be short.' Top Cat took a deep breath. 'I doubt this adoption would happen but *should* something so extraordinary occur, we need to be prepared. Decide whether to stay or go.' Top Cat looked at all three of us, gave a slight yawn and then stood up. 'I had better be getting back to Birgu Square to start scouting for new talent to help us. You're expecting the arrival of the yacht sometime tomorrow. I should like to be near when it happens and see for myself how things are taking shape and indeed be a witness to this happy event.' With that, Top Cat was gone in a trice, no doubt on his evangelical mission.

Mouser seemed in a trance as he saw Top Cat flee the scene at break neck speed, racing under the arch leading out of the Marina and out of view.

'Well that was quite a speech.' I said. My brother and sister sat in awe of all they had heard. They looked at Mouser with a new reverence. He had been raised up in their estimation and his promotion was surely well deserved. Maybe just maybe they could all stay together as part of the wider happy family, sharing new adventures on land and sea, but only time would tell.

'Yes this was all out of the blue, I must admit. Nevertheless it has made me feel much happier. I may have underestimated Top Cat's opinion of me as he holds me in greater esteem than I might ever have guessed.' Mouser looked at us and gave a wide grin. 'So plans for today. I thought we might take a visit to the village of Kalkara. It is a short walk away and I know an old man who takes his pony and trap out along the Kalkara sea front. He really likes cats, and sometimes I hitch a ride. Maybe he could cram all four of us aboard. So what do you say? Fancy a local trip, nothing too far. I feel we should be back reasonably early, in case there is any further news from your owners Licky about their progress back to Malta. Besides Top Cat may need some help later on and I suspect he will be back looking for us later this afternoon.'

It was agreed and the four of us set off along the quayside towards Fort St Angelo. Mouser chose the route carefully, avoiding the more obvious choice, via Birgu Square. 'We don't want to risk any further encounters with that Mr Stick. We shall use the steel steps between the new block of flats next to Fort St Angelo which take us into the secret alleys at the back part of Birgu.' Mouser continued to lead the way, and some ten minutes later we were filing down wide and shallow ancient stone steps cut through fifteen feet thick fortress walls. Mouser pointed out the shallow depth from one step to the next. 'These steps were made hundreds of years ago to help heavily clad soldiers pass rapidly from place to place. The soldiers wore heavy armour, so their ascent or decent was made easier for them to manage with these extra wide steps.' Where Mouser had acquired such knowledge, none of us really knew but the Museum was a likely source. We just felt so comfortable being in the company of someone who seemed to know everything about the past and the present and even sometimes a bit of the future.

Our walk took us along Kalkara Creek, with a view across the bay to the Bighi Hospital. We walked through a boat yard as a crane whined above us, teasing a small craft upwards, then around until it came to rest on blocks of wood. Its bottom encrusted with shells where the paint had badly flaked. We passed cans of liquid which would in time protect this hulk once the scraping and sanding had been done. Men were steadying the boat and pushing tapered wood around these blocks so it would stand upright and firm against gale and wind. We moved onwards until we reached the village of Kalkara. A silvery dome sparkled in the sunlight and we walked slowly towards it.

'Now not much goes on around here, as it remains a sleepy old village, with a few bars and band clubs. However it is a lovely quiet residential and historic small town within the Grand Harbour.' Mouser continued to fill us in on points of interest as we went. The Kalkara Chapel set in the midst of the village and facing directly out towards the Grand Harbour was central to the town. Mouser made us sit down on the steps of the church and take in the views.

'I have to say, I find this place very peaceful. Not I fear a place for a guaranteed lunch. No restaurants to speak of where tourists might rest and throw morsels at us. Hopefully you have all had a good breakfast.' Mouser took a brief pause before announcing that he himself had eaten well that morning. His tally of mice deposited behind the reception desk had improved that night. A large piece of fish, placed on a large chipped cream coloured plate had been his reward for a job well done. He smacked his lips at the memory and I hoped he would not dwell on the detail of chase and kill.

The clip clop of a horse' hooves could be heard in the distance. All four of us turned and looked around. 'There you are! Didn't I tell you so? That's the cat lover and his carriage. We'll try to hitch a ride.' Mouser was appeared extremely pleased with himself, as he urged us to get up and cross over the road to the seaside pavement.

A four wheeled carriage came into view, drawn by a splendid looking and well cared for dapple grey horse. 'Are you sure he will stop and give us a ride Mouser?' I could not disguise the incredulity in my voice.

'Yes of course he will. Now all three of you raise your right paw and do what I am doing.' With that Mouser raised his right paw, stuck it out in the air as far as it would go, and commenced waving it from left to right. All three of us copied his strange ritual. 'We are hitch hiking,' Mouser informed us. Sure enough our performance halted the passage of this transport.

'Easy there. Steady up.' The old man, wearing a cloth cap and clothes from decades past, reined in the horse. 'Well if it isn't old museum Mouser. And you've bought along some friends with you. Come on then, hop on board for a bit. I'm taking Trigger up to the small sandy beach in Rinella Bay.' The horse' ears pricked up on hearing his name. 'Going to give him a nice dip in the sea and cool him down.'

'Here we go then, follow me.' With not another word, Mouser leapt up onto the black, fully lined folded hood at the rear and he beckoned us up. We followed in quick succession. The old boy gave a slight twitch of the reins, and Trigger moved off into a trot, rolling his head – thinking no doubt about those cool waters and the treat that was to come.

'So what do you think, a good idea of mine or not?' Mouser looked as pleased as punch as he had the right to be. Who could have believed that all four of us would be riding in such style? The carriage itself was beautifully maintained, sprayed in royal blue with shining solid brass lamps and lamp holders, a whip holder and other brass furniture. The seats were fully upholstered, front and rear and the carriage floor boasted a fully fitted carpet in light blue.

'I think you have some marvellous ideas Mouser. I'm so glad Licky found the likes of you.' William's words echoed all our sentiments. As we sat perched regally on the back of the carriage we clearly became a sight for sore eyes with the locals of Kalkara. Some people stopped and stared. Others waved at the driver and shouted *Bon jour*.

A bit of a climb for the horse it may have been, but he appeared to handle it with ease. We reached the brow of a hill and then raced downwards. Moments later we arrived at a small deserted sandy beach, Rinella Bay. We came to a halt and the old man told us it was time for Trigger to have his promised dip in the sea. Trigger reared up ever so slightly and nodded his head again, knowing full well the heat of the day would be expunged by those cool and blue waters he loved so much. 'Up to you what you and your friends want to do now. Hang around and get a lift back in say half an hour. The choice is yours.' With that he started to uncouple the cart from the horse.

'What do you say Licky? Shall we just stay put and take in the view?' Mouser turned his attention to William. 'What about you and Mary?'

'Oh I would rather like to try walking on these deserted sands.' Mary's idea met with instant approval from her brother, and I suggested they both go and try out this new experience for themselves. I needed a moment alone with Mouser.

'A good idea for you both of you and meanwhile Mouser and I shall stay put right here on the carriage. You go ahead and enjoy yourselves, but keep clear of the water's edge and remember to be back here in time for our lift home. We will keep watch from here.'

I intended to use the moment for a private word or two. Mouser showed no suspicions of my intentions and so William and Mary hopped off the carriage and strolled gingerly down the concrete ramp to the sands below. Moments later they were followed by the old man leading Trigger down onto the sands and then gently into the sea.

Mouser still had a look of contentment on his face as he spoke. 'Well this is lovely Licky.' He said this as he gazed towards the horse and the shimmering azure sea just beyond. 'Just you and I keeping guard of this carriage, together with playing lifeguards over a solitary horse and two small cats, and with not a care in the world. It seems a long time since just you and I had our own space together.' Mouser turned his face towards me. 'Do not get me wrong. It is lovely having your brother sister with us, though sometimes I value your company alone, without worrying about William and Mary. You see they are not as worldly as you and we need to keep a close watch. Your experiences of being ship wrecked in my museum and then having to use your wits to survive afterwards, stripped you of some of that *domestic cat* veneer. No doubt that will return in an instant, once you are back with your owners on the yacht.' This last sentence uttered by Mouser had an unmistakable ring of pathos about it. Mouser was not quite finished. 'But I shall be very happy for you to be reacquainted with your home and of course with your brother and sister. I hope you may all find sanctuary there. Together.'

A feeling of great sadness overwhelmed me but it made it easier to move onwards. Talk about the future and the changes we might need to make together. 'Mouser I have wanted to say something to you for a long time and time is suddenly against us.' Mouser's expression changed from contentment to puzzlement.

'Well Licky, you know you can tell me anything. There is nothing you can say or do could ever cause offence. In my eyes you are....' Mouser looked away. He appeared as if he was in a trance. His head was slightly cocked as he turned back to look into my eyes.

'I am what in your eyes Mouser?' I needed to understand his thoughts, before opening my mouth and saying something that might damage everything.

'Oh Licky you know what I am trying to say. I'm not good with words, you know that. It's that you are everything in my eyes.' Mouser paused for a moment. 'There I have said it. I think you have known that for some time. But I don't regret having said it.'

'That is very kind of you to say so Mouser.' I felt safer to say what I knew was coming. I turned my head towards the sands to where Trigger was standing still, up to his belly in water. He was attached to a long rope held loosely by his owner. William and Mary were sitting upright on the sand, a few yards away. Mouser looked out to sea.

'Mouser, I have been thinking for some time about what I should be saying now. The time has come.' Mouser looked at me sideways, puzzled but not concerned. 'Fire away Licky. Please don't leave me in suspense a moment longer.'

'I think it is time that you took the plunge and became a *domesticated* cat.' Mouser's jaw visibly dropped. 'I am sure that with no urge to scratch human beings my owners would take you on board. That will need a change of attitude towards people - a change that brings with it trust. We could then all be one happy family.' Mouser rolled his tongue slowly around his lips. I knew my suggestion was being received very poorly. Mouser's mouth may have even turned to sand paper as he struggled to reply.

'How can I turn overnight into a domesticated cat? Please tell me more Miss Licky.' *Miss* Licky, a very formal choice of address. I had maybe gone too far and retreat might be the best way forward. I chose to persist.

'I think you know the answer to that Mouser better than anyone.' I paused. 'We may need to see a vet to fix things for the future, just as they were fixed for all three of us so many years ago.' Mouser held his gaze out to sea. I could not risk pause for thought even though I knew my words were painful. 'You need to get fixed. Have the chop. Then you shall be as right as rain and ready for a life of serenity. Human affection will be yours and human hands will never pose a threat. Constantly stroking of your hair will not offend you. Life will be easy, calm and tranquil.' I took a deep breath. 'In time you will come to love the affection as I did. Most important of all, with all being equal, we might all live together, on the yacht.'

I shut up and said no more for the moment, waiting for a response to my unrehearsed and poorly stated idea. This was a lot for Mouser to take in and I feared his response would not be a kind one. Maybe I had crossed the line. A parting of the ways seemed a likely outcome if what I sensed became a reality. I continued my silent gaze over the creek.

'Licky, I do not understand why I should ever need to see a vet. I can adapt to circumstances as they arise. I can change things myself. I hope I have proved that with you three cats.' You three cats! Was there a sound of annoyance in his voice? 'I have also I believe proved myself worthy and trust worthy in the eyes of Top Cat and with the Museum. I *can* learn not to scratch people who suddenly seek to stroke me. It may take time but I can do it.' Mouser shuddered from tip to toe. Quietness followed as he then composed himself. 'Licky I am a *mouser* and a visit to the vet would destroy my usefulness in the Museum. My instincts would fail me with the flick of *that* knife. Do you really think this would help anyone at all? How could I return to life here on my own without the support of my own instincts? I cannot risk losing that – it makes no sense.'

'But Mouser, you are missing the whole point. You would not be reliant on the museum for employment any longer. You would retire on your own terms.' I began to realise I was being very selfish. I also sensed there was some greater logic here which Mouser understood in a way that I could not. Mouser looked shocked. Even I was surprised by what I had just said but continue I would. 'You would truly be one of us, domesticated. I still have a hunting instinct though it is subdued. You would not lose that, not entirely.' By now even I had doubts about my own argument. What hypocrisy to cripple someone's ability to survive should they be left in the lurch, as could easily and might happen.

Mouser continued to avoid my gaze and look out to sea. 'Well Licky how could this operation ever happen, even if I ever contemplated such a thing? Do I just turn up at some local vet surgery and scratch them forcibly? Turn really feral and dangerous? Be captured and then neutered. Or even worse, be put to sleep as I know can happen to cats. The vet would think I was rabid. No animal takes itself along to a vet willingly for any reason. A human would need to take me there. At risk would be the loss of my position in the museum, loss of all interest in catching mice and loss of my food allowance.' Mouser turned and looked me directly in the eyes. 'Licky it just wouldn't work. There are too many ifs and buts and the biggest one is ever being given sanctuary on the yacht. You will have your work cut out simply to get William and Mary on board. Let alone me and let alone Top Cat.'

Mouser was probably right but I felt I needed to say more. It had taken me so long to discuss this I was certainly not going to be felled at the first hurdle. 'Mouser I hear everything you say, but one thing at a time. I would make sure my owners would meet you and then they might well decide to take you to the vet, if you are invited on board. Then you would have to make the decision, to go along with what you and they want or abandon ship and escape back to the Museum. You need to keep all of these thoughts in mind.'

Mouser remained in deep thought. Mouser turned and held my gaze. He would think over what I had just said. 'My mind is in turmoil but *if* I could stay on the yacht, then maybe.'

'I think you are right to leave things as they are and wait and see. You must prepare for whatever my owners decide and agree or not as you see fit.' I was choosing my words more carefully now. 'Maybe you should be thinking what is best for the *two* of us. Does that make more sense to you Mouser?'

Mouser eyes lit up as a slow smile appeared on his face. The old man had started to lead Trigger out of the water and back on to the sands. William and Mary were now standing up and getting ready to follow.

'I think it does Licky. You may be right and I may need to make a choice. Let us see how things turn out in the days ahead. Then I can tell you what I need to do. Thank you for letting me have a ponder on these things in all good time. Prepare for whatever will be. Then do whatever I must for the benefit of all five of us.'

We prepared to hitch a lift back to Kalkara town and then make our way back to Vittoriosa. Both Mouser and I agreed not to breathe a word of our discussion to my brother and sister. We would let time and circumstance dictate the future and see if fate would take a hand in making us one big happy family.

CHAPTER 28

We strolled onto the quayside around three o'clock, and half expected Top Cat to be there, waiting for us. No sign of him and no sign of Margaret either. All seemed quiet until an odd resonance of song filled the air. A party on the rented yacht was gathering pace and small groups of people were making their way along to Quay B carrying bottles and bags which clinked in time with the footsteps and dance steps of happy people, laughing and joking as they twisted their way forward.

A full bodied lady sported a hula hoop revolving precariously as she led the throng forward, her hips gyrating wildly to keep the hoop aloft. Just above her own plimsoll line as it threatened to collapse onto the ground below. At each threat, her gyrations became increasingly frenetic. The hoop would suddenly rise upwards.

'Well, maybe they are high on just more than drink and music. Perhaps they are on Meow.' We three looked curiously at Mouser. He responded. 'I once came across some youngsters, who saw me and began to meow. They started to laugh and one told me they had all had a bit of Meow. Now, I should have understood but I thought they were being friendly. Maybe they had been stroking cats and this had created their calmness and good humour. However something was not right and I wondered if they were perhaps mad. Anyway they left me alone and moved off. Dancing and laughing. Just like today. No doubt they would share their story with another passing cat who would be as perplexed as me.'

I looked at Mouser and then towards my confused brother and sister. 'Well Mouser I am glad these youngsters did not try and tempt you with any of this Meow rubbish.' Mouser turned and gave me a disdainful look.

'If you think for a moment Licky that I would fall for something like that, then surely you have underestimated me.' He finished off his comment with raised eyebrows, perhaps not quite understanding what I had said. As I was confused as him, so I said no more.

'Oh not at all Mouser, Licky would never do that. Underestimate you I mean.' William was quick to my defence.

'Oh absolutely dear Mouser, you are far too sensible a fellow to do anything silly.' Mary too was now on the defensive though she too could probably not understand what on earth she was talking about. She was looking straight ahead at the partying on the yacht. 'I do think we would all be prudent not to do too much meow meowing in their direction. They might take it the wrong way and throw us into that bin I see over there or worse into the sea beyond!'

Mouser smiled and we all chuckled. Even though we did not really know what the joke was. If ever there was a joke. Mouser paused and let slip he had once been given some catnip which was some sort of herb. One of the museum staff had bought in this plant and Mouser sniffed and licked it. Moments later he was laughing and singing and racing around on the museum floor for several minutes. He could not stop meowing, whilst rolling over and rubbing himself with the herb. 'I think she bought it at a pet shop. I became what they call *off my head* and a real spectacle. Fortunately the effect wore off after a few minutes, and then I regained my senses. Not before all the staff had laughed their heads off at my antics and my expense. I am sure these people over there have been sniffing on a catnip plant.'

We continued to be amused by the antics of these *catnip* people now assembled on that yacht. The blaring music could hardly disguise the laughter and merriment of the people on board, all dancing together and clinking glasses as they shuffled around the deck.

Margaret appeared a short time later with Terrance in tow, both throwing glaring glances in the direction of the noisy yacht. Their glances turned to smiles as they saw us all sitting together.

'Well there they all are Tel, all sitting as pretty as a picture.' She looked over at the party goers. 'Well I see they are all at it again, holding another rave up as usual. No peace for the wicked, I'll be bound, with that lot around for a full week.' Margaret turned and spoke to me. 'Now listen up here Miss Licky. Your fortunes are about to change. We had a phone call only about an hour ago from your owners. Didn't we Tel?'

'Oh yes we did Ma. Yes indeed we did.' Terry was a man of few words and with the good sense to support Ma whenever she prompted his consent. He found the easy life lay in fond acquiescence and that had never yet let him down. 'Are you going to tell Miss Licky, Ma?' With that he shut up as was his custom.

'Yes your owners have just arrived in the port of Pozzallo in southern Sicily, and they intend having an early start tomorrow morning at first light. They reckon with everything being equal, it will take them around eight or nine hours to cover the distance back here to Malta. They should arrive around two or three o'clock. Then Miss Licky you shall no longer be a ship wrecked cat!' With that she gave out one of loud howls of laughter but which could not over awe the noise from that yacht. She turned and scowled at it. Tel did the same in harmony and she respected his good judgement. She asked Tel to hurry up and they rushed back to their yacht. Margaret had before departing, promised us all a fresh dinner at six o'clock.

'So it is really happening. This time tomorrow you will be back on board.' Mouser's voice was subdued, giving it an air of inevitability over a veneer of sadness that could not be unglued. He was looking directly at me. He was unable to hide that sadness in his eyes. I was unable to say much but I knew much needed saying.

'Well indeed and this is the news we have all been waiting for, so it should be a time to rejoice and be happy.' My words sounded hollow. William and Mary looked on nervously. Mouser's expression was downhearted. I needed to say something which would give us all hope for the day ahead. We had, a little earlier, already made Mouser aware of the retrieval of the golden chain. Top Cat was to be informed of this and the part he would play regarding this treasure.

'Well come tomorrow, on the return of my owners, that is when the real work starts. By real work, I mean *our* real work.' I took a pause for breath. Mouser, William and Mary remained expressionless, whilst all looking at me intently. 'We have to carry out our plans tomorrow with precision. We should all stay together and I will lead all of us through the introductory stage, as great first impressions shall be needed. Mouser will recover the Will and race over with it and give it to Eric. Then Top Cat will bring those two golden cats on the chain and give them to Daisy or Eric. That will help us get on board and create the right impression.' Mouser's expression showed some degree of thawing. He actually appeared to believe in what I was saying. It might just come true.

'William and Mary, you are obviously at the greatest advantage, due to the old lady's Will. My owners should fairly quickly cotton on that we three are related and that I am or was the long lost sister. The old lady alludes to this very matter in the Will. If all three of us have to have DNA tests, then so be it. But at the end of the day, the Will is the thing that holds the clout, and to all intent and purposes, shall be your saviour. Hopefully if there is any ambiguity, then Top Cat and you Mouser shall hopefully get the benefit. I remember distinctively as I scanned the Will that the Marchioness alluded to other immediate cats that may be friends and who should then also be taken care of. It all depends on the finer points as to how that Will was written and how it shall be interpreted by the Notary, that horrible Mr Stick and of course Eric and Daisy.'

My sudden and unrehearsed speech had the desired effect. William and Mary were more than happy to go along with the plan and Mouser was suddenly galvanised into action.

'Now Licky, good on you for lifting our spirits and making us do things which might be helpful.' Mouser was back on board with us and that wonderful twinkle in his eye had returned. 'Tonight in the Museum, I shall retrieve the Will from the stockings of the Admiral. I shall have that ready to be carried out of the Museum tomorrow morning.' Mouser was now wholly back in his stride, and it warmed my heart. 'Correct me if I am wrong, but Top Cat shall visit us tomorrow and shall also be present as part of the *welcoming* committee when your owners sail back into harbour? He shall then deliver the golden cats on board personally?' Mouser gave a short pause followed by a lick *and* smack of his lips. Possibly all brought about by his still thinking of his recent and unexpected elevation to first lieutenant under Top Cat. Clearly he sought no answer to his questions as he continued. 'Yes we shall not leave a thing to chance and as you have mentioned earlier Licky, it must be precision all the way.'

It is funny how spirits can sink so low and then almost at a toss of a coin, rise to new levels of hope and aspiration. However curious that may be, that is exactly what happened that afternoon. When Mouser left us for his nightly duties at the museum, he left with a definite spring in his old step. He gently stroked the back of my ear with a flick of his paw, and then he was gone. Tomorrow was the day we had all be waiting for. Some of us with hope – others with apprehension if not real fear for the future.

And as William, Mary and I settled down for the night, we drifted off to sleep with music drifting from the party going yacht. Then I heard that old song.

Que Sera Sera

I fell into a fit less sleep at last. The omens were improved.

CHAPTER 29

William and Mary slept well throughout the night, curled up next to me under the lamp post. My sleep was by contrast, disturbed, partly by strange noises coming from the partying yacht of wailings and loud hysterical laughter. Also by nightmares where hawk eyed Mr Stick with night vision binoculars, would appear in darkened places with his net and carry us away before the yacht arrived. I wanted this night to end quickly so I could make and enact all my carefully laid plans into positive fruition.

Margaret arrived shortly after eight that morning with breakfast for the three of us. She was *splashing out* today with a full tin of Whiskas with lamb, which she promptly divided into three plastic bowls. 'We can't have your owners thinking anything bad of me. You have been fed only the best cat food that money can buy. I'll leave the tin here so they can see the truth. Make sure you are around here from two o'clock onwards.' She looked us keenly in the eye. 'You Miss Licky, need to be here as part of the welcoming party.' With that she gave her deep bellow of a laugh and she was away, back down the causeway leading to her yacht.

Sometime later and a bit before Mouser would be out of the museum, Top Cat appeared. He arrived in haste and did not look his usual composed self. There was no quiff touching from him. We soon learnt why.

'That Mr Stick is up in Birgu again with his confounded butterfly net.' My nightmare had come to life I thought. 'This is a break from his usual routine. I can't recall seeing him searching those streets on a Saturday.' Top Cat looked over his shoulder from whence he had come. 'What is the ETA of your owners?'

We were perplexed and could not answer. Top Cat expanded his odd abbreviation. 'ETA, which stands for the estimated time of arrival of your owners.

'Oh yes Top Cat, probably around two or three o'clock. They left Sicily early this morning and it is likely to be about an eight or nine hour crossing back here given calm seas and a good headwind.'

'Right well that is good news. The sooner you are back on board the better. That Mr Stick is becoming a real problem. Not just for you. Anyone else he tries to ensnare. He sought, mistakenly I can only imagine or perhaps not so, to grab old Biscuit, a ginger cat who has been living peaceful on my territory for years. She does not look anything like you three apart from her ginger coat. She has no fine white patches as you all three sport. She was too quick for him thank God. My lucky and indeed loyal subject raced past me just as I appeared on the scene. Mr Stick gave me a most odd look, as if he knew something. His actions of today clearly show he is getting desperate. Any old cat shall do for his evil purpose.'

He turned in a circle, checking for signs of Mr Stick. All was well. 'Today is your day Miss Licky. The day you seek to persuade your owners to adopt your brother and sister on board with you.' Top Cat gave us all a stern look. 'That shall be the test. Mouser and I can and will back you up, with that Will and with the golden cats, to give what strength we may to the cause. Once we are known to your owners then Mr Stick's machinations will be broken. He might try to substitute any one of you with an alley cat if he could. There is something in that Will that draws him back time again to these streets and alleys, something of great importance. A time to be cautious and get our plan finished. Then Mr Stick will be dumbfounded and will leave us all alone. That includes all my feral subjects in the alleys who have become more fearful of his net by the day.'

Mouser crept across the road as though he realised Mr Stick was still on the search. He slowly pawed his way towards us looking left and right, whilst carrying a rolled parchment in his mouth. Top Cat looked over in astonishment. 'What on earth has Mouser got in his mouth?' William, Mary and I gave no response, as Mouser grew closer. 'Mouser has a surprise in his mouth' said Top Cat. As Mouser hopped up onto the quayside, he gave Top Cat a salute with his right paw touching his quiff. Top Cat returned the compliment.

'Good morning Mouser and pray whatever have you got stuffed between your chops?' Top Cat's brow was furrowed. 'Have you *stolen* something from your employers at the museum such as an old artefact for instance? We need no trouble this day.'

Mouser gently lowered the rolled parchment on the ground in front of him. 'Good morning Top Cat and no trouble here. Later we must go recruiting around Birgu for other cats we can train as our auxiliaries. I do have several in mind.' He then looked at the three of us. 'Licky, William and Mary. Good morning to you all.' He then turned back towards Top Cat. 'Yes well this is the all important document concerning William and Mary. It is the Will which we have spoken about. It has absolutely nothing to do with the museum. I have just been storing it there for safe keeping.'

'Ay yes of course, the all important Will. The very document you Mouser are to deliver onto the yacht.' Top Cat now appeared back in the loop. 'I have to say how very clever of you Mouser to have chosen the Museum for storage purposes. This only reinforces my own belief that I am always right in life and only make sound choices. How would I know that? It is clearly borne out by my decision yesterday to choose you as my First Lieutenant.' Top Cat really did seem rather full of himself today. Mouser though seemed delighted to hear Top Cat's very own self appraisal of *his very own self*! Mouser I was certain felt praise was being heaped on him. Anyway it hardly mattered as Top Cat moved back to more important things to hand.

'So then Mouser, what did the old lady actually propose in this Will regarding William and Mary's future care? I assume that she had set aside some funding for tins of cat food from what I remember of it? Would that be correct Mouser?'

Mouser bit his lip. He worried about reminding Top Cat, knowing what he did not know, that William and Mary had inherited the equivalent of a fish food canning factory. Millions and millions of best quality tins of cat food would hardly be tipping the scales to say the very least. 'Yes in essence you are probably correct Top Cat. It seems whoever administers this Will *must* ensure William and Mary are provided for in every sense of the meaning. That is why we distrust Mr Stick so much. We hope Licky's owners will be able to carry out the instructions, which indeed might in time prove to be a benefit to us all.'

Top Cat looked puzzled. 'How could it possibly be to the benefit of us all?' Whatever thoughts Top Cat might now be harbouring, these were quickly squashed by Mouser. Only human beings could act for William and Mary. We cats could not! Top Cat listened intensely as more detail emerged and he realised human law gave no rights to cats wanting to act as guardians. Any danger would come from humans wishing to exploit this odd situation.

The discussion came to an abrupt and chilling halt.

It was Top Cat, forever on high alert that first spotted the immediate danger. He howled instinctively as he saw the approach of all our own nightmares rolled into one. Mr Stick was fast approaching, with a mean purpose to his stride, butterfly net held aloft, leading to Top Cat hurling a blood curdling hiss in Mr Stick' direction. I sensed a great hatred there and shared it. He took on the mantle of the leader that he was and would manage this emergency as best he could.

'Move it now!' he bellowed in our direction. 'Run for Fort St Angelo. Get up on the bastions.' There was not a moment to spare. Clearly Mr Stick had spotted all five of us, and his special targets were clearly in our midst.

'I'll join you up there later and take the god damn Will away. Don't let it out of your sight.'

With that agreed in duress, the four of us hurled ourselves at break neck speed along the Vittoriosa water front. If we had wings we would have flown. Mouser lagged behind us as he grappled with that parchment. We reached the apron of Fort St Angelo as Mouser pursued us.

We reached the small bridge crossing the creek and here Mouser pulled us up. He dropped the parchment from his mouth.

'Phew well that was a close shave and no mistake. We've lost him.' Mouser looked back into the distance. There was no sign of Mr Stick. 'We need to reach higher ground and settle ourselves at a vantage point overlooking the Grand Harbour, which has to be the perfect vantage place for seeing the arrival of your yacht, Licky. After which we may safely return. I hope.'

I knew exactly where we should go, which had to be the most obvious place in the world, the very place where we were born. Our first home in happier times.

I led the way. Fifteen minutes later we were there. William and Mary instantly recognised the place. Memories came flooding back. It had not changed in all these years. The dungeon lay untouched in the background. Birds sang from their perches in the brambles. To the most discerning eye, the magnificent view out onto the harbour could never lose its appeal.

Only one thing had changed. Or rather it was no longer there for us to greet. William and Mary said nothing but I knew what they were thinking. Mother did not live here anymore.

It was William that first spoke. 'This used to be our home, but so long ago and in such happier times.' Did I detect a tear in his eye as he said these words? 'You remember Mary. Of course you must remember.'

Mary was slow to answer. She looked first at William and then me. 'Yes I remember. How could I not, with those summer days playing in the sunshine, under mother's watchful eye. Not a care in the world as we skipped and made up games. I thought such bliss would never end. Oh how could I ever forget?' William's eyes were misting over. 'The only thing that is missing is our dear mother.' Tears started streaming down both their faces. 'I miss her so terribly.' The loss was infectious and we all began to cry. Even Mouser turned his head into the breeze – hoping the gentle wind would dry away his own tears.

313

Mary's tears were a floodgate of emotion. 'Oh William don't. Please don't. The past is the past and there is no turning back. Mummy is gone forever and we shall never know what happened to her. She may have died of a broken heart, through the loss of all three of us.'

I fixed my gaze on them both. Now was not the time for any more tears. A cloud briefly passed over us as the sun peered through, turning white and orange into a silvery mist above. 'Every cloud has a silver lining' I said as I pointed with my paw. The tears desisted. My owners were destined to return soon and a new future would be mapped out for all of us, just as long as we all played our part. This was no time to overhaul the past, but a time to rehearse for this afternoon performance of a life time. There were things to do. I glanced over at Mouser. He was looking ahead. Planning and scheming no doubt. There could be no room for sentimentality at this moment of potential crisis. The here and now was all that mattered now. Mouser cocked his head towards me and whispered these words to my brother and sister.

'William and Mary, look at me. You have a new life ahead of you, together with your sister Licky. Everything is going to change for the better.' He paused for thought. 'You also cannot be certain that your mother is lost forever. Nothing, as we have said before, is certain in this life. I will forever pledge to make enquiries about her welfare. When we have this day under some control, when hopefully all three of you join the yacht, I shall have time to double my efforts. Search out the truth. Involve other cats in the effort. It is time to dry those tears and think of happier days ahead.'

With that said, the tears changed to smiles as we planned our next critical move. All four of us looked out across the Grand harbour, awaiting sight of the *Sun in Splendour* to come in to view. We had to plan how best to leave this sanctuary safely and get back to the Marina and start a new life together.

CHAPTER 30

So we sat waiting, peering out to sea, with excitement rising and falling as boats came into view. We spoke very little knowing fate would decide our next steps. I had made a private decision to jump ship should there be any question we three would be separated or even us four? New plans would need to be hastily made at that time. We *could* have another life here on land in the comfort of knowing that Mouser and Top Cat would be there for us. Inwardly though I knew this would be the least favourable option. The waiting in the meantime coupled with silence appeared to have a calming effect on us all.

That calm was eventually broken as Top Cat appeared behind us, from a secret entrance and certainly unknown to Mr Stick and far too small for him to navigate.

'Aha, it did not take me long to find you. I know my way backwards around Fort St Angelo.' Top Cat had doffed his quiff in Mouser direction. 'I used to come up here for peace and quiet – away from noisy people and rebellious cats. My best thinking moments lay here amidst the history of corroding limestone blocks. It has been a while since I have lain here and relaxed in a pensive mood. Calls of duty down in Birgu have grown much more burdensome over time. It is nice to be back. Such lovely views from here, with such peace and quiet too.'

We all looked at Top Cat, keen not to interrupt his thoughts. However we were gagging to know about Mr Stick and his odd activities. We were not to be disappointed for long. The tale he had to tell only added to our worries about his intriguing guile.

The moment all four of us had fled, Top Cat had immediately impeded Mr Stick's progress along the quayside as he tried to catch us. He arched his back and hissed menacingly – taking care to dodge that swinging net. Mr Stick froze where he stood and lowered the net to the ground. Then he used his right hand to gently stroke his left cheek. That cheek still bore the scar from Top Cat's previous heroic leap towards his nose which managed to avoid the full force of those sharpened claws. The commotion of Top Cat's hissings and Mr Stick's shouting brought Margaret and Terry out on deck and then onto the quayside. They asked Mr Stick what was happening and he was keen to share his woes with them.

He explained that he was a *notary* and William and Mary, were two cats that sought to evade him thereby preventing him from carrying out his duties. He was in charge of a Will that needed to be discharged, once those two cats were netted and in his custody. A large inheritance was involved and with that came a generous fee for his time and effort. He gestured in Top Cat's direction referring to him as that nasty cat, hell bent on getting in his way and obstructing him wherever he went.

Mr Stick elaborated further. Those two cats were now without owner and were for all intents and purposes waifs and strays. Their owner had died suddenly however and everything she owned was effectively theirs to enjoy, subject to conditions. 'What conditions are those?' Terry had enquired in a softened tone, not to sound excited, but simply interested and concerned maybe.

Margaret had tilted her head and frowned, portraying deep concern. She realised Mr Stick was in a state of shock. At such times, people would say much more than was wise. At such moments, listening with no prompting bore the greatest fruits. She looked at Terry and he understood what she was doing and was content to go along with her subterfuge.

Mr Stick readjusted his fedora, shuffled his feet awkwardly then volunteered the information Terry and Margaret were craving to know. He mentioned a *finders-fee* for the safe recovery of those two cats which he intended to claim, once they were caught. Of course he would share that with anyone who could successfully ensnare them should his efforts fail. Margaret thought that very likely. That net was a ridiculous cat catcher. It was surely a butterfly net with no great strength to it.

Any cat with a life would surely bite and scratch its way out. Probably snap the frail stick between hand and net. Mr Stick sought to move the conversation forward and said there could well be a gentlemanly agreement about money changing hands if only these two *pesky* cats could be delivered safely into his hands, by any means possible. Of course there might be other benefits to anyone wanting to adopt these animals. 'They have caused me no end of trouble these past few weeks and I would not give them house room, for all the tea in China!'

'That's the word he used about you two. Pesky cats he called the pair of you!' Top Cat's indignant tone rose to a higher level. 'And that's not the end of it at all.' Top Cat stopped dead in his thoughts. 'Much worse thoughts were to come from his quivering lips.'

Terry had asked whether the capture of one cat would warrant a reward. Mr Stick quickly dismissed this out of hand. *'No I need a pair. One cat is no good. No good at all!'* The conversation then became deeply troubling.

Margaret decided it was time to talk about the Miss Licky situation and how she had become extremely friendly with two other cats. She explained how so similar all three of them looked. You could not tell the difference between them. Perhaps they were related. Who would know one from the other? This in turn set a train of thought which shocked us all to the core.

'Margaret has set up a new line of enquiry for Mr Stick to follow.' Top Cat noted. While he knew it was not impossible to keep Mr Stick at bay, he realised an alliance of these three people could prove disastrous. His duplicity allied with this couple's guile could easily lead to an unwelcome capture. 'If we are not very careful, your days could be numbered Miss Licky. Disaster could take over events and make no mistake about that.' Top Cat looked more severe than ever I had seen. 'This must never happen, and the sooner your yacht comes in today the better.'

Mouser's hairs were standing on end. He stared at Top Cat with disbelief.

'Top Cat please tell us anything more we need to know. We cannot have come this far to have all our

efforts thwarted and wiped out by this lunatic Mr Stick.'
Mouser waited for a response.

'We now have more than Mr Stick to deal with. There is now the enemy within, that pair, Margaret and Terry. Even now they will almost certainly be plotting other matters, knowing full well your home Miss Licky is fast approaching the harbour. Since I left maybe other agreements are being made between the three of them. The last suggestion Margaret made before I came away was if she could only capture William then you Miss Licky, could be substituted for Mary. No one would know the difference and then the three of them could benefit. Easy to catch you she said - easy to grab one of your siblings too while you were eating by the quayside. She would put some food out later in the hope you all would be attracted back. She would stay there awhile as she already had all of your confidences!'

Top Cat paused a moment. 'They would have to substitute your name tag Mary onto Licky's neck. How could they do that without getting hold of you Mary?' Mouser continued looking intently at all of us. 'Maybe grab it and break it off should you try to escape. It is looking bad. Those three even now are probably hatching a plan this very afternoon to capture you all in good time. All they need do is await your arrival and patiently watch as you approach those food bowls which shall no doubt be filled with delicious prawns and the like to lure you in. We must all avoid any temptations they place ahead of us. Simply wait here, until we are sure the homecoming yacht is safely at anchor.'

Mouser was the first to respond. 'You are right. We need to act together now. Abandon our plan to wait as the welcoming party. Arrive at the very last moment when we can welcome them with the Will and the two golden cats. Catch this trio of traitors off guard, before they could say or do anything to impede us.'

'So, the plan of action will stay as it was but all must happen at once. Mouser will race down with Licky, William and Mary down to the jetty. You will race onto the boat evading those three – with the Will in your mouth. Meanwhile I shall be close behind with the golden cats in my jaws. We are reckoning on an arrival time of something between two and three o'clock this afternoon. That shall give me time to sort things out. I shall be there by two o'clock and will hide close by holding those two golden cats. Meanwhile should anything unforeseen happen, I can race back here so we can plan a different means of attack. There is a little thing I alone need to sort out but that not need bother you now.' Mouser did ask to know more but was put back in his place.

'You shall see Mouser, but it is at this vital moment in time that you must earn your stripes as my new First lieutenant. You are the protector of these three and that is your focus for today. I shall take care of other matters. So now I have my work cut out over the next couple of hours. Remember not to make an appearance before two o'clock near that lamp post. Better still, wait until you have spotted your yacht entering the Grand Harbour, before starting to make any move from this safe point down to the yacht's final mooring. And do not be tempted by fish offerings that might appear by your lamp post that could entrap you all!'

Top Cat raised himself up. 'I will be off now and I shall see all four of you from two o'clock onwards at the quayside.' With that Top Cat gave a solid salute in Mouser's direction and left.

We all turned and looked to Mouser. His brow was furrowed. 'I think we all now know why he is called Top Cat. He is a strategist after all and we should be grateful he is working with us.' He gave us all a wry smile and turned his head towards the sea.

CHAPTER 31

Top Cat had left us guessing as he went on his way, to some unfathomable mission, cloaked and daggered in mystery. That was all we were allowed to sense. The more we wondered, the more we worried. Mouser had nothing to add. No words of comfort. He had been told nothing and perhaps secrecy was the essence of Top Cat's plan. Being left in the dark perhaps had its own virtue.

'Top Cat is Top Cat and with him on our side we need not worry. Everything shall pan out for the best.' Mouser gave us a reassuring smile. 'He knows how to call the shots. Indeed he has made me his trusted First Lieutenant.' Mouser licked his lips and a feeling of great pride overwhelmed us all. We surely had nothing to fear. 'Lieutenant Mouser!' He raised his eyebrows, simultaneously looking in our direction. 'Now that is impressive and in theory that makes you all my subalterns!'

Mary and William looked at me to say something. I would respond, if only to raise their spirits upwards. I looked to the sky and noticed a swarm of birds following their leader, trusting in his own good judgement, flying in harmony, twisting and turning, back and forth with such unity of purpose and yet so carefree. Higher and lower they patrolled their skies, until they disappeared from view.

'Mouser, you are our leader and with your help we can reach for the stars and overwhelm those that would try to bring us down. No slings and arrows can ever deter us. We are indeed as one.' Had I said enough to bring keep our spirits high I wondered. Mouser looked towards the heavens and I sensed he knew what I was saying.

'Those birds know and do more than we ever could,' he said. 'We shall fly fast. Evade the hunters with their buckshot. Duck and dive this day forth. Keep any of those human traitors at bay. Cunning and precision will be our guides, as we approach any menace this very afternoon may present. I thank you Licky for your inspiring words which were so nicely put. I hope in the hours to follow I can lead us from yesterday's veil of tears into a new dawn tomorrow - for you and for us all. What becomes of me is anybodys guess and Top Cat too. Still, one step at a time and those steps may need the very greatest leap of faith. Who knows, with boldness we might all yet endure together.'

Little parts of conversation flowed between the four of us as we waited for the precise time to come and act in unison. Inwardly I sensed we were each rehearsing what we needed to do at the last moment. Top Cat would surely strike the note at just the right moment. Each time a yacht entered our sight sailing into the mouth of the Grand harbour I strained my eyes against the fierce sun rays, with disappointment following disappointment as the hours sped past.

Mouser fixed his gaze in my direction every time I spotted another vessel approaching. These looks were unnerving. I sensed hope mixed with despair despite his brave words. 'Does this one look familiar Licky?' When my answer was no, Mouser became withdrawn. I knew what was happening. Mouser was lost in his own dark thoughts. Thoughts swamping his very own aspirations, after I was reunited with my owners. I had to stand away and not share my own worries with him. It is odd how fear swallows sense at critical moment likes these, as time approaches and tests us to the hilt. The clock struck two times and I steeled myself to say something.

'Mouser, you remember our many talks we have had? The one's about you and I, of lasting friendship and the future?'

Mouser looked towards me and then back out to sea. He gave a gently nod of his head. 'Yes I remember.' That was all he said. There were small tears forming in his eyes.

'Mouser, come on. Look at me. There is no need for this.' William and Mary could see what was happening but sat just far enough away not to intrude, but near enough to hear. 'Everything I said in the past was true. I shall always be your true friend and we shall not be parted.'

Mouser turned and held my gaze with watery eyes. I fought hard to think what to next say. If things went wrong I knew I would need to leave my home, the yacht to be with my brother and sister.

'Mouser, hear these words I learnt on board the yacht. They are framed above the couch. They are especially for you.' Mouser head tilted slightly to the left, his right paw quickly dispelling a glimmer of a tear.

'Mouser, don't walk in front of me. I may not follow. Don't walk behind me, I may not lead. Walk beside me, and just be my friend.'

If I thought I had chosen soothing words, then I might have thought again. Mouser burst into a flood of tears. A Mouser I had *never* seen before. My brother and sister became alarmed and ran over – shocked surely by this fragile sight that threatened to fracture all good intentions, with everything that was about to be done.

'Oh Mouser, you must not cry.' What else could I say?

William and Mary began to cry. It was then William who turned to Mouser and said we needed to be calm. The time for action was upon us. We should save any tears for much later. Mary nodded with approval. I was speechless. Mary placed her paw gently on Mouser's shoulder, something she had never done before.

'You know my sister means every word she says. We agree with everything she says and thinks about you. All the good and joy you have brought to us, ensuring we can never forget the debt *we* owe you. Mouser you have been so good for us. Words can never tell of our gratitude.' William nodded in solemn approval.

Mary lowered her paw from Mouser shoulder and sat back. 'Things shall be wonderful for all of us Mouser. Licky, William and I shall be your true friends for life.'

Mary had turned misery into contentment and had surprised me. Normally so acquiescent, but now suddenly taking the lead. Bringing us back to reality and infusing that with hope. Despair she had battered this day and I saw her with new resolve. Mouser dried his last tears away and then he spoke.

'Thank you Mary. Thank you so much. No it was those last lovely words your sister said that made my spirits melt, but that done, back to the task in hand.'

'You know Mouser; there is nothing wrong in sharing our emotions. It does not make us weaker, but maybe a little more human. We all have these feelings inside us and they are better out than in.' I looked at Mouser who thought for a moment, and then came that lovely smile that humans never can see.

We all resumed our gazing across the Grand harbour. A yacht could be seen in the distance, sails slowly lowering as it approached the harbour entrance. I gazed intently.

This yacht continuing advancing slowly, coming closer into view. The hairs on the nape of my neck were on end. The time had come. My eyes were not deceiving me. My dreams were coming true. I knew I was right. The vision was the reality and this was indeed my home was at last returning. I could now confirm my sighting with the rest and tell them that our time would shortly be upon us.

'It's them. That is the *Sun in Splendour*. Eric and Daisy have made it back safely.'

Mouser followed my gaze. 'Are you sure Licky? That is your home coming?'

'Yes! There is no mistake. Eric always has the sails down as he enters safe harbour. Look can you see now? You can see the name of the yacht on the side.'

Everyone was peering downward as the yacht neared closer to our viewing point. 'Oh yes I can see it. Can you William?' Mary's voice sounded higher than normal. 'I can Mary. I can. *Sun in Splendour* it says.'

'Well I can't say I can make it out. My eye sight and age makes the detail so blurred.' However, Mouser's optimism rose above worries about his eyesight. We could see and we would be his eyes. 'I take your word for it. That means we must make tracks, carefully, and cautiously. The next hour may well settle our futures.' He rose and stretched himself before taking command. His instructions were clear and precise. He knew what had to be done. We would follow his words to the letter.

Mouser collected the Will carefully in his mouth from behind a small rock where he had hidden it. He would lead the way downwards.

Mouser warned us to track the yacht's progress along the Cotternera water front. We had to arrive as it was berthed and not a moment sooner. We would be in time to meet with Top Cat before our final approach. He would be there as we had planned. Danger lurked if we arrived too soon. Mr Stick would probably be there to intercept us and do whatever else he, Margaret and Terry might have already planned. Had he curried enough favour with Margaret and Terry to include them in his kidnapping plan? Nothing could be left to chance.

We carefully wound our way down through Fort St Angelo reaching its apron and the small bridge across the creek. It was when we crossed the bridge that Mouser called a halt and released the Will he carried in his mouth.

'I can see your yacht quite clearly now Licky.' We all peered back to where Mouser was looking. 'Yes she is veering left into the Cotternera water front if my eyes no longer deceive me. We can be there in a matter of minutes moving up to the Casino da Venetia where we shall have a full view of the yacht's mooring progress. Top Cat will be in position I know.' Mouser took hold of the Will and he led us onwards.

On reaching the Casino da Venetia, Mouser called a halt. 'We are a little ahead of the yacht, so we shall stay put here for a moment. Stay close to this building site next door that you know so well.'

We sat down beside a mound of mottled sand that camouflaged us from view. I looked straight ahead and wondered if my eyes were playing games. 'William, Mary, do you see what I see straight ahead?'

Mouser gave them no chance to reply. 'What do you see Licky? Lend me your eyes. What can you see?'

'There are hoards of cats. That is what I can see.' It was Mary who spoke first. William quickly confirmed what she had said.

'It looks curiously like a cat army! All assembled beyond our old lamp post.' I blinked as I said this as indeed it was an army. It almost blanketed the pathway. People were crossing the road to avoid them. The noise raised by this cat army was intense.

Mouser disarmed us in a moment. 'Aha. No surprise whatsoever and just what I suspected. Good old Top Cat. Oh he's the ticket.' Mouser was grinning from ear to ear. 'He has summonsed his troops. He has assembled his Birgu foot soldiers here for your protection. Come on now. We can close in closer towards your lamp post and get a better view.' Mouser collected the Will. I wondered how he could know these things but my trust remained strong and resolute.

Mouser called a halt as we reached our own beloved lamp post. 'This will do. We can see everything from here. No need to embrace danger now.'

Mary and William looked on edge as they sat down close to each other. I sat slightly ahead of them next to Mouser. He seemed to know what was really going on whilst I remained fearful. So much was happening, with so many cats and so many confused families, ushering their children away.

The *Sun in Splendour* was now silent, alongside the jetty. Eric was at the helm, barking out orders. 'You idiot, the lines are tangled!' Of course his wife was no idiot at all, merely someone who against better judgement had taken on these hazardous chores.

Daisy was scurrying forward gathering those securing ropes. 'Secure the ties,' he screamed and Daisy did her best to tie down whatever ropes were loose on deck. Never quite understanding his nautical talk she always strived to do her best. Music could be heard playing from the rented yacht nearby. Eric appeared to take little notice, until Daisy called back to him. 'Oh Eric, what an appropriate song I hear coming from that yacht. They must have put it on especially for us.' He stopped what he was doing for a minute, which was turning off all electrical switches and the likes, and listened for a moment. 'You are right Daisy, most appropriate.' It was the sounds of Rod Stewart with perhaps his best known song of all time.

I am sailing, I am sailing
Home again 'cross the sea
I am sailing, stormy waters
To be near you, to be free

Close to the yacht party, I spied Margaret and Terry standing on the quayside. They were arguing. I could not hear what was going on. More importantly Top Cat continued to rally his troop of fifty or more cats, all hailing from the back streets of Birgu. Ready to go to war though they probably had no real idea what sacrifice that might mean. So it all became a muddle. Mouser interrupted my thoughts.

'Boys and girls, I am going up to see Top Cat to see what is going on. You three wait here and Licky, guard this paper with your life.' He dropped the Will at my feet and was off. He shot over to the other side of the road where he sensed Top Cat might be laying.

'Top Cat we are here. Licky and her siblings are nearby now and simply waiting. Do you need any help?'

'Phew Mouser, well you can see the problem right ahead of you, but I have it all under control. That Mr Stick is quite hemmed in and fearful of another hammering.'

Mr Stick held a new butterfly net in hand. He became as visible as an arch deacon above the frenzied army of cats that were by now besieging him. Top Cat had already parted his troops as surely as Moses had parted the red sea, right here under the arch leading into the Marina. A further battalion of cats had appeared as Mr Stick approached and he saw the hoard ahead. His fear and loathing of cats now probably knew no bounds. He realised they had the upper hand. He swaggered forwards occasionally swishing his net which simply made matters worse.

'Right troops, one two three!' Top Cat was fully in command, stimulating the throng of hissing cats. Sounds of Rod Stewart from the partying yacht had long been extinguished. Every noise was directed at a very shaky looking Mr Stick. He tried to pace forward, whilst appearing in the moment to be worrying too much about

326

his loosening fedora. It was not the moment to be squaring that back on to his head. He needed to spend as much time as possible protecting his legs from cats' claws and his arms and head from the wrath of savage bites. His enemies had learned too much of his dangerous ways. He was to be treated as a treacherous man who would live to learn a curious lesson in humility.

'Two paces forward men.' Top Cat looked swiftly to his left and right. 'Every pace he tries to take, we take two forward.' And they did. Mr Stick was retreating and losing his one step, whilst faltering midst the melee. 'You see Mouser; I have a perfect *pincher* movement here. We have him hemmed in. He shall not enter the harbour! We will have him on the retreat moments from now.' Top Cat looked to his right, past Mouser. 'Ah Scraggy you are doing well. I may have under estimated you. Hold your position, follow my orders, and you shall all eat well tonight. Even earn a legendary position as lieutenant in my army! Good lad Scraggy.' Scraggy lowered his eyes in Top Cat direction and whispered a cry of thanks.

'Now Mouser, all is in control here as the final part of my plan takes place. The yacht is berthed, so you need to get back to Licky and her company and keep them there by the lamp post. I shall join you for the final leg of this journey, onto the jetty where the yacht is berthed.' Top Cat paused for a moment and looked puzzled. 'Where is the Will Mouser?'

'Totally safe Top Cat. Licky has it.'

'Well get back there and take possession of it. Remember your part in delivering this Will. Take great care of that pair over there, stalking the gangways. I wouldn't trust them further than I could throw them.' He was looking over his shoulder at Margaret and Terry, standing on the quayside, deep in chatter. 'I am going to fetch the golden chain shortly. They have told me where it is buried. You get back by Licky's side.'

Mouser started scampering back towards us and suddenly stopped where Margaret and Terry stood. Top Cat continued to regale his troops with orders. 'Forward two paces. Easy and hold back you Gingers. Hold your position.'

Mouser stayed still for just a moment; head half cocked looking intently at Margaret and Terry. They looked down at him, weary of his presence.

'And what do you want black cat? Don't think we know anything about this madness! You tell him Tel. It's all that Mr Stick's fault I'll be bound, trying to get us involved in his dirty work. As if we would! We love Miss Licky and whoever her two friends are. Don't we Tel?' Margaret stared accusingly at her husband. 'Well don't just stand there you fool. Support me. Oh my god. Eric and Daisy are almost upon us. Come on Tel, let's get back onto the jetty and lend a hand. Catch a securing rope from Daisy. She is at her wits end. Look useful, concerned and away from all this commotion. Nothing of our making and that's what we stick to.'

As they turned to make their way back along the jetty, Mouser said nothing. He appeared to be in deep thought. I sensed he was trying to add up in his mind the truth about Margaret and Terry. After all they had shown kindness to us in all the weeks, whilst being homeless. He turned and faced us.

'That's all taken care of. Top Cat wants us down on the jetty pretty well now.' He looked over his shoulder. 'The time is right. The yacht is practically moored. Ready?'

We were as ready as ever we might be. We all stood up. Mouser grabbed the Will and led us along the walkway and onto the jetty. The timing was perfect. The *Sun in Splendour* was reversing inch by inch into its berth. Daisy was there at the back, a large rope in hand. Margaret and Terry were there too – looking to grab anything they could to help stabilise the vibrating yacht. They remained oblivious to the document held in Mouser's mouth. Perhaps worried much more about that reward and keeping in favour while the yacht settled in its berth.

'Welcome home my friends. Throw us the rope Daisy.' Terry's voice was full of a new bonhomie. Margaret was waving her hands in the air – as if welcoming two very close and long lost friends back to safety.

The four of us approached cautiously until we were directly opposite the yacht. Mouser brought us to a halt and placed the Will on the ground. 'This is fine. Let us wait for the lowering of the gangway.' The words were hardly out of his mouth before Top Cat raced down the jetty beside us, with the gold chain dangling either side of his mouth. He released it as he skidded to a halt. Top Cat sat for a moment looking for recognition and we acknowledged his efforts.

'Everything all right your end Mouser?' Top Cat gave no chance for a reply. 'My work's pretty well complete. Mr Stick has retreated, minus his new butterfly net. The troops captured that and it shall join his old one where he shall not be able to find it. I have disbanded the troops who are now returning back to Birgu. They are all keen to know the eventual outcome now that the yacht is back. With luck, I should be back within the hour with a story to tell. Everyone is waiting for good news after the successful repulsion of Mr Stick. Things did go well don't you think?'

'Well Top Cat, better than we could ever have thought, with the enemy dispatched and the Will intact. Now it's up to us. You have made this all possible and we will not let you down.' Mouser paused to allow Top Cat the chance to smile. He did, but was waiting for a little more appreciation, Mouser thought.

I stirred myself to say something. 'You have been absolutely brilliant today Top Cat. We are so indebted to you. Aren't we William and Mary? I mean every word I say. My brother and sister thank you with all of their hearts too.'

Mouser bowed his head. 'The last episode is now with us' he said. Top Cat drew our gaze to the now berthed yacht. The gang plank was being lowered. 'You know what has to be done Mouser. Just wait for me to give the word.' Mouser nodded his head in acknowledgement, his eyes firmly affixed to the Will lying at his feet. He appeared forlorn. There was a look of foreboding but I had no intention of enquiring what he might be thinking. This was neither the time nor the place.

'All well Daisy. We've kept Miss Licky as safe as houses.' Margaret was in full flow. 'You see she's right here as part of the welcoming committee. Together with that pair of new friends I have told you about.'

Daisy was now looking from the yacht in our direction. 'Oh my goodness yes, but which one of those three is she? Which one is Miss Licky?'

'Mouser do your bit. Go!' Top Cat barked out the order and Mouser leapt to his feet, grabbed the Will and shot across the quayside and in a moment was racing up the gang plank and onto the yacht. Daisy took a step back and let out a squeal. 'Good God what is that!'

Mouser paid no heed but raced up to Eric, who was standing just outside the wheelhouse, looking over in the direction at his startled wife. He skidded to a halt at Eric's feet and placed the Will there. He sat down and looked up at Eric.

'What on earth is going on here?' Eric looked utterly bewildered. 'What is this?' He bent down and picked up the parchment. He gently untied the red ribbon and unfurled the content. He produced a pair of reading glasses from his shirt top pocket. 'Hmm, let us see what the dickens this is all about.' He scanned the document for no more than thirty seconds before saying anything.

'This is quite extraordinary. It's a Will, a Last Will and Testament. It seems to be all about cats. It refers to a William and Mary as the sole beneficiaries together with some codicils about a missing sister, who if found must be reunited with William and Mary and equally taken care of. It also goes onto to say that further provision must be made for any other cat friends they may be enjoying the companionship or company of. Well blow me down with a feather.' Eric began to roll up the document and then stopped. He looked down at Mouser who remained seated at his feet. 'Yes well thank you very much cat for this more than interesting document. I shall need more time to read it in detail.'

'And what the hell has it got to do with us Eric.' Daisy was shaking her head.

'Oh I can help you out there Daisy. Can't we Tel?' They were still standing on the quayside at the bottom of the gangplank. Margaret clearly wanted to get in on the act. She now knew too much through the avarice Mr Stick. Tel looked away and said nothing.

'Mouser! Back here now. You've done a good job.' Mouser turned towards Top Cat and as quickly as he had made the journey onto the yacht, he was back down the gangplank. He paid scant regard to Margaret and Terry, before he was then back by our sides.

'Licky, the time has come for you, William and Mary to take your leave. You know exactly what to do now, but before you may care to have a private word with Mouser?' With that Top Cat moved a yard or two away from the pair of us. William and Mary respectively lowered their heads and looked away.

I held Mouser' gaze - his eyes appeared misty. I needed to say something, quickly and for this moment.

'Mouser, today is the start of a new dawn. One we can and should share together for the future.' Mouser looked unconvinced, turning his head away in the direction of the yacht. His darker thoughts would be hard to shift. 'Just because I may return to my home tonight, does not mean anything has changed in the days ahead. We can see each other whenever we choose.'

'How do you work that one out Licky?' Mouser turned his head half in my direction. 'After all your owners shall never accept me as a casual visitor.'

'Mouser, it is all very simple. When you leave the Museum each morning, you come down here and see us. I am allowed to come and go as I please from the yacht, and the same shall apply to William and Mary.'

'And then what Licky?' Mouser was raising hurdles.

'We shall continue our friendship and companionship. That is what Mouser.'

'I have your word for that Licky? I am just so fearfully of being lonely again in life. I have found such great happiness in these recent times. This is all because of you Licky.' Tears were starting to appear in his eyes.

'Mouser I have told you before and I say it again. I will never let you down. You have come to mean the world to me. I still have thoughts about you joining us for good on the yacht in time. But that is all another story yet to be fully fathomed. But trust me; it shall come to pass, with my efforts, the Marchioness statements in her Will regarding friends of William and Mary and most importantly your willingness to comply to certain *adjustments* in your life.'

'Licky, Mouser, the time is right. You'll have to wind up now and you Licky, with your brother and sister must now seize the day.' Top Cat had spoken.

'See you tomorrow morning Mouser. I must now go.' Mouser moved his face closer to mine. I knew what was coming and it just seemed right. Mouser gave me a quick kiss on my nose and I instinctively did the same. 'See you tomorrow Licky.' I moved to stand up and at the same time felt very weak at the knees. 'This merely Mouser is an *au revoir* in my vocublary. Never shall we ever say *goodbye.'*

I called to William and Mary and the final part of the plan was carried through. Top Cat gathered the gold chain with its two golden cats in his mouth and raced ahead of us and straight up the gangplank. Moments later he had laid the golden chain squarely at Eric's feet. He then took a step back from the startled Eric, looked up at him and promptly with his right paw, touched his wonderful quiff. I was certain I saw Eric's right hand slightly move to his own forehead in response as he eyed Top Cat in amazement. Top Cat then turned around and in no great haste, walked along the yacht' decking and back down the gangplank. He walked over to Mouser who sat a few feet away from William, Mary and me.

'It is truly time for the three of you to make your entrance. Lead the way Licky and take your brother and sister straight up onto the yacht.' Top Cat looked extremely solemn. Mouser appeared to be in a world of his own. He was staring into space.

'Daisy!' he exclaimed as he picked up the chain. 'Daisy, this surely has to be solid gold! What a wonderful piece it is, adorned with these two dangling cats.' He pulled out his spectacles from the top pocket of his shirt and examined the pieces. 'Twenty four carat gold! Made in Birmingham so the hallmark says! The weight of it is unbelievable.'

I trotted pass Margaret and Terry and up the gangway with my brother and sister directly behind me, wondering if ever we would *all* be invited on board.

If I had overwhelming worries about all three of us boarding the yacht, all such fears vanished in a trice. Daisy rushed over to all three of us, took one look, then picked me up in her arms, quickly glanced at my name tag, before giving me the cuddle of my life.

'Oh Licky you are safe! Thank God you are safe. And you look none the worse for our long absence. You still look beautiful.' She continued in this vein for some moments and then put me down and turned her attention to William and Mary. 'Well the next thing is for us to work out who you two are and what is to become of you.' William and Mary sat there on the aft decking peering up at Daisy. Inwardly I felt the dye had been cast and everything would work in our favour.

I looked to the quayside where Top Cat and Mouser were slowly pacing their way back off the jetty and onto the marina. But not without witnessing Mouser turn his head several times in the direction of my home as they walked away and eventually, for this day, out of sight. He looked as if he was carrying the world on his shoulders. Oh poor Mouser.

Over the next few minutes, Margaret and Terry had been invited up for a drink on the yacht. Daisy scurried around producing a bottle of wine and four glasses, all laid out on the table in the open space at the rear of the yacht. Moments before, Eric had taken a moment to stroke both William and Mary and take a look at their name tags. 'Just as I thought,' he said to anyone that cared to listen. 'These are the cats surely named in the Will, the very same William and Mary.'

Eric now had the Will laid out for all to see and was now studying it closely.

'Well, well' said Eric. 'If we take in these two cats, we in turn become their official guardians. William and Mary inherit the estate of the Marchioness, and everything that it may entail. There also appears to be a plot of land on the Island of Gozo.'

'A plot of land in Gozo did you say Eric?' Daisy eyes had lit up. 'Well that would be a fine place for cats to have a home, should the land be put to use by building a house there.'

For a number of years now, Daisy had wanted to broach the issue of this dammed boat which she considered was nothing but pain and trouble for her. Eric would say nothing, even though for a number of years his back had been playing up, and inwardly he knew this yachting business was no longer an old man's pleasurable hobby any more. She would keep her own council for the moment, but ideas were certainly rattling around in her head from the expression on her face.

'Clearly this *Marchioness* had a great love of cats. This gold chain says much about that. She has had it specially commissioned I am sure. What should we do?' He looked at us three cats with genuine affection. Daisy suggested she defrosted some prawns they had bought in Sicily and Eric agreed. 'Those cats need looking after,' he said. Daisy was heartened. Maybe her sudden feelings about the future were taking hold. Maybe Eric would listen to her if and when the time was ever right.

Eric continued to examine the Will a bit longer, reading out aloud most of the time. He found the section appertaining to any friends or companion cats of William and Mary to be of some interest. He looked over in our direction. 'Do you have any new friends or companions, William and Mary?' He let out a chuckle of laughter. 'After all if you do, we may well be finding ourselves running a cattery!' He stopped briefly and looked at Terry and Margaret. 'And what do you make of our cat Miss Licky? She really does bear every sense of resemblance to William and Mary don't you think so? Is she the lost sister mentioned in this Will?'

Terry and Margaret were quick to respond, with Margaret taking the lead. 'Oh now you come to mention it Eric, it does start to make so much greater sense. The three of them have been inseparable these past weeks. They just suddenly appeared one day in the company of Miss Licky and the three of them have remained together ever since. Yes I would put my money where my mouth is and say that in all probability they are related and are immediate family.'

'Oh yes and I would heartily second that,' said Terry. 'Anyway you could always have blood tests done and get a full DNA test result.'

'Well I suppose at any rate it would hardly matter whether they were related or nor, going by the terms of the Will. William and Mary are clearly smitten in the company of Miss Licky, so here is certainly the first friend or companion to be looked after as per the Will.' Eric looked pleased with his assumption.

We listened to everything so far that had been said and it was proving music to our ears. The Will had indeed been delivered into the right pair of hands, those of my devoted and loving owners. William and Mary kept smiling at me as they too listened to everything being said.

Daisy, who herself was now seated at the table, a glass of wine in hand, next spoke up. 'Well the logical next move to get things moving and formalised, must be to contact the Notary and have him execute the terms of the Will. There is also a mention of the Marchioness maid and her inheritance that needs to be recognised and adhered to.'

'Indeed yes Daisy you are quite right and this shall be no problem.' Margaret produced a calling card. A calling card with the name Mr Stick on it, a telephone number and his office address in Valletta. She passed it over to Eric who glanced at it and then put it in his shirt top pockets. 'Thank you Margaret and that is very useful. I shall give him a ring first thing Monday morning.' He showed no interest as to how she might have come by the calling card, which was probably just as well. It might only have led to distorted truths and further deceits.

'Now you two have been stellar in keeping our beloved cat alive. We posted a reward without naming how much, but we shall certainly be doubling that. What are neighbours for? Once things are settled here then we can post you a cheque. Of that you may be certain.' Eric raised his glass in their direction and everyone joined in. I smiled at this event. My smile was also brought about by the subject of *reward money*. Since in Eric's very own words, they had not mentioned on the reward notice the *amount* that was being offered, who knows what that amount might have ever been in the first place, that was to be so generously doubled! How long is a piece of string?

'Oh the pair of you are too kind by half.' Margaret took a fair swig from her wine glass, as a second bottle had now been opened, before continuing. 'It was our pleasure to take care of Miss Licky and ensure she had two square meals a day. We quickly found she had a preference for tinned Whiskas, so that is indeed what she had every day. Oh yes and on top of that some fairly frequent helpings of fresh fish as a treat. Just to keep her spirits up during your *long* absence. Remember we can always look after Miss Licky and indeed her friends whenever you are away from Malta. It would be our honour and privilege.' Margaret looked at Terry and he nodded with a passion.

I looked at William and Mary and all three of us smiled contagiously. Well in all fairness, Margaret had been pretty good as an ally in my time of need, and she had even then taken on board extra mouths to feed. So who cared about her little indiscretions and the odd white lie concerning tins of Whiskas. She deserved some poetic license. I was pleased however that neither Eric nor Daisy sought to question where I had been living these past times. That was as anyway, now all water under the bridge.

Margaret and Terry took their leave to return to their yacht, nearing the end of the consumption of the third bottle of wine. They stood up and looked happy and merry. Hands were shaken all round and we three too were bid farewell from the leaving guests.

Daisy stayed to clean up, whilst continuously smiling at us. The sun was fast setting and Eric had gone down below.

'Miss Licky. If you and your brother and sister, as I am sure they are, can help us find your two friends then we can make a home together. *Not* on this blasted yacht. *Not* in that claustrophobic flat but in a country house with gardens to play in. Keep this very secret and with your help all of our dreams may well come true. If I can talk sense into Eric flogging the yacht *and* the flat, we can perhaps all go and live in Gozo!' Daisy stroked us all and whispered. 'While there is hope, there is everything.'

In due course with everything tidied up on deck, she then went below, but only to return moments later with those prawns. Two bowls of water were placed on deck. She then made quite a fuss of bidding all three of us goodnight, turned off the lights on deck and went below and to her bed to sleep.

We were now peacefully alone and safe, all three of us sitting up on the outside cushion benches. I sat opposite William and Mary with just the small outside fixed dining table separating us. We talked and talked amongst ourselves as the evening light faded into darkness. So much had happened this day. We started to reassess our thoughts about Mr Stick and indeed Margaret and Terry. Maybe better souls all round than previously imagined. We thought about what tomorrow might bring. We thought and expressed our views constantly about dear Mouser and Top Cat. They must be given the offer of a new life, a better life void of loneliness and all its uncertainties. One thing remained constant in our thoughts. Eric and Daisy, if no one else in this world were by far the most reliant and trusted conduit to have in order to possibly create, in time, one big and happy extended family.

A very happy William and Mary eventually went off to sleep around midnight, drifting no doubt into dreams of their future hopes to come. For me I could not help thinking of Mouser. My last sighting of him as he left the quayside had been a sobering one. He looked so dejected, miserable and down hearted as I had never even closely seen him before. Had he convinced himself that things would never be the same again? That he would never be able to see me again? I wondered what he was doing right now in the museum. Was he thinking about me? Was he thinking about how things *might* have been for us both, had my home not returned to harbour?

337

I will myself to sleep, convincing myself I would see Mouser again tomorrow and plans would be formulated from then on about his future, about *our* future.

THE END

Acknowledgements

I would like to thank the following:

Marcelle d'Argy Smith, for her inspirational encouragement to me in pressing me to finish the book.

My editors at Woodlord Publishing and eBooks-UK:

Jane Mason for her first edit of *Cats Brigade.*

Kate Mason for her patience and helpful responses in correcting the final proofs, and for her work in typesetting the book and designing the jacket.

For details of books published by Woodlord Publishing
and eBooks-UK, go to:

www.ebooks-uk.com
www.woodlord.co.uk

Woodlord paperbacks and eBooks-UK Kindle eBooks
may be ordered from Amazon websites.

If this book is not available also
in your local bookshop,
please request it:

ISBN: 978-1-906602-36-9

Available in Kindle eBook format:

eISBN: 978-1-906602-33-8